South Philly's 7th St.

By: Red-Bone

First print 2018 July

First print 2018 July

This is a book of fiction. Any references or similarities to actual events, real people, or real locations are intended to give the novel a sense of reality. Any similarity to other names, characters, places and incidents are entirely coincidental.

ISBN-13: 978-1727033571
ISBN-10:1727033574

Book Productions: Crystell Publications
You're The Publisher, We're Your Legs
We Help You Self Publish Your Book
E-mail – cleva@crystalstell.com
E-Mail – minkassitant@yahoo.com
www.crystellpublications.com
(405) 414-3991

Printed in the USA

DEDICATION

LAVERN & GRANDMOM JEAN MOORE

AND TO THE MIXSON FAMILY

CONTENTS

It's Bone-Crusher, Bitch!!!

Pictures

PROLOGUE

South Philly, 7th Street.

I was raised on 5th and Snyder Avenue with my grandmother, Jean Me, my mother Lavern, and my older brother, Wyan. Her house, is where I was born. 2036 South 5th Street, was my living space until I was about 6 years' old. Then, my mother got into one of the project houses down 5th Street with her boyfriend, and me and Wyan moved in with them, 1021 building 16th floor. The good part of my mother moving, was that it was close to the area we'd already made bones in. 7th Street. So every day, me and my brother would walk from our mother's apartment down to 7th Street. And when it became dark, me and him would walk back to 5th Street.

I don't know if my mother ever wanted to move to 5th Street. But, when the Government is giving your assistance you don't have much of a choice where you want to move.

There is a park me and Wyan often walked through as a shortcut to get from 5th Street to 7th Street faster, and a few dudes from 5th Street used to hang in that park and play tough. I'd fought a few of them before for picking on Wyan. Wyan is a bitch for real, but he's still my brother.

One of those times me and him were on our way back to our mother's apartment, and we were walking through that park. Those 5th Street boys were out there on the park benches. They saw us and we saw them. The next thing you know, they came with the bullshit.

"Wyaaaan Wyaaaan! What's up Wyaaan Wyaaan?" the younger one started it.

He was calling my brother's name in his cry baby voice like trying to say my brother was a cry baby. His brother a goofy brown skinned boy who looked just like him sat next to him, grinning like they'd just caught a victim.

My brother Wyan tried to act like he didn't hear him. But I knew he did, because I did, and I was tired of them fucking with him. We'd already passed them by now. But that made me stop to turn around and say something.

"Naa chill yo, don't say nothing." Wyan was bitching already, trying to stop me.

"Naa FUCK that!" I yanked my arm out of his hand. I knew these dudes. Squeaky, and Russy. We'd been through this before and it was always Squeaky, the younger one starting shit. I was fucking him up today.

"What's up Bull? Fuck y'all want with my brother?" I managed to force a few words out. My jaw muscles were clenched tight, and I was ready for whichever way this shit was about to turn. "Y'all nigga's always fucking with my brother, we ain't having that no more!" I added.

Me and Squeaky are face to face by now, and I'm staring Squeaky dead in his iris. He's bigger than me, but I don't give a fuck! On my right side, I can feel Wyan shaking like a leaf while he stood next to me.

"So what'chu saying nigga?" Squeaky stepped closer to me.

"What YOU saying?" I stepped closer to him.

Nothing stood between us but air and opportunity. And before you knew it, we were tearing it the fuck up! I'm trying to take Squeaky's head off, he's trying to take my head off. Of course, I'M going to tell y'all the truth I was winning. But, as soon as I started winning, I felt a hand grab me from behind. I could tell it wasn't my brother Wyan's hand by the feel of it. I know his touch. So, I turn my head to see whose hand was on me, and I see THIS nigga's brother, RUSSY!

Automatically I'm looking for Wyan. Because I'm thinking he should've moved on Russy, as soon as HE moved to touch me! I spots Wyan after a few seconds. And guess where? RUNNING! At TOP speed across the park! This boy done left me out here, fighting HIS fight! Smh.

After fucking Squeaky up, I made it home a short while later with a few scratches on my face. You know me, it's nothing. Wyan was already in the house, and he's looking at me all dumb as I walked in. I went right in on his ass.

"WHY the fuck you leave me out there by myself?" I snapped.

Mind you, while I'm getting on him, I'm sweating because it's hot in this little ass apartment. Our mother doesn't have any air conditioning, and we're in the middle of the summer!

My mother didn't have air conditioning, but she did have a personal hand fan. And since Wyan pulled that bullshit, I got a trick for his ass. The hand fan sat right on the table in the living room. Yup, this will do.

Wyan was still sitting there with that dumb ass look.

"Yea, and since ya bitch ass did that bullshit, grab mommy's personal hand fan, and fan me!" I commanded Wyan. Pointing my index finger at the fan, Yea this is the type of shit a nigga like ME, does.

Wyan looked at me like I was talking to him in Russian.

"HUH?"

"Huh WHAT? I ain't stutter nigga! GRAB mommy's personal hand fan, and fan me! Fuck wrong with you?" I ordered him again. Then, stood there with my arms folded across my chest and waited for him to obey me.

I remember Wyan looking at me like I'd lost it. Might have. I'll tell you what though, 2 minutes later, Wyan stood in front of me waving that fan on me like I was the Prince of Philly. Yea, his ass knew!

We still went through shit with them 5th Street boy's. Although it was never with Squeaky or Russy again. One of them died R.I.P through other hands. The other one went to jail. But like I said, we still had our run ins with them. Through the years, the same fist fights would turn in to deadly shoot outs. I could have chosen 5th Street over 7th Street. But naa, I'm from 7th Street.

Anyway, back to how I came about. My father died when I was 4 year's old. After that was when my mother met her boyfriend. I guess he did alright. Together they had my little sister, Ameenah. Whom I love, but don't really mess with too much because she gets on my damn nerves. This was after we moved to that project house on 5th street. Keep in mind, me and Wyan would manage to make it back down 7th street no matter where we moved to.

Don't get it confused, we're still in with 5th street. We have family there. Bone-Neck and Kaleen are from over there. They're our cousins. Our family is big. Our uncles have a lot of children. My Grandfather had about 7sons. Three to my grandmother, Jean and four to another beautiful lady whom I've never met. He was a stand up man. He also had about ten daughter's, five to my grandmother, and five with the other woman. All of those uncles and aunts of ours are crazy! But I love them. They all have children. My uncles on my grandmothers side alone have 16 children. My mother had 3, and Vicky had 4. Though 2 of her boys died before I was even born. I grew up with Key and Mone.

Geno, Sha, and Ty was 'Move Members'. Move Members, was a name Philly gave the people who had to move out of Southwest Philadelphia. See, Southwest Philly around that time was horrible. So the Governor dropped a bomb on that part of the city! Fact. You can check this in the history books of Philadelphia. The Governor dropped that bomb because of the mayhem that was going on in that part of the city at the time. Of course that destroyed almost everything around it. Just in Southwest Philly. And the people who were there had to move. But that didn't make Geno, Sha, or Ty dirty. They were dirty BEFORE that. They grew up dirty. After that my folks had to take them in.

Lloyd, that's my oldest cousin. He grew up on Dickenson street. That's in the middle, between 5th and 7th streets. Lloyd could go between both areas, but he considers himself 7th street.

My uncle's Nut-Nut, and Kareem are from Germantown.

That's Uptown Philly. They come down our way to south Philly all of the time.

We have a few girl cousins too. Not many though. Kareema, Chae, Rodnieka, Quindeis, and Ameena. They all hang around each other. We have a few more female cousins. They live up North Philadelphia somewhere. They come through sometimes.

One day, some of us are on 5th Street watching the girls jump rope. Me and Wyan are watching the girls titties jump up and down. Birney, Linda, and a few other females are out there. It was a good day, until Kia, Tina, Marlow and Mike came walking down 5th street acting like they wanted to fight our cousins. You know us, we weren't allowing that. Even though it did get loud. Neither side was backing down. Me, and Wyan stood in the middle of it all. Everyone, knew everyone. And eventually, our aunts came outside to calm down the commotion.

In the midst of it all, my grandmother calls me and Wyan in the house, to tell us that the girl Marlow, is our cousin!

"No she not!" Me and Wyan said at the same time.

"Yes she is! That is your uncle Cider's daughter," my grandma corrected us.

"She do look like uncle Cider. And Lloyd too!" Wyan said as he studied her.

"Yea. She do!" I stood next to him, and looked out of the same window at Marlow. I had to agree.

Me and Wyan went back outside to tell Marlow what we'd just heard. She didn't believe us. We told her we'd just found out. See, Marlow's mother always denied who her father was to her because of my uncle Cider's drug doing, and dealing with other women on her. As a result, Marlow never knew who her father really was.

That was just an example of how we had family we knew, and didn't know of.

In the end, the girls never fought. And Marlow, of course went back to her mother asking her were we related. She told us her mother told her no! But, Marlow knew she was lying. The main reason was because every time she saw Cider, or Lloyd after that day she realized just how much she resembled them. After that no matter what her mom said Marlow grew up agreeing that we were cousins. That was crazy. Memories.

That same day a bit later on I walked up to Marshall street. I left Wyan on the block and went to see my father's side of my family.

Me and Wyan have different father's. My father's side of the family took care of me. Bought me clothes, bikes and gave me money if they had it. I wasn't doing bad back then. I always had nice things.

My father's name was Monroe. I was told he grew up down Oregon Avenue with the Italians. Back in those days when you were from Marshall Street, you couldn't go down 7th street. But my dad had heart. He would go anywhere he pleased. Eventually, he'd made his way down my way. That was where he'd met my mother. She was at a store on 7th street trying to buy some candy. My father paid for it. They ended up together.

My folks said my father used to always come to my grandmother's house looking for my mother. He started staying over soon after that. Then eventually hanging with my uncles.

One day my father and his best friend Frank were standing on the corner in their neighborhood. Marshall street. That is still considered 7th street, but on the other side. Anyway, they'd witnessed two white men commit a homicide. The two white men that did it, saw my father and Frank. At that time, the rule to live by was 'Kill all witnesses'. This would fall on them.

So, a few days later some men caught Frank at the bar and blew his head off.

My father found out what happened, and came down 7th street to lay low with my uncles. They had each other's back. By that time, Frank's killer was long gone.

Weeks later, my father was alone on Broad Street coming from a party. He went to take the subway home. When he got down into the subway station, a white man appeared behind him and pushed him on to the train track's as the train was coming. The train killed my dad.

Word got back to my family. Everyone met at my grandmother's house. While they were downstairs figuring it all out, my mom woke up and came down the stairs to see everyone, except Monroe. She saw the commotion, but she didn't see Monroe. This told her something was wrong because she knew he would normally be there when she awoke.

"Where is Monroe? Where is Monroe?" she began asking, as she went from face to face and room to room.

No one wanted to be the bearer of bad news.

"Lavern somebody killed him last night," her sister had to take the weight.

My mom stared at her in disbelief for a few seconds. Then shock set in, and she ran upstairs crying. That was a bad morning for everybody. My father was a good dude. They say the whole 7th street was at my grandmother's house, showing their respect.

A little me at that time, was too young to understand it all. Though when I got older, men and women who knew my father told me he was a good man. I used to love to hear them stories. I still do. Sometimes I'll go to one of the Mom and Pop stores, to buy some of the older folk's drinks and just listen to them tell me their stories, or memories they had with my father. They all say I look, and act Just like Monroe.

I remember one day, I was over my father's house chilling with my aunt Shirley and a few cousins Donna, Tina, Nikki, and Vernon. Now, me and my aunt Shirley were real close. I mean tight. Shirley had a sickness, but I didn't care. I loved her.

The family used to play cards at her house all of the time. I did almost everything with my aunt. My cousins called me Lil Earl over there. Sometimes they played too much. They knew I don't like that shit.

This day, we were at the dinner table. I'm the baby out of the bunch. I'm sitting under Shirley, and my cousins are playing around at the table. I don't like it. And you know me, as soon as one of them get crazy with me OR my aunt Shirley, I gotta do something. And guess what they do? Call me LIL Earl!

I looked at Shirley cause she knows I don't like when they do that and she gave me the 'go ahead do whatever you feel face'. That was all I needed. I got up out of my chair and walked up behind them.

I walked upon Donna first.

SMACK!

Then Tina…

SMACK!

Then Nikki…

SMACK!

Vernon was last…

SMACK!

I smacked him as hard as I could, because he was the boy. And of course, he was the one to get tough.

"YO ni…" Vernon jumped up like he wanted some work. I was sure ready to give it to his ass too.

"Boy, sit the fuck down!" Aunt Shirley snapped at him. Told y'all she had my back.

After that my cousins started calling me Big Earl. They called me that all day too. Yea, I was feeling that. But I had bigger plans.

"Naa don't call me that no more. Call me, "The Bone Crusher!" I poked my chest out.

My cousins started laughing like I was being funny or something.

"Oh yea?" I looked over at my aunt Shirley.

She looks back at me, and she sees I'm serious. That made her serious.

"What y'all laughing for? Y'all got a problem with what he said?"

"He said call him The Bone Crusher, I'm not doing that!" Donna kept laughing.

"Oh, you goin do it!" I snapped my eyes at her. The look

on my face, was the same look it had when I smacked them a few hours ago.

Donna seen it and got with my program.

"Ok, I'll do it."

After she fell in line, they all fell in line.

"We'll call him "The Bone Crusher," they stopped laughing. They didn't want me firing off again. They knew.

As we got older, we all went our separate ways. And my best friend, and FAVORITE aunt Shirley passed away on us. (R.I.P).

Pardon me y'all, I gotta take a quick moment for my aunt.

Aunt Shirley, you are a good woman. You will always be loved and missed. I want to thank you, for opening your doors up to me. THANK YOU, for allowing me to play cards with you. And THANK YOU, for leaving me in your home, when I didn't have anywhere else to go.

GOD BLESS YOU!

Chapter 1

Shopping at Forman Mills

(Years later)

Alright check it out and pay close attention because I'm only saying this once for you. Yes, YOU. Whoever YOU are, reading this book. YOU. I have 6 main females in my circle. Some of them I'm creeping with, and some I'm not.

I got Vita, Aisha, Shaleen, Shatema, Tasha, and Shakeah. Then I have my girlfriends. There's Jada, Ericka, Tiffany (Muff), Porsha, and Pooh. ALL at the same time! Yea, Boss moves. All of these chicken heads love me. And I love them too. They all have different personalities. But I keeps their asses in check.

I met Jada back in 1991. I was driving down Front and Snyder Avenue on my way to Wendy's to grab a bite to eat with a few dudes I knew.

"Yo pull over! PULL over!" One damn near jumped out of the moving car with his thirsty ass.

I pulls over thinking there's a Rolls Royce for sale for a price I just might have in my pocket! The way his ass was yelling it had to be something close!

"Fuck you yelling like that for?" I looked up to see and saw it.

Two of the prettiest twin girls I think I'd ever laid eyes on. At least up until that point. "Ohh," was all I could say. They were worth the stop.

They were so bad I had to get out of my car and go and talk to them! And I was driving the 91 Honda accord with the 20-inch rims on her! (Aight, aight, they were 10 inches. But I kept them clean!)

I approached the prettiest of the two immediately. Meanwhile, her and her sister saw me coming toward them, and both of their eyes got wide. I know they were thinking I'm a rapper or professional athlete or something. Because I was shining hard. Yea Philly nigga.

"If one of us get this nigga we'll be out of the projects for good!" I know both of them are thinking as I step closer.

My other homies stayed in the car. They knew this level of the game was out of their league.

"Excuse me, can I holler at you for a second?"

"Yes." I got both of their attention.

"My name is Red Bone and I'm from Seventh Street." I introduced myself.

See saying I'm from 7th Street after saying my name, was like saying the name of the basketball team I played ball for, after mentioning I played ball. (I hope you caught that reader.)

Anyway, after I said my fly shit one of the twins said some whole other shit. "My name is Jeva. It's so grateful to meet you."

"HUH? It's so grateful to meet me? This chick sounded like a white girl was the only thing on my mind. I'd never heard a black woman use the word grateful in that way before. Not in Philly, "I hope this other twin don't turn me off." I looked at her next.

"Hi. My name is Jada You look so good," the prettier one said.

"Aight, that's more like it. You look good too. Where y'all sexy ladies headed to?"

They both spoke at the same time, "To Boston Market" Jada said. "To model," the other one said.

In the back of my mind I know they're lying. But at this moment, her lies are not my business.

"Ok, cool. Well look, here's my number. Give me a call whenever," I handed my cell number to Jada.

"I will give you a call," she nodded at me.

***

"Them bitches look good!" Pugie was saying back in the car.

"Hold up Pugie," I had to check him. I was feeling that chick Jada. She didn't seem like the average 'hood rat' I ran across, and I could picture her in my future. So, I had to let him know his boundaries. "That chick Jada might be my wife, so don't ever call her a bitch again," I looked at him.

But the look I gave him was like a warning shot from a sawed-off shotgun. And Pugie knew what that meant coming from me.

Pugie put his hand in his mouth and put his head down.

He knew if he jumped out of line I'd smack the shit out of him.

So anyway, we hit Wendy's. And since Pugie disrespected my new wife and her sister, well, free food on him. My other homies Lenny and Hoarse are both in the backseat laughing because they know I'm about to get some free food. Lenny is my 'Down south' 7th street homey. He's from 7th street, but he's so dark you would think he's from down south. And Hoarse, he's just my young bull from my block. Anything can go down when I'm with these dudes. They're with whatever I'm with, and they stay with a gun and a pack on them.

Ok we got our food. Pugie paid for it. And as I'm driving away from Wendy's, Pugie turns around to look at my homies. "That's the LAST time I'm paying for y'all food!"

Lenny and Hoarse kept right on eating, smacking on the food purposely, so they could aggravate Pugie! Ha! Trouble maker's! Their faces said what they were thinking.

"Yea right nigga. FUCK outta here, you goin' do whatever Bone-Crusher tells you to do!"

Pulling out from Wendy's, I hit the back road where I first saw the twin's walking. I wanted to see if I saw them again. And I did. Hoarse spotted them first.

"Bone look, there go them twin's again."

"Where?"

"Right there. They're walking toward Forman Mills," Lenny saw them too.

"Yea, the cheap store." Pugie added in. "Oh, shit them bitches lied to you Red Bone," this nigga Pugie had the nerve to say out of his mouth.

Smh! This nigga don't learn!

Hoarse and Lenny just looked at one another. They knew I was about to teach homey a little lesson. He forgot what I had just told him. But he's going to remember after I finish this class with his face and my hands.

"Slap! Slap! SLAP! SLAP!" were the sound of my hands on him. I back hand slapped him, then front hand slapped him, then BACK handed him, and FRONT handed him again! All with the SAME hand! Fuck wrong with him!

Now, he's holding his face and looking at me all dumb.

"Bone, WHY are you bitch slapping me like this?" Pugie's hollering.

I got him screaming like the bitch he is now.

"DIDN'T I tell you not to call my future wife and her sister bitches again?"

"Damn old head, I forgot. I'm sorry," he's whining.

Hoarse and Lenny are in the back seat, laughing. "Yo Bone, tell that nigga to buy us some pizza!" Lenny whispered in my ear.

He knows I got Pugie now, and he wants to see how far I can take it with him. "Make that nigga get us some chips too!" he adds.

I can hear the humor in his voice. He's funny.

"Didn't he say he ain't buying y'all no more food?"

"Yea, that's what he said, but that bitch slap you put on him goin make him forget ALL that! He don't want to get slapped like that again. I know he don't! Pugie's going to do whatever you say right now."

I looked at Lenny through my rearview mirror, then I turned to look at Pugie. His lips are bleeding and swollen like fried sausages. And his eyes have tears in them. Yea, Lenny's right he's going pay for that food.

"Yo Pugie, when we get to my house you're going to have two choices to choose from."

"Ok, but what are those two choices Bone-Crusher?" Pugie's asked curious.

"You want me to tell you now, or when we get to my house?"

"Now," he sniffled.

"Ok Pugie, tonight you either buy my boys some pizza and chips, or you clean my dog's shit up?"

I revealed the choices. Sounds harsh yea, but Pugie does things in the hood niggas don't approve of anyway. So, yea, those choices fit his grimy ass.

Pugie's looking at everyone. Lenny put his head down, Hoarse is rubbing his stomach, and I'm waiting for his answer. Pugie's still thinking hard on what he wants to do. As he should. I know he's not going to clean my dog's shit up.

"Pugie, what are you going to do?" I looked at him.

"Didn't I tell y'all two dirty nigga's that I'm not paying for y'all food no more?" Pugie turned to Hoarse and Lenny. Then he turned back to face me and swallowed his spit before he spoke "Bone Crusher, I would rather clean that dog's shit off of the ground before I feed one of these nigga's again!"

"It's a done deal then Pugie. You've made the right choice," stepped on the gas pedal.

10 minutes later, I pulled up in front of my house. The homies immediately jumped out of the car and went to tell

the block Pugie was about to clean my dog's shit up. The next thing you know, the whole 7th street was at my house watching Pugie clean my dog's poop.

Me, I'm in my car. Thinking hard about the twin's. Seriously, they were beautiful. I can make things happen with Jada. But the only way me and her are going to work is if she stops shopping at Forman Mills.

ITS BONE CRUSHER, BITCH!!!

CHAPTER 2

These girls are Thieves!

Nephatia...

It was 1994. I was posted outside of one of the corner stores on my block. Now it's our strip so the owner of the store knows us, and of course we all know him. So, I'm caught off guard when I hear this young girl voice screaming, and the sound is coming from inside of the store.

"Get off of me! Let me go! GET OFF OF ME!"

"What the fu--?"

I went into the store to see what was up. I saw Lee the Chinese store owner holding a young girl from around my way by the arm. And by the looks of his grip he isn't letting go.

"Lee why are you holding her like that?"

"This bald head bitch been stealing out my store every month, around the same time!" Lee forced out in broken English. Which was funny because his ass barley knew English any other time.

"Every month Lee, are you serious?" This man is buggin'.

"Yes, Red Bone, EVERY month!" Lee said, while he was still struggling with the dirty little chick.

"Let her go Lee, let her go," I told Lee. Lee did let her go, and when he did as soon as she got loose she ran out of his store and snatched something on her way out.

"Hey YOU!" Lee was about to chase her down. I stopped him.

"Chill Lee let her go. Whatever she took I'll cover it," I cooled him.

Lee smiled at that.

"Take a walk with me to the back Red Bone," Lee motioned me.

I walked with him to the back. He took me to a room where he played a video tape for me. On the tape, it was Kia, Marty, Netta, and Nephatia. The one he'd just had in his grip, was Nephatia. Kia and Netta seemed like they had started an argument with Lee's wife at the counter, while Marty and Nephatia were in the back of the store stealing. I see Marty taking eggs, bacon, bread and some butter. Then I see Nephatia taking tampons. "Oh sh--, THAT'S why Lee said she stole every month around the same time." The Tampons!

Lee was 100% correct! It happened around the same time. Every month she was there. March, 8:30 in the am. April, in the am. May, in the am. June. July. I'm seeing 2 years straight of them doing this. Consistently.

"Ok Lee, how much does she owe you?"

"Three hundred and forty-five dollars," Lee says as he's looking into his notebook. He's fronting, he's trying to overcharge me because he knows I got it.

"Lee stop playing, now you trying to rob me!"

Lee got quiet. He's caught. Now he's thinking about what a man like me will do to him if he tries to push it. Lee saw me beat up Dor, Grimise, and Pig before, and Lee doesn't want the treatment I gave them.

"Red Bone, if you give me two fifty I won't press charges on her."

"Ok Lee, that's a done deal." I reached in my pocket and gave Lee the money right then and there for Nephatia.

"What about the bacon and eggs the other girls stole?" Lee asked me. But like I said, we all know each other, so I know Lee knows who those other girl's folks are.

"You gotta hollar at their folks about them Lee," I left him with.

"Red Bone, don't get mad if I don't let them bitches back in my store again," Lee said to my back as I walked out of his store.

"It's coo cool with me," I said over my shoulder.

I walked out of the store looking for Nephatia. I ran into her cousin Karon. "Karon, did you see Nephatia?"

"Yea, she just ran into the house without saying anything," he said. In the back of my mind, I knew she ran to put the pad on she'd just stolen. "Why are you looking for my little cousin?"

"She left her change in the store," I told his nosey ass. I didn't want to get Nephatia in trouble by telling him the truth. Plus, it wasn't his business anyway.

"Change?" Karon screwed his face up. He knew something. He ran off into his house. I guess he went to go check on his money.

See, what I didn't know was Nephatia was a thief. I mean

a real thief! Stole everything she could get her hands on, and from whoever she could steal it from! Of course, that was until she met the Bone Crusher. Y'all know I had to step her game up. At first it was just me wanting to aid her. And, she appreciated it, and showed me she appreciated it. And her showing me she did appreciate it, made me appreciate her because that is all any real man wants to feel. We fell in love. I had her looking like she hit the neighborhood lottery! This chick was buying her own tampons and all after that. Yea. That's how a 7th street nigga do it!

IT'S BONE CRUSHER BITCH!

CHAPTER 3

This Nigga Malcolm

Let me tell y'all about Malcolm right quick. Now, Malcolm was a good dude, don't get it wrong. But it was just hard to get money around a nigga like him. He was the type to give you some work, then rob you for it after he got snorted! Or, shit just rob you, period! Take HIS money and YOUR money!

Anyway, this was a day most of us were waiting at the park, to get together and go to a basketball game While we're there, Malcolm walks up like he's about to shoot somebody.

"Yo Bone?"

"What's up Malcolm?"

I'm hesitant, because I already know it might be anything with this bull. He was crazy. So, I'm on needles about what he wants.

"Did you see your brother Wyan, or Bull Dog?"

"No, Not yet."

"Well, if you do tell them they're dead men if they don't have my money when I see them!"

"Damn! What the fuck did my brother and Bull Dog do

to this killer?" I'm thinking. Because when Malcolm said something like that, he meant it! I had to ask.

"Yo Malcolm, why are you looking for my brother?"

Malcolm just eyed me and walked off. Malcolm was the type of dude who did reckless shit, but you didn't ask him too many questions. Type nigga to say something, and that was it! He said you owed him, you did. If you didn't owe him, you paid him like you did, to keep him from taking what you had! Seriously, this boy was one of the reasons them J.B.M boys did not come through South Philly with that 'GET DOWN or LAY DOWN' shit! HIM, his cousin Kenyatta, and a couple of other goons is from uptown, South Philly.

"Fuck that! Whoever see my brother Wyan, or his man Bull Bog, tell em Malcolm is looking for them!" I announced.

"Man, FUCK Malcolm! He ain't killing nobody!" Lavon said.

See, Lavon and Malcolm were both fucking this chick named Nell at the same time. Nell was a regular hood chick from 7th street, but her cake must've been good because a few men got into it over her. Anyway, Lavon was mad that Nell was fucking Malcolm, so he was using this situation to downgrade Malcolm. Little did he know, Malcolm wanted an excuse to do something to him.

"Bul' YOU tripping!" everyone who'd heard Lavon, looked at him.

Pugie's bitch ass walked off. Hoarse saw him.

"Yo Lavon, let's take a walk. Pugie's snitching ass is going to go tell Malcolm what you just said," Hoarse warned him.

"Fuck PUGIE too!" Lavon snapped, and continued with his dice game.

Sure enough, 10 minutes later Malcolm came walking down the block. Lavon's back is turned to him while he's squatted, shooting dice. Malcolm grabs my pedal bike, lifts it above his head walked over to Lavon, and brought the bike down on his back!

"WHAT the fuck!?" Lavon jumped up ready to work.

Malcolm stood there looking at Lavon. Waiting on him to move. Lavon realized it was Malcolm and froze in his act. You could see it in Lavon's face he was thinking about swinging but he'd left it alone because he knew Malcolm was going to take it where he didn't want it to go. And TRUST me, if it was ANYBODY else, Lavon would've went! But when it came to Malcolm, Lavon tucked his lions tail in and put his head down! When Malcolm was done with my bike, I went to get it.

"Get the fuck off the bike!" Malcolm jumped at me.

"You got it playa," I put my hands up. Fuck that bike. Wasn't mine's anyway. I took it from Lenny.

Now Malcolm is looking for some shit to get in. Once he starts, there was no stopping him. And, I wasn't the only one who knew it. Within five minutes the whole block cleared out. Hustler's, gambler's and all had walked off. The block was dead, and there was no one out there for Malcolm to rob.

"Yo Malcolm, be careful out here. The police are out here heavy looking for J Bird because he walked out of Toys-R-Us with some toys," old head Brandywine told Malcolm just to get him off of the block. It was hard to eat with that kind of dude around. This is my point. Malcolm got scared and walked off. He had some warrants for who knows what, so he was smart enough to leave.

"Good looking man, Malcolm was about to rob all of us," I overheard old head Mark tell Brandywine.

The old heads knew how Malcolm was. When Malcolm came around, you would see them old head stuffing their money in their socks!

***

I'ma share another quick story with y'all.

One day me and Arron, (another 7th street homey) were on the block chillin. All of a sudden, Arron saw Malcolm approaching.

"Malcolm coming!" he warned me and began stuffing his own money in his ass!

I didn't like the idea of that. Not out of fear of no man.

"Man, I ain't doing all of that, I'm cool. I'm Bone Crusher, Fuck I look like?" I'm saying to myself. But I'm talking to Arron.

And yea, I knew who Malcolm was and what he was about. But at that time, I was just fed up with his shit, and I wasn't going for him taking nothing else from me. Fuck that! I wasn't stuffing nothing in my ass for this nigga. And if he came to me with that bullshit, I was going to tell him straight up, "I ain't giving you SHIT!" That's it, that's all! Fuck I look like? ME! Letting another nigga take something from me. Yea, not this time. We ain't young no more! COME ON!" I hyped myself.

Malcolm walked up. "I need my money," he went at Fitz first.

Yea, Malcolm aint even come at me with that shit. He know! I wish a nigga would!

"I don't owe you nothing," Arron's bitch ass is pleading.

I'm standing on the side of this nigga thinking to myself "Fitz you are one soft dude! You'd better not give this man your money. I'ma tell the whole neighborhood! Watch."

Without another word Malcolm pulls his gun out. His eyes met Arron's. Shit just got real. We both knew Malcolm did not care about life!

"Here man," Arron went right in his ass and gave Malcolm his money.

ALL of it too. $1's, $5's, $10's, $20's, quarters, nickels, and dime. Everything! Malcolm stood there with his hand open as Fitz emptied his pockets in it. I just stared in shock, at Fitz. When Fitz (Arron) was finished giving Malcolm his money, Malcolm turned his gaze to me.

At that moment, I had a choice to make. I just watched a grown man give his money to this man. What was I supposed to do? Fuck all of that imaginary shit I was talking to myself, this was real life! Shit, I had to do what I had to do. So, I did what was best for a man like me TO do.

By the time Malcolm realized it, I was in the wind! Half way down the block at full speed! Fuck that, Malcolm wasn't getting this $1,500 I stood out there for hours to make this!

Hell yea, I took off! Down 6th street, right through the alleyway on McKean St, and came out on Dugley street. Later for Malcolm. I ain't got time for his shit.

"Young Bul' what you running for?" one of them old

heads asked me, after he'd seen me come of out the alleyway.

"Malcolm on the loose!" I warned him. That was all I needed to say.

A few minutes later, after I caught my breath I decided to just chill down this side of the block for a minute. I didn't know what the hell Malcolm was up to, or if he was still on my side of the block. While I was over that way, I saw J-Lip. J-Lip is a player from 7th street. He was standing on Dugley street out front of Shocku's garage, talking to some chick I knew named Sania.

Sania was a thick, brown skinned young girl from around our way. The first thing I noticed was how good Sania was looking. Immediately my mind set its wheels in motion to work for me.

This was perfect I ran into J-Lip, for 2 reasons. 1st was because I just ran from Malcolm, and I needed somebody to feed to him if he found his way to me again. And Malcolm already didn't like J-Lip. Well, that man didn't like anybody for real. And the 2nd reason this was so perfect was because of how good Sania was looking.

Sania was thick, and I guess J-Lip caught her before she made it to school, because she still had her school uniform on. We were all young, so we were supposed to be in school too. But school was in the way of a young hustler's success, so later for school.

Anyway, Sania was built like Tiffany, but thicker. Big round butt and some fleshy legs. Yea, I can have fun with that. And if I can get J-Lip out of my way, I could have her to myself. J-Lip is slow I can do that.

"J-Lip, what's up young bul?" I greeted him.

"Bone what's up young bul?" J-Lip walked over to me.

"Aww ain't shit, what's going on?"

While I spoke to J-Lip, I was checking for a door I could use to work my way into the equation.

"I got Sania ready to go! I just don't have nowhere to take her," J-Lip looked at me.

That was my door!

"Well, y'all can use my crib if I can fuck?" I offered J-Lip.

"Aight hold on I'll be right back," J-Lip went to propose it to Sania. He was back within the minute..."Yea yo, she cool with it."

Of course she was. We were known hustler's. "Cool. My crib is on Eighth and Segal," I lead the way.

J-Lip drove us in his car. What J-Lip didn't know was it was Darryl's place. He just gave me the keys to it. Yea, I was winning all of the way around the board! All I had to do was get J-Lip out of my way now.

A short while later, we were pulling up to Darryl's. It was my last chance to get rid of this dude and I just came up with a way.

"J-Lip, run to Seven Eleven right quick and grab us some rubbers!" I thought fast and laid the bait for him.

"Aight!" J-Lip took the money out of my hand. He went right for it. Smh!

"Yea, go get that DUMMY!"

Meanwhile, me and Sania got out of the car and went inside of the house. As soon as we both were in, I shut the door, locked all of the locks and put the keys in my pocket.

J-Lip can't get in, and this bitch can't get out!

I turned to Sania. "Listen, I told him to run to Seven Eleven, but I already got the condoms in my pocket. I'm just trying to fuck you right quick, then let y'all do y'all because I gotta leave." I laid the game down to her before she could even think straight.

"Well why did you send J-Lip on that ghost mission?" this bitch had the nerve to ask a 7th street nigga like myself! Like she gave a fuck. Smh!

A Ghost· mission was a dead mission around my way. A mission that lead whoever was on it nowhere! Because it was unnecessary to begin with. But I was appalled at the audacity of her asking me some shit like that. Bitch, didn't I just tell you why?

"Because I wanted you to myself," I sweet talked her.

"You're wrong for that Red Bone."

"Yea aight, whatever." This bitch is acting like she really cares I dumped this nigga. Hah! I just ignored her ass and fixed the condom on myself.

Meanwhile, the whole time she's talking about me being wrong, she's wiggling out of her clothes. Smh! See what I mean?

Sania had one of them K. Michelle asses. I mean, as soon as I stood behind all of that ass I was hard. I had to pull her ass cheeks apart just to get in that. I know J-Lip is going to be mad. He'll get his turn, after I get mines. Ha!

So we're getting it in. This little dick is in her guts for about the next 5 minutes, and right when I'm about to bust my nut I hear the door!

"Knock, Knock, knock!"

"Knock, knock, knock!"

I'm trying to ignore it and get this nut off. This nigga wasn't having it.

"Knock, knock, knock!"

"Yo Bone!" this clown is calling me.

I continue doing me. I'll open the door as soon as I bust this nut.

"KNOCK, KNOCK, KNOCK!" He knocked harder on the door. Then he went crazy.

"DOOM! DOOM! DOOM! DOOM!"

"Yo BONE, I got these CONDOMS!"

I can see him out my window, in the middle of the street yelling! I can't help but laugh. That nigga wants some of this. "I'll bet YOU do got them condoms. Ha! Just a few more sec---"

"Doom! Doom! Doom!" This nigga kept kicking the door.

I can't bust with him doing all of this wild shit. He was about to get the neighbors involved! I looked out of the window, and J-Lip had all kinds of shit. Soda, Chips, Cigarettes and some more shit! This nigga was so ready! Ha! Not tonight young Bul'.

"Yo, go get us something to eat. By the time you get back we'll be done. My word!" I pushed him off again. "Get ya silly ass out of here, you ain't get the picture yet?" I'm thinking.

"What do you w---?"

"Clack!"

I shut the window on him. Fuck out of here!

Now I'm back in the pussy. 5 more minutes, and the

mighty Bone-Crusher is done. Time to get me some sleep.

Sania was on the porch, waiting for J-Lip by the time he got back.

"Knock, knock, knock, knock."

I hear. I know it's this nigga. I know its him, because I told him he could fuck her after me in this crib. And he must've believed me. Yea, picture that.

"KNOCK, knock, knock!" he was getting louder!

That was it, I snapped on him.

"Yo, what the fuck you want?" I looked at J-Lip with my crazy look. This is when I back hand people. But J-Lip wasn't in my palms reach. Damn!

"Yo, what's up dog, I thought you said can fuck her in your house?"

"Listen you ain't fucking her in here. I don't care what I said. No. You got some money?"

J-Lip looked at me, "Money? You serious?"

"Yea I'm serious! Matter of fact, get the fuck from out here or I'm telling Malcolm you around here!" I barked on him.

"Ayo. You's a dirty nigga Bone," J-Lip tried.

"Oh you think I'm playing?" I reached for my phone. When I looked back out of the window J Lip was gone.

"It's ok. We can do something in your Benz," I overheard Sania say.

"Yea aight! Better get the fuck out here!" J Lip snapped on her.

He was already heated that a playa like me overpowered the both of them. Seconds later I heard J-Lip's Benz screech off. Shortly after I heard police sirens outside.

"What the fu--?" I looked outside and saw a few squad cars, and they had Malcolm in handcuffs! Damn. It's fucked up, but I know people will be happy. One of them old heads might have called the cops on him, to get him out of the way.

The next day, I saw Arron. Well, Fitz same person.

"Yo, why did you run yesterday?"

"Cause I didn't want to kill Malcolm! That's why!" I talked my shit.

Fitz frowned his mouth at me. He knew I was lying.

"Look, don't worry about Malcolm no more, aight? He's locked up."

"I know he's locked up. I'm the one who called the cops on him!"

This man had the guts to admit this, to a certified 7th street nigga like myself.

"What?" This nigga must be high. I checked his eyes Nope, he didn't look high. I had something for his ass. Right then and there I pulled my gun out, and placed the barrel on his chest.

"Yo Bone, what the fuck are you doing?" his eyes got wide. If he was high, he isn't now.

"SLAP!" I open hand smacked him. "I hate snitches!" I leered at him. Then went into his pockets. "Forty-six dollars? Forty-six d—"

"CRACK!"

I hit him with the front of my pistol. "I don't ever want to see you out here again!" I stepped off on him. "$46.00 damn dollars!"

With Malcolm out of the way, 7th was wide open for a young man like myself to take over. The first thing I had to do was get my money up. Then buy a ton of guns to get my team right. 7th street needs to go to another level. I needed to recruit 1 or 2 thorough Young bulls. I knew who I had in mind.

CHAPTER 4

Saigon Projects

7th. St.

Farrej is a young bul' off of Moore St from around my way. I'd been watching him. And I know he's been watching me. I pulled up on him days later.

"Farrej what's up young bul?" Today was his day. I was about to see if he had it or not.

"Whas' sup Red Bone," he greeted me back from his porch. His eyes are glued to my Acura legend. My rims are shining hard.

It was that look in his eyes I wanted to groom it.·

"What's up young bul', you tryna roll down to Thirteenth Street? It's a party over there?" I offered him.

His face lit up. "Yeah we can roll Bone." He says. His eyes still glued to the car.

"Aight now, if you goin roll with the Bone crusher you can't be scared," I checked his temperature. It wasn't the party I was offering him. It was the position of being associated with me and everything that came with it.

"Na, I ain't scared Red Bone. I know what it is," he joined

Ty Ty, the other young bul' I'd recruited about an hour before him, in my backseat.

"Aight. We're going to enjoy ourselves at this party. But we're goin strap up because some dudes don't like the love we get when we go places. We gotta have each other's back. Yall hear me? Yall got my back?"

"Yea, we got ya back Bone!"

"Aight. I got yall's too It's about time we all looked out for each other. I reached down into my pocket. "Here!" I gave them each $200.00 apiece.

"Yall don't ever have to go nowhere without no money again. Like I said, have my back, I'ma have yall's," I bonded with them.

The both of them were busy stuffing money inside of their pockets. But I know they'd heard me. Loud and clear.

"Here, grab them guns from under that seat."

They did.

"Ohh shit!" They each stared at the handguns.

"Yeeeaa," Ty Ty said. Ty wasn't new to it. He liked this sort of thing.

After being amazed by it all, their eyes told me everything I needed to see. They were ready to be tested.

$...$...$...$...$

We parked on 13th Street. As soon as we did, I spotted a dude I had issues with in high school. Well, I didn't have any issues with him. He had an issue with me because I was fucking his girlfriend, child mother. It's an old beef but I still don't trust these boys. Pussy make niggas get crazy.

"Yo, y'all see the boy with the red hat on? His name is Back To Back. Watch him. And if he looks like he's going to make a move, y'all squeeze first. Because these bul's are sneaky. Just like us I told the both of them.

"I'm ready to buss at him right now," Ty Ty looked at me.

I smiled to myself. I knew I'd picked a good one.

We're on 13th and Christian Streets, looking at Sagon projects from that view. People don't really come through these projects for real. These boys act crazy over here. But, we're from 7th Street, we go where we will. So toward the building we headed.

***

"Yo Bone, don't come in here starting nothing," someone said right before I stepped into the building.

I turned my head to see Chester. I know Chester from up 31st Street. He used to stay with my cousin Don. I did too sometimes. Chester was a goon, who'd had a bad accident on his Banchi bike. Now he has pins in his leg.

"What's up Chester? You got my word I ain't going to start nothing. But if these niggas start hating, I'm going to give them what they want!" Me and Chester started laughing.

"Did Malcolm really get locked up?'"

"Yea, he booked." I told him and gave him dap at the same time.

With that, me and Chester were done greeting, and me and my boys headed to the party.

Once they realized where we were headed, Ty Ty was the

first to speak.

"I know this party ain't in Sagon's?"

"Yes it is," I confirmed.

"Aight. Fuck it," Ty Ty agreed.

"And y'all know me, as long as I got my baby on my hip I'm good!"

The projects smelled like piss and fried chicken. I don't know how these people party like this, but if they can do it so can we.

The party was on the 9th floor. It was either the stairs, or the elevator. Of course, we took the elevator. And that was where we ran into our first encounter. And it wasn't with Back to back.

When the elevator door swung open, I saw Diq smoking ass and Ebony (from down my way?) and they were in there with, John John. See, Ebony was fucking with Diq. But neither him, or John knew she was getting high.

Shit, Who was I to put her out there?

You could almost hear a pin drop as we walked on the elevator. I could see Ebony shaking, because she knows it might pop off. I pressed 9 on the button panel, then put my eyes back on Diq and John John.

Dig was a big dude. 6 foot 6 but sloppy. John on the other hand was just big. But all muscle. Football player type nigga. But the elevator is small, and me and my boys are strapped. And I know some stomach shots will break all of that big boy shit down. Let them get stupid.

Okay, so we made it to the party without a problem.

"Seventh Street is out there y'all!" one of the girls saw us. Once she blurted that out, a few of the other girls came out to the hallway.

"Hey what's up?" they came polite.

"Red Bone what's up boy? I'm glad y'all made it," Shatema came out. It was her sister, Sharon's party.

"What's up? You know I'm coming. Thanks for inviting me." I smiled And before we knew it we'd shut the party down. Most of the girl's that were inside the party, were in the hallway, partying with us!

That made the boys mad. "Who the fuck is that?" I overheard.

The first face I noticed at the door was Butter. Another dude I had went to school with. I can't remember why we beefed, but we did.

"The fuck are you doing here?" he peered at me.

"The fuck are YOU doing here?" I voiced right back. I see Ty Ty and Farrej reaching for their guns out of my side eye. So did Shatema, and she knew where that was about to go.

"Whoa whoa, y'all are here for Me!" she jumped between us, and pushed Butter and his people backward.

Butter screwed his face up, but he didn't say anything. Him and his squad stepped back. They knew us, and they respected Shatema.

Me, Farrej and Ty stayed in the hallway. It was too many people in that little ass apartment. But we had plenty of fun. The females kept coming out to party with us when they saw us out there. We were on point though. They were hood rats, and they would set you up for one of their own boys quick. After about an hour, we'd left. The party was dead. We just came to show our faces.

"Hold on Bone, I'ma walk y'all to the car," Shatema and some other girls said. The problem was, they were the baddest ones in the party. So when they followed us, Butter and his boys, followed them!

"So when I'ma see you again?" Shatema kept talking as I sat on my car. One of her friends talked to Ty Ty, while Farrej talked to another.

Meanwhile Butter and his boys, stood out front of the projects and watched us the WHOLE time! The animosity they had for us must've been in their weed because I could smell it with every puff they took.

"Aight. Listen we're going to go ahead and roll out, make sure y'all give us a call," I told Shatema, after I seen Ty Ty and Farrej pass their numbers to the ladies they were speaking with.

I know we were looking like stars to these boys driving cars they aren't driving, and the girls they were after, are after us. And right in front of them! We knew it would be like this. That was why we had new gunz. Just for situations like it. We were waiting to try these out. All we needed was a reason. And guess what? They gave us one.

PSHHHHH... PSHHHHH... We'd heard it just as we were about to pull off!

"Oh shit, yo these niggas throwing bottles at us!" Farrej looked, out of the back window. "Yo I think it was the light skinned one. The one they call Butter," he turned back toward us. That was it. It was on!

I got out of the Acura first, then Farrej, then Ty Ty. Butter and his boys scattered! They were fast too. But not faster than these bullets.

Pop! Pop! Pop! Pop! Pop! Pop! Pop! Pop! Pop! Pop! I went crazy! Then Farrej and Ty Ty. Now we're each side by side, busting at these clowns.

I spot a few heads trying to duck that heat. We tried not hit Shatema, because when the shit was about to pop, she was with us. "Don't worry about them. If they try anything I'm riding with y'all," she told us. Then after she'd walked back toward the building, one of these chumps had the nerve!

"AAAGHGGH, my ASS, they hit me in my ass!" I heard Fudge screaming. Then he began limping real fast. That shot didn't slow his ass down, I'll tell you that. Probably because it didn't stop us, from shooting!

We had everybody out there ducking! Niggas was trying to squeeze behind car tires and everything. C more, I seen you ducking boy! Hah! We aight now, but at the time you knew what it was! Hah! The boys were screaming louder than the girls out there!

Butter was hiding behind a rock, so I couldn't hit him. I tore that rock the fuck up though. Yea, 7th Street nigga!

Alright, we jumped back in the car. I looked up as I was changing the gears, and saw Chester looking at me shaking his head at me like; Bul I told you.

I'm looking at him like; Naw Bul, I told YOU! Chester also knows his boys are young and dumb. And like I said, when 7th street goes places, it's always something.

#...#...#...#...#

The next day, I'm on 7th Street chillin...

"Who that yo?" my man Farrej was looking behind me. Indris, Toby, and Lenny was out there with us too.

"I turned around and saw a red Nissan Pathfinder with tinted windows parking slowly on my block.

We all reached for our gunz. Beep! Beep! Whoever it was tried to get my attention, before we got to them gunz. He knew what it would turn into.

"Redbone! Redbone, it's me, Shar u deen!" a voice shouted out of the trucks window. Yea, he knew.

I squinted my eyes now, trying to see if it was the Shar I knew. Other than that; Chop chop! Shar pulled up further and parked in front of us.

"Yo, chill. I came to make Peace!" he stressed, showing both of his hands to us.

"Oh, aight. What's up?" I ask, still clutching the tool, and keeping it behind my leg. I was waiting for him to try something. Anything.

"Hey man, what happened yesterday man?"

"Man them niggas got stupid! They threw a bottle at my car when I was leaving." I looked at Shar with my crazy look.

I really didn't want to wreck with Shar. I knew Shar was a good dude for real, and he was about his money. I'd met him when we were both dealing with females from North Philly. They were sisters, and he was dealing with the older one. We started talking one day, and got aight with each other. He knows I'm not on no bullshit, so it was something his homies did to start that war. And like I said, I didn't want to go at Shar, but if Shar acted like he wanted it, I was sure ready to give it to him.

"They threw bottles at you?" Shar screwed his face up.

"Yea they did wild shit."

"Aight man, don't worry about it. I'ma hollar at them niggas later. I didn't know they did all that," he looked away from me. Then looked back at me, "But damn all of that, listen man; who got that work around here, I need a brick?" He turned war into money. That's what I liked about Shar. The man was about his business.

"Aight, I can get it. I don't got it, but my man do," I told him.

"Aight, I want it."

"Aight bet," I pulled out my phone and called my man J.C.

***

30 minutes later, Shar had his brick, and J.C had his money.

"Aight Bone. I'll get at you," Shar nodded at me with respect before he pulled off into traffic.

"Aight," I nodded back. Then turned to walk with J.C.

"Aight Bone. Word. We can do that EVERY time. Straight money," J.C said, holding that $24,000 in one of them hood grocery store bags.

"Yea nigga, get me my cut! I'm trying to buy this house on Winton St." I smiled.

"Hah, yea I got you."

We got to J.C's house and he counted me out my share of $6,000 cash. That was the first-time I had held a brick. I've probably had more than that in cash, but that wet my tongue.

It was on from there. I'd bought my first house, and began spreading the word around that I had that work!

CHAPTER 5

Jay Shot Me!

(weeks passed)

Things are good for me right now. And just as they're about to get better, something came up. My youngan Farrej is waiting on me at the corner.

"Come on dawg!" I walked past him. I'm moving with a purpose, and Farrej can tell it isn't a drug deal.

"What's up? Where are we going?" he started walking with me instantly.

"We goin around Seventh Street to handle this pussy!"

"Who Jay?"

"Yea, Jay."

"Yo, Bone."

"What?" We're still walking. And by now, we made it to the part of the block Jay hangs on.

"Ms. Brenda told you if you kill her son she's going to call the cops on you."

"Fuck them cops. This pussy got's to go!"

"Well, fuck him. Let's go then," he stepped in sync with

me.

We there now. My eyes are scanning the block for Jay. My blood is rushing and my heart is beating fast. I know I have to catch Jay before he catches me, because he knows how I'm coming. He will drop me if he catches me first, out of fear of me. Just then I spotted him!

"There he go right th…"

Boc! Boc! Boc! Boc! Boc! Boc!

I threw 6 shots at his face. He ran. I missed.

"Damn! That pussy is fast as hell! I don't know how the fuck he got out of the way of that," I said. Looking through the gun smoke the few shots I threw left in the air.

I hear police sirens less than 5 minutes later.

"Yo, you hear that?"

"Hear what?" I wanted to see if Farrej had heard what I'd just heard.

"The cops is coming," he looked around for the red and blue lights.

"Oh shit, that's Ms. Brenda. She must've seen us and heard them gunshots."

Ms. Brenda is the neighborhood town watch lady. So she is always peeking out of her window, and in everybody's business anyway. Her and Markeem. There was a chance of her seeing us. But fuck that. When you shoot the Bone Crusher in his leg, you're getting gunned at! The whole Philly knows that!

"Jay! Jay! Jay!" We hear Ms. Brenda calling her son.

"Damn. I know she gone tell now." She knows about me, and she seen me checking her son a ·day ago when he shot me.

"Fuck it!"

"Yea, fuck it. Her ass better mind her business."

"Jay ain't gone tell."

"He better not fucking tell!"

"Na though Bone, he might."

"Fuck you mean he might?"

"Yo, that is Pugie's cousin. And you know Pugie is a rat," Farrej commented.

"You got a point. It's in his blood. Pugie is a rat. A HUGE rat!"

"That is crazy yo, who did he tell on again?"

Me and Farrej are up on part of 7th Street now.

"Man, the bul Pugie done told on the whole South Philly and a few boys up North too. He mentioned so many names it was crazy. And for no reason too. Ain't get nothing out of it. Then he mentioned my name!"

"Oh word?"

"Yea that pussy did. Fatty showed his statement. He's lucky I don't put one in his head. Nigga like that don't got no morals. He even told on his own grandmother back in the day for a weed case. It all good though. Them dudes uptown are on his ass. His days are numbered."

"What did Jay shoot you for?" Farrej curious. He knows Jay must've been high to even consider some shit like that.

"Because he thinks I'ma shoot his brother for fucking up that work I gave to him."

"Ohh Yea," was all Farrej could say before his cell phone rung.

"Yo?" He answered it. Then looked at me, "Yo Bone, Jay on the phone."

I took the phone from Farrej's hand, so I can hear Jay beg for my mercy. Yea, Jay know.

"What's up bitch?" I came straight at him.

"Yo Bone, I'm sorry man. I'm sorry! I'm soo sorry for shooting you in ya leg yo. I didn't take my medication that day," he started.

"Na, fuck that. You knew what you was doing!"

"No I didn't Bone. My first reaction was to protect my brother. And I know you know how to fight. Bone, You know I can't beat you. And I didn't want you to bitch slap me around like you be doing them other niggas. We can't even take it there. You my old head. I'll eat shit off of the floor for you!"

"Yo Jay, I know you'll eat shit off of the floor for me. Because you know what will happen to you, if I told you to do it and you don't! But listen, I'll let you live if you give me twenty thousand dollars, and buy me a bike," I laid the rules out for him.

"Ok Bone Crusher. What bike do you want?·You know Vince got that nice ass C B R Seven Fifty. Bone, you goin look good on that ·shit!" This nigga jay is bitching. Now he's trying to help me spend his money. Yea. He knows.

"Let's go and get it Jay," I said.

"Huh? Right now?"

"Yea, right now."

"I gotta pick my daughter up from school in a half hour."

"No Jay. We gotta go pick that bike up for me in a half hour." I corrected Jay then hung up on him.

"Bul you crazy," Farrej tapped me as I gave him his phone.

"I·ain't crazy. I'm tryna ride this summer. Bike on Jay, Fuck·that!"

About an hour later, I met Jay at Vince Motorcycle place out in North East. And guess what? This nigga Jay's scary ass brung Brenda, Pugie, KJ, Marion, and smoking ass Ebony with him.

"Damn homey, Fuck is all of this about?"

"Na Bone, they just making sure you don't do nothing to me."

"Jay, I told you, if you do what I tell you to do I won't do nothing to you," I reminded Jay.

Now we walks into the shop. Damn it was some nice bikes in there. Deep down, I understand why Jay shot me. He knows what I'm about and he was scared to death for his little brother. And if a nigga like me was mad at my brother, I'd have shot him too. Just like I fucked Squeaky up for messing with my big brother, Wyan. But I'm still making Jay pay for squeezing on me.

"I think I want this one right here." I stared at it. 1994 R-1000. It was yellow and white. Yea, this is going to look good on them streets. I'll definitely allow Jay to live for this one.

"Bone Crusher, Bone Crusher?"

"What? Damn, who is that?" calling my name like she was a fan of my music. And I don't even rap!

I turned around to see smoking ass Ebony sitting on 1 of the bikes.

"My ass look right on this bike?" she's grinning all goofy. Bitch don't even got no ass.

"Bitch, you'd better get your no having ass off of that bike before you get us kicked out of here." I crushed her dreams. Then I turned to Jay, "Yo get this bitch out of here," I commanded him pointing my finger.

This nigga Pugie had a nerve to turn around and say, "Don't call my sister no bitch." With his thumb in his mouth! Hah I can't even take a nigga like him serious in any kind of way. At all!

I looked at his dizzy ass like he'd lost all of his marbles. See, Pugie knows we know he told; But we don't have no proof of him telling. The minute we do get that proof? Off with his head!

"Shut the fuck up with ya tattle telling ass." I checked him.

Pugie got quiet and walked away with that same thumb still in his mouth. Just as I thought he would. He knew me better. Pugie didn't want to get embarrassed, so he grabbed his smoking ass sister and they both went and sat in the back of the car they came in.

Now back to Jay. "I want this bike right here."

"Ok Bone Crusher," he's nodding. "I can see you coming down the block right now on that joint wheeling the whole block." Jay trying to be all friendly. Scary ass.

"Yo Jay, shut the fuck up," I commanded him.

"This bike will be ninety five hundred dollars, tags, title, and insurance included," I heard Vince say as I studied the bike.

"I'll take it. I'll pay it all right now. Cash," Jay said.

"Ok Jay. That's what I'm talking about." That was my thank you. And it was all he knew he was going to get out of me, so he took it humbly.

With that, we all left the store.

We're outside now. I'm rolling my new baby as I pass Jay's car.

"Yo Jay, is that mines?" I spotted an envelope in his backseat. He still owed me $20,000 so I was on point.

"Yea that's yours," he went in his car and handed me the envelope.

"Is it all here?" I held it in my palm. I know money and it didn't have a $20,000 feel to it.

While I'm talking to Jay, guess who came outside yelling?

Ms. Brenda! Talking about some, "Yea it's all the fuck there!"

"Mom chill mom!" Jay got to her before I did.

Now with her, I really ain't have no comeback. Ms. Brenda does voodoo and the hood knows it. Plus she knew my mother. But I still was looking at her like she had a 3rd eye! I couldn't believe she wasn't afraid to speak to me like that! What, she forgot?

"What are you doing? What are you trying to get us killed? Yo, Bone Crusher, don't pay my mother no mind. She didn't take her medication yet," he apologized for her. Yea, Jay ain't crazy. But Ms. Brenda? I don't know. She might be touched. One of them spirits might've gotten her.

I put the envelope in my back pocket and hopped on my new baby.

"Yo Bone! Bone!" I hear Jay before I cut the bike on. "Fuck he want?"

"Yo?"

“Yo, can you sign these papers before you leave?”

“Sign what papers?” I'm confused.

“These papers saying you won’t do nothing to me.”

“Yo Jay, get the fuck out of here. I'm not signing no papers. I told you, you cool. Just make sure you take that medication every day from now on. Or somebody might kill your ass,” I left Jay with.

Now back to my baby. I cut her on.

“HHHUUGhh, HHHHUGhh,” she came to life. I threw her into 1st gear and let the clutch go. “WWOGghhoom!” She took off. I'm loving her. She’s going to ride good. I know bikes and I was about to get to know her real well.

It was time to lift her up. I held the clutch with my left hand, and revved her up with my right hand. And right before I'm about to willy off in their faces I see Pugie in Jay's backseat with his thumb his mouth, and Ms. Brenda looking at me with the evil voodoo eye like she was wanting me to fall off of the bike.

I let the clutch go, and as soon as I took off, I hear Ebony’s groupie ass behind me screaming.

“I love you Red Bone!”

What? I almost crashed when I heard that dizzy bitch! And I know the hood heard her too! “Better get ya dizzy crack smoking ass outta here!”

IT'S BONE CRUSHER BITCH!

CHAPTER 6

You Clown!

7th Street.

I'm pulling up to the block riding the new bike I just made the nigga Jay pay for. As soon as I shot the bike off, I hear them clowning on Meech.

"Fuck is you talking about Goat mouth?"

"Hell yea, Nigga mouth look like it belong on a goat!" They're going in on him. Well we on Meech then, fuck it! I'm getting in on the fun.

Meech is standing by the edge of the sidewalk with the Gucci look on his face. The 'Gucci look' is a name we made up for a sour face. Every time someone had a sour face, that's what we'd say he had. 'The Gucci look'.

So I'm creeping up behind Meech as he's standing on the curb and they're grinding him up. He doesn't see me coming. Yall know what I did.

"BOO YOW BITCH!" I kicked Meech dead in his ass. Everybody went off laughing.

"Get ya nut ass outta here Meech! Niggas chased Meech home after that. That was wild. Meech stayed in the house for days after that. He had to pay taxes to come back outside.

Meech paid Puerto Rican Rick, Garsh, Lodge, Sean, Mike, Darryl (aka Funk), Kamille, Markeem, (we call him Mark Madness), and Meech might've paid some more people too. That shit broke him. He ain't have no money after that! 'YOU CLOWN', and that 'BOO YOW BITCH!' was crazy down 7th Street. I told y'all I made that Boo yow shit up? Yea, I'll tell you what though kicking a man in his ass bul. It's embarrassing. Especially when it's done to you.

I remember one time Puerto Rican Rick was at this dice game I started, and he was down like $7,000. This bul' was sweating like a slave, and looking like he just lost his best friend. All dumb!

This shit was funny because he was holding on to that last $100.00 bill so tight. It was the hope he was staring at it with! I mean I could almost literally see the last string of that hope in his eyes, before he kissed it and laid it on the ground to bet. It was fucked up, because he had to bet it, because no one would give him change for it, because they wanted to see him lose it! Ha. Niggas aint shit! Rick knew if he didn't hit, it was over. And guess what? He Didn't Hit. Ha!

Yall know me by now I was already standing behind him waiting for that! As soon he lost, I came creeping up behind him while he was kneeling down staring at the dice. I guess he was trying to make them shit's magically roll back over to a winning number or something, and I rocked his ass!

"BOO YOW BITCH YOU BROKE!!!" I kicked him right in his ass. And yo, this nigga pissed on himself! Yea. Crazy.

The next day; I took 7th Street to Doctor Denim's on me! Well, on Puerto Rican Rick, for real but on me. And I had Rick with me so he can watch me spend his money. Yea, that's how I does it. Yup!

"Big spender, Big spender, Seventh Street here! Everything on me today. Go get the new shit out of the back of the store and all that. Ay Rick, go get ya self an outfit or something, it's on me." I came in strolling. Rubbing the both of my hands together, and dipping my knees with my walk.

"Hi, can we help you?" Two pretty lady females offered me.

"YES y'all can! I need that whole top shelf, size eight. Then get me every outfit you think I'll look good in," I smiled at the female on my left.

This nigga Puerto Rican Rick was heated standing next to me. I could feel the heat coming off of his eyes. He knew I was being funny. And I was.

"Yo man, Go head and get ya self an outfit or something told you it was on me!" I smirked at him with his money in my hand.

By that time, the female who was on my right side was back with a new line of clothes from the back of the store.

"Ok cutie, I got all of these for you. And I got this blue I think will look so good on you," she flirted.

"Aight, aight cool. I like all that shit take it to the register," I pointed in the way of the register without even looking at the clothes.

"Ok cutie," they're blushing.

Yea, of course I'm cute. I got this toilet paper sized roll

of money in my hand. I'm on my way to the register, and I got damn near half of the store in clothes, and I didn't try a thread of it on. Barely even looked at it. And my walk is saying its Nothing! I can buy all of this right now, and do it again tomorrow! Yea, y'all got a 7th Street nigga in here!

Now we're at the register. The ladies placed everything they were carrying on the desk. "Aight, thank y'all pretty ladies. Here, this is for y'all." I tipped them both $100.00 bill a piece, since that's how I like to do it.

"Thank you cutie!" they both smiled at me. They were grateful.

"Here, why don't you take our number?" they offered me, together! Both of them! Yea, they know. They see it.

Now, that got the lady at the register smiling at me as she's ringing me up! Shit. I'm smiling at her too. She can get it.

"Here, here, here, you ain't gotta do all that!" I waved her off of the register. Fuck you ringing my shit up for anyway? You know who I am? My other name is Hood Rich! Fuck wrong with this Dizzy bitch? This is what I'm thinking to myself. It felt like an insult to see her scanning my things with me holding this knot of money in my hand. I could've paid for the store, let alone this pile of clothes!

"I hear you cutie, but I gotta do it this way," she continued doing her job. Then she was done. "That'll be seven thousand, two hundred dollars," she smiled at me.

I gave her my money. Well Puerto Rican Rick's money. She blushes and begins counting.

I'm just looking at her. Smh. Now I have to wait for this. Smh!

After a while, she had 6 piles of $1,000 separated across the desk, and was on the last pile. She stopped counting. This isn't enough. It's two hundred dollars short," she looked at me.

"What?" I looked at her. All I brung in here was Rick's money! The whole store is stone quiet. Damn near half of them are people I invited, and are all standing at the register holding clothes I promised to pay for! And they're waiting on me to say something. I was stuck!

Puerto Rican Rick hating ass must've been in the wing. Waiting for that second, because I didn't even see where he came from. But I felt him.

"BOO YOW BITCH! YOU AIN'T'HOOD RICH, you BROKE!" he kicked me right in my ass.

The whole store laughed at me. I had the Gucci look on. Shit, that was probably why those females didn't answer their phones when I called them a few days later. Dizzy bitches. It's because of them I was short at the register in the 1st place.

Rick got me good though. I wouldn't have been able to explain that to them bitches anyway. It was a dumb ass game I made up. And as a matter of fact, Rick might've put more clothes on that counter than I agreed to pay for on purpose! Just so that could happen! Hating ass nigga. We ain't playing that Boo yow shit no more. Fuck that.

ITS BONE CRUSHER, BITCH!!!!

CHAPTER 7

I Boo Yow Rick, then Rick Boo Yow me…

After that bullshit hating ass Puerto Rican Rick pulled, I went and bought a mink for myself. I wanted to hurt their feelings with this one. Trying to stunt on the Bone Crusher. Smh. Let me remind their asses. Shit, I'm Monroe's son. Fuck I look like?

"Hey Earl, it's been awhile huh? How you been?" the owner said when I stepped in the fur store.

"Yea man, I been chillin. What you got new in here for me, I need something exclusive!" I shot straight at him. "I'm talking about REAL exclusive. I don't care what the price is, You know me!"

"I got you bro. You know I got you. Here come on with me to the back," the German said. "Hold on, let me..." he went to lock the glass front doors.

This is my boy. He knows I am here to spend BIG. All of my jewelry, watches, furs, and exotic shit I don't want anybody knowing where I bought I come to him to buy. Every time we go to the back, he's got something for·me he hasn't shown to anyone else yet.

Two minutes later, we're back there. "Wait one second for me Earl, I've got something I KNOW you'll like," he looked at me. "Cindy! Earl is out here," he called his wife.

"Earl! How are you doing? You haven't been to see us in a minute, I'll be right out hold on," Cindy greeted me from further in the back. She was where the hot shit was.

"Ok Cindy, I'm here. We got something going on tonight. Yall know I had to come see what y'all had for me," greeted her back.

Minutes later, Cindy came out of the back of the store holding it in her hands.

"Damn!" was all I could say.

"This is our newest one. This is 'Sable Gold' right here. This one has silk lining. It's not like the other three you've already purchased from us. Or the one you bought for Jada when she came in," Cindy was holding the mink coat out to me.

I grabbed it from her hands and immediately tried it on. I was checking myself in the 3 full body mirrors they had in the dressing room.

"Hell yea, fuck they think I am?" I commented at the million dollar reflection staring back at me.

"How much is this one?" I asked Cindy still not taking my eyes off of the fur. I was ready for whatever number she came at me with. I stopped at my house and grabbed an extra stack of bills out of my stash spot to bring in here with me.

"That one is sixty four hundred. We have a few pieces of jewelry you haven't seen either," Ron threw on. He was funny. Always found a way to try to make me spend at least $10,000 with them.

"Oh yea? Bring it all out, I wanna see it!" Fuck it. I was here now. Plus I had big plans. Everything I bought right now, was for an event that was going on later on that night.

CHAPTER 8

7th St. Stars

17th and Mckean St.

“There they go y’all! That's them in that stretched Benz, they're here!” someone yelled as we pulled up on the scene.

Yea, this is what it’s about. The Life... The ladies screaming at us like we're movie stars. We weren't in Hollywood, but, we were the stars of Philly. This party Lenny and Markeem threw proved it. It was so much love out there. The party was for 7th Street. And you know us, we showed up in all kinds of wheels. We even had a bus out that join!

Me? I'm in 1 of the stretched Benzes. You should already know that by now reader, I play hard. I remember looking out of the limos tint and seeing it! What did Rick Ross call it? Uhm. Pandemonium! Yea, that was it!

Ladies everywhere, looking right! High heels, super tight skirts and leggings on, Gucci bags, furs, stilettos and all of that fly shit.

The D boys were diamond down. I mean big boy Breightlin watches hanging off of niggas wrists, chains swinging off of necks everywhere you looked. Yea, this was some real playa shit. Markeem and Lenny did this thing.

And it was all for us. 7th Street. And they loved it. They loved us.

"Yall ready? Yall good?" somebody checked was we ready to step into our fame. Hmh. I could see the camera crew waiting in front of the club for us.

The scenery reminded me of a scene from the movie 'Paid in full' when the main character Mich and his 2 partners went to a party. It was the main party in the movie. Well, This is what it looked like. Real shit. Ask any Philly boy about 7th Street. Then ask them about me, Redbone! They'll tell you. We were stars.

"Yea, we out!" We stepped out of the limo, and into our world. The second we did, it was on.

'Snap! Snap! Snap! Snap! Snap! Snap! Snap! Snap!' camera flashes went off. It was crazy! Bitches calling me, or him, or him all of us. Niggas posted around us strapped, and making sure we enjoyed ourselves. The dark blue sky smiled on us that night. The moon was out, the snow shined its white glow. The stars in the sky were bright. I mean, damn. They say Hollywood is the most addictive drug in the world. I don't think it's the actual city they meant by that. It's the fame they were referring to. And seeing all of this, I have to agree. Damn.

"Red Bone what's up cutie?" a female shouted me out as we hit the red carpet. Then, I felt a hand on my fur. Then another hand. Yea, Cindy came through with this one. That sable will get a woman's panties wet!

"This is soo soft."

"I know right," another hand came out of nowhere. It was all love though. Especially when I turned my face to see Bia and Tanisha. They're Muff's peoples. I told y'all Muff is one of my girlfriends. One of them.

Meech was behind me. I didn't know until one of the females grabbed his coat. "Meech why your mink feel so hard?" was all I heard. "April, feel this," Bia called her girl to inspect Meech's coat.

By now, I had turned around to look. This shit was funny.

April touched Meech's fur. "Yea, it feels rough. Like a dog." April screwed her face up at me.

"Aww shit, Meech caught." I hid my smirk. This shit was funny because we all told Meech to get a new mink. Everybody bought new minks for this 7th Street playas ball. Meech's ass got cocky. "I don't need no new mink! I'm from Seventh Street! My name MEECH! These bitches can't tell!" he said rubbing on Herbie Luv Bug's old black mink.

"I don't even know why you let him rock that old ass mink Herbie Luv Bug?" I commented to Herbie.

"He paid me to Fuck that mink!" Herbie said, rubbing on his own new mink.

Any way, we told this nigga Meech. Don't get me wrong, it was still a mink. It was just old. Real old.

Meech heard the females talking and played it off like he was drunk. "Huh?" he swayed side to side in his act.

I laughed. 'Naa nigga, we only had a few bottles of champagne in that car. You ain't drunk And I know you heard these bitches because I did, and I'm standing right next to you!' I thought about screaming at that nigga.

But, he's from 7th Street. I can't do that. Plus, he was feeling enough backlash.

After a few more photos, and more of my squad arriving it was time for us to make an entrance into the club. We were here.

"Alright fellas enjoy yourselves," security lifted the ropes.

"Aight," we go in.

***

'SNAP! SNAP! SNAP! SNAP! SNAP! SNAP! SNAP!' more flashes snapped as we entered the club.

The inside of the club, was just as crazy as the outside.

"Red Bone!"

"Rafiq!"

"Jariek!"

"G Rap!" We got shouted out as soon as we stepped in. They kept shouting our names out. I'm telling y'all, it was so much love.

I know Meech was happy to get out of that grill them bitches had his ass on out there. It's a lot of people here, and they were going to embarrass him.

Meech didn't say another word. And as soon as we got in the club, he ran upstairs to take that mink off. I saw him a few minutes later, in the club with no coat on.

"Yo Bone, you were right. I should've bought my own," Meech looked at me all dumb.

"I know I'm right young bul'. You see this rich ass mink I got on right now? I know I'm right!" I talked my shit to him. Because I knew it was going to come down to this. Him standing in front of me, looking like the odd ball in a pool of player's.

Meech walked off. I know he felt stupid.

For the rest of the night I just enjoyed myself.

***

Alright, the party is over. We're filling out into the parking area. Sidewalks, streets, all of it. We were deep. It's freezing outside and EVERYONE has a coat on except Meech! We all knew why. One of the females just couldn't resist.

"Meech where ya animal at?" she screamed out. Everyone fell out laughing. They knew she was talking about that ruff ass mink he showed up in.

Meech played it off again, but like he was pissy drunk now. Wobbling to the car and all. Yall should've SEEN this nigga! Acting like he didn't hear the bitch. I know he heard her because I heard her. And I was halfway inside of the limo!

Meech couldn't wait to get his crusty ass away from that club. That was a bad night for him.

$$...$$...$$

The next day, I'm rolling through Uptown South Philly to pick up my man Jimmy. Jimmy is on 16th and Catherine Street. So I'm riding down Catherine, and before I even hit 16th Street, I see Big Lip Nate standing on the corner of the block, where all of the passing traffic can see him wearing my man Herbie Luv Bug's old mink. The mink Meech just threw in the trash last night! SMH! It wasn't even Meech's mink to throw away! Like I said before, Meech rented that mink off of Herbie. Ain't this some shit!

"What's up Nate?" I rolled up on him, and positioned myself to park. "I see you got my man Meech's mink on," I fronted for Meech.

Nate is funny. I guess he said 'Fuck that !That's a mink!' and took the shit out of the trash, after Meech threw it in there. You can tell Nate forced himself into the coat, by how small it is on him. But, Nate doesn't care. He had a mink on. That's all that mattered to him. He was right too. Who was I?

"Yea man, I feel like a ·real Seventh ·Street nigga!" Nate smiled pulling at the collar of the coat, with a cocky look on his face.

'Slap!' Nat's man, Carl Carl slapped the back of Nate's head. "Why would you say some dumb shit like that in front of him?" he barked.

"I do feel like a real Seventh Street nigga!" Nate fired back. Carl Carl got mad at Nate and stormed off.

"That nigga hatin! Just mad because I beat him to the trash can to get this coat first!" Nate said, and literally skipped off down the street like a little kid.

"What's up young bul'?" Jimmy jumped in the passenger seat.

"What's up young bul," I shook his hand. "Yo y'all be, easy!" I peace his block before I pulled off.

Weeks later, y'all won't believe this shit. This nigga Meech, done told my man Herbie Luv Bug that someone stole his mink from him. There was a big argument between them about that. Herbie didn't believe him.

"Yo, I just seen Big Lip Nate wearing that mink you threw away!"

"You serious my nigga?" Meech was surprised later on that day.

"Yea. I'm serious. He just had it on when I went through there."

"Nate tryna play me!" Meech went for his gun. Though I knew he was fronting. He wasn't doing nothing to Nate.

"Meech cut the bullshit! You threw the coat away," I checked him. Meech knew he was going to have to pay Herbie back for that mink.

That was at least $2,000 he wasn't trying to peel off, so he was going to put the blame on Nate. Smh. Right is right, and wrong is wrong. I made Meech pay his own tab. He paid it. In full.

ITS BONE CRUSHER, BITCH!!!!

CHAPTER 9

Toby shitted in the pool.

7th St.

Months done passed. It's summertime now, and the pool is open.

“I'm driving this one.”

“Aight, I'm driving this one, and before we go to the pool stop by Pathmark,” I told Rafiq.

“Aight.”

It's like ten or twenty of us in the two vans. We reach Pathmark in like 15 minutes.

“Yo, make sure you get the lunch meat,” Hoarse told Toby on our way in.

10 minutes into us being there, dirty ass Jariek and Rafiq are in aisle 9 eating the candy out of the buckets. I'm in the other aisle opening up bags of chips. Hoarse, Black Nate, and big ears Geno are all in aisle 6, trying to avoid Lenny go on and on about how he loves Hayleen. He'd told everybody how he was going to take Hayleen out of the hood, and raise a family with her. Lenny is crazy. This miserable nigga was only 16 years old! And Hayleen was 40! Now I’m not the

one to hate, but damn! Lenny took Hayleen personal and had a baby by her. Smh. His business.

Anyway, so we're done shopping. We're in the parking lot now, and this nigga Toby done dug into one of the packs of bologna, and is eating the meat RAW! His hungry ass couldn't wait. We'd only heard him because of how loud he smacked as he chewed. After a while all of us just stared at him a second. You know somebody had to say something.

"I guess your dad Cuffy didn't make y'all lunch today," Black Nate broke the silence. Everybody started laughing.

Toby tried to comeback at Black Nate (and no Black Nate isn't big lip Nate) but he was corny.

Now we're in the van riding. And here come my man big ears Geno with some wild shit.

"Man, I can't wait until I can drive planes and fly the bus!" Yup, he said it just like that too! Like it should've been happening already.

The whole van looking at him now. Trying to let him clarify himself. I don't know how? He couldn't! And he didn't try to! That was it.

"Get out! Get the fuck out, for that dumb shit you just said right there!"

"Yea Geno, get out! You gotta walk for that dumb shit you just said!"

"Hell yea!" we all went on him. Yall know we go hard.

"Yea aight!" Geno tried not to go for it. But he had to go for it. That was what we did when niggas said dumb shit. Even 'I' myself had to walk back from a few spots. So, Geno you got to go!

"Aight. Say no more!" Geno got out of the car heated.

Then somebody rolled the window down and threw a piece of meat at G Rap.

"Here take that G Rap!" Aww man, niggas really laughed off of that one.

G Rap was so mad he wanted to fight.

"Naa fuck that, Yo y'all niggas gotta give me a fair one. Everyone of y'all," he fumed.

We all laughed harder. That got G Rap angrier. "I'm serious!" G Rap took his shirt off. But we all knew G Rap could fight.

'VVVvvooommm!'

"Fuck outta here nigga!" Indris pulled off on him.

That's when G Rap snapped and chased our van on foot!

"YOU BITCH ASS NI!" he took off after us. Top speed! Full throttle! The look on his face was like a mad man's! Like he would've torn those doors off of that van to get anyone of us if he'd caught it.

"Lenny I'ma beat you and Idris the fuck up! Then I'ma slap the bullshit out of Nate! And I'ma Kill Bone nut ass! ·Cause I know it was him who threw that meat at me!" Geno ran behind us yelling.

##...##...##...##

So we'd made it to the pool.

"Damn yo, my stomach hurt, Toby told me.

"I know it does. Eating like you don't have no home training!" Is what I wanted to say to Toby, and then laugh. But what came out was, "Drink some water. It might be gas."

He did. 5 minutes later, he was back.

"I'm good now." What I didn't know was, Toby was lying to me.

Now me and Toby fall in line after a train of other people for the diving board. Lenny and Hoarse started it off. Lenny did some ole' down south shit. Hoarse doesn't know how to dive, so he just jumped in. Black Nate did a nice dive. Indris did a funny white boy dive.

"Oh shit, look at dirty ass Pig!" someone shouted. "Noo PIG! DON'T do it! NOOOO!" Everyone is yelling.

"FUCK y'all!" Pig yelled back before diving in.

The reason everyone was screaming at pig not to dive in the water, is because Pig is a complete dirtball! I mean FORREAL! The shorts he'd had on that day, he'd already had on for the last 6 days in a row! Them shorts was dingier than I could ever try to explain. Chlorine couldn't clean them shits!

Following Pig came J Bird.

"Yo, watch out y'all, here comes the Seventh Street rapist!" a voice yelled out. The whole pool fell out laughing.

"Man FUCK y'all! I don't knock what y'all do, don't knock what I do!" J Bird defended himself. Although it wasn't really a defense. J Bird isn't a rapist in the literal defense but he deals with really young girls. Too young we all felt, so we'd made it known.

The lifeguard Robby had his face balled up. Evidently he didn't like what J Bird said. I think he would've left J Bird to drown in that water if he couldn't swim on his own.

Toby went up. Mind y'all, it's 2 diving boards at this pool. One by the 6 foot deep end, and one by the 9 foot deep end. The pool itself stops at 12 feet deep. Everyone is at the

6 foot diving board of the pool! Here comes Toby on the higher one at the foot side of the pool.

"Watch out, watch out! It's T MURDER on the BIG BOY board!" He's talking shit. Hand over his jock as he's walking all cocky.

Toby looked good for a second. He bounces once, then twice, then. I knew he shouldn't have went for that 3rd bounce. He was too high. Toby was so high in the air off of that last bounce. I remember him looking down from the sky and seeing how high up he really was and that was when it happened.

"Bbblggh" the fart came out. His pants went brown instantly! The crowd went silent. We weren't sure if it was what we'd thought it was. Then one of the neighborhood females confirmed it.

"Toby shitted on himself!" she didn't even shout it. But it was so quiet her words were loud and that made everybody listen and look.

I guess Toby thought the water was going to clean his shorts off for him while he was in the pool. So after he'd dived in, he came out of the pool and played it off like nothing happened. Ha! That brown stain on the back of his Polo shorts told us everything!

Robby, the lifeguard saw that stain too.

"Everyone out of the water! Everyone out of the water NOW!" Robby came down off of the lifeguard stand immediately.

"Damn Toby!" was all you'd heard.

'Mch,' Maan!" children whined, females were cursing. Everyone glaring at Toby with the evil eye. There was at least 100·people inside of the pools walls, and another 50 outside in the parking lot.

Mind you; our pools are like events. I mean we got the baddest, prettiest females, the livest hustlers and the baddest neighborhood kids coming through. The females all know they're getting dumped in the water by one of them fly hustlers and it's their way of trying to catch a nigga. So they actually want a nigga to dump one of them. Because if they didn't get dumped they probably weren't pretty enough. Then we got the hustlers in there showing off their shit. Whips are parked outside with the loudest, latest music blaring, and niggas is sitting on them fly cars waiting for the pool to let out so they can catch the pretty girls. So these pool visits are like events for us. So when Toby shitted in the water, he ruined all of the fun! He cleared the whole event out!

So we're walking out the exit, Toby was not walking out with us. He lingered in the back while everyone walked through because he knew we were going to grind his ass up. So he was trying to wait until he was last to leave.

I looked back to see him, and saw Tanya his girlfriend standing there with him. Tanya had taken Toby's sock off and was wiping the shit off of his leg with it!

Toby just stood there with a boot on, 1 sock on his left foot shaking his head. I will say this though that woman stood by her man.

By the time we made it outside, word had already spread that Toby had shitted in the pool, and fucked the party up. I mean kids were running out of the gates yelling, "TOBY SHITTED IN THE POOL!" Even while we sat in the lot.

Finally, Toby came out of the gates.

"Damn Toby, you shouldn't have ate all that lunch meat!" the fellas attacked him.

"Get ya shitty ass outta here!"

"Bone, BOO YOW that nigga!" they went.

"Hell no! I wouldn't dare get no shit on these fresh boots." I looked down at my new Timberlands. "You do it!"

Toby heard us. He just kept his head down and continued walking to his car. It was only a·30 second walk to his car but that day 30 seconds probably felt like 30 minutes for Toby's ass.

That isn't the first time that's happened either. I know of another time, I've personally witnessed myself! I'ma share this with y'all right quick. Real nigga shit.

Back in the day The 7th Street Barber, Joe Joe, shit in the pool!

I remember it as clear as day too. I was about 13, 14 years of age. Robby our same lifeguard now saw it. But, Robby didn't see it on his own.

I showed it to him. I had to!

See, it happened like this.

I was swimming next to Joe Joe in the water. When me and Joe Joe reached the edge of the pool, I went to get out first. Next thing you know I feel Joe's hand on my shorts trying to pull me down as I'm climbing up the ladder to get out of the water. Joe Joe was trying to rush passed me.

I turned around. "Joe what the fuck you doing?" I asked him. By this time Joe had bumped me in his rush to get wherever he was going.

Joe had a German Shepherd that he took everywhere with

him. The dog was on the other side of the pool, tied up to the fence. Joe looked like he was headed straight for her. And fast!

I looked back to see what his rush was, and I saw it. Scattered in the water. SHIT!!! Like, the diarrhea kind of shit! Floating all in the pool.

Then it hit me this nigga Joe Joe was trying to beat me out of the pool, so it would like maybe I shitted in the pool instead of him!

Oh no no no, he can't do the Bone Crusher like that! I got a reputation to protect!

"Yo Robby, Robby, he shitted in the pool look! Get him!" I shouted to our lifeguard Robby. Yep, the same lifeguard was even there back then. While I screamed that, Joe Joe never broke his step! He hurried his walk that whole time, knowing we would see his shit. He unhooked that big ass dog as fast as he could and bolted out of the gate while Robby was screaming at everyone to get out of the water.

The funny shit was this, If Joe Joe wasn't in a rush to get passed me and pin the case on me, I wouldn't have noticed it, and I was the only one who seen it, so he might've got it off if he'd played it right!

I went back to the hood and told everybody what Joe tried to pull. I had to protect my name before Joe Joe finished trying to destroy it! He was plain old Joe Joe the barber. I'm the Bone Crusher! Fuck is wrong with him?

I seen Joe later on that day.

"Yo, I'll give you a year worth of free haircuts if you don't tell anybody what happened at the pool," Joe offered me.

“Hell yea, It’s a bet.” I shook his hand. He just doesn’t know. You don’t make a deal like that with the Bone Crusher. He’ll learn though.

Joe·kept his word too. He kept me fresh every week after that. Of course I made him keep his word.

“Joe Joe, I’m next,” I would walk into the shop. I’m talking days when his barber shop would be packed!

“Bone I’ve got eleven heads to cut,” Joe would plead.

“Joe, I’m next Joe,” I would repeat with a firm threat in my gaze.

“Aight man. Yo, Bone is next y’all!” Joe would submit to my threat.

“How does he get next? I’ve been here since nine o’clock? I would hear them whining. Hmh. Because I’m the Bone Crusher that’s why!

Yea, that was how that went. And it went like that for the whole year too. On the last day of that year, Joe tried to get cute with me in the shop!

“Yea, this is your last cut for free too Bone·”·he smirked at me.

“What? No. No, You goin keep cutting my shit unless you want me to tell these people what happened at that pool!” I stopped all of that.

“Are you serious? Alright, say no more. I got you.” Joe Joe got serious and wiped that smirk off of his face real quick. Yea. He knows.

After about 2, maybe 3 more years passed then I took the pressure off of Joe Joe, and started paying him for my haircuts. Yea. That’s what he got. Shouldn’t have ever tried to pull that stunt on a nigga like me. ME? Me? The Bone

Crusher? Yea Aight. Not down 7th Street!

CHAPTER 10

These pions set me up!

Let me rewind this back...

That same day Joe the barber shitted in the pool we had a basketball game in McDaniel's school yard for the championship. This wasn't a high school game or anything. We were still in high school, yes. But by this time we were knee deep in the streets too. And the corners were teaching us way more than any school or teacher. So that's where we'd spent most of our time. But no this wasn't a high school game. This was one of our neighborhood things.

It's packed with the school females, parents, coaches, other teams who didn't make it this far, and us 7th Street. We're playing 24th Street for the championship.

I'm on the bench. Jeff, Spud, Karon, Jay, and Tex are on the court. Tex and Jeff are our lead players, and Tex is better than Jeff. But Jeff can ball. The problem with Jeff is, Jeff has a bad anger problem. And he's 1 of those stocky young boys that is twice the size of the average dude his age. And he always wants to throw shit around when he gets mad. Like he's Hulk Hogan or somebody. And I told y'all he has an anger problem, so he's always throwing shit, because he's always mad at something. Or someone!

So right then, it's second half of the game. 4th quarter, 3 minutes left to play, with 7th Street up by 13 points. Jeff is at the foul line preparing to shoot 3 free throws. Time for me to start some shit.

Jeff is focused. He bounces the ball once. Twice. Takes his pause, breathes deep. Raises both arms, positions the ball to shoot his shot, and right as he was about to release it. (This is his 2nd shot now mind y'all, the 1st one he made.) And right as he was about to release his shot. "DAGGH!" I noised. And he missed! Just like I wanted him to!

Yea I'm hating today. Fuck that!

Jeff turned looked over at us, trying to see where the noise came from. We quickly put our heads down like we didn't do anything. Jeff screwed his face up, but went on to take his last shot.

"Do it again Bone. Jeff goin get mad!" my boys piped me up. That was all the Bone Crusher needed. And these 7th Street niggas love to get Jeff started!

So, for the rest of the game, every time Jeff got the ball and tried to shoot it, I made that noise. And my niggas kept right on piping me up too.

Here goes Jeff, running past the bleachers, "Who made that noise?"

"Focus on the game Jeff!" Coach yelled at him.

Jeff was so heated he couldn't even think straight. Then he was fouled again! Now he's at the line.

"Do the noise Bone," the coach said this time. So I did. I was going to anyway as soon as Jeff went to shoot the ball.

“DAGGH!” I went from behind Darryl’s shoulder.

Jeff whirled his head in my direction, “I know it's you Bone Crusher, now keep it up!” he threatened me.

“What? Fuck YOU nigga!” I thought. He'd still had another shot to take. And he took it. “DAGGHH!”

He missed!

This time Jeff stared me down, and put his right fist up to his left eye while he was running toward the other end of the court. Like he was going to black my eye. Like I was just going to let him. Like we were back in school on some 3rd grade shit. I don’t know who the fuck he thinks I am.

“Jeff wants to fight! Aww shit, Jeff wants to fight!” Everybody's saying. They just want to see some action. We live for that.

“Yo, if he comes over here with that dumb shit we goin jump him!” Darryl said.

“Yea. Hell yea, we goin roll on that nigga!” everyone else agreed. “FIVE, FOUR, THREE, TWO, ONE!” The crowd goes off as Jay releases the final shot.

'BAAAAHP! the buzzer sounded.

‘CUFF!’ Jay made the game winner. Jeff is heated he didn't get to shine. “WHHHOOOAAA! YEEEMM! YYYEEEAAA!” we rushed the court floors celebrating. We’d won the championship.

Jeff wasn’t with us on the floor. He went straight outside to the station wagon coach drove us to the game in. When we finally went outside Jeff was already out there. He saw us coming, and started cracking his knuckles and punching the palm of his left hand with his right fist. He was mushing his knuckles into his palm. Like somebody was supposed to be scared of that or something! Smh! This nigga! (On the low I was kinda shook though, but I wasn't about to show it. Naa, not the Bone Crusher.)

Now we're outside. This nigga Jeff done took his shirt off, and is bouncing his chest muscles! "All of y'all gotta shoot me the fade." He's mad breathing through his nostrils. This man is bugged out.

"What?" Everyone looked at Jeff like he was crazy.

We're not about to be wrestling with his strong ass out here.

"Calm your ass down Jeff. It's just a game. Get in the hatchback!" coach told Jeff.

We all respected the coach, so we go in the hatchback. But I was ready though. All he was going to do is try to wrestle me. I was ready.

We're on 10th Street a short while later. Everything is on ice for the moment. Jeff is still heated. But he's not saying anything. I guess Jay was still mad I made him buy me that bike cause now he wanted to start shit.

"Damn Jeff, How you miss all of them shots? Jay asked Jeff. I can see Jay squinting his eyes out of my perennial, and I can hear shadiness in the undertone of his voice.

He's trying to size Jeff up so Jeff can come at me. Jeff was already steaming, so his dizzy ass went right for it.

"Because one of these niggas want to be a clown!" he beamed, looking dead at me.

I'm looking Jeff back in his eyes. Yea I did it. If he wants to rumble, fuck it!

"W…" Before I could say anything, Jeff jumped out of the hatchback as the car was about to pull off from the Stop

Sign.

Now he's in the middle of 10th Street looking like he's about to fuck something up. I got quiet.

"Get the heck back in the car Jeff! Now!" Coach is telling Jeff.

"Naa I don't want to get in the car!" Him and coach are arguing.

"Well stay here then!" coach snapped. Jeff lives close to 10th Street, so he didn't care.

"Aight I'll walk home then. Fuck outta here!" Jeff stormed off.

"Well walk then," coach pulled off.

Keep in mind that the hatchback is still raised up, and Jeff is still mean mugging me as we're about to pull away from the stop Sign. As soon as coach pressed that gas pedal, I went off!

"DAAAGGHH! DAAAGGHH! DAAAGGHH! DAAAGGHH!" I was as loud as possible, and looking dead at Jeff. Taunting him now, because I knew we were going to jump him!

Jeff, sees it was me the whole time and that was when he blanked out.

Jeff shook the shock off of his face to make sure he wasn't high. He wasn't. "I knew it was you, yo Bit..," he took off running after the car.

"Here he come, here he come, here he come," we all yelling at the coach, while we're laughing at Jeff trying to run down this car! It was hilarious! His face was so serious. His head is tilted back and his body posture was like that of a track stars. And he's running like he knows he can catch this automobile.

The whole thing is funny to me. I have the upper hand, and y'all know me by now. I kept right on making that noise. Yea, fuck you Jeff! And we're going to roll on your ass if you get crazy out here was my attitude.

10 minutes later, we're all back down 7th Street where the coach dropped us off. I know Jeff will be around here soon. And when I see him, I know we're fighting. Jeff is the type of dude to come to your house, knock on your door and ask you to fight in front of your parents! So I knew he was coming through here to get some work for sure.

"Yo Bone, get ready. You know Jeff is coming through here," my boys are starting shit again. But, they're saying this, like it's about to be just me and Jeff. Huh?

"Whoa, hold on hold on! Yea I'm ready. But uhm, did y'all forget we agreed to roll on this nigga?" I reminded them.

"Yea, uhm. About that," they started bitching.

"What?" I should've known these soft ass niggas was goin. "What about it?" I didn't want to jump to conclusions.

Darryl was the main one hyping me up, and I see him trying to hide his smirk.

I look at Tex, and he isn't trying to hide his smile! In fact his smirk is hiding his smile. "Damn, I should go grab some chips and a soda. Or something for this shit," this nigga said. Like it was about to be a show.

"Huh? For what?" once he said that, I instantly knew something was wrong. Fuck he wants some chips at a time like this for I'm thinking. I still can't put my finger directly on what's going on. I'm looking at their eyes. Their eyes will tell me everything.

I look at Tex, then Darryl. Then Tex, then Darryl, then Jay. Jay is grinning.

"Fuck is Jay grinning for?" Then it hit me they got me!

"Aww. Aww y'all some dirty niggas. Yall some dirty niggas! Yall goin do the Bone Crusher like that? Yall tryna feed me to this nigg?" I looked at all of their faces.

They're not answering me now. I figured their little plan out. They tried to feed me to the wolf. That's fucked up. They know I'm only 5 foot 2 barely 130 pounds, with my boots on!

This man Jeff is a muscle head! I mean for real. This nigga got muscles everywhere! Muscles in his head, muscles in his jaws, muscles in his neck, muscles in his finger so! Yo, this dude was just l of them muscle bound type of dudes. He was at least 6 foot 6', 185 pounds of lean, mean killing machine type of muscle! Been through juvenile bids mostly all of his life, around the toughest, roughest young bul's in America probably, and this man has anger issues? Yea, it's obvious. They're trying to get me fucked up! Probably because I be talking my shit. Aww, man they got this 1 off.

I don't even know how I let them get this shit off. I'm way smarter than these pion's. I'm supposed to be the 1 laughing at them. Damn, I can't believe this shit here. It ain't over though. I still got time before Jeff gets here to turn this around.

"Yall niggas ain't going stick with the plan?" I said, breathing all hard. "Darryl, that's how you riding ? Huh D? D that's how we playing? What is this about that chocolate milk I took from you in second grade? I ain't mean it like that bro. I just wanted something to go with my pizza. That's all fam. Let that shit go man! We boys!" I spoke my piece to Darryl.

The look on his face said he wasn't trying to hear me. He had me. Right where he wanted me. Spud, was one of my homey's that was already on the block when we got there. He came over to us to see what's up, because he sees the friction. "What's up Bone, you aight?"

I looked over at Spud, glad to see him. "I'm tryna be! Mu'fuckas playing dirty out here," I shook my head at him then looked back at Darryl and them.

I'll explain to Spud later. I turned my sights to Tex now.

"Tex you with this shit too?" I'm breathing harder now. They're laughing. I guess this would be funny to them. I'm not laughing at all.

"Rumble young bul' rumble!" Tex shook his head side to side grinning

"Aww, what is this about Aisha? Come on dawg, she was mines first anyway!" Tex wasn't trying to hear me either.

"Aww, aww I can't believe this! I can't believe this shit here! Yall some dirty niggas for this shit here! Yall some philthy niggas for this shit here! But you know what ? Fuck y'all! And Fuck Jeff too!" I snapped. They must've forgot who I am!

"When he comes around here I'm going at him like I would any other man! Fuck I look like? Matter of fact I should go to his house and tell him. I wanna fight! Yea, as a matter of fact That's exactly what I'm about to do!" I pump faked them, and turned like I was walking toward Jeff's house.

We know I wasn't going to Jeff's house. I was going home! But I had to make it look good. And I did too. Yall should've seen the way I walked off on Darryl and them! Now I'm strolling like the gangster I am, and guess who turns the corner. Jeff!

Damn! The look on his face says he isn't trying to hear shit! I was still acting like I wanted to fight him But now, I'm stuck in character. So fuck it then, we gotta get it!

As soon as I got close to Jeff, I cocked my strong arm back and gave him everything I had!

'WHAAP! WHAAP! Whaap!' I'm trying to take Jeff's head off. I'm throwing lefts, rights, uppercuts, hooks, everything! Jeff is swinging punches back. We brawling. I was good until 1 of his hay makers hit me. Then I got dizzy! In the midst of me swinging, I seen Spud swinging on Jeff with me. My nigga! Out there rocking with me. Spud was shaking like a leaf when he'd first saw Jeff walking toward me looking like he was going to bench press me.

"Bob and weave Bone, Bob and weave!" I hear Darryl and Tex in the background laughing. It's cool though. I got something for Darryl ass right after I'm done with this big nigga.

Me and Spud got Jeff backing up to the wall. Jeff is trying to grab us now. He's trying to stop this heat we're throwing. If he grabs us it's over. Me and Spud are like 130 pounds apiece! So no matter what, we really couldn't let him grab us. Right before he did, Tex broke the fight up.

"Chill! Chill y'all," he grabbed Jeff from behind him.

In my mind I'm saying 'good looking Tex!' But my face

is saying 'Fuck no, let us fight!' I see Spud on the side of me, drinking some crackheads water bottle.

Darryl, still in the background laughing. It's a front though. His face is saying he should've helped me, because not only did Jeff not do what he thought Jeff was going to do to me, but now he knows I'm liable to get his ass next. Jeff walked off toward Mckean St.

"You fight like you uncle Chew Red Bone!" Burned Nate bul whose drink Spud was drinking said throwing his own punches as he shadow boxed.

"Yo Bone, you aight?" Pugie and Chad walked over to me.

"Hell no I'm not aight! Your homie Darryl tried to play me!" I told Pugie.

"How did he play you?" Pugie asked.

"He was supposed to help us roll on Jeff, and he just stood there laughing like shit was funny!" I told Pugie while he stood there with his dirty ass thumb in his mouth.

"For real? He didn't help you at all?"

"Yea I'm for real! But it's cool. I got something for that nigga." Pugie shook his head. He knows whatever I have in store for Darryl, he won't like it.

#...#...#...#...#

It's night time, and we're going Up Town to the local bar located on Tasker Street. Janeen, 1 of our 7th Street chicks is throwing a party there. We're like 30 soldiers deep loading into our wheels.

"Yo take this walk with me right quick to Mercy street,"

I told Hoarse and Karon. That's where Darryl's house is.

"Aight come on," they both leave with me.

So we're on the way there. Karon is talking about nothing, Hoarse is quiet. He's riding with me no matter what. That's my boy. And plus his girlfriend Bia is on his mind. The both of them know I'm up to something.

I slowed down my pace, and stopped when we got to Darryl's car. I pulls out my knife, squatted down, and bust every one of Darryl's tires.

'POP! POP! POP! POP!'

Hoarse took off like I'd just killed someone. Me and Karon walk off laughing. Fuck Darryl. His ass won't be driving that Honda tonight, I know that!

We're back on 7th Street, in our cars and were about to pull off. Toby and Markeem are both looking at me like they know I did something.

"Yo Bone, I know you didn't do what I think you did?" Markeem is trying to fish information out of me.

"Get your nosey ass in the car and mind your business!"

"I know you ain't do that Bone?" Toby had to add his dizziness in it.

"Toby, what are you talking about?"

"I know you ain't do nothing to Darryl's car?" he's stares at me. He knows Darryl loves that car.

Yup. That's exactly what I did. But Toby's ass doesn't need to know.

"Hell no! Me, Hoarse and Karon walked up to P and P to grab a cheese steak. Hoarse bought a cheese steak for Bia, and I ordered some French fries," I gamed him.

Toby just looked at me like he knew I was lying.

We're all at the party now. Here comes Lenny on his way over to me and Hoarse on the other side of the bar.

"Ayo, how is Darryl calling my phone saying that Garsh's girlfriend flattened his tires?" Lenny looked at me confused He shook his head and walked off.

I smiled to myself. That told me Darryl was clueless on who had flattened his tires.

Hoarse tapped me. "That nigga Darryl shouldn't be fucking his homey's girlfriend."

"Ha! Yea." Me and Hoarse laughed at that, and the fact we knew what Lenny didn't know.

Here come Toby pulling me to the side. "Bone you're wrong Bone! You're wrong! You flattened that man tires!" He's damn near screaming all loud and drawn!

This nigga! Damn! Can't even enjoy a shot of liquor, and some pretty women around these nosey ass·niggas. It's cool. I know how to handle this. I got something for his ass.

I cocked my head to the side, and looked at him with my crazy look.

Right then and there, Toby knew he'd went too far. Too late for that though!

'SLAP! SLAP! SLAP!' I front hand slapped him, then back hand slapped him, then front hand slapped him again. All with the same hand! Yall know me!

His dizzy ass just stood there, holding his face.

"Get your dumb ass in the car and mind your business!" I told him. And that was just what he did.

CHAPTER 11

I flattened Darryl's tires

7th St.

We stayed at the bar for a while longer, supporting Janeen. It was her event. It was cool too.

When it was over, me and Spud both headed back to the block.

***

Its 3:30 am. Me and Spud are on the block still. See, Spud doesn't have a stable place to call home, so he was going to be outside regardless of what the night brang.

Me, I was just chilling with him. He didn't leave me earlier, so I didn't leave him later.

Out of nowhere some crack head rolled up to us riding a Harley Davidson motorcycle. "Hey man. You guys know anyone who wants to rent a bike?" He'd parked in front of us, and sat on it. 1 leg on the ground.

"Hell yea, you talking about this right here?" Spud's eyes lit up, and he was pointing at the bike.

"Yea, this one. I just want to get high man." the fiend began.

That was all we needed to hear! "I got a dime for you?" I shot at him. I didn't really want the shit. But the way Spud was looking at it, I had to get it for us, before he offered his whole pack for it.

"Aww man! Come on dude, it's a freakin Harley. It's gotta be worth more than that?" the fiend came out of him. Isn't he something? A second ago, he might've took a nickel bag of weed for this thing. Now, he sees Spud is geeking to ride it, and he wants to make the rules? Hah! People!

"Man, I really don't want the shit. I'm cool!" I told the fiend.

Spud snapped his eyes on me.

"Chill nigga," I shot my crazy look at him. I knew Spud wanted the bike, but I couldn't let his thirst for it give the fiend the power to overcharge us. Plus, I was paying for it anyway.

Spud stayed quiet. I needed that. Let me do this.

"Aww man. Is that the best you can do?"

"Yep!"

The fiend is thinking now. I'm eying the bike while he does. I know it will be fun to ride. I can ride this. Spud just wanted to learn how to ride. I can dig that too. But its 330 in the morning. Price goes down.

"Okay man. I guess I have to. Alright then, I'll give you guys one hour! And we'll meet back here at this spot right here. Cool? He set the rules. Or, so he thought.

"Cool!" Yea, aight. Fuck outta here. The minute we get this bike, we're gone! It's too late for all of that shit Spud got planned, but I got something for us.

***

20 minutes later, we're riding the Harley from South Philly to West Philly in the cold! (Yea, I forgot to tell y'all it was winter time!)

We're on our way to Jada's house. I'm going to get some lovin', and I'm taking Spud for the ride. I'd left my car on the block to take this ride.

We were cruising past cops and all. They didn't fuck with us. Plus I told y'all, I can ride a Harley. Shit, I can ride any bike I sit on. The cold air did feel good on my skin. We didn't have Helmets, but our knitted winter hats kept us warm. The heavy motor of the Harley also felt good beneath me.

We were almost at Jada's house. The 7 Eleven close to her told me so. I'd stopped in there. "I gotta get Jada some Cheese Dogs," I explained to Spud. "If I go to her crib with no food she's going to be mad."

10 minutes later, we were pulling up to her house.

Jada lived on 36th and Melon in West Philly. And I won't lie these boys lay niggas down out here. It's crazy because you can sense it when you're there.

"It's creepy out this joint," was the first thing Spud uttered.

He was right. The streets were dark from some of the street light's being shot out. The dudes were dressed in all black. You saw their dark shadows in the crevices of the scenery. You felt eyes on you. Like some Vultures waiting for a body to drop.

But none of that mattered to me. I'm from 7th Street. I go where I will! Just like Monroe did.

Plus, Spud is about to sleep in the jungle, and he don't even know it. Ha Ha!

***

Jada had her face in the window. She knew we were coming. She smiled as soon as she saw me. I knew she'd seen that bag of food in my hand too. Her face lit up like it was Christmas, and I was Santa Clause.

"Hey baby!" she opened the door.

"What's up Babe?" we hugged.

"Hey Spud."

"Hey Jada," they spoke. Jada lead the way into her home. Me and Spud followed behind.

"What the fu..?" Spud stopped in his tracks.

Jada and her family are pet freaks! I'm serious! It's like 30 animals in her house. Snakes, Rabbits, Cats, Dogs, Lizards, Iguanas, Birds and all. This bitch might've had a Lion in the basement!

Spud was stuck standing by the door!

"It's cool Spud, they don't bite. Come in," Jada urged him.

Spud must've heard me snickering to myself. "What you laughing for Bone? And why you ain't tell me she had a Safari in this joint?" he whispered in my ear, slowly walking in at the same time.

Jada went straight into the kitchen, focused on her food.

"Cause I ain't wanna hear you bitching!" I'm still laughing to myself. Between me and y'all, Spud is scared to death of animals! But he's from 7th street and I knew he wasn't going to let the animals shake him up in front of Jada, because he likes Jada's sister, Jeva!

Yea, y'all knew the Bone Crusher had a plan. As soon as I heard Spud liked Jada's sister, and I already knew he was scared of animals? What? I had to get his ass over here. See if he likes her after tonight! Plus, on some real shit I knew Jeva was involved with somebody, so Spud would've never got her. And this, was my chance to see how scared I can get my nigga. Yea, yea, I know he was there for me earlier when I fought Jeff, but Fuck that. I'm getting this nigga!

Meanwhile, Spud is looking around like a scared fox. The animals has his head turning, trying to keep his eyes on every one of them. His eyes are so wide open you can almost see his whites!

"You aight young bul'?"

"Yea I'm aight!" Spud responds without taking his eyes off of his surroundings. "I'ma Seventh Street nigga! Fuck you mean am I aight?" he added.

He's fronting. I know he's shook. But long night left buddy. It'll come out. For now, it was time for me to go upstairs and do what a man came to do.

"Jada! Where yo ass at?" I called out.

"I'm up here Bone!" I'd heard her voice from her room.

"Well that's right where I was headed." I reached in my pocket and wrestled my money to get it out of my pocket.

"Yo, I'm going up here Spud." I balled my money up, preparing to give it to him.

"Up where?!" Spud looked at me.

"Up there with Jada, nigga!" Where the fuck you think?

"Where am I going?"

"On that couch!" I pointed. The couch had bird feathers, cat fur and all kinds of stuff. Hah! He'll be aight though.

"Here hold this money for the night. Keep it down here with you. Jada likes going in my pockets when I'm sleep," I forced my money in Spuds hands, and headed up the stairs.

"Yo, hold up I don't get no pillows? A sheet or something?"

"Naa nigga, you be aight," I chuckled at Spud. "Sleep tight!"

In the end, I knew Spud would be cool though. That was my boy.

Long story short, I left Spud to go love on Jada for the night. Yall know how the rest of that evening went.

***

I woke up to Jada staring at me. I'd felt her eyes on me. Mind you, I barely slept anyway because I'd been hearing a lot of moving around and some thumping coming from downstairs over the night. I knew it was Spud. That kept me from complete rest. So I was already restless sort of. Then I'd felt Jada's focus on me.

She was sitting on her bed, one leg folded naturally, facing the other. While the other hang loosely off of the edge of the bed, her toes touching the floor. Her arms were folded across her chest, and she was not smiling.

"Fuck you look so mad for?" "What's up Babe?" I had to

ask. Then it hit me! I gave Spud my money last night! She probably tried to get me and got fooled! HAH! Yea. Dummy! You ain't getting none of these dollars!

"What you mean what's up?" Jada fired back at me. Yea, she was heated. I could tell.

A smile broke across my face. The thirsty young girls think they have all the sense. You got me once Jada, you won't get me again! That's what I was thinking anyway. Jada had other plans.

"I'm pregnant," she stared at me seriously.

"Aww shit." I stared at her. Yea, aight she's tryna get me. She want some abortion money. She think the Bone Crusher sweet! Bitch, what I got dummy written on my face? You went right from plan A to plan B huh? You must need some clothes or something. I ain't going for this shit. I started looking around her room.

"What are you looking for?" Jada's confused.

I was looking for signs of her needing new clothes or something. Anything that would tell me her motive for this head game she is playing right now. Shit, for all I know she's trying go shopping at Forman Mills again, on ME! (Forman Mills, is the thrift store I'd caught her walking to the day I'd met her!) I guess she wanted some new dresses or something. Na, not on me Boo.

Now you're pregnant huh? Now you're pregnant. After you couldn't tap my pocket's. Now, you're pregnant? Tsss, ain't this some shit.

"I'm serious Bone," Jada repeated.

I felt confused and targeted. "Yea, how many weeks are you?" I needed a way out. This was too much.

"Six weeks."

"Is it a boy or a girl?"

"I don't know yet Bone. It's too early to tell," she whined.

Yep! I knew she was lying! I knew it! "Yea Aight! Call me in nine months!" I got up and hurried my ass out of her room.

***

I came downstairs to Spud sitting on the sofa. His hand was holding his face up. Its elbow was supported by its knee. He looks like he hasn't slept a single second in weeks! Like a crack head who had been on a crack binge, and was at end of his adventure.

"Spud, what's up you cool?"

Spud was just staring at the wall in front of him. He ignored me and continued staring at the wall. One of Jada's cats must've heard my voice and poked its head out of Spuds Timberland boot. Spud ignored that too. Defeat was written all n over his face.

"Spud! You aight nigga?" I bothered him.

"Yea I'm aight! Da fuck!" Spud snapped. Then went in on me. "Couldn't get no damn sleep! You knew I wasn't goin get no sleep! Look at this shit!" he motioned at the cat who'd made one of his boots his new home. Fucking cats sleeping in my boot, birds flying around dropping shit everywhere, snakes crawling on my legs, dogs chasing rabbits. What the fuck!" Spud went on. "Then homie come out of the basement walking around in his Superman drawl's and shit, looking at me like I'm crazy!" Spud finally looked at me.

“Oh nah, that's Gregg, Jada's brother.”

“I don’t care! Shit, it's their house. I can't say shit. I'm just saying! Where the fuck am I? A gay club or a fucking zoo?” Spud waved his hand around, gesturing at his surroundings.

Yall have to vision this nigga at that moment. I’m talking, 3 cats laying on the couch with him. 2 on the top back part of the couch, dogs laying at his feet, and some Iguanas on the other side of the room, just listening to him vent his problems to me. And Spud sitting in the middle of all of us, stressed out! 1 sock on, 1 sock off. And the animals are wearing the rest of his clothes. Hah! This shit was hilarious! Evidently, these pets of hers don’t really have company. And we see why!

But later for that. There’s bigger fish to fry.

“Aight Dawg. I hear you. Enough of the jokes. We out! Jada tryna get some abortion money,” I headed for the door.

“HUH?”

“Jada said she pregnant!” I kept walking out the door and to the bike. The 1st thing I noticed was the bright sun shining.

Oh shit. I know this fiend is going to be heated. Oh well. I’ll throw him another piece. He’ll live.

20 minutes later, me and Spud are on our way back to the block.

“Yo, you think Jada is lying about her being pregnant?” Spud asked from behind me. We were almost home, so we’d slowed down enough for me to hear his voice over the bikes motor.

"I don't know," I told him. But the more I'd thought about it, Jada wasn't the type of girl to be with too many men at once. She was raised different. I had to be honest with myself. And when I was something deep, deep inside of me told me if a child was in her stomach, it was more than likely me.

"Damn," I muttered to myself. All I knew at that point was if Jada really was pregnant, I had to get my shit together. I would have to buy a house and furnish it with appliances. I needed help with that, and I knew just who to holler at. Lenny. Yea, his hating ass had what I needed.

***

"Hey man, what the fuck dude! I know you guys got something for me!" the white man said when I rode up on his bike.

I just laughed. "Yea man, I got something for you," I cooled him. I knew that was all he would want. More 'get high'.

"I've been out here all night dude. What happened to Three O'clock? I've gotten rained on, stopped by police, shitted on by some birds, and…" the smoker went in. Granted, he may have been telling the truth but it wasn't getting him anymore than I was giving him. He could whine all he wanted. Fuck he thought I was.

Alright, after I gave the fiend what he had coming, I called Lenny a few hours after that, and told him my situation, and what I needed.

Lenny gave me what I wanted, and I got situated. This

was all around the same time Malcolm got locked up. Time to turn it up.

ITS BONE CRUSHER, BITCH!!!!

CHAPTER 12

My 1st Robbery

7th Street.

"Yo, Bone Crusher what up?" a dirty ass blue pinto rolled up on me. I can remember this as clear as day.

I knew it was money. I automatically began running toward the car with my work in my hand. Shit, I'm trying to hustle some Reebok money up for my girl. This might just be the drop I been waiting for.

As I'm jogging to the sale, I see Korey running up beside me trying to beat me to the fiends. "What you want yo? I got it right here! I got it right here!" he's fingering his bags of coke.

"Na nigga he called me! He called me!" I picked my pace up and raced with him to the money.

When we got about 2 feet from the car, the window rolled further down, and we realized who it was. My brother Wyan, his man Bull Dog and their dirty ass third leg, Pig.

My brother Wyan was driving. "What's up man? What'chu doing?"

Korey had turned around and headed back to where we

were posted up. "What's up y'all? I ain't doing shit. Chillin, tryna get this money."

"Cool. Just what we wanted to hear. Take this ride with us," Wyan instructed me.

***

20th and Morris, South Philly.

20 minutes later, I'm with these niggas up Morris Street. We pulled up to a Chinese store right there on that corner of those 2 streets.

"Yo, you see that Chinese store right there?" Wyan said through deep tokes of whatever he was inhaling. Never know what he's smoking. Turbo's and all kinds of shit.

"Yea," my young self said, looking through the thick clouds of funky smoke. I told y'all they smoke turbos. Them shit's stink.

I was a kid. I mean for real, like 12, 13 years old. But I was in the streets, but of course Wyan was deeper in the street's than me. And this mission he pulled me on was about to prove it.

Remember when I told y'all Wyan was a bitch? Well, not when he was with his man Bull Dog. Them 2 together? Vicious! "It be a lot of dudes hanging in this Chinese store. Go in there, order some food, and come back out and tell me how many of them are in there."

"Aight," my dumb ass got out of the car, and went into the store. Not seeing the game he had planned.

I see 2 young dudes and a young girl, as I make my way

to the thick bullet proof glass window. There's 1 of the young men on each side of the store and the young girl is with the young man on the opposite side of entrance door. Yall know me! I assessed it, and placed my order at the window like Wyan told me. "Lee, (we call every Chinese man in Philly Lee. I don't care what part of Philly we're in. Lee! And they answer to it too.) Let me get three chicken wings and fried rice," I spoke through the holes in the window.

"Okay," Lee wrote it down.

After that I went back outside to tell Wyan what it was. "Three people. Two boys, one gir1."

"Aight cool. Look go back in there, act like you're waiting on the food, and we goin come in a few minutes behind you and jam them niggas."

"Aight bet."

10 minutes later I'm in the Chinese store. Lee give that Duck sauce up too! Stingy mu'fucka. And Gimme an extra-large Tea too!" I played it off while fishing in the side pocket of my black fatigue pants. "Oh and Gimme some Loosies and a Black and Mild too Lee," I ordered.

As soon as I did that, 3 masked robbers stepped into the Chinese store with their guns aimed."

I was at the ordering window, homey on the left side of the store was flirting with the young girl, and homey on the right side of me was rolling up some weed. I had a split second of seeing them before these robbers came in.

"Get the fuck on the ground! It's a robbery! Don't fucking move!" a voice boomed.

“Who the fuck is these niggas?” I'm thinking to myself as I get on the ground. Wyan and them said they were coming to rob them, but they didn't say they would have on mask's. I don’t know Who the hell these dudes are. Let me get my ass on this ground too. I laid on the ground as we were ordered.

“Maan get ya dumb ass up!” a hand grabbed me by the shoulder. I realized my brother's voice, and remembered what the plan was.

Keep in mind, this is the only robbery I’ve ever been on up until this time. I’m a small time hustler, trying to find a lane so I can survive in these streets. Selling drugs on them corners is cool, but I need some extra money. I hope these niggas in here got some for us. I gotta make at least $100.00 if I left the block for this.

So I got up, and went in the 1st man’s pocket. I pull out a knot of money, and stuffed it in my pocket. I went to the girl next. Patted her down, she didn’t have shit.

In the middle of it, we hear the 1st nigga talking shit. “Do y’all know who I am? My name is Jihad! JIHAD! Yall fucking with the wrong one!” he threatened us from his face down position.

Bull Dog went right at him. ‘CRACK! CRACK!’ he butted him in the face with the 357 magnum he was holding. “Shut the Fuck·up! Give a Fuck who you is nigga! Kill ya dumb ass in here!” he growled at him.

Jihad or whoever he was, got quiet.

“Back up and turn around!” I commanded the girl I just patted down. I know she was scared, but from what I can see she didn’t pee on herself.

On to the next victim. It's as quiet as ever now, because they know we aren't playing. I patted the next man down and took whatever was in his pockets. He had a ring on his finger. I took that too.

"Check his balls too yo!" I heard Pig say to me.

"What!" That was an ambiguous statement right there.

Pig could mean that 2 ways. He could have really wanted to see if this nigga had some money in there. Or, he could've been checking to see if I had any type of gay way's, at all. Knowing that's what he was into.

I made up my mind instantly. They weren't paying any attention to me. I couldn't do that. Fuck that. That's a molestation charge. I wouldn't dare go in the youth study center with a rape case! Fuck that money. All Wyan said when I first agreed to the mission, was to go in their socks and pockets. I'm cool with that. All of that other shit? I'm good. And since they were so focused on aiming their guns, they won't even notice what they don't already have.

I thought fast. Instead of going in the man's pants, I went in his sock and pulled out another stack of money. "I found it!" I fronted like I did what I was told. I put that in my other pocket. He also had a chain on him.

I looked at his chain. "Goomba loves Sara," it read.

"Ok lil baller, you in love huh? You in love?" I fingered his chain. "Man Gimme this shit you sucka fa love ass nigga!" I snatched it off of his neck.

After we got them all, it was time to make an exit. "Yo we out!" I let them know I was done.

Every one of us started backing away from the scene, heading for the door. "If y'all come out of this store, I promise you, I will shoot y'all!" Bull dog threatened.

The bul' whose chain I took started crying. I did feel sorry for him. But fuck him. Stop crying nigga, go buy another 1.

We walked out of the store like nothing ever happened. "Oh shit, I forgot my food."

"Man fuck that food! We goin to Geno's tonight."

"Shit, aight bet." I hopped in the car with them.

"Bone how much money we got?" Wyan asked me.

The streets are in me, so I got's to think fast. I peeled 2 separate stacks of bills off of the money. "The girl and the first nigga didn't have any money," I lied to them.

"Aight, count it up and spilt it between us," Wyan instructed.

"Damn these niggas razors are dull. They trust me with all this money? Shit I wouldn't trust me with all this! Then something dawned on me, they can't count! Aww yea, I'm about to work these niggas. This is Reebok money for Porsha and Tiffany. Ha! I can tell them any number, and they gotta believe me. Shit, I can buy Jada a whole new wig with this·shit. I'm up!

Damn, I got 2 stacks of money here. This is $1,400.00. "This is eight hundred dollars y'all, We get two hundred a piece." I passed everyone their money.

Mind y'all, I didn't tell these dummies about the other knot of money I stashed on them. I hope it's a nice amount.

***

7th Street...

"Yo, you ain't tryna go to Geno's?"

"Yea Bone what's up, you ain't tryna eat?" they asked me as I got out of the car on my block.

"Na I'm good. I got's to finish this hundred pack," I lied.

"Aight, be easy nigga."

"Aight," shit for real I was just eager to see what I had.

As soon as they pulled off, I pulled the money out I'd just made from our move. I counted it. $760.00. I recounted it to make sure I wasn't tripping. Nope! $760.00 it was! I did good. I'll sale the drugs tomorrow, fuck that.

I rode my bike to Wa-Wa's to get something to eat, then took it in for the night.

Before I drifted off to sleep, my mind roamed on how easy that move was. I was still high off of it. And the rush from it had after effect's on me. I knew I could do it again. I could put together my own team, and we could rob niggas.

ITS BONE CRUSHER, BITCH!!!!

CHAPTER 13

Pig left Bull Dog for dead.

7th Street.

Later on that night, me and Wyan at his crib asleep.

"Yooo, Bone!"

"The fuck is that?" I looked outside of my window to where the voice was coming from.

I see Pig standing in front of the house looking up at me.

"What up?"

"Yo let me get them guns in there yo?"

"Hold on," I knew what he was talking about because Wyan kept the guns. So I just went and grabbed them from the stash spot. I threw him the same 357 Wyan used earlier in the robbery.

"Here." I tossed it out of the window. "Wait, I'ma get you some bullets for it right now." I went to turn around.

"Naa, I don't need no bullets. It's only to scare this girl's baby's father," Pig informed me.

See, Bull Dog was dealing with a female, who'd had a child. And that child's father was very jealous. He just never crossed his boundaries. He knew Bull Dog, Pig, and my brother Wyan. They all hung together. They all knew him as well. Evidently, this day was the day he pushed his limit's. I would get the full story after the bloody event.

"What? You don't need the bullets?" "Huh?"

"Na, we good. I just need to let this nigga know we got guns too!" Pig explained himself.

I'm thinking to myself, it's one o'clock in the morning. What the fuck is going on?

"Na man, this chick's baby's father is talking crazy. Talking about he'll be through her crib for us," Pig mimicked the man's voice and demeanor.

From my ears, it did sound like a threat. I know the guy knew my brother and his men chilled with Bull Dog at the mother of his child's house, because Bull Dog was dealing with his child's mother. I'm guessing he's fed up with it? It's too much to look into for me right now. I know dude isn't really trying to take it to death over a female. So he may not need the bullets. Either way, Wyan is in his room asleep. If it was that serious, they would've woke him up. Or so I thought.

"You sure you don't need these bullets?" I checked with Pig 1 last time.

"I'm positive man, this nigga don't want no wreck."

"Aight," I watched him walk off with an uneasy feeling.

***

"Yo BONE!"

"Yo WYAN!" I hear Pig calling me and my brother.

"Yo, what up?" I answered him peering out of the window.

"Bull Dog just got shot!"

"WHAT?"

"WHAT?" Wyan appeared next to me out of nowhere. I didn't even hear him behind me.

Without words, me and Wyan instantly began grabbing more guns to head to wherever Bull Dog was.

***

Dressed, strapped and with Wyan 5 minutes later, me and him are in the car with Pig.

"What the fuck happened?" Wyan was on go.

I'm in the passenger's seat loading the guns up, Wyan is driving, and Pig is telling his side of the story.

The whole time Pig is talking I'm thinking to myself, If Bull Dog was shot, were the fuck were you?

And even though Pig was telling his side of the story, I wouldn't get the full scoop until I got to Bull Dog's girlfriend's house. When we did get to her house, Bull Dog was already in the ambulance truck fighting for his last few breaths of air.

***

Cindy's house, Mifflin Street...

By the time we pulled up on the scene, the paramedics had Bull Dog on the gurney, and was wheeling him into the back of the ambulance van. There were police everywhere.

The million watt blue and red lights continued to illuminate the block as police cleared the scene, for paramedics to do what they had to do.

Me and Wyan, caught Bull Dog just in time. "Bull Dog, what happened?" I got to him first. Pig stood behind me and Wyan.

I knew it would be hard for him to speak. The front of his chest was covered in blood. It had soaked through the sheet the medical staff placed over his body. The Iv water tank was hooked up to him. He had tubes all in his arms and upper body traveling beneath his shirt, taped into his veins, and an oxygen mask covering his mouth. It pained me to see him like this, and I can't type in the words that would explain how Wyan felt.

"What happened Bull Dog?" I asked him again.

Bull Dog was fading in and out of consciousness. But he'd heard me and fixed his eyes on me. His stare was weak. Almost blank. It lacked life. The life I knew Bull Dog to have, wasn't in them. Damn. We really might lose him. I bent over, and put my ear to Bull Dog's mouth to hear him. "Pig left me," he said weakly. I mean, barely audible. "He left me. Pig left me. He just left me. Pig. He left me. He just, left me," was all he could say.

Wyan stood next to me, and we both watched as life eased its way out of Bull·Dog.

"He just, left me." were the last words we heard from Dog, as his eyes rolled to the top of his head and his lid's closed.

"Excuse us sir, we have to get him to the hospital!" the medic said hurriedly.

Me and Wyan removed our hand's from Bull Dog's gurney and stepped out of the way for them.

Bull Dog, was lifted into the ambulance, its doors were closed, and he was hauled off.

Now the whole time me and Wyan were trying to hear Bull Dog tell us what happened, Pig was behind us talking to 1 of our homey!

"Did you hear what he said?" I looked at Wyan.

"Yea, he said somebody left him."

"Yea, he said Pig left him."

At the exact same time, we both looked behind us for Pig. Pig was gone. Instead of Pig, Wyan spotted Cindy, Bull Dog's girlfriend.

"There goes Cindy right there. Cindy, come here Cindy!" Wyan called her over to us.

Cindy left the group of people she had been talking to, and walked over to us.

The weather was a bit breezy, but it wasn't the reason I'd felt a chill crawling up my skin. I paid no mind to the neighborhood on lookers, as I readied myself for the story Cindy would tell me. Surely it was she that would fill in all of the empty spaces for me.

CHAPTER 14

We found Cindy. Cindy told us the story.

"Hey Wyan. Hey Red Bone," Cindy greeted both of us with a hug. We greeted her back, comforted her, then got right to the business.

"So what happened?" we both said.

"Ok," Cindy took a deep breath, and the 3 of us began walking toward Wood's Chinese store at the corner of her block.

There were too many neighbor's standing around, and me and Wyan needed to get the full scoop without anyone's input. Especially since Pig left so many spaces in his side of the story.

"Tone called up here to talk to his son, and his son was sleep. Pig answered the phone. I don't know why Pig answered the phone. Shit, that was what set Tone off in the first place. You know he's jealous of them being around me and his son all day to begin with. Anyway, Pig told him his son was asleep, and I guess he felt like Pig was lying to him. I'm in the kitchen and I heard bits and pieces of the argument."

“Dawg, what'chu calling me a liar? I said the little man is sleep. No I don't tell you he's always sleep. You always call at these awkward ass times trying to talk to him. Twelve o’clock at night, you calling here talking about some put Tom Tom on the phone. I tell you he's asleep, you get mad at me! What's up wit'chu fam? You What? You’ll be around here? Fuck you mean you'll be around here? Aight, well come around here then, I bet you I'll knock you the fuck out! You ain't coming to do no fighting? What? Well bring it then nigga, we got guns too!”

“I wasn’t even going to get involved with it at first, but then I heard them talking about guns. I know Tone. I was with him for two years, he is the father of my child. I knew he would come over here with a gun. He is crazy about me. I know Pig might not take it where Tone will take it, but I know Bull Dog will. And if Tone came to my house with a gun, I knew Bull Dog would get involved, regardless if Pig was there, or if it was his fault or not. So I… HHhh, I tried to...Mch Oh my goodness mann... Damn, now Bull Dog is...” Out of nowhere, Cindy began falling apart.”

The realization that her man was shot by the father of her child was breaking her up.

Me and Wyan stood in front of her as she told us the chain of events that took place. With tears in her eyes, she went on. “I came out of the kitchen and tried to cut the argument. Tone don’t come to my house with that bull shit, I’m telling you!” I’m screaming in the background.

But Pig is still on the phone acting like he’s built like that.

“So a few hours later, we hear a knock at the door. All me and Bull Dog hear is “Who the fuck is that?”

"Tone!"

"Oh you really came over here, you bitch ass nigga!" I heard Pig say, then I guess he had opened the door, because I heard it open. I hear Tone come in the house.

"What's up now! What's up now? You was talking that shit, what's up now?"

"You know what I mean? Like, he was daring Pig to jump at him. So that's when me and Bull Dog came out of my room. When we came out of the back of the house, Pig was holding his gun, but Tone was holding a bigger gun. It had to be like a Tech Nine. And when Bull Dog seen him, he went straight to him and tried to take the gun.

"Fuck you goin do with that?" he reached for it. But I don't think Bull Dog was trying to shoot Tone I just think he wanted to get the gun from him, so Tone didn't shoot him!

"But Tone ain't give him the gun. So all Tone kept saying was "Let go yo! Let go of the gun!" but the whole time they both are wrestling for the gun!

"Bull Dog got the gun by the barrel trying ·to take it from Tone, and Tone got his finger on the trigger, holding the gun by the grip, telling Bull Dog to let it go. The barrel is pointed at Bull Dog's stomach."

"Bull Dog was doing good too! He had him yo! Bull Dog had him! He had the gun like pointed away from him. Holding it with both hands. Fucking Pig was just standing there.

"Hit him!" Bull Dog told Pig when he had the gun. "Hit him Pig! Pig, hit this nigga!" he kept saying while he was wrestling with Tone. Pig was just standing there. I guess he was scared to hit Tone, and Tone pulling that trigger by mistake or something. But the gun wasn't even facing Bull Dog at that moment. They had the nigga! Bull Dog had him! All Pig had to do was hit Tone! Punch him in the face, or Something!" she looked at me and Wyan with despair in her gaze. "You know what I'm saying?"

"Yea."

"Yea," me and Wyan both acknowledged. "So then what happened?"

"While they was wrestling, Tone got the gun loose and aimed it at Bull Dog's chest. I'm in the kitchen with my sister screaming STOP! STOP put the gun down! Put the Gun down! They just ignored me and kept fighting!"

Then Pig left him. While Bull Dog was wrestling with Tone over the gun and Telling Pig to hit him, Pig ran right by him out of the house! Bull Dog looked at him like. Confused. Like what the fuck? And that's when Tone got the gun loose, and aimed it at Bull Dog's chest."

"So I'm like STOP! STOP! from the kitchen. But I seen Bull Dog reach for the gun again, and as soon as he went to reach again I heard it go off. BOOOOM!"

"It seemed like everything just stopped. It was sooo loud. Oh my goodness," Cindy covered her eyes to hide her tears.

"Tone backed up, and looked at Bull Dog. Because Bull Dog fell straight down to the ground holding his chest. So, Tone stepped back with his eyes wide open and was like "O shit!" Like he didn't mean for it to go that far. Then he looked at me and was like "I'm sorry. I'm sorry, then he turned around and ran out the house."

"Bull Dog was still alive, so I called the ambulance and the cop's came with them. Then y'all came."

"Where Pig at now?" Wyan asked her. Knowing she didn't know.

"He left again! I don't know where his ass at! He's the one who started all of this shit! Then goin leave Bull Dog in it by himse1f. He…" she started going off.

"Chill, chill, chill. We got Pig. We goin find him. Don't worry about that. Look go back to ya house, clean yaself up and try to get some rest. Ok? Call me if you need anything. Ima be right there," Wyan reached out to embrace Cindy.

CHAPTER 15

We caught Pig in bed with a Man!

6th Street.

After we comforted Bull Dog's girlfriend as much as we could, we set out to find Pig. We started on 6th Street. The first people we ran into was J.T and Harvey. I guess they were arguing about something because I heard bits of the discussion as I was walking up to them.

Harvey appeared too high and drunk. J.T seemed heated about it. Harvey was slouched over while sitting on a small crate. Too intoxicated to move. His head rested against the bumper of a car.

J.T stood over top of him with an empty bottle of Hennessey in his hand. "How the fuck is you just goin drink all my shit like that? Fuck type shit is you on? You Just smoked all the weed, now you going drink all the liquor? That's some real crack head shit right there! You got that. Don't worry about it. You got that. When I get my S.S.I check this month don't ask me for shit! And I man that! You fucki.."

"Yo J.T did ya dirty ass see Pig?" I butted in his

argument. He wasn't talking about anything important anyway. These 2 always go through this. Who drunk who's liquor. Who smoked who's bag of weed. Who wore who's sneaker's. Who smoked who's last cigarette. You know, dirt ball shit.

J.T stopped arguing to look at me. Harvey didn't budge. He kept his eyes closed and played sleep. J.T looked upset with me because I'd just butted into his argument about his liquor. Smh! Fuck that liquor, my man just died.

"Yea I seen him. He just came through here. He followed Donald in Poncho's house," J.T told me and went right back to Harvey, who still wasn't budging. "Wake ya drunk ass up! You ain't sleep!"

Me and Wyan kept it moving. Yall know where we were headed.

Poncho's house, Mercy Street.

"KNOCK! KNOCK! KNOCK!" Wyan knocked on the door with the butt of his gun.

"Who is it!" we heard Poncho moving around.

"It's me Poncho, open up." Wyan said. Couldn't tell him who it was in case Pig told him he was hiding from us.

Poncho opened the door a few seconds later with his crack pipe in his hand. When he seen Wyan, his eyes got wide, and he instantly put his pipe behind his back.

Wyan's eyes followed the pipe behind his back, and I saw his eye ball peer at me out of its corner as I stood beside him.

"I don't got nothing for you Wyan! You too greedy! You hog my shit every time I let you hit it, and you don't never wanna put up. Nope!"

"Poncho where's Pig at!" Wyan tried to shut him up quickly.

Poncho's eyes darted side to side real fast, I don't know?"

"Poncho, we know he's in here. Here take this for yaself and stop playing, where he at?" I showed him a little $5.00 treat.

Poncho looked in my hand. "Aight man, he upstairs in one of the rooms," he held his hand out. Yea, a nickel bag worked wonders around here.

Poncho's house is a party house. So I know he went days straight partying with no sleep, shower, or anything close to it. All in all, Poncho was a good dude.

"Who he up there with?" Wyan inquired.

Poncho's eyes got big.

I still ain't give him the coke yet, so he knows he has to help us to get it.

"I'm not answering that. That ain't my business. I been with women all my life, other than that I mind my business." Poncho looked away from me. A sense of churn on his face.

"He up there with the faggot bul' Don aint he?" Wyan let him know we already knew.

"Poncho come on, stop playing. We gotta hollar at him," I came in.

Poncho looked at me now. "Yes, he up there with him. But I don't know what they doing. I told y'all, I mind my business. When I see two men together like that! Make my stomach turn." Poncho turned his face away again. Then turned back to me, "Give me what you goin give me, so I can go about my way."

"Aight, here. Go to the Chinese store or something. We'll be gone before y'all get back," I hinted at him taking his girlfriend Val with him.

"Aight Bone, This better not be the same shit you had last time. That shit fucked up my pipe! Val let's go!" he looked back at his woman.

As soon as Poncho left me and Wyan crept up the stairs toward the rooms. We didn't know which room he was in, so we listened for sounds. We probably shouldn't have done that knowing what Pig was into. But, we did.

I heard Pig's voice close by. "Yea, just like that. Ssss, yea." like he was in full enjoyment.

It was all coming from the 2nd room to our left. Wyan·moved past me and opened the door. Since Bull Dog was his right hand man, I let him go in the room first.

He opened the bedroom door and this nigga. Pig was laying on the bed with his eyes closed. The faggot bul Donald was pleasing him.

"You left my man? You left my man. You bitch ass ni…" Wyan walked toward him aggressively and raised the barrel to his face.

"No, Wait hold on," Pig held his hands up!

Donald moved out of the way, just like he should have. Smart move. The look in Wyan's eyes told him shit was serious. Deadly serious.

"Hold on! Hold on! Walt a minute! Don't sh.."

His sounds were muffled out by the sound of Wyan's gun. The back of Pig's head exploded and his brain matter splattered all over the beds headboard behind them.

Wyan turned his gun to Donald. Donald now lay there holding a sheet across his chest with 1 hand, looking all feminine.

"You say anything about this and Ima blow ya fucking brains out!" he promised him. "Then Ima kill ya people Easy Earn and Jariek!"

On the way out of the door, I seen Wyan make a phone signal to Don. I ignored it but caught it. I was on the phone with the cleanup boys, Silk, Monty, and Kev. They didn't do the dirty work. They just cleaned it up.

"Yea, come get this faggot ass nigga Pig and dump his ass in Cobbs Creek or something." Yea, R.I.P Bull dog.

ITS BONE CRUSHER, BITCH!!!

CHAPTER 16

My Stick Up Team

7th Street.

I remember when my boys were headed to a Mike Tyson fight in Las Vegas.

"Yea young bul'. That shit goin be crazy," J.C was excited.

This was before most of our other trips. At this time I barely had the money to just up and shoot on events like this. I was getting money, but I was fucking it up on other things. You know, young bul' shit.

"Damn yo, I'm tryna go with y'all man, fuck."

"I told you to save ya money young bul'! Shit you only goin need like a thousand, two thousand dollars."

"I know but that's all I got!" I said between tokes of my weed.

"Well we leave in two days if you figure it out let me know."

"Aight bet," I hung up.

Damn. Niggas been telling me to save money. I just got

used to it coming so fast it started running from me. But I knew 1 thing. I was still trying to go to Vegas to see Iron Mike. I was a kid but I knew what I wanted. Another thing I figured out by this time was whatever kind of money, I touched I could touch it again.

My brain began storming on how can I get the money for this trip. The fellas were leaving in 2 days, so I had until then to figure it out.

But, I had a plan. That move I did with Wyan and them taught me something.

Hmh, I say it's time to use what I learned.

$$...$$...$$...$$

"A few hours later, I'm on 7th Street looking for a few homey's to pull this master plan I devised.

First 4 people I saw was Black Nate, Indris, Hoarse, and Buck Shot.

Now these are some niggas I can work with. I know they're with my plan. But I also know I got's to find a nigga to search the inside of the pants of whoever will be in the store I had plans for, because these niggas won't be doing that.

Just then, guess who I see diddy bopping down the street sashaying all gay? J Bird! The 7th street rapist. Perfect. He's definitely going in niggas drawls. He goes both ways, so he don't care. On some real shit, he might enjoy it.

As soon as J Bird got near us I opened the floor. "Yo, y'all niggas wanna go to Vegas?"

"Hell yea!"

"Hell yea, what's up?" they got excited. By this time J Bird was next to me.

We were all looking at his mouth, because it was lighting up like a disco ball every time he went to speak. Or even when he wasn't talking.

"Yo, What the fuck is that in ya mouth?" Indris looked at J Bird wildly.

"Shut up, it's my tongue ring. It glows!" J Bird defended himself.

"You always got some gay shit going on. Tryna catch. Fuck outta here." Black Nate scowled at him.

"Fuck y'all!" J Bird snapped back.

"Shut the fuck up! Yall niggas tryna go to Vegas or what?" I snapped.

"Yea nigga!"

"Yea mu'fucka!" Black Nate and Hoarse answered me.

"You probably like it! J Bird still argued with Indris.

"Yea aught! Better take ya gay shit to ya girlfriend Marlow!"

"Indris, Chill dawg. I'm tryna help us get this money," I looked at Indris.

He shook his head at J Bird and shook his head. "I don't know what you got planned with his fruity ass anyway," Indris mugged J Bird.

"Listen! We goin hit these niggas in this Chinese store. The one up there on Thirty First and Tasker. I need y'all to do what y'all do, and I need J Bird to go in them nigga's drawls and check for that money they might have stashed in there."

"OHhhh. Yea, aight," niggas nodded now getting the

picture. We all knew that was the part they wouldn't be doing.

A few other people heard my mission and wanted in. "Yo ·Bone, What's up I'm tryna go to Vegas too. I got money nigga!"

"Doc get ya dirty·ass outta here. You don't got no Vegas money!"

"Yes I do got Vegas money! Fuck you talking bout. My dummies move!" Doc called himself correcting me and pulled out the money he'd hustled up off of selling fake coke.

Now, I know money. Doc was holding about $97.00 at the max, and it was piled in $20's, $10's, $5's, and he had bulk of it about $48.00-$52.00, was in $1 dollar bills, which made the stack appear thicker than what it was. And Doc was shuffling through the bills like he was on for real!

Here comes his man Omar behind him hyping him up. "Show it to him Doc, Show it to him! Fuck he talking bout, It's the WU out here!" this nigga had the nerve, grinning at Doc's money like they was about to blow up.

I just put both of my hands on my head and rubbed my face.

"These niggas." I didn't ignore them, but instead I paid more attention to task at hand. "Aight y'all, we going roll out in like ten more minutes."

"Aight bet."

"Aight."

"Aight, I'll be right back," all of the responses came.

CHAPTER 17

Our 1st Mission

31st and Tasker.

The Chinese store.

"Aight J Bird go in there order some food and see how many people are in there..."

"Alright," J Bird mouth lit up.

"Hold on, take that fucking thing out ya mouth, before you get us locked up."

"Alright dang!" he obliged. Sounding all faggoty.

After removing the tongue ring from his mouth he left the car to go and handle business.

He was back minutes later.

And minutes after that, we were in the store.

***

"It's a fucking stick up! Everybody on the ground before somebody gets hurt!" I came in 1st.

Indris, Black Nate, and Hoarse came in behind me. All of us were masked up and our guns were aimed.

Seeing 4 masked men with guns made everyone get on the ground. Even J Bird's goofy ass. Couldn't blame him though. I did the same thing my first time around.

"PFF!" I kicked J Bird in his ass. "You, get up and check their pockets one by one!" I commanded him.

We had burst in on·a dice game they were shooting. Its 4 of them. They are all young bul's and their money spread all over the floor.

"Yo! Put that fucking money down!" I caught Indris trying to stuff some of the money off of the ground. I wouldn't dare let them stash on me. I know the game. I done stashed on nigga's before. Ha! Nice try nigga. "Matter of fact; Watch these niggas," I ordered him while I bent over to pick up the money.

It's about $3,000 on the floor from what I can tell of my street adjusted eye.

Meanwhile, J Bird passed me everything from the 1st bul' pocket.

"Aight, cool. Go in his pants now," I ordered J Bird.

Through his mask, I see J Bird's eyes light up. "I got you!"

Dude was already on the wall, because J Bird had made him stand up so he could pat him down. His hands were spread open, and his face had fear in it.

J Bird then went into the bul's pants. Man I can tell y'all right now, the way J Bird groped dude I could tell he wasn't looking for no money. Not at first anyway. Ha! That was fucked up.

This nigga J Bird palmed this man's whole sack, then moved his hand up and down like he was messaging his baby maker!

Bul' didn't like that shit. "Yo, Yo dawg! What the fuck you doing?" he jumped back but couldn't move because I had the drop on him. My 44 revolver was dead locked on his face. But I felt his pain. The pain of being violated.

I looked at Indris. He looked at me. His eyes are saying, "What the Fuck?"

So are mine. That was crazy.

J Bird acted like he was sticking to the script. "Shut the fuck up! I'm robbing y'all niggas!"

"Yea, but you don't have to rub my dick!"

Now all of us Me, Indris, Black Nate, and Hoarse are looking at 1 another trying to make sure we aren't tripping Or high. "Yo, here goes some money right here!" J Bird played it off and pulled the man's money out of his pants like he accomplished the goal.

"Aight," I took the money from his hand.. "Check the next nigga, and don't go in his pants this time!" I tried to protect the next man. I can see now, J·Bird is a savage.

"What? What you mean?" J Bird shot a hot heated look at me.

"Don't search their pants nigga!" I repeated.

I could feel J Bird's anger waving off of him on to me. He was mad I wouldn't let him violate these boys. "Well I ain't doing it then," this nigga yelled in a high pitched voice, then stomped out of the Chinese store!

What the fuck! I know I didn't bring these sloppy ass nigga's with me on this mission. I'm thinking. I had to act fast. "You pat these niggas down!" I motioned Indris.

Indris moved as I said. We robbed all of them and got the

fuck up out of there. This nigga J Bird was sitting in the car mad as hell. His arms folded across his chest like a stubborn child! Smh. These niggas here. In the end, we came up a total of $6,000.

I thought about not giving J Bird shit for the craziness he pulled. But I thought against it because he did play his part at first.

"Here," I broke him off when we got back down 7th street.

He took his take and put the fruity ass tongue ring back in his mouth. "Yall do what y'all do, and let me do what I do!" J Bird acted like he was checking me, put his little gay sailor's hat on got out of my car. Me and the other fellas pulled off. "Fuck outta here."

That sexual molesting shit ain't cool! If that's what you are into? Stop!

***

2 days later, we all went to the Tyson fight. Tyson won. 1st round knockout. 30 second's was all it lasted. I'll give ya'll the details in my next book.

ITS BONE CRUSHER, BITCH!!!!

CHAPTER 18

Meech's fake Rolex

Back down the way.

I remember when Meech did this sucker shit. (Meech, you Bitch! I'm telling the readers about this shit! You still my man.)

Check this out y'all 7th Street was too much for Meech after I boo yow him (that was when I kicked him in his ass after I pulled up on my new bike I made Jay buy me) so he started hanging out with them boys Up Town, in South Philly.

Don't get me wrong, Meech is still a 7th Street nigga, and he is about his money. And as I've said, robbing a dude from 7th Street was like hitting a good lick. So·1 day when Meech wasn't with us, somebody tried him. I'd got the news after I'd come from the Masjid on a Friday late noon.

A few of us were just walking up on 16th and Christian.

"Ahhhhhh, Hah! Meech is fucked up for that!"

"Haha!" someone else joined in."

"Yea he's wrong for that!" I hear everyone is laughing and clowning Meech again!

“What the fuck is so funny?” I’m curious.

“Na Bone, the nigga Meech almost got his watch took by Edmond,” Toby whispered in my ear.

I’m instantly heated. It’s funny because Meech is kind of soft, but he is still my man.

“Where did you hear this from?”

“Everybody's saying it! They said Meech was Up Town at the Masjid, and…” Toby filled me in on what he knew of what took place. Pretty soon people who were around Meech when it happened were hitting me directly with it.

“Yo Bone, let me tell you this shit. The bul’ Meech...”

“Yo Red Bone, ya man Meech is out of pocket! Check this shit out...”

“Ayo nigga! Listen to this wild shit!”

I got it from everywhere. Supposedly it happened like this...

***

Meech went to Jum’uah service on 16th and Christian that's Up Town, with his 4 year old son. Mind you, Meech has 1 of the realest fake Rolex watches I've ever seen. This shit was ill! It looked real. Almost too real. The man had everyone in the neighborhood thinking it was real.

“Somebody's going to think that watch is real one day, and try to rob your ass for it,” my man used to tell Meech.

Well, that somebody was Edmond. And that day was this day I'm hearing it all.

“Yo, take that watch off!” Edmond walked straight up to Meech after Jumu’ah.

"What?" Meech paused looking down at his son.

"Don't make me tell your bitch ass again," Edmond lifted his shirt and showed Meech his gun.

Meech's eyes got big. He knew the watch wasn't worth his life. He also knew he had the hood thinking the watch was real because he's from 7th Street where the playa's over there wore pieces like that Edmond wanted it. And he stood there waiting on Meech to hand it over.

Meech on the other hand couldn't try no dumb shit because he knew Edmond was going to shoot. No if's and's or But's about it!

So, Meech tried something else. "Chill yo, put your shirt down. Police is creepin up behind you," he warned Edmond peeking behind him at the same time.

Meech sold it. Edmond bought it. "For real?" Edmond looked back. We all know you never look back. Never. In this case Edmond had to.

Because if Meech was serious he was booked! So Edmond turned his head to see where the police were.

As soon as he turned his face away, Meech bolted! Took off running! "Dad wait!" Meech's son took off after him! His little legs pumped as fast as they could. No use. He wasn't catching Meech.

Meech's fat ass was so fast, Edmond didn't·even·try to chase him. Nor was he trying to keep Meech's son. That was when Edmond took Meech's son to Jamilla's house up the street from the Masjid. He knew·Jamilla was cool with me.

I got the call from Jamilla herself about·Meech's son.

"Are you serious Jamilla? That little boy is really at your house?"

"Yes I'm serious Red Bone. People don't play like this. Meech ran like he was trying out for the Philadelphia Relay Race. Left that little boy out here like that."

"That's crazy. Left that little boy like that. I'll come get him though. I'm on my way right now," I hopped in the Acura.

Meech was dead wrong for that. He should've gave that watch up. Now it's looking like he chose his watch over his child. Yea, he's going to hell for that. But, wrong or right, I got's to scoop his son from Jamilla's for him.

ITS BONE CRUSHER, BITCH!!!!

CHAPTER 19

Meech lied to P.G.

Meanwhile, while I shot to Jamilla's crib to pick up Meech's son, Meech found his way down 7th Street. (Yea, now you wanna come back down 7th Street. Smh!)

“Hold on! Hold on! Calm down nigga, damn! Here drink this,” P.G (an up and coming young goon from our block. In fact this boy was another Malcolm!) handed him the water bottle he was drinking from.

Meech was still running wildly, and breathing heavily when he ran into P·G. A familiar face and a comforting drink was just what he needed. Meech guzzled the water down, then told P.G his version of what happened.

“Edmond put a Glock to my sons head and took my son!”

“What? For real?”

“Yea! And he had eight of them Up Town nigga's with him!” Meech spiced it up. He knew how P.G got down for his peoples.

“What happened after that?”

“I walked off and call my people's.”

"Who ya peoples Meech?"

"Walt and Musty."

"Where them niggas at now Meech? It don't matter where they at Meech, Seventh Street is supposed to be your peoples. You gotta stop being Up town and start being around ya real folks. Niggas who goin rock for you when shit go down!" P.G checked him.

In the back of Meech's mind he's not hearing that. He love the bul' Musty's sister too much to listen.

"Don't worry about Edmond. I'ma take care of that," P.G promised him.

***

Later on that night.
5th St.

A few of my boys were suiting up to go pay Edmond a little visit. He was another 1 of them 5th Street boys. Yall know of our history with them. Gun play! They had to go and pay them a visit. The news had spread around the hood by now about Edmond trying Meech.

The shit that had me heated was the fact that I knew Edmond would have never tried no shit like that if we were around! No one would've, because they know how 7th Street get down. I'm not bragging, but if you throw shots at us then you're asking for a war. And if it's a war you want, it's a war you will get. And if we didn't move on this situation it would send a message to an outsider that they could try, or do anything they wanted to to a 7th Street playa. Na. Wasn't happening!

I wasn't on this particular mission I don't think I made it back in time. But my homies filled me in on what I missed.

***

"Fuck is this nigga at!" P.G said in frustration.

Him, Rafiq, and Farrej had been in Edmond's part of town looking for Edmond for the past 20 to 30 minutes. Evidently Edmond wasn't in any of the places he normally hung.

"Yo, matter of fact go through Sixteenth Street. He be out there too," Ty Ty remembered. He also joined them for the mission.

"Bet," Rafiq made the turn toward there.

Rafiq was driving. P.G, Ty Ty, and Farrej were in the minivan with him. Rafiq turned on 16th Street.

They spotted Edmond. "There that pussy go right there!"

"Fiq, park up right quick and let us out," Ty Ty and P.G advised him.

Rafiq didn't park the car, but instead kept right on driving.

Edmond stood on the sidewalk, not even aware of my boy's creeping up on him.

"Where he at?" Rafiq's scary ass said looking dead at Edmond, and purposely driving.

"He's right there!" P.G pointed at Edmond with his eyes and forced himself not to yell as Rafiq rode past him.

"Oh. Ok. We'll get him. Not right now though. Some old lady was standing beside the house he was in front of. Ya'll ain't·see that lady?"

He knew damn well they didn't see a lady because there was none! Ty Ty and Farrej opened their mouth to scream on Rafiq, but didn't feel like arguing with him.

"Damn!" P.G was heated. His trigger finger itched so bad he still wanted some wreck. "Yo since we up this way, go through thirteenth Street and see if we see this nigga Boo," he told Rafiq now.

Boo was another one from around that way we've been trying to get at. And since they were up that way, and couldn't get to his man; ·today was his chosen day.

Rafiq reached his block in no time. "Park right here on the corner," Ty Ty told Rafiq as soon as they hit Christian Street. "Listen we'll walk around here on foot and see if we see this nigga. You stay ya scary ass in this car and don't go nowhere!" he scorned Rafiq.

Ty Ty, Farrej, ·and P.G got out and walked around to Webster street. That was connected to that area too. All of those blocks are within walking distance from 1 another. And all of the people who hang around that way, you might catch on any 1 of those blocks.

As soon as my boys turned the corner of Webster, they'd caught Boo walking through the projects. Show time.

"BOOM! BOOM! BOOM!"

"POP! POP! POP! POP!"

"H'd'd'd'd'd'd'd! H'd'd'd'd'd'd'd'd! They all let off shots.

Boo did like any wise man would do, and took off running through the projects.

At that exact same time, the tables had turned in Boo's favor.

"H't't't't'tat! H't't't't't'tat! shots rang from above my boys. Whizzing past Ty Ty's ears and rocking the parked car behind him.

"Oh shit! (he looked up) somebody on the roof shooting at us!" he warned P.G and Farrej.

"H't't't't t't'tat! H't't't't'tat!" more shots came.

"BOOM! BOOM! BOOM! BOOM! BOOM! BOOM! BOOM!" Farrej covered them while they backed out of the projects and headed for the car.

They had the advantage of being on the roof because my boys couldn't see them directly. Boo got away. We'll be back for him though. He knows.

***

"Look at this nigga," P.G commented on Rafiq's face.

They made it back to the van, and when they got there Rafiq was sitting in the car with his eyes so wide it looked like he just hit a crack pipe! He was sweating like an athlete at a competition, and breathing hard like he'd done something besides sit in the car scared. Shit, he might've been about to pull off!

"You good man?"

"Yea I'm good," Rafiq played it off.

Rafiq was still shook as we all piled into his car. P.G was a bit behind us, so he was the last to get to the car. He'd only got 1 foot in.

Rafiq's scary ass couldn't wait. "SCCCUUGRRRRrrr Vrooomm!" he screeched off while P.G's other leg was still on the ground!

"Damn nigga, Slow the fuck down!" P.G yelled at him after he damn near dove in the car.

Rafiq was gone. He ran every red light in sight. "Nigga, this how we get home. Safe! We almost killed them niggas!" Rafiq yelled back. They couldn't argue with that.

***

After they got away, it wasn't long before Rafiq was talking his shit. "Yea! Fuck is wrong them niggas! Seventh Street ain't playing games with nobody! Them niggas don't wanna go to war with us! Na mean? We Seventh Street! They know what the fuck it is with us! We'll kill them niggas! We almost killed them niggas!" Rafiq burst through Lenny's door all hyped up. "Yo, who in this mu'fucka?" he came in, looking around like he just tore a block down.

Me, Darryl, and Lenny were playing monopoly with our street money on Lenny's pool table. I was shaking the dice as I was about to roll them. "Fuck happened?" I looked up from the game.

Rafiq was pacing back and forth through Lenny's house like he done had enough of the bullshit and he just snapped. That's how he was acting.

Farrej, P.G, and Ty Ty all came in. "Bone, what's up young bul'"

"What's up Young bul?" they greeted. us. We all shook hands. Rafiq kept pacing. "Aww ain't shit, just came from Thirteenth Street. I ain't goin brag about what we did. I'ma let Ty Ty tell y.., Ay Ty Ty tell these nigga's what we did to them bul's down there!" Rafiq waved his hand around.

"Darryl, bring ya soft ass on if you want a ride home! And get ya hat! (Rafiq turned to me) I'm out Bone! Watch ya mu'fucking back! Them pussies might come back aro… Darryl come the fuck on!" Rafiq went. He was everywhere.

"Bone that bul ain't do shit!·Ty Ty burst out laughing when they left. "Let me tell you this shit; This nigga rode by Edmond like he didn't even see him! So we had him park for the next hit. His ass sat in the car with the mask on like he was shooting! Then he almost pulled off on P.G's foot!"

"That's crazy!" I laughed. This bul' done fronted like that. "Well why y'all let him front like that then?"

"Bone, that was his story. We just let him tell it."

"Hell yea," we all laughed it off.

20 minutes later, Lenny's house was crowded. Lenny's house was the clubhouse, so everyone who was squad had normally just walked in. Before we knew it there was Hoarse, E boogie, Rollin and Buck shot.

"I got next! I got next!" 1·of them was yelling at whoever it was that turned the PlayStation on.

"Knock! Knock! Knock!" Knock! Knock! Knock!" the door sounded.

"Who is it?"

"Craig Mack and Markeem!"

Lenny then opened his door to the both of them looking like some dirty young bul's.

"What up? What up?" they'd come in greeting the house.

"Fuck y'all want? That's what's up?" Lenny joked, in truth.

"Na, yo I just seen two cars deep riding through Seventh

Street masked u just now."

"Oh Shit. Aight, come in. Mark Madness go upstairs and get your dirty ass in the shower!" Lenny told Markeem. I laughed at that.

"Fuck you laughing at Bone?" Markeem said on his way up the steps.

"Get ya dirty ass upstairs and wash up nigga," I laughed more.

Craig Mack walked in the living room and quietly gazed at Hoarse. Him and Hoarse are real close. Craig Mack is Hoarse's young bul'.

"Ay Hoarse, can I hollar at you right quick?" Craig Mack asked Hoarse. Hoarse knows what Craig Mack wants. Hoarse is looking at Craig Mack, while Craig Mack is still staring at him. But, Craig Mack isn't looking at Hoarse, he's looking at Hoarse's Coogi sweater. Craig Mack loves Hoarse's Coogi sweater. And like I said, he's Hoarse's young bul' so they have a big brother little brother relationship. Hoarse always allowed Craig Mack to wear his sweaters. So, Hoarse knew what Craig Mack wanted. He just wanted to hear him say it.

Craig Mack knows Hoarse wants to hear him ask. He also knows the whole house is watching, and as soon as he asks everyone in the house is going to burst out laughing like they always do. It's like a role in a movie we all know our parts to. Now, everyone is silent, waiting on Craig Mack to play his part, and ask Hoarse to rock his Coogi.

Mack looks around the room. Then looks at Hoarse. "It's Sunday, and I go to school tomorrow, So can I rock that Coogi sweater?"

That was it the whole house went off in laughter.

"Hah! I told you he was goin ask!"

"Smack! Smack! hands smacked each other's, ·nigga's·were jumping around and all. It was all love though.

See Craig Mack gets money but he don't get money like Hoarse get money. Craig Mack get small money. Like, for sneakers and things like that.

Hoarse on the other hand, get money like a real 7th Street hustler.

He's blowing $500.00 to $600.00 on sweaters just to hustle in. And my block is like a fashion show as it is. You'll pull up on our strip and see all kinds of styles, so it was normal to us.

Craig Mack is viscous. Although he knew Hoarse would let him rock his sweaters, and he'd soaked it up every chance he'd got. Every sweater Hoarse gave him, he'd worn it for at least 4 days straight out of the week to the clubs, dinners, wherever! And Mack knew everybody knew he was from 7th Street so he could get it off.

Long story short, Hoarse gave Craig Mack that Coogi sweater that night. And before we'd left the house, Craig Mack took his shoes off and funk the whole house up. Had Lenny's pad, smelling like corn chips!

ITS.BONE CRUSHER, BITCH!!!!

CHAPTER 20

Craig Mack fronted, Hard!

I remember Craig Mack got one off! Check this shit out.

Me and him are downtown 1day, and we had met some girls. They were pretty. We gave them our numbers. That was on a Friday. Craig Mack had had 1 of Hoarse's sweaters on.

So the next day Mack came at me again.

"Come on Bone, I'm tryna step out again tonight," he said while stroking his head with the wave brush.

He'd still had the same Coogi sweater on from the day before for about 3 days now and he was fresh. I won't lie. He knew how to dress. But he wasn't always that fly, so when he did get dressed he wanted to show off.

To me, getting fresh was a normal thing. I really wasn't up to stepping out.

"We went last night. I ain't really trying to g... You know what fuck it, where you wanna go?" I gave in. Let my boy shine his shine. I couldn't let him go out alone.

"We can go to Red Sky."

"Aight bet," I agreed.

20 minutes later, we're pulling up to Red Sky. I didn't have to get dressed. 7th Street is a fashion show. We stay ready.

As soon as we step out of the car, I automatically walked toward the bouncer so I could pay our way in the club. Craig Mack's funny looking ass just wanted let everybody know we were here.

"Seventh Street here! Seventh Street here! Whas sup y'all?" he stepped out of my Benz.

"Smh." I just shook my head and smiled. I mean I get it because it's like we're living a street dream. And it feels good to be living it! But, it's always the ones who aren't getting any money, that do the most fronting like they're getting all of the money! And like I'd said before, they the ones that keep fronting know we won't expose them so they keep right on doing it. They're some funny dudes.

Anyway, he's over there fronting hard on the ladies in line. All I hear is "Oh this? This ain't nothing. This is my Saturday shirt!"

I laughed. There was a lot of pretty women in the line, and they all were believing him.

By the time I'd gotten to the Bouncer, 1 of them had called my name. It sounded like a familiar voice.

"Hey Chris!"

I'd turned my head to see Shakeah and her girlfriend. The females me and Mack had met the day before! And by now, I know they'd seen Mack on the other side of the line flirting with the crowd. And Mack is a funny dude, so he has them laughing and enjoying themselves.

“Yo what’s up? “I walked over to Shakeah. Me and her had already known each other before we had traded numbers the day before.

“How y’all night going?”

“Good, and yours?”

Their gaze is locked in on Craig Mack, and I know why. But lucky for his ass, I got a nice excuse lined up for him since I know what it takes for us to rock this fly shit, and what it takes to get here. So I knew just what to say if they’d asked.

“I'm good.”

“What’s up with your boy Mack?” I knew that was coming.

“Mack is aight, why what’s up?”

“Didn’t he have that shirt on yesterday?” Shakeah asked for her girlfriend.

“Yea. That’s what Mack does. But check his left front pocket when he comes back over here. Between me and you Mack got a family and bills to take care of,” I went in.

I’m lying. Craig Mack don’t got no fucking bills in his name. Mack is a bum. But the Bone Crusher can’t tell this bitch that.

“Hold on right quick y’all.” I’d 1eft them to go holla at Mack. I had to put him on point.

I can hear Mack talking shit as I walk up on him. “Yeah, this ain’t nothing. I got a sweater like this for Wednesday, I got a sweater like this for Thursday, I got a sweater like this for Friday, one for Saturday, and one Sun…” I’d cut him off by tapping his arm.

Craig is funny. I can’t wait to see his face when I drop

this news on his fronting ass. "Yo, Shakeah and her girlfriend is here, and they asked me if that was the same shirt you had on last night!"

Mack's eyes grew wide. "Huh?" he'd stopped counting, but his fingers were still positioned like he was. He peeked behind my shoulder then looked at me, "When they g..., how long were they here?" he studdard panic took over his expression.

I smiled to myself. "Look, we're walking over there right now. Here, put this in your pocket." I gave him my money. "When you go over there, make sure you stand in front of them on that side so they can see it through your pants. Act like you'd just came from the block," I saved him. I had to. Like I said, 7th Street nigga. Me and him "And when we get there, make sure you tell them you gotta get back to the block to grind!" I schooled him.

"Aight bet. Good looking out!" Mack said. "Is my pocket fat? Do it look like I got a lot of money on me?" he asked me. He's smiling now. The size of the knot of money I'd gave him did that. He knew it was a lot because he'd had to fight it into his pocket.

"Yea. Hell yea. But act like it ain't nothing." I had to admit, his pocket was bulging.

Craig Mack smiled extra hard after that, looking all goofy and shit. I shoulda knew he was going to do some whole other shit when we went over there. Craig Mack never had thousands in his pocket before.

As soon as we got over there, his crusty ass ignored everything I'd just told him and turned into this hood rich coke connect! I mean, this boy fronted so hard, it made me look like the broke $10.00 nigga that he was and made him look like the $250,000 nigga that I was!

“WHAS’SUP, WHAS’SUP y’all? Seventh Street over this mu’fucka! (there was a few more ladies in the line by now.) Damn. All of y’all lovely ladies in line? Aight, Craig Mack got something for all of y’all! You, you, you, you, you, you, you, you, you, you, and all of y’all friends are on me! I got all of y’all door fee!” he’d fronted fighting to get my money back out of his pocket.

Then he’d looked at me. “I got you too young bul’, just make sure you hold the door for all of us!” he waved me off with a hand.

I can't front, it was a good look for him. The door fee was $50.00 per head to get in. Them females forgot about his shirt real quick after he paid that.

“Seventh Street here!” Craig Mack walked in the club strolling so hard it was crazy, and he was headed straight for the bar. “Ladies! Yall want a drink (he looked at the ladies, then looked at the bar tender.) “Hello pretty, Gimme the whole bottle of the best thing y’all got!” he waved his hand at the liquor wall.

I’m behind the bitches now, trying to get to Craig Mack while they follow him to the bar because they think he's about to buy it out.

No he will not! Not with my money. As soon as I got around them hoes, I went right up to that nigga and took my money right out of that broke nigga's pocket. He is something else! Had me holding the door like I'm him. It's cool, he's going to pay me my money back when we get back down 7th Street. Shit, he’s lucky I don't tell them bitches about his funky ass feet.

Then of course, after he got the bitches to the bar, him and Markeem dipped off somewhere until we paid for the drink's. Smh! Those 2 are never around the bar because they know they'll have to buy drinks. I'm telling y'all them 2 nigga's are something else!

Anyway, me and Puerto Rican Rick had the bar. You know us, drinks is nothing. Party on us. So, awhile later the liquor settles in and everyone is feeling good.

"Yall enjoying yallselves?" I check with the ladies.

"Yes, and thank you Red Bone. You and your friend," they smiled.

"Aw that ain't nothing sweetheart. I'm glad y'all had f.." and right when I was about to say something else guess who showed up! Smh!

"Seventh Street here, Seventh Street here! What's up ladies! Yall cool? Yall enjoying yallselves? Craig Mack came strolling over to us smiling.

"Do y'all want anything else to drink?" Markeem was next to him, fronting like he had some money!

'Say yea! Say yea! Say yea!' I wanted to tell them to call Mack and Mark Madness's bluff so bad. Damn They're fronting at an all-time high tonight! I knew they were somewhere watching us, making sure everything was already paid for before they came back. They're pro's with that. Every time we go out. I'll tell you, them 2 7th Street niggas there ain't shit! And if you meet them, you'd better watch them!

Alright, the club is about to close. Suddenly we hear some

commotion. Tables moving, glasses breaking, and yelling. “You goin pay me my money Walt! You’re going to pay me my money!” was all I’d heard.

By the time I’d turned around, I’d seen Walt laying on the ground knocked out, and Lil from 13th Street standing over the top of him, pointing his finger in his face, still talking trash. “I told you! I told! And I still want my money!” he was saying to a sleeping Walt. After he’d knocked him out!

“Yo, Red Bone, what’s up bul’?” I heard Mike behind me. Mike was an old time friend of mine, that hasn’t been down 7th Street in years. I just seen him with Walt! They were together! “Where y’all going?” Mike pushed.

“What’s up bul’? We’re leaving here. It’s over,” I brushed him off. You ain’t going with us. I’m thinking to myself. “Weren’t you just with Walt?” I asked him.

“Maan, Walt got his own shit going on,” Mike looked at me and walked off. Leaving Walt still on the floor asleep in the club. Smh. Dirty bul'. Tried to act like he was hanging with us. I'd heard police had to use smelling sauce to wake Walt up.

Anyway. Club let out. We’re outside in the parking lot choosing who we’re taking home for the night. So, we’re talking to the females and you know its popping. Jewelry flashing. Dudes got watches, rings, chains, and bracelets shining. All kinds of Benzes, and other exotic wheels. Some are parked up, some are blowing on horns trying to get some pretty females attention. Music knocking. Yea. This is Philadelphia.

Me, I'm talking to Tina. This little dick got's to go

swimming tonight. I have the Magnums in my pocket, and the Bone Crusher is about to do his thing.

"Yo, Tina meet me at Lowes hotel. Here," I gave her the room key and number.

See, me giving her the room key was telling her that the room had already been paid for. And those rooms were $400 to $500 per night.

"Aight. I'm on my way right now," she smiled.

"Aight. I'ma drop my man off and I'll meet you back here," I smiled.

Craig Mack is trying to get the chick he was talking to, to go with him.

"I'm with it. Where are we going?"

"To my crib."

"Your crib?"

"Well, it's my mom's crib but I stay there."

"Can we just go to Lowes hotel?"

"Lowes on Thirteenth and Market?" Craig Mack's mouth dropped. He knows he can't afford one of them rooms. He was fronting like that wasn't the case. "Na, I'm trying to get back down Seventh street so I can make these runs."

The chick knew something was up but she couldn't put her finger on it. Lowes was expensive. And a nigga like Craig Mack ain't the Bone Crusher, so he can't afford no shit like that.

"Naa Mack, we·chillin tonight dawg. Come on, we out!" I smoothed him.

"Aight man, fuck it," Mack didn't hesitate a single second. He knew that meant we were paying for his room too.

Me, Puerto Rican Rick, and Craig Mack are headed to the hotel with our dates. That's when Craig Mack changed up on Markeem.

"Aight Markeem. Take your dirty ass home," Craig Mack stunted on Mark Madness in front of the bitches, after he was with him all that day!

"Yea aight," Markeem said walking off. "Fuck outta here, Bone paying for your room! Shit, you must don't know doing a deal with Bone, is like doing a deal with the devil. Cause believe me, he's charging, you just don't know what his price is!" we heard Markeem's voice in the wind.

He's right. Craig Mack owes me for this 1. Big too. I might just have him clean my dogs shit up next.

ITS BONE CRUSHER, BITCH!!!

CHAPTER 21

Tricky Nikki's

"Yo, take me to Tricky Nikki's," I ordered Craig Mack later on that night. It was time for him to pay up.

See what Craig Mack didn't know was; Markeem was right. Because doing a business deal with the Bone Crusher, was like doing a deal with the devil. You never knew how I would make you pay me for whatever I gave you. As for Craig Mack, I had just the thing for him. Yup.

"Tricky Nikki's?" Craig Mack looked at me.

"Yea nigga!"

For a second, it looked like he was about to ask me some dumb shit. Like why did I want to go over her house? I folded my arms across my chest and waited for him to.

His question never came. I knew he knew better.

##...##...##...##...##

10 minutes later we're in front of Tricky Nikky's house. Yall can pretty much gather why we call her Tricky Nikky.

"Beep the horn young bul," I instructed him.

Before Craig Mack could beep the horn, Nikki's door swung open and she came running out of the house toward us. She was already expecting me.

***

"Hey," Nikki got in the car smelling exotic, and looking ripe like fresh fruit. Yeah, I'd bite that apple.

"I need my normal," Nikki looked at me.

Her normal was·$20.00.

My normal was some head. "Come on Nikki, I ain't goin keep giving you no twenty dollars," I tried her.

Yall know I had to try to wiggle my way around that. Whether I had it or not, fuck that.

"Come on Red Bone I need you! I'm tryna go back out Wilson," Nikki seduced me.

Wilson was a project out in South Philly Nikki hung in. The way she was looking at me right then was like she was going to suck skin off of me for that $20.00. Yea, I needed that. Treat this little dick right. "Aight I got you," I whipped out on her. "Get to work," I grabbed her by the neck soft, but firmly.

And that was right what Nikki did. Went to work!

That was what Nikki did. WORK. She was a beast, and I loved her for it. No arguing, no complaining, no crying, no gagging. Just WORK! WORK! WORK! Damn she was good!

Damn. Ssss Damn!Ssss Shit! Stop using ya teeth. What I tell you about using ya teeth!" I reminded her.

The crazy part was she was past all of that beginner shit.

This bitch was PRO! Something was causing her to do that. Right then and there, I felt the car swerve.

I look up and Craig Mack is looking at me instead of the damn road through the rear view mirror. Trying to adjust the joint so he can see!

I cocked my hand back, and full palm slapped him across·the back of the head. "Young bul drive this fucking car! Stop being so damn nosey. You making this bitch scrape my shit dick head! Bout to get us killed with that dumb shit.

"Matter fact, drive up Grey Ferry bridge. Go over the hump, come out the bottom, and do it again! Do it til I'm done! With that dumb ass Kango hat," I went on his hat too.

I didn't have to go on the hat. I know. As a matter of fact I liked the hat. Matter of fact, I'm taking it when I'm done with this bitch. This nigga don't even know how to rock the shit right. Got it all tilted to the side like he's cool. All dumb. I tell y'all, these fake ass chauffeurs.

Craig Mack looked at me like I lost my mind.

I looked at him with my crazy look.

"Aight old head," he put his head down, then focused on the road.

I know why he was trying to look though. Nikki was a gun! She cleaned up all mess, took in every drop and sucked out whatever was left.

Aight, so 15 minutes later we were done.

"Here you go," I gave Nikki what she wanted. Fair exchange, no robbery.

"Yo, go back to her crib Mack."

"Aight." Mack hit the blinker.

***

“Aight Bone,” Nikki got out when we arrived at her house.

“Aight,” I peace her.

“Yo who that?” a jet black Maserati parked across the street from Nikki's house caught Craig Mack's attention.

I seen it. Before him. I knew who it was. “Oh that's the Broad Street Bully.”

“Beanie Seigal?”

“Yea.”

“Fuck he doing way over here?”

“Tryna get his dick sucked. Told you, that bitch Nikki is serious!” I joked.

Sure enough, Nikki was walking toward his car.

“Bean’s! Whatever you do, Don’t kiss that bitch!” I joked. Me and Craig Mack laughed at that.

Knowing Beans, he might’ve been doing more than just kissing.

ITS BONE CRUSHER, BITCH!!!!

CHAPTER 22

Pugie is a Savage man!

7th St.

"Bone, do you remember when you said Pugie fucked his own daughter?" 1 of the young bul's asked me on the block. This was after·Pugie left the block 1 day right after a shootout.

"Yea I remember me saying that."

"Why you lying Bone? Pugie didn't do no wild shit like that," the young bul said. Really, he just wanted me to tell him the history. I can do that.

"Fat Cat, do you remember Rubin's sister? The one that was killed by Rubin's dog?"

"Yea, I remember that."

"Well, back in the late eighties, she was getting high smoking crack, and Pugie was tricking her. She was a trick, but Pugie was her main customer. Pugie was a kid himself, mind you. He was about thirteen, she was about seventeen. Well anyway she became pregnant, had the baby, but since she was in such a messed up state of living foster care took the baby from her.

"We all knew she was pregnant, but we never put it together of that being Pugie's baby. Like I said, he was a kid. Years later, when Rubin's sister got herself together, she'd went back and got her baby. Pugie never saw the girl though. Now she's almost grown. It's been years.

"One day, Nikki and the girl are walking through Seventh Street together. Then I noticed how much she looked like Pugie, still didn't put it together. The girl had a phat ass. Me and Pugie were both standing on the corner. So, you know me, I went to see what's up.

"Hey Nikki, what's up? How have you been doing?" I spoke to her first.

"I'm good Bone. I been okay. This is my daughter, Nikki."

"Oh, your name is Nikki too? How are you doing?" I greeted her.

"I'm fine."

"Damn, you look good shorty, where are you from?" I shot at her. That was when she'd went into everything. About herself and her life story.

"I don't know my father though. All I know is he's from Seventh Street."

"So, that was all I'd heard right then and there. It was all I needed to hear. She already looked just like Pugie and everything matched up so much. That's when I went to Nikki.

"Ayo, is that Pugie's daughter?"

"Yes Red Bone it is. But PPPLLLLLEEEEAAAASSEEE! Don't tell Pugie. I just don't want him to know," she damn near begged me. So I didn't say nothing.

"But, me and the shorty got cool. I started fucking with her as a friend. I mean, as a real friend. She would always tell me stories about her life in Foster care, and being away and all of that. So one day me and her were having one of our talks on the block.

"Yea, so I'm just trying to get somewhere new. Start all over and get myself some money."

"The only way you're going to make any money around here is tricking. These boys love to trick. That is where the money is at for girls."

I kept it real with her.

"Ok I'll do it," she perked up. She wanted that money for real.

"Yall know me, I let the hood know what she wanted to do.

The next thing you know she had all the player's coming to me about her. And pretty soon, here came Pugie. Thumb in his mouth and all.

"Who's that Bone?"

"Some shorty. She's tricking. But you ·can't have her though."

"Why not?"

"Because Pugie, that's your daughter!" I tried to shut him down. Because I knew Pugie wasn't going to stop unless I forced him to.

Pugie still wasn't trying to hear it. "What you mean that's my daughter?"

"You remember when you were fucking·Nikki back to back like that back in the days?"

"Yea?"

"Well, remember back in the day when she got pregnant?"

"Yea?"

"Pugie, that's your daughter."

"Get the fuck outta here!" the reality of it hit him.

Now the whole time Pugie is talking to me he's sucking his thumb, and eying Nikki's body. I told y'all she was thick. And she'd had on some nice clothes, so her body was showing. I mean, showing. You could see her thong's through her pink windbreaker pants. Pugie was still staring at her.

"Pugie, I know you're not still thinking about it?" I looked at him.

"Bone, I didn't raise her though," Pugie looked at me seriously.

"So what nigga. That's your daughter!" I reminded him.

"Man, I didn't raise her," Pugie brushed me off, and walked over to where she was standing. A few seconds later, I see him and her walk off together. And I heard Nikki had a child later, and the baby was retarded and looked just like Pugie." I finished the history.

Fat Cat just sat there, wide eyed. "Pugie is a vicious man," he screwed his mouth up.

"Yea, who you telling? It is what it is. That's on him."

ITS BONE CRUSHER BITCH!!!!

CHAPTER 23

Bone Neck is the Funniest

7th St and 5th St.

Bone Neck is the funniest! Let me give y'all a real quick story about Cuz. Its more to it than him, so I'ma give y'all the whole movie clip.

Check it out.

In case y'all didn't notice I was always at some kind of party or event. Shit once I had things running smooth on the block, there were many places a fly guy like myself had to be seen in. Like now, there is a party down South Street. Well, later on anyway. I remember trying to get a hold of Rafiq on the phone before the party.

"Yo Fiq?"

"What's up Bone?"

"Where you at bul'? And who's that in the background?"

"I'm at Lenny's crib. That's P.G, G Rap, and miserable ass Lenny," Fiq say.

He's right about how miserable Lenny is. That bul' is a complete hater! I'm telling y'all, all of our girlfriends love Lenny. Because he tells them every fucking thing we do! I mean for real! But, when shit gets real, he's with us till the end. That's why I fucks with him! But still, he be doing too much. Yall ain't seen nothing yet!

"Oh yea? Lenny's dizzy ass is with y'all?"

"Yea, but I'm about to drop him off though. He's getting on my damn nerves."

"Yea, drop him off Dawg. I'm not trying to be around him," I let Rafiq know.

"Why? What he do now?"

"That nigga showed Jada that prom picture of me and the chic Mia, from North Philly!"

I could hear Rafiq turning to face Lenny. "Why would you show Bone's girlfriend that prom picture?"

I could hear Lenny in the background, "He shouldn't be cheating!" this nigga had the nerve.

"How are you going to tell Bone that he shouldn't be cheating? Ain't you cheating on Hayleen with Ebony? Rafiq addressed him.

Lenny got quiet.

"Damn Lenny, that's some bull shit! You're wrong for that.!"

"Mind your business," I heard Lenny say.

"Yo Bone, where you at?" Rafiq turned back to me.

"I'm walking through the park." Once I said the park, I know Fiq knew where I was. It was the only park around our way.

"Aight bet. I'll be there in ten minutes."

"Bet!" I hung up.

When I hung up, I stopped walking and posted up on the wall waiting for Rafiq. While I'm there, I see some commotion going on. I see dirty ass Pig and dirty ass Damien arguing over some food! Like, really? Food though?

***

"Na nigga, give me some of your chicken wings!" Pig demanded. I told y'all Pig is gay, but I never said he was a punk.

"No!" Damien snapped! (Damien, is Spud by the way.)

The way Pig was going at Spud, y'all would think Spud owed him, right ? Na, Pig was just a greedy nigga, and was trying to force Spud to feed him his food. Spud wasn't no bitch either. I remember all of this so clear.

'"SPLACK!" Spud's plate of chicken hit the ground. Pig smacked it out of his hand. It hit the floor instantly.

"You goin pay for my shit!" Spud jumped in Pig's face.

"I ain't paying for shit. I'm broke!"

"You bitch ass nigga!" Spud shoved Pig to the ground.

Pig got back up, and went wild on Damien! Unleashing a fury of punches. Upper cuts, left hands, right hands, hooks. You name it!

Spud was doing him. Well, trying to anyway. Ducking, weaving, bobbin, and trying to take Pig's head off with his own punches. They were going at it until Pig landed 1 of them upper cuts on him.

"Ah!" Spud stopped swinging, covered his eye, then took off running from Pig. "You better not be here when I get back!" Spud threatened Pig.

Pig looked around. His eyes landed on me. "You got your gun on you?"

Of course I did. But I wasn't getting in their shit. "You better get up and get your dirty ass out of here before Spud come back and blow ya head off!"

"Fuck Damien!" Pig flared up.

Pig was fronting. Spud is a cold killer and he knows it. Within the next few minutes Pig made his way through that park. He knew 2 of 3 more minutes and Spud was coming back clapping And not with his 2 hands either.

Pig got me fucked up...Asking me for my gun.. I should've shot his ass for that.

Rafiq pulled up with a car full. G Rap was in the back seat.

"G Rap move over before I put paws on you!" I opened the rear door. I forget who was in that front passenger seat but I'd decided to be merciful and let him stay there. Because I could've moved him!

"Bone, you can't beat me no more Bone," G Bap shook his head while he moved over.

Yall heard that? "No more." Yea. G Rap knows. I used to fuck him up!

"G Rap you remember that day I slapped you in your ear? And you got mad? Yea, That's how you got them big ass ears. Shit's look like dinner plates nigga!" I joked with him. We'd had a family moment then.

In the midst of us joking, Rafiq's phone went off. (Yall won't believe this shit!)

***

"Hello?" Rafiq answered his phone.

"Was sup old head?" Craig Mack came over the line. He was locked up, and the call was from the county jail.

"Mack, what's up young bul'?"

"Yo Fiq, this nigga is up here trippin! He's trying to kill me up here!"

"Who tryna kill you?" Rafiq cut the music down.

"This nigga Boo, from Thirteenth Street! This nigga stabbed Dontae in his leg and took his food. Then he came to my cell with three niggas and took the sneakers Hoarse bought me! Then told me to tell somebody from Seventh Street to put thirty five hundred on his account," Craig Mack was bitching.

"Craig Mack you lying!" Fiq burst out laughing.

The reason he was laughing was because no one would ever expected Craig Mack, or any Seventh Street playa to be saying words like this. It had to be a joke. Especially coming from Craig Mack.

"Fiq, I'm serious. This nigga tryna kill us. Yall laughing like this shit is funny!"·He'd heard us roaring in the background by then. "Yo please man, put that money on Boo books and I'll pay you back when I get home Dawg," Mack plead.

"WHAT?" Rafiq's face said as he stared at the phone. "No! FUCK Boo! I'm not putting no money on Boo books! Fuck I look like? You better get some fucking heart!" Rafiq screamed into the phone receivers.

"Yea nigga! Better pay that nigga before he kill yo ass!" G Rap Joked from the backseat.

We all laughed at that. Smh. Mack in jail for a fucking bike fine cold bitching. Hah! That's what the fuck you get.

Out here fronting in Hoarse's sweaters like you like that. Hah!

Mack turned from Muslim to Christian in them walls. Geo a homey from 7th Street said he saw Mack in the hallway holding a bible in his hands saying "Jesus is good. Jesus is good." Mack is trying to keep the wolves off of his ass.

"Don't call me no more with that shit," Fiq prepared to hang up on Craig Mack.

"Rafiq, don't do this to me. Don't leave me in here for dead. We all we got!" We hear Craig Mack bitching while Rafiq is trying to press the end button on his phone. "Ay Rafiq! Ay RAFIQ! RAFIIIQQ!" his voice trailed into its end. Rafiq hung up on him.

"Bone, what's up with ya cousin?" Rafiq looked at me in his rearview mirror.

"Yea aight That pussy ain't my cousin," I joked back. We all laughed at Mack. Wild bul'.

***

Back to the part Bone Neck played in this movie.

"Yo Fig, take me down South Street. I got's to pick up this linen set for this party tonight," I moved on with our day.

"Aight," Fiq agreed.

We're riding down 7th street. "Hold up, Let's go through here," Fig turned down 5th street projects, just as we were about to ride past 5th street.

We were still beefing with them 5th Street boys heavy. Needless to say, that was a war we were always ready to start or finish! As soon as Rafiq made that decision, we automatically went on enemy alert.

"Look! Look!" P.G and G Rap pointed to their right side. The'd spotted one of the Twins. I did too. It was on.

"Pull over, Pull over!"

Rafiq pulled over and parked on Christian St. and he wasn't bitching like he was the last time we went through 16th St with him. (That time I told y'all he acted like he didn't see our target standing on the corner.)

"Bone, you got your gun on you? P.G asked me.

"Hell yea I do."

"Aight look we're all going to get out and walk. Bone, you walk on the left side. P.G you walk on the right side, and I'm going to go and post up by the parking lot in case Twin runs to his house," G Rap laid the roles for everybody.

"Aight bet," we all went with it.

"Rafiq, you keep this car running!" G Rap looked at him.

***

I'm walking down the left side of 5th Street, on some "We're lost, we're not from this area shit. I see P.G out of the corner of my eye trying to get my attention. I look his way, and he's pointing at something. It's my cousin, Bone Neck! In his wheel chair trying to trick some crack head chick! I can only hear bits and pieces of what he's saying.

"Just suck it for me, please. I'll give you Ten! Ten, and I got the money on me right now!" He reached for her hand. Cuz is wild. My nigga though. Bone Neck is on my side of the street, so I'll have to watch where I'm shooting.

We got closer. The Twin is talking to 1 of the females. I can hear Bone Neck clearer. “I'm telling you, I can still eat that pussy.” He doesn’t see me, Twin doesn’t see me, nor does either of the females they’re talking to.

I hear P.G go off, “POP! POP! POP! POP! POP! POP!”

Automatically Twin ran. To the same side of the street I was already on, waiting for him. “Come here young bul’!” I took aim at him.

“POP! POP! POP! POP! POP! POP! POP! POP! POP! POP! POP! POP! POP! POP! POP!’I let the whole clip off at Twin.

P.G hit like 5 of them clowns. I hit Twin a few times. I know I did, though his ass kept running.

Its scrambled now. People are running for their lives.

“CLAK! CLAK! CLAK! CLAK! CLAK!” I hear G Rap bussing his A.K off.

Me and P.G turned around to head back to the car. I see my cousin Bone Neck trying to shelter the crack head chick from getting hit!·Ha ha! Yall should’ve seen this shit I guess he was going to get him some pussy 1 way or another.

The 3 of us made it back to the car.

“DHUM!”

“DHUM!” we jump in and slammed the doors. “Pull off! Go!” G Rap told Rafiq. We’d just emptied most of our shells. If these boys turn this corner, and spot us with their guns full of bullets. Na, Rafiq needs to pull the hell off. Not fast though. Nice and calm.

“SCCCUURR!” Rafiq pulled off like he was afraid, Again! Not as crazy as the last time. But, still wild.

Rafiq got himself together! Then as usual started talking

his shit. "YEA! Fuck them 5th Street niggas! They don't know who they fucking with! 7th street is the Big Dawg's in South Philly!" he went on. And on. And on. And on. And on. And on. And on. And on. Like he was the main man out there doing the shooting! Rafiq is something else.

***

Now, we're on South Street about to shop. (Yes we still went shopping. This was normal for us.)

"Yo, we gotta hurry up and change clothes before the police get on us," Rafiq was right back to his scary self again.

"We good nigga! Stop being paranoid," I brushed him off.

"We had that nigga Twin running for his life out that·motha fucka P.G joked.

"Hell Yea," G Rap burst out laughing. And yo, I think I might've hit Precious too cause she took off with them Christian Street niggas limping. G Rap looked at me.

I just shook my head. Casualties of war. Precious is 1 of my cousins. G Rap is crazy. He doesn't care who he hits. He just loves squeezing that trigger until his clip is empty. And P.G's psycho ass is just the same. Me, I like to hit my target. And Rafiq is getting his driving skills up for hits like that.

***

We're finished shopping now, and moving along as if nothing ever happened.

"Yea, just come through the spot. I'm here," Lenny's telling Rafiq over the phone. Lenny was trying to make sure we're good. News was getting around that 5th Street has been shot up. He knew it was us and called Rafiq.

"Aight, cool." Fiq hung up the phone.

***

20 minutes later, Lenny's house.

"P.G took the other side of the street. Bone pretended we were lost. They ain't see us coming. P.G let the first few rounds off. I'm way behind them, with the K cocked ready to let that mu'fucka dump. So," G Rap was explaining to Lenny.

"Hell yea, had em running for life out there," P.G told the story with him.

I wasn't saying shit to Lenny. I still wasn't feeling him from that bull shit he did to me, with Lil Mia and the prom picture. So, I walked off. Lenny sensed it to.

"Don't come back around here no more neither!" Lenny yelled at my back.

I just shook my head and kept stepping. I felt like fucking Lenny up for.real. I know we're bigger than that but he was pushing it. Its cool though. He's right. Pay back is a Bitch.

***

I'm walking through the park now. Thinking to myself how we had them running for dear life. A smile crossed my face. We got them 5th Street niggas good that time.

Ivan and Nai came to my mind. Hmh. They were funny.

"What's up Bone?" I'd ran into Dor in the park. Dor is a

7th street homey.

"What's going on Dor?"

"Nothing. Be careful out here. You heard what happened?"

"About?" I'll let him tell it.

"It was a shootout on 5th Street. Five niggas, and three bitches got hit! And one of them bitches was Pooh!"

"Yea? Damn. Make sure Pooh aight for me cuz," I looked him in his eyes.

"I got you Bone," he promised me.

Dot knew Pooh was my peoples. But it is what it is. She shouldn't be on them corners. That's a man's place. Damn, let me give Bone Neck a call. Make sure he's cool. I dialed him.

Bone Neck answered on the second ring, ring. "Hello?"

"Yo cuz, this Bone. You good? I heard shit got crazy down there? People getting shot and all that?"

"Yea cuz whoever them niggas was they was trying to kill us! Them niggas had army guns! But you know me! I still get down! Them niggas didn't expect a nigga in a wheel chair to be bussin back at them!"

"Oh yea cuz? You was getting down?"

"What? Was I getting down? Hell yea I was getting down! Shit, I'm the one who got them niggas the fuck up outta here!" Bone Neck really went in then.

"Hah!" This nigga is funny. "Oh yea?" I urged him on.

"Hell yea cuz! See cause first I had one of them by his dreadlocks. I was holding him so I could get the join out and do the nigg. Right? So he wrestling all wild trying to get out my grip. Now I'm holdin the mu'fucka, but the mu'fucka strong, so the mu'fucka got loose." Bone Neck went on.

I'm just listening to him lie. This is crazy.

"By the time I got to my gun, that nigga was already hauling ass! I bussed at him anyway! Na mean? Had to let them niggas know they ain't coming around here with that shit! Fuck wrong with them?"

"Yea. Yea," I can't help my smirk. Bone Neck didn't have a clue how much I knew.

"Yea cuz. I'm still a killer. But now. I'm on wheels. You shoulda seen how I chased them niggas outta here!"

"Yea. But I heard you was down there trying to trick one of them smokers while that shit was popping off?" I couldn't help it. He was going too far.

Bone Neck got quiet. "Huh?" Now he ain't hear me? Yeah Aight!

"Huh?" I could play dumb too.

"Oh naa, I definitely was tryna trick but when I seen them niggas, I started bussin'," he still tried to convince me. But, this time, his voice didn't have that same fire behind it. Hah!

Fuck it, might as well let him know now. "Bone Neck, you lying You wasn't bussin no gun. That was me shooting at them niggas!"

Bone Neck cold switched characters! "Ohh, that was your crazy ass cuz? You damn near killed me! Good thing I'm on wheels and I was able to roll outta there."

He didn't mention him covering the smoker chick. I didn't even ask. He knew I'd seen him. "Naw, I saw you. That's why you didn't get hit! Anyway, let me know what's going on down there," I let him go.

"Aight cuz, I'll let you know."

Smh. Cuz is funny. Lying ass nigga.

ITS BONE CRUSHER, BITCH!!!!

CHAPTER 24

#1, Porsha

7th St.

Let me tell y'all about these 2 chicken heads. Porsha and Tiffany. I'll start with Porsha 1st. Dig how I met this wild 1.

Porsha was standing on 20th and Tasker St. with all of her chicken head friends. She was the typical hood rat. Knock kneed, thick and she resembled the soul singer Jill Scott, but with a loud mouth. She had full breasts, thick legs, and fluffy light pink lips. Those lips was her catch. I couldn't help imagining what she was able to do with them.

As I'd said, she was with a few other girls. I didn't know who they were at the time but I'd later came to find out. It was Cherika, Taria, Mi Mi, Andrea, and Fat Ass Channell. All of these chicken heads looked hot and thirsty!

At the same time, I just happened, to be down their way pushing 1 of my new cars. Uncle Luke boomed from my customized Sony System.

"DOO DOO BROWN! D'. D'. DOO DOO BROWN!"

With my windows down, Porsha heard my music loud and clear and started dancing to it while I was at the stop sign. I told y'all she was thick. And she'd had some moves too.

By this time her and all of her friends are dancing. Mind you, they all have on daisy dukes, and they're all trying to twerk. I'll say this; everybody don't belong in no daisy dukes! Especially none of them chicken heads! I'll bet any amount of money you couldn't tell them that though. Not judging by how they was dancing that day.

Porsha looked like she knew what she was doing though, and I'd told her that.

"Damn shorty, you look like you know what you're doing for real," I flirted with her.

"I do," she'd flitted back licking them lips and still moving in rhythm to the song.

She was young. I was young. A little more flirting, and I'd gave her my number. I'd decided she was going to be on the stable.

"Aight Porsha. That's your name right? Porsha?"

"Yes, Red Bone."

"Yea boo, make sure you call me. Aight?"

"Aight. I will," she blushed.

"Red Bone, can you hook me up with someone from Seventh Street?" Cherika jumped in out of nowhere.

"Aight I got you," I laughed. Glad she understood our status.

"Can I get some of your chicken nuggets?" the other 1, Fat Ass Channell had the nerve to ask me. These bitches won't let a nigga breathe!

The whole time I was flirting with Porsha, I was snacking on some chicken nuggets I'd scooped up on 1 of my rounds.

I·was enjoying them too. But, the Bone Brusher ain't a stingy dude. I share. So, I did.

"Yea, I got you. Open your mouth," I'd told Channell.

The next thing I knew, all of them were standing next to Channell with their mouths open! Oh well, guess I got's to feed the birds then.

"Here catch," I said and began throwing nuggets into their mouths from my car.

Porsha and Mi Mi, picked theirs up off of the ground and ate them.

Taria and Channell were both professionals. They'd caught their nuggets in the air then put them in their mouths.

That was enough. I pulled off and as I'm pulling off I heard all of them chicken heads yelling.

"I love you Red Bone."

"I love you Red BOne."

"I bet y'all do love me," I'm saying to myself. "I just fed ya'll."

Even though they were chicken heads, they'd all turned out to be good girls. Well, for the most part. You know women. Smh.

Aight, on with the wild shit Porsha pulled.

After I was with Porsha for only 24 hours, this girl got dick whipped! Now she always came to my house around the late evening. Same time most of the time. It wasn't every day but it was constant. Only because she was damn near stalking me already. Told y'all she was dick whipped.

One day 1 of my old flames just decided to show up at my crib.

"Knock! Knock! Knock! my door sounded.

Me thinking it was Porsha because I didn't get a phone call, so I didn't expect there to be anyone else at my door, and it was around the time Porsha always came through when she did come through. I opened the door like it was her.

"Come in," I'd left the door ajar and walked back to my couch.

Mind you, I still think its Porsha, because this is the slot I'd left for her. See, I had my women trained. They knew their places. Not knowing this woman at my door wasn't one of my women.

"Hey," Shaleen walked in. Looking good too!

Shaleen was tall. I mean 6'3 at least. Sexy as hell. Brown skinned like a Sanaa Lathan sort of look. And she'd had on regular jeans and a white blouse.

"Hey girl, what's going on stranger?" I piped up. I was genuinely surprised to see her. It had been about 4·to 5 years since I'd seen her face. We used to deal with each other back in those days, but the universe had its own way of separating us.

"I'm doing alright, how've you been?" she'd out stretched her arms for a hug.

"I've been good, its good to see you. You got thick as hell too girl," I embraced her as I flirted.

I was wondering what she was doing here, but I didn't want to be rude and flat out ask. Now a few things had stood out to me right away; 1st off if she had a boyfriend, why would she even bother to come and see me? After 5 years? 2nd thing; her reaching out to hug me, meant she'd wanted to touch her. And she'd wanted to touch me. Now all I had to do see how far it is she would allow my hands to go and that would tell me everything I needed to know.

"Aww thank you. You looking good too boy. All cute and sh.." that was all I needed to hear. Before she could finish her words we were kissing, touching, caressing, and undressing.

Our chemistry was always on fire for 1·another. Time, just had me uncertain for a small second. Her body language told me it was still there. She'd still belonged to me, if I would have her. And a man like me, took what he'd felt like belonged to him. So I took her. She allowed me to take her. Wanted me to. Needed me to even. Because the men she'd been around, didn't possess the masculinity I possessed. It's been years since she'd felt it. But she remembered it her body, remembered it, and yearned to feel it again.

Meanwhile, my phone is going off crazy, and so is my doorbell. It's Porsha!

"I know you're in there Red Bone, pick up the damn phone. Come and open this door! I'm not playing with you boy, I'm telling you!" Porsha's going off.

She's going off because I'd been ignoring her for the last 15 minutes. Shit, what was I supposed to do? Shaleen had some good good, and I was close to busting in it. I wasn't getting out of that ass. Porsha could've knocked all night, fuck that.

"Hold on Porsha, calm down! He might not even be here," I hear my neighbor, Princess.

"He's here! His fucking car is parked right there. He's got some Bitch in there, that's what the fuck it is! All of his fucking lights are off, and he got slow jams playing! I'm not stupid! Fuck I look like?" Porsha shot back.

I hear it all. But, I'm finishing this exercise. I know that! And the main reason Porsha know it's someone in the crib is because I have all of the lights out and the slow jams banging when she's here. So she knows what this is. But I was determined to bust in this bitch.

Now just as I was to bust that nut, Porsha was just as determined to stop me. Smh.

That was when I'd heard the window break.

"BBLLIINNG'GGN."

"I'ma fuck you up!" I'd heard her voice inside of my walls now.

I'm still in the pussy. I told you, I'm determined to bust. So I'm still stroking, but I'd slowed down when I heard the noise. Sounded like she threw a brick through my shit. I know she didn't just do what I think she just did?'

I hear her footsteps on my stairs. That made me bust. Just not at the peak I was expecting. Now I'm heated, because she just fucked it up for me. I'm tensed at the same time because I know Porsha is a wild one.

"I know she ain't just come through the window? You got that girl acting like that?" Shaleen huffed between squeezing back into her clothes.

"Yea. I…" I never got another word out.

Porsha burst through my bedroom door, saw Shaleen and went straight at her!

Porsha threw a 2 piece at Shaleen that landed on her face. And Shaleen, not being the slouch, threw a 2 piece right back at Porsha landing both on her face.

"Hold! Break that shit up!" I stopped it by stepping

between them and shoving them both away, 1 from the other. I don't like that girl fight shit They'd stopped swinging.

"Go head Shaleen," I permitted her leave.

Shaleen walked past me and Porsha. Porsha eyed her like she just wanted to tear her hair out of her scalp. She took that anger out on me.

"Why the fuck you got that bitch in he.." she swung for my face. That was it! I went off now! I don't hit women, but this bitch? Got's to get it!

I was already heated. 1st of all this girl done came to my crib, climbed through my window, fucked my disco time up, and swung on me? BITCH! Are you serious?

As soon as her little punch hit my face, I looked at her with my crazy look. She knows she done fucked up now. Too late.

"No," she tried to get away. Uh uhh, you paid for this!

I grabbed her by the wig and front handed her, then back handed her, front handed her, back handed her, and was about to front hand her again! Dumb bitch! I just put you in the stable, and you're acting all crazy!

She calmed her ass down after I knocked some sense into her damn head. She was laying on the bed crying a short time after that. Then I heard, Shaleen outside.

"Yea, bring that bitch out here! Tell that bitch to come out Red Bone."

"Yea, tell that bitch come out Red Bone," another voice joined hers.

They're all loud and shit outside of my spot. I can't have this goofy shit out here. "Yo, y'all drawn. Go head man, get the fuck out of here," I tried to wave them off.

"No, Uh Uh. We ain't going nowhere til that bitch come out here!"

"Yea, send that bitch out here! We're going to whoop her ass," they both got louder! Shaleen and hood rat ass Tasha. Tasha is a 5th St. girl.

I'm the Bone Crusher and I'd already told these bitches once! "Oh yea? Yall ain't leaving? Aight, stay right there, I got something for y'all."

"Na, fuck that I'm going outside. These bitches want it they're going to get it!" Porsha was already started. On the inside it was good to see she stopped that fake ass cry she was always trying to give me.

"Na, na, chill. I got em! I got em! I got something for their ass," I hurried off.

***

I'm in my kitchen a few seconds later. Yea, these bitches wanna play? Come to my crib, screaming outside of my shit! Trying to fight my chick and then don't want to leave when I ask y'all to? Hmh? HMH?·I was in my head.

I'm at the sink filling up a jumbo sized pot full with hot water! Big 45 pack hot dog pot. I h=got something for these bitches. I got something for their asses!

"We goin fuck her up! She's going to come out. She gotta walk home, she don't live here," their still outside talking shit. They'd talked shit the whole time I was preparing for them.

Now, I was ready. I went back upstairs. "Watch out, watch out," I moved Porsha. She had been arguing back at them the whole time I was getting ready.

She'd moved when she saw that pot of hot water. I had the old school heating system, so my pipe's got real hot too! With Porsha out of my way, I had both Shaleen and Tasha in clear view. Keep in mind this pot is huge. I couldn't just simply throw that joint. I had to heave it!

So, I did. SSSPPLLAASSHH! That shit poured from my 2nd floor. All I'd heard was, "AGGHH! My wig got wet!" That was Tasha.

"Told y'all get the fuck outta here! Bounce! Fuck wrong with y'all!"

IT'S BONE CRUSHER, BITCH!!!

CHAPTER 25

Tiffany

7th St.

Now let me tell y'all about Tiffany.

Her nick name is Muff. So, when you see that name in this book, that's her. It's really Muffin, to be exact.

This chicken head, calls me 10 times a day. Just to see where I'm at and what I am doing.

Now, when I met Tiff she was a bad little young joint on her way to school. I was young, she was young, and she'd had her school girl uniform on. Skirt, white blouse, and stockings. Her stockings had had a hole in the calf part of her right leg.

The first thing I'd noticed was the shape of her calf, because it was fighting its way out of that hole. That's when I saw how thick she was.

"Damn boo, you're shaped for real I see," I couldn't help saying.

"Huh? What you mean?" she blushed clutching her school books to her chest, and acting like she didn't know half of her calf was exposed.

"Them stockings can't even hold them legs in. You shaped for real, huh?" or some cool shit like that Id said to her. After that we'd traded numbers.

The wild thing about it was, I still didn't realize how bad Tiffany was until I ran into her again, and bagged her again. It was then I added her to the family. Made her stop buying them cheap stockings. Upgraded her got her 7th Street ready. I was about to sport her around. And I did too. And it messed her mind up. Check this wild shit she pulled.

One night, I did not answer the phone out of the 10 times a day I told y'all she calls me, because I really just kicking it with my children this day. And since Tiffany can't reach me on the phone, she decides to have her best friend April come with her down 7th Street to look for me.

Now, as I've said I'm in the house with the babies. So when Tiffany doesn't see me on the block she comes to my door. April stays in the car waiting on Tiffany.

Tiffany jumps the neighbor's yard and gets into my yard. She's dressed in all black like she's trying to creep up on me. She thought I was with Porsha, and she'd planned to see for herself.

Mind you, my dog is in my back yard. I had a vicious red nose pit bull! Born and bred killer from an alligator bloodline waiting on her ass. Or anyone who'd came back in his territory. The yard. I mean this dog was only bred to destroy any intruder on our premises (because I'd needed him like that to protect all of the money I was getting. Yall know me.)

Anyway, this woman managed to calm this flesh eater

down somehow. And then she was in the back yard with him! She got him on her side. How? Smh! Now her and the dog were looking through my kitchen window trying to see who was in my house. Scared my daughter Peyton with that craziness!

"DAD! Somebody's in the backyard looking through the window!" she ran into the living room screaming.

I instantly grabbed my gun. I ran into the kitchen and cut the backyard light on so I could see.

I see Tiffany and my ·dog running into the dog house! (The dogs house was spacious enough.) Still I·wasn't·having that.

"Tiffany, get your big ass out of that dog's house!"

Tiffany then crawled out of the dog house on her hands and knees. "Why aren't you answering your phone?"

"Bitch, You did all of this to ask me some dumb shit like that?"

Tiffany was wordless. She just shook her head. I was still heated.

"You got's to be out of your dizzy ass mind to do some creep shit like that. You could've just knocked on the front door. You scared my daughter!·Tiffany, you're sick. You know that? You need some serious help," I told her crazy ass.

Tiffany knew she was out of pocket with that. She burst out crying then.

"Red Bone, I love you. I love you Red Bone."

"I'll bet you do love me if you're willing to hide in the dog's house!"

Smh. I don't know what I'm going to do about their dizzy

asses. I cut them both off after they pulled that bizarre shit.

IT'S BONE CRUSHER, BITCH!!!

CHAPTER 26

Lenny is a Creep!

Back down 7th Street.

Normal shit. Lenny's bugging me again. I can't wait to get away from his ass. "I'm just saying, who do you think that nigga was?" he's still going on about the dude he saw at that shorty's house in Delaware!"

I actually almost forgot about it. I remember now. "Lenny, take me to the park. I got's to talk to somebody about your creep ass," I ignored his miserable ass question.

Lenny knew I was right. He was a creep. He doesn't even try to deny it. Like now. "Whatever. Just don't tell Rafiq and Darryl," he mutters then looked out of the driver's side window. (Rafiq and Darryl probably owe his ass for telling their girlfriends on them about something. Lenny is some shit.)

Bul', as soon as I see Rafiq and Darry they're the first ones I'm telling.

Pulling up to the park, I see a few heads. "Aight young bul'," he stuck his hand out for some dap.

"Aight young bul'," I dapped him and stepped out of the

car. Lenny pulls off. I know he ain't going to do nothing but go back and stalk Lenda some more.

"P.G, what's up young bul'? You seen Rafiq ?" I'd started my search. I was going to tell Rafiq this shit. It was time to let the young bul's get his ass. Grind him up.

"Yea, he's over there stalking Quilla!" P.G pointed his way. Quilla left Rafiq, for Rick 23rd Street.

Quilla is on the benches. And sure enough, Rafiq wasn't far from her. Looking her way, but acting like he wasn't. Everybody knew him.

"Rafiq, get your dirty ass over here before Indris kills you for messing with his sister," I called him.

"Bone, what's up young bul?" he'd spotted me and came right over. "Let me tell you 'bout this bul Lenny's stalking ass!"

"What's up?"

"Your man is out of pocket, stalking Lenda with binocular's! He took me out to her house and..." I briefed him. At the same time, Rafiq was cutting me off, waving his hand like he knew where I was going with it.

"Bone, that clown took me and Darryl out there to that same house one in the morning to see who was inside of her house with her!" Rafiq went into his own story.

"Did he pull out the binocular's?"

"He did something worse! This man snuck into the neighbor's yard and stole their ladder! He gets the latter, sets it up alongside Lenda's house, and climbed that mu'fucka to her window and was peeking in her house!"

"For real?"

"Yea I'm for real! He almost fell off of that mu'fucka!

Had the latter wobbling side to side and shit, scraping all against that woman crib man. Me and Darryl was in the car laughing so hard I almost pissed in my pants! We almost lost that nigga!"

I couldn't believe this nigga Lenny went this far with it!

"You should've seen that nigga, tryna balance the ladder in mid-air! He's scattered Bone, I'm telling you!" Fiq looked at me seriously.

"That's crazy," the vibrating of my phone cut my words. It was a text. From Pooh, asking me was I still coming through.

"Anyway though, fuck him. You going to that fight tonight?" Fiq changed the subject at the same time.

Philadelphia was the place for boxing. Amateur, pro, and everything between. Local fighters, and high level celebrities came out to see the fights a lot. Lenny's uncle is a fighter. Earl The Pearl. He is a pro too. Although he'd got knocked out in his last fight. This man is 51, still fighting. Its over!

"I don't know dawg. Lenny's uncle Earl got knocked out the last time he'd fought. If he gets knocked out again Lenny and G Rap is going to be mad!" (Lenny and G Rap are related to each other through Earl.)

"I already know it! They think he still got it! They won't listen to me. That's why I hope whoever he fight's tonight crushes his old ass!"

"Well, I'll let you know if I'm still going. If I do, I'm riding with you. Riding with Lenny, we might end up at Lenda's house again. Fuck all that! I can't play with him tonight. Anyway, I'm trying to see what's up with Pooh," I let Fiq in on my plans.

"Pooh? Pooh from Twentieth Street?"

"Naa, not that Pooh. "Hood rat Pooh from Fifth Street.

"Yea, shorty nice Bone. I ain't goin front."

"All my chicks is nice nigga," I corrected him.

"Ay Bone, I got a question for you," his face had a depth to it.

He probably had a relationship question for me. Rafiq knows I'm the Don Datta. The man these girls chase relationships with, want to take home to their mother, introduce to their father, tell their brothers about, and beat their girlfriend's up for staring at too hard type of nigga. Yea, Rafiq knows.

"Did Porsha and Muff ever bump heads?"

"Of course. A few times." Now we're just kicking it like real homey's. Heart to heart shit.

"How did that turn out?"

"At first they tried to fight. But you know I wasn't allowing that."

"How did you stop it?"

"What you mean how did I stop it? You know the Bone Crusher, I slapped them. Both! Then told them both to get the fuck outta my face!" I looked at him.

"Bone, you're lying!" Rafiq searched my face.

See, now he's forgetting who Monroe's son is. "Nigga, I'm Bone! If I tell them dizzy bitches to jump off a cliff, they're going to jump!"

"I don't know about Muff. But I know Porsha, and you're right, she's going over that cliff!"

"I'm telling you, Muff is too !"

"So, what's up with Jada?"

"Rafiq now you're asking too many questions."

My phone was ringing now. Its Pooh. Wondering why I haven't hit her back yet. I ignored it still.

"Na nigga, you know Jada my people's. Yo, do you remember when you were teaching her how to ride that motorbike and she'd bussed her ass on Mckean street?"

"Yea, I remember that Fig." My mind drifted back in that moment as soon as Rafiq mentioned it. I remember it as clear as day.

***

I'd came and got Jada this day to take her for a ride on 1 of my new bikes. Jada was in love with bikes, so I knew she would like it.

"This one is nice, when did you get this one?"

"Girl, shut up and get on!" I laughed at her and·reved it up.

"Aight boy, don't be acting all crazy either!" she jumped on the back. I peeled off with her behind me.

"Let me ride Bone. Teach me how to ride it," she'd told me after driving around for a while.

"Aight, I got you." I took her to 2nd and Washington Avenue. A regular city street. It was big enough and not to far from our block.

***

"Aight, keep it straight! You in first gear, take it slow, and…" She was off. Gone. She'd got the hang of it real quick. Not long after that, I was chasing behind her making sure she didn't crash.

"WGGhlmooomm,"·she sped up. She had it. I was proud of her because I knew how much she loved bikes so I knew she was happy. Then she left me! Took off!

"I know this gir1 didn't leave me," I stood in the middle of the street saying to myself as I watched her so. 3rd Street, 4th Street, 5th Street, 6th Street. She was all good. Until she'd got to 7th Street.

Traffic was heavier the further up the street Jada rode the bike. Mind y'all, Jada was still riding the bike at a beginner's speed since it was her first time. Evidently her speed was too slow for some drivers. Suddenly she was in the way of a Nissan Maxima trying to turn off of Mckean Street. And whoever that was didn't take Jada being in his path too kindly and tried to cut her off.

Jada was still on Mckean Street coming up 7th street. I know her ass was trying to get around the hood, so they could see her riding. It is a 1 lane street, but had enough room for another car to either keep going straight, or turn right onto 7th street.

Some people feared stopping on 7th Street because they know it's the gutter. Whoever was in that Maxima, didn't want to stop there at all!

"Get out of the damn way!" "SCCCUURR!" he'd drove around her.

"Fuck you!" Jada screamed back.

That was when it happened. The bike wobbled in her grip.

I couldn't see her by now because her ass done went too far out of my sight. I heard it though!

"Sssccuuurr!" "BOOOOM!" "I know this·bitch didn't just crash my bike!" was all I could think. That was like $10,000 right there! My emotions are mixed now. Fuck did she leave me like that to begin with! Goin ride my shit all the way up there. I ain't tell her ass to go way the hell up there! She paying for that. Fuck that! I'm telling me.

Meanwhile I'm jogging my way to her. I still didn't see her, but like I said I knew it was her dizzy ass.

$....$....$.....$

I saw it as soon as I hit 7th and Mckean. My baby, my precious sweetheart, my boo was all busted and bruised up. I was hurt.

Jada, was on her feet by now. Rubbing her butt real hard. Her wig was crooked, and her face had strawberries on it. (Bike burns.) As I said, I was hurt. She saw it in my face too.

"My baby! Damn my baby! Fuck happened to my baby!" I ran to my boo with open arms.

Jada saw me coming toward her and opened her arms for my embrace. "My baby!" I kept on running right on past her ass and stopped at my bike. Left her arms open and all! Dumb bitch!

"You aight boo? Daddy here, come on, we're going to get you fixed up. Don't worry, I ain't letting her touch you no more!" I stroked my bike. Then stared at Jada, like she hurt my child.

Jada was looking at me like I'd lost it.

“Na Bone, it wasn’t her fault! It wasn’t her fault!” my homey’s came out of nowhere it seemed like. They’d been there. I had just been too zoned out on my bike to notice.

“Na Bone, it was the nigga in the Maxima’s fault! Jada was at the corner, and dude went around her on some fast shit ! He caused that to happen!” Buck Shot defended her. Him and George. Both 7th Street boys.

“Yea?” A Maxima? It was only·1·Maxima in my neighborhood. A black one. The bul Tim who was dealing with a chick named Peaches from around my way had owned.

Now, it wasn’t the fact that the man caused Jada to crash. But that he’d kept driving after the accident happened, that had me heated now. Looking at Jada now, standing there all beat up, wig crooked, patches of skin missing from her face, and arms, and still trying to brush dirt off of her body, I felt sorry for her. Then I ran to her with open arm.

“My baby! You ok? You hurt? Where does it hurt?” I comforted her, rubbing on her body.

Jada was slow to embrace me back. She was still in shock. What the fuck is wrong with her? Shit, she left me! That is what the fuck she get! Trying to show off in front of my homey’s. Dizzy·bitch! It was her fault. I told her to control the bike. The fuck! ran through my mind. Even still, I’ma see Tim about this. He caused the wrong woman to crash.

***

“That was funny,” Rafiq said. Knowing what I knew about that.

"I'll bet it was. Jada was fucked up that night," I admitted.

"Na, it was when the car went around her that was when she got paranoid and fell. Before that, she was riding. I was surprised to see her on that joint. She didn't even bother to get back on the bike after that."

"Na, she didn't."

"She just had the Gucci look on, waiting for you to come get her."

"Yea, she was embarrassed."

"You tell her what happened?"

I looked at Rafiq like he was crazy. Tell her? Tell her what? That that was dude from 23rd Street? And how me and my man Farrej had went through his area, hit him the fuck up, lit his Maxima on fire, and left it in flames as we got away! And now, Tim is wearing a shit bag because of that gangsta shit we did? I should tell her all of that? Is he serious?

"Na, I can't tell her that Rafiq."

"Why Bone?"

"Cause she don't need to know all that nigga!"

"Bone, you're wrong."

"Rafiq, you're high! Fuck I need to tell her that for?"

Rafiq thought about it for a second. "You're right Bone."

"I know I am."

My phone is ringing. "Hello? Who this?"

"It's Pooh."

"Oh, what's up shorty?" I'm smiling at the call. I been waiting to buss Pooh's ass.

"Nothing."

"What'chu mean nothing? Where you at?"

“I'm at home.”

“Oh yea? Can I swing through?”

“Yes Bone, you can come through,” she says. All sweet voiced. The 'tone of her voice had invitation in it. That aroused me.

“Where’s your mom?”

“My mom is at bingo.” She didn’t mention her father and I didn’t ask.

“Aight bet, I'm on my way.” I hung up the phone. “Aight Fiq, I'm out!” I stuck my hand out for some dap.

“Where?”

“Swimming!” I smiled.

“Swimming? It’s too cold to go swimming!” Rafiq responded, with a dizzy look on his face. Rafiq is slow, so I gotta work with him.

“Not swimming at the pool! Swimming in some pussy!”

“With who, Pooh?”

“Yea young bul’.”

“You’d better have on a life jacket cause I heard that pussy deeper than the whole Broad Street!” he snickered at his own joke.

“It’s cool. I’ll drown in that ass! I won’t drown in none of them fiend’s you be fucking!”

Rafiq got quiet. Later for his ass. This little dick is about to go and drown! Because I’m damn sure about to see for myself if Pooh pussy is as deep as Broad Street, or any other road around here! Take me under. Pooh! I might not even wear no life jacket. I’m feeling freaky tonight!

As soon as I was leaving, something caught Rafiq’s attention. “Bone! Bone! stopped me.

"What!" this nigga is cock blocking now.

"Lemme hold five dollars?" he spoke fast. Like the faster he spoke, the faster I was going to peel off the dough.

If I was still a young dummy, he might've got that off. Not now. I'm curious now. "Why?"

Now it was about to get funny. Because I can see it in Rafiq's face he was trying to do something. I know he like's tricking crack head's, but he's always denying it. I got his ass now. If he want this money, he going to submit to my questions and admit it like a real nigga!

"Because I'm hungry. I wanna get something to eat," Rafiq tried me. I knew he was going to. Smh.

"Fiq, why you keep lying to me. You just ate! What you need five dollars for?"

"Aight. You're right. You want me to keep it real?"

"Yea nigga! Keep it real! Why you want it?"

"Aight you see that crack head across the street?" he nodded her way.

"Yea?"

"I want to buy her something to eat."

I know Rafiq ain't just say no dumb shit like that to me? I just stared at him for a second. I should've made him buy me a cheesesteak for that goofy shit he just tried. On a nigga like me. The Bone Crusher? Huh?

"Get the fuck out of here Rafiq, you're going to go and trick that bitch!" I blew his cover.

"Na Bone, it's not like that," he stood on his bullshit.

"You lying! We don't celebrate Christmas nigga, and it ain't her personal holiday! Come on with the dumb shit Rafiq! Fuck you wanna buy her something to eat for? And if you keep lying, I'm not giving you nothing!" I put the squeeze on him. I got his ass now. I, got, his, ass!

"Ok Bone. Aight. You're right. I'm trying to trick the bitch. Damn! Quilla ain't been loving on me, and I'm backed up! Aight? There it is Damn!" Rafiq looked stressed that I'd made him tell me his business. But fuck that. He'll live. You want my money, I want the truth!

I stared at the crack head lady Fiq was geeking for. Trying to see what was so desirable about her. She did have a phat ass. Smh. In the hood, that was enough. "Yo dawg, why do you want to trick her?" I smirked now, reveling in the power I had over him at the moment.

"Yo, for real dawg. I got's to see what it's about. Indris, Lenny, Nate, Toby, G Rap, Geo, Rollin, George, and Puerto Rican Rick said that pussy was good," he confessed now.

"For real Fiq?"

"Yea I'm for real, and I'm trying to hit that."

"Yall some dirty dick niggas bul'!"

"Bone come on, hurry up!" Rafiq rushed me now, looking her way.

"Why are you rushing? That bitch ain't going nowhere?"

"Yes she is look!"

I'd turned my head to see the crack head lady talkin to Jariek and Nate. They were both trying to get her.

"Aww shit! You for real! Them niggas is crazy!" Kelly is going to kill Jariek! "Here," I gave Rafiq the money.

"Good looking out young bul', you just saved my night!" Rafiq hurried over to the fiend chick. Walking like he'd had just what she needed.

"Whatever nigga. Just please, Don't eat her ass!"

"Bone, I don't do that no more, I stopped two months ago!" he kept right on strolling.

#...#...#...#...#

I'm on my way to Pooh's house. I think Ima like this little chick. But I got's to hide my money in this glove compartment when I got inside of her house. These 5th Street girls will rob you. I'm not sweet. Fuck that. If Pooh go in my pocket tonight, all her ass is going to get is $2.00 and some change.

"MUAH!" I kissed my money before placing it in one of the stash spot. This hood rat won't see these dollars. The women from 5th Street, and 20th Street are known for going in a man's pockets.

I remember when Porsha got me!

I had fell asleep at her house, and her dizzy ass got up at about 3a.m in the morning to go in my pockets. The crazy part is, I'd caught her getting up that night too!

"Where you going shorty?"

"To the bathroom," she sweet talked me. My goofy ass fell right for it. I was young and naive.

I was also drunk the night before, so I didn't pay the theft any mind. She'd peeled about $75.00 off of me. But I had about $3,000 on me, and you know when you have a lot you don't worry about a little.

Porsha had got me a few more times too. She was a good thief. She knew just how much to take. That 1st time she had done it. I saw her later on that day on 20th and Tasker Street with her hair and nail done, Stuntin! Looking good too!

I'm saying to myself, where the fuck did she get money from? When I'd left her this morning she was crying broke. But it was all good. I let her thieving ass be. In the coming future I would set her ass up with the dummy pocket. The same way I'm doing Pooh right now.

Muff tried me before too. Though by the time I stayed over her house I was hip to the game. Muff had only got $2.00 off of me. Hah! I know, because I'd played like I was asleep the night she'd did it! I'd kept 1 single eye open, and watched her go in my pocket.

That was funny. It was even funnier, because the next day Muff didn't want to give me no pussy! Hah! She was just mad her ass couldn't get her hair and nails done.

I'm on Pooh's block now. Waiting for her to answer her phone.

"Hello?"

"Two twenty three, right Pooh?"

"Yes. The white door. Come in. No one is here, and I'm upstairs in the room. The door is open," Pooh sounded all sexy.

I listened to her directions, and they'd lead me to her laying naked on her bed with a sheet covering part of her body. Her ass cheeks were out. This bitch looked good. I got's to represent. I got's to put on my best performance and last longer than my normal 6 minutes!

'Fuck that, if this pussy is good, I'll be here all night. This little dick can swim forever,' I'd made up my mind right then.

"What's up Pooh? Damn, you looking right girl," I

palmed her fleshy ass cheek.

I began fore playing with Pooh. I wanted her waters nice and warm by the time I got in. I wasn't messaging her. But I was gripping her bare ass roughly. Manly. (The men reading this, know exactly what I'm talking about.)

Pooh was loving it. Her eyes were closed in enjoyment, and she was biting on her bottom lip. Then the moans came.

"Hmhh," she'd began.

I paused to take my clothes off. She opened her eyes and saw me removing my clothes. "Yea, bring it to me," she smiled. Pooh was nasty, and I was about to find out just how much.

She was mine. She was waiting for me to come and get her. She'd turned to her side now. Her nipples were hard, her lips are full, and she was already breathing heavy. This was going to be a good one.

I wasn't sure about eating the pussy, caught in the moment. My other girls flashed my mind. I don't know who I love more.

All of the other chicks I'm fucking fit between them.

"Ohh. Ohh. Sss," I got Pooh moaning. I decided to eat her box I wanted to turn her ass out! I was a few minutes in, and she's rubbing her hands through my head as I lick the insides of her pussy walls. My tongue is behind her labia majora. I follow it, up to and around her clit. Once, twice, then once more. Then use the tip of the bottom row of my teeth to brush across her clit, then came back down full face into her. She went crazy!

"Oww! MY G! Mmh Hmmm." she's shaking now.

I got her! I'm doing this on purpose because I don't want

her monied out. I don't think I'ma wife her, but I want her thinking about me until I make up my mind.

"Bone. Bone," Pooh is screaming my name. And every time she does, I'm licking it better. I'd ate her box for 20 minutes. Now it was time to put the hammer down.

I slide's in her. Damn this little thing is tight. "Ohh. Sss," she's moaning as I push. I'm stroking now. And before we know it, I'm digging in her ass full-fledged.

"Plop! Plop! Plop! Plop! Plop!" are the sounds as our exercising grew. She's holding me so tight she scratching my back. Her hold feels real. Maybe it is.

"I love you Bone. You in my stomach. You in my stomach!"

And for the moment, I was there with her. "I love you too."

With passion in her eyes, Pooh stops me from stroking her. Pushes me back against her bed, and gets on top and begins to ride me like. I was her bull, and we were in a rodeo!

"Ssss, damn Boo. Damn! I love you!" Now she got me going. I don't even know if I meant it. It just came out. Heat of the moment.

Pooh is going crazy on top of me. She's trying to turn the Bone Crusher out! Shit, go for it. Damn, I'm blessed tonight.

We change positions. Pooh gets in Doggy-style. I got behind her. She pokes her ass out, and arches her back for me. "Beat this ass up daddy. You hear me? I want you to beat this ass up!" she forced out between deep breaths.

Yall know ya boy did that! "PLOP! PLOP! PLOP! PLOP! PLOP! PLOP!" I went on that ass. I tried to wake the neighbor's up! I'm pounding her now. She's running. Her pussy is so good, I'm staying the night over here. Fuck that. Then when I wake up tomorrow. I'ma hit this again before I leave!

I fucked Pooh for 11 minutes, and 10 second's! 11 minutes is long for the Bone Crusher. Next time, it might be an hour! But right now, that pussy was so good I had to buss that nut.

Pooh is staring at me. "I love you," she whispered. Then put her head between my legs, and started kissing the veins on my dick. Then she took me into her mouth. All mouth, no hands. She's going like a pro now.

This little soldier got back to attention real fast. That's what I'm talking about. Go for yours boo. This woman is making me feel like I can go all night!

I'm back! Round 2, here we go! I'm back swimming in her ocean once again. Yall know the 2nd climax takes longer, so I'm working extra hard. Sweating and all that. I'm 47 minutes in, and I ain't tired. I might go all night with this pussy.

"I'm cumming ! I'm cumming!" Pooh keeps screaming. Every time she does, I go harder.

"PLOP! PLOP! PLOP! PLOP! PLOP! PLOP!" Now I'm cumming. "I love you."

"I love you. I love you," Pooh breathed out.

***

I'm tired. Time to get a quick few minutes of sleep. I hope Pooh doesn't try to go in my pockets, because I'm trying to fuck in the morning.

If she goes in my pockets tonight, she's going to be mad tomorrow, and might not be in the mood to hump. You know how chicks are. Smh.

***

It's morning. I woke up and rolled right over into Pooh's pussy.

"Uhhh," she moans. "Yea, it was waiting for you." she tells me as I go in her.

That's what I'm talking about. This pussy is so good. I got's to make sure Pooh have money whenever she need it. No lie. I'll fuck around and take this bitch out of the projects. I know she'll like that. But first I might just get the bitch's hair done or something. I think I like her ass.

ITS BONE CRUSHER, BITCH!!!

CHAPTER 27

Tobi and Ali shot it out.

7th St.

Today is going to be a good day. Its sunny, I got that shit on, and I'm walking through 7th Street feeling good.

I see Ali and Toby arguing with each other. I know they're arguing about some dumb shit.

Old head's BrandyWine and Uki are on the other side of the street shooting dice with Lil Zeke.

Lil Zeke is busting his head losing his pack money. Them old heads there don't give a fuck about Nobody! If you put those dice in your hands they're coming for you. So you better have a shot.

Lenny is over there. I know he's not going to shoot them dice. He doesn't gamble. Fuck is he over there for? And then the next thing I know, Lenny had jumped on the dice!

"Bet a thousand!" I hear him talking shit.

"Bet it young bul'!"

"Bet my thousand too!" Uki jumped in on the money.

"Bet it nigga! Fuck y'all talking bout! I'm Lenny nigga! I'll bet this whole block!" He looked at Lil Zeke, "You wanna bet too lil nigga?"

"Yea, fuck it! Bet it!" they're all hyped up now.

Lenny rolled the dice. "OHHHHH!!!" was all I'd heard. Lenny stood there with the Gucci look. Not believing what just happened.

"That's Seven nigga!

You lose! Let me get All of this," Uki was the first one picking up his money. Then BrandyWine, then Lil Zeke.

"Thank you young man. You have a nice day," Brandywine smiled at Lenny. He knew Lenny was going to crap out. That was why he'd baited him in.

"Oh I'm back now! I'm done for the day, fuck that," Lil Zeke was stuffing his pockets with Lenny's bread. Lenny had bought Lil Zeke out of the loss.

After watching all of them stuff his money in their pockets, Lenny walked off. Before he walked off he pulled out his famous chapstick and rubbed it around his lips real fast like he normally did. Lenny's lip's get dry. And not the normal dry either! So he'd stood there for every bit of 2 minutes just moisturizing his lips. Then he'd walked off like he was going to get more money. He never made it.

"Nigga, I'm telling you! Try that shit again!" Ali and Toby began arguing again.

"I will! Fuck is you talking bout!" This is the typical day on my block.

I'm standing next to Doc and his man Omar. "What they arguing for?"

"Toby took Ali's sale," Doc tells me.

"For real?" I asked, but I didn't expect a reply. That was wrong. If Toby did that he's out of pocket.

Toby has like 10 kids between 3 women. He is still with Tanya. That's the girl that was with him when he'd shitted in the pool. And if he doesn't come home with no money, Tanya is going to kick his ass. So, Toby was thirsty. And he wasn't giving a fuck about nobody right then. Still, it didn't make his action right. People get shot for shit like that.

"So, you goin make that right, right?" Ali was giving Toby the opportunity to straighten his wrong. It was a warning.

"Toby, come here." Lenny pulled Toby away. He was trying to diffuse the situation before it escaladed.

Toby walked off with Lenny, and a few homey's pulled Ali toward a separate direction. Neither Ali nor Toby were soft. But, you may have thought we could've calmed them down. Problem was, we were all young, and we went hard! And sometimes at each other.

"Fuck you looking at?" Ali eyed Toby.

"Fuck you looking at?" Toby shot back from across the street.

I'm still standing across the street chillin. I could've tried to intervene. Though honestly I can see where this encounter was headed from the chemistry of in. I was right. Before we knew it they'd took it there. All the way there.

"Watch out! Move!" was all Ali said as he raised his P 90 in Toby's direction.

"POP! POP! POP! POP! POP! POP!" shots rang off.

"BOOM! BOOM! BOOM! BOOM! BOOM! BOOM!" Toby immediately opened fire back at Ali. This is in broad daylight! Kids riding bikes, old ladies pushing food carts and all!

While those 2 are going at each other, trying to take 1 another out. People are screaming, ducking behind cars, diving on the ground, you name it!

“Get the dice! Get the dice!” BrandyWine yelled to Uki.

“You get them!” Uki turned to run. Hah! Uki said fuck them dice. BrandyWine hurried to get the dice. Got them, and ran off to catch Uki. Who half waited for him. It’s like a movie to me out here.

“Sai, get on the ground!” Lil Zeke pulled her down. Sai was his girlfriend. So it was like he was jumping in front of bullets for her. That was a good look for him. He'll get that hero love from her later on.

In the middle of all of the commotion, I see the smoker bul’ Burn Nate and his girlfriend Honey arguing!

“Come on, we got the work!” Bum Nate was telling her.

“But he got my change!” she pointed at Doc. Honey just spend $10.00 with Doc, and had gave him a $20.00 bill. That was a big deal for her and she wanted her change.

“Girl damn that change! We got the fucking coke!” Burn Nate was pulling at her hand to leave. Evidently he’d pulled some fast shit. “You tripping! Bout to get us killed over some damn twenty dollars! You'd better come the hell on!” Burn Nate screamed on her.

“But, I gave him twenty,” Honey shut down, and reluctantly obeyed her man.

This is too funny. I took another sip of my Pepsi.

My son Pizza Pretzel, (he earned that name because that was all he ate) kept right on riding his bike through. His scary ass ain’t stopping. Him, or his man Heem.

Lil Wyan, my nephew, is under a car shaking like a leaf.

Ha! He just came off of the steps. He's never been around 7th Street before, so any loud noise his soft ass is going to drop and roll.

I'm across the street laughing. A day on 7th Street is like no other.

I see my daughter Monae and her scary ass boyfriend Boo Boo running up the block all fast and looking all scared.

Markeem (Mark madness), and Ms. Brenda are on 7th and Mckean St. I can hear them saying shit.

"That shit ain't right. It ain't right. Somebody going to jail tonight!" he's bitching. He's the worst.

"That's right. That's right," Ms. Brenda's agreeing with him.

"Toby! Toby! Toby!" Tanya came out ·of the house screaming for her man.

"Tanya get your ass back into the house and watch them kids! I got this!" Toby snapped at her. Tanya ran back in the house crying. She didn't want nothing to happen to her man.

Ali walked off after he seen Tanya.

"What happened, y'all? What happened?" Pugie's asking everybody. No one is answering him. We know he's trying to get information to tell the police.

"Somebody is going to kill Pugie one day for that shit!" Cheese muttered to Khalifa.

"Hell yea. Somebody, goin drop his ass one day," Khalifa agreed.

A day in the life of 7th Street. Smh.

ITS BONE CRUSHER, BITCH!!!!

CHAPTER 28

Bus Almost Hit Cherika

7th St.

Let me tell y'all about Markeem and Ms. Brenda. Now in the summer the government funds the city of Philly free lunches for the neighborhood. Its good stuff too. Chocolate milk, sandwiches, cookies, and juices. Snacks really, but it's appreciated.

Now, they give it to the town watch, who is Ms. Brenda, and the person who helps her. The block captain, Markeem.

People hate it when Markeem give out the free lunches. See, this is how it works.

The government delivers the lunches right to Ms. Brenda and Markeem's doorstep. From there, they each pass out the lunches to the people. Their supposed to pass it out anyway. But Ms. Brenda, and Markeem, both always keep a few lunches for their family and themselves.

Markeem is the worst! This ·boy keeps all of·the·fruit·juices! "They didn't give them to me!" he would lie, after we'd see him take the juices into his house. Boxes of them! And he might be sipping on 1 of them!

"BGHURRP!" he would burp, and keep right on sipping. "Well, where did you get your juice?" 1 of the kids would ask him.

"I saved mine from yesterday," he'll lie. He had all his lies already ready.

"Well, can I have some cookies?"

"Ain't no more cookies either! Listen, y'all lil kids better get the fuck outta here!" Markeem would get frustrated and threaten them. Acting like he'd paid his own money for that shit. He's something else.

One time, Hoarse and Shock went in Markeem's apartment to chill and Hoarse wanted something to drink.

"It's something in the freezer," Markeem bragged.

"Bet!" Hoarse went into the kitchen. "Yo nigga!" Hoarse yelled. "This where you got all the juices at?" He'd found his stash.

"Get out my freezer man! Get out!" Markeem rushed into the kitchen.

"I saw all lunches in the top, in the refrigerator half and all juices in the bottom, in the freezer half!" Hoarse explained to us later that day. Markeem is foul stealing from the hood like that.

That was why Markeem took the block captain job anyway. Trying to feed his family. That's why his sister is getting fat now too.

I see Cherieka coming up the block. O shit, I forgot I'd hooked her up with Markeem after I'd met Porsha.

"I'm treating her to lunch today," Markeem smiled at me earlier today, after the shootout happened with Toby and Ali. (Oh yea, nothing happened with that. I told y'all, that's a regular day on 7th Street.)

"Oh yea?"

"Yea man, you know. Tryna show her a good time."

***

"Hey boo," Cherieka was dressed all nice. She was ready to go wherever Markeem was willing to take her.

"Heyy shorty. I see you all dressed up," Markeem hugged her. Then eyed Cherieka again. "Damn you look good girl. You came to see me all dressed like this?"

"Yea. You said we was going to Warm Daddy's, right?"

Markeem's face froze. Warm Daddy's? I didn't say I was taking you to Warm Daddy's. I said I was treating you to lunch," Markeem popped her fantasy bubble.

Cherieka had the Gucci look.

"Come here, don't look like that," Markeem grabbed her by the hand and lead her away with him.

Twenty minutes later Markeem and Cherieka sat on Markeem's step eating free lunches. I'll tell you what though, Cherieka was fucking them cookies up! And Markeem is just having a good time because he was feeding his girlfriend. And Cherieka and Porsha are cousin's .So if Cherieka eats that shit, I know Porsha eat that nut ass shit!

Anyway, I'd seen Cherieka go in the house with Markeem a short while ago. Now, I could hear Markeem through his open window.

"Get out! Get the fuck out! In here eating up my shit, and drinking up all of my juices like that! Then wan' act all stuck up! Get the fuck out?" And hurry up too!"

"Whatever Markeem, fuck you! You cheap ass nigga!" Cherieka opened his front door screaming.

As soon as she came outside, I was standing across the street. Me and the smoker bul' Burn Nate. I guess he'd smoked all of that coke he'd came up on earlier. He was damn sure adamant about getting off of the block with it.

Cherieka saw me as soon as she came out of Markeem's house. "Bone. Bone, can you take me home?" she has the nerve to ask me!

I looked at her like she'd lost her marbles! Then I gave her my crazy look! I was about to front hand her, then back hand her, then front hand her again! Fuck is wrong with her! But, I didn't. She's Porsha's cousin, so I couldn't. Or wouldn't rather.

But, the reason I'd thought about it was because this chick had the nerve to ask me for a favor, after she puts all of her 2 cents in me and Porsha's business every time me and Porsha disagrees!

"Aww nah Porsha, you need to leave his ass! He ain't nothing but a dog! Just like everybody else! He ain't no different! And don't think he is just because he's getting all of that money! Them diamonds don't mean nothing!" Yall should hear her hating ass. With her whiney voice. So I know she didn't just ask me for a favor?

"Ohh, you need me now? Now you need me?" I stared at her. I was being sarcastic too. "You know I don't fuck with you like that! I ain't driving you nowhere!"

"Bone, are you f or real?"

"Yea I'm for real!"

I did f eel Cherieka. It was a far walk to her house. But, I was not giving her an easy ride. I looked at the 10 speed pedal bike in front of me leaning against the light pole. “You see that bike right there?” I told her.

“Bone I ain’t riding no damn bike home!”

“Well, you won’t get home then!” I shrugged my shoulder’s. It was as simple as that.

“Mch!” Cherieka sucked her teeth and walked over to the bike.

“Whoa, Whoa, that's my bike!” the smoker bul’ Burn Nate spoke up.

Cherieka looked at him. Her shoulders sank. “I’m tryna get home,” Cherieka whined.

“I know you are, I am too. And that’s my ride. I need my bike. If you take my bike, I need something for it. And I don’t need your money,” Burn Nate stared at Cherika his eye’s wide open, hoping she would bite his bait.

This bul’ is funny as hell. The bike is about to fall apart as it is. It has 1 pedal, no reflector's, no back break, and a banana seat! And he’s talking about he want's something. Ha. What the fuck does he want? Shit, I can’t hate. It's his bike. I had to let him shoot his shot.

“What'chu mean?” Cherieka’s eye's sharpened at him.

Burn Nate stared at her.

“Mch! Boy please!” she waved him off. “Bone, you goin let him act like this about a bike?”

“It's his bike! Fuck you want me to do?” I enlightened her. “That's that man’s property, you gotta talk to him.” When I defended the crack head, he really took it to the head then!

“Yaa, Yaa. Shit, that's my property!” he got all goofy.

Nodding his head up and down with what he'd said. "I need something for mines!" he looked back at Cherieka.

This shit is so funny. This crack head is a prime example, you give a person just a little bit of power and watch how they'll act!

"I don't got nothing to give you!" Cherieka whined now.

That was it, that's was all I'd wanted to see. I needed Cherieka to understand it was not about burning bridges; it is about building them.

"Go head Nate, give her the bike. I got you," I promised him something. And my promise was like a credit card; you didn't know how much it would come with! "You better thank your aunt Tracey!" I told Cherieka.

Of course Burn Nate gave her the bike. I gave him a dime of crack.

"Bone, I don't know about this Bone," he starts pressing the rock all hard in the bag. Trying to see if the rock would turn into shake or mush. "You gave me this little small ass Pebble," he looked at me.

I looked at Burn Nate with my crazy look.

"Na this is cool Red Bone! This is nice," he changed his words real quick. Yea, he know.

Cherieka got on the bike. She wiggled a little, then she was off. I don't know how her petite self even managed to get on top of the bike. But she knew she had to make it work, or her ass wasn't going home.

Me and Burn Nate were in the middle of the street, watching Cherieka. She was cool after her wiggling phase. She was pushing that 10 speed.

"Go Cherieka Go!" I yelled being funny.

"Fuck you Red Bone!"

"BBEEEEEPPP!" the bus just missed her! It came out of nowhere as soon as she got to 8th Street.

"Ooohh Shit! You see that? That bitch almost got hit by a bus!" Burn Nate laughed.

Cherieka, swerved right around the bus like a professional.

"Yea, dumb bitch! That's what she get!" Markeem was in the window now. I guess he must've heard the bus blowing its horn.

"Ay Markeem, why you put that girl out the house like that?"

"Red Bone, I told the bitch, DON'T DRINK THE RED JUICE'S! Those are for me! She didn't listen!" Markeem slammed the window shut.

"Ay!" Burn Nate hit my arm, "we gotta have a community meeting about that nigga! Check this shit he did I came to his house. Me, my girlfriend Honey, our daughter Michelle, and our baby son. I'm trying to eat lunch with my family. I knock's on Markeem's door. First of all, he answer's the door eating one of the lunches. Cool. "Hey Markeem, what's up man me and my family are trying to get a few lunches," I asked him. Politely, Bone.

"Hold on!" Markeem slammed the door in our faces, and left us on the steps! Then when he came back, he acted like he was aggravated about it. "Here!" he gave us a sandwich a piece! No juice, No cookies, No napkin, No bag, Nothing! Just 2 pieces of bread, and 1 slice of meat! "Where the cookies and juice at?" I asked him. "Man, this ain't no fucking restaurant!" he had the nerve to tell me!

Now I'm heated. He done embarrassed me in front of my family! "Nigga, what the fuck did you do? EAT it all? What the fuck! Why you eating all of the free lunches anyway? Ain't you getting money? Out here rolling around in this red Acura, fronting like you getting money, but you in the house eating up all of the neighborhood free lunches!" I went in on him. "Then I took my family and left before we got into something. But, I'm telling you Bone, we need to have a community meeting on that nigga!"

"I feel you," was all I could say.

ITS BONE CRUSHER, BITCH!!!!

CHAPTER 29

Virginia Beach

That swindle Craig Mack pulled wasn't nothing to us. Partying was our thing for real.

I remember we all drove to Virginia Beach for the Labor Day weekend. It was about 40 of us!

"Yo whas'sup? Yall wanna go out Virginia Beach for the Labor Day?" our old head J.C came through.

"Hell yea, why not?" I jumped up. I'd heard it was popping. We're young bul's running around with untold thousands of dollars, and all of the energy in the world. Hell yea!

"Aight look, we're going on a Friday. And we're coming back on a Monday," he'd laid the blue print for us right then and there.

A week later, 7th Street is on the highway 15 vehicles deep, maybe more, back to back on the way to Virginia Beach. You know the Bone Crusher, I'm driving my own shit. I'd had a Lexus at the time.

The highway was dead for a good minute. Shit, it was a long drive. Then after about 4, maybe 4 hours we began seeing signs for visitors of the Labor Day holiday come into view. And that's when we all of the traveler's filled the lanes. Suddenly the highway was packed! Earthquake loud systems blared from big boy trucks. It was Benzes, Escalade's, Lexus's, Jaguar's, and all kind of crazy vehicles riding in traffic with us. Super bad bitches y'all! And we're in traffic, with cars that have rims on them as tall as the car its self damn near! These boys had coupes looking like trucks! Old school Dunk's and all that. Yea. This was exactly where we wanted to be.

"Wwoooooommm! Wwoooooommm!"

"Wwoooooommm! Wwoooooommm!" bikes challenged one another, bitches with thongs on the backs of them. Asses hanging off of seats.

"BEEEP! BEEEP!" Horns went off at women flashing their titties. Virginia plates, New York, Jersey, Washington, Detroit, Miami, Atlanta. EVERYWHERE! Cats were coming from EVERYWHERE! Women dancing to the loud systems, popping their asses out of windows, off of the flat bed of trucks with thongs on. It was crazy, Already! And all of this, was before we'd even got into the city its self, where the actual event was taking place!

I'm going with the flow of traffic, trying not to crash while all of this action is going on. My boys driving in front of me and their blinkers are flashing left. I throw mines on. We exit the highway.

The plan was, the Holiday Inn has our hotel rooms. "Yo dawg, peep that shit!" my young bul' pointed out.

As we're pulling in the parking lot, we see bitches fucking on the side of the hotel. Fellas are getting blow jobs, people screwing on the balcony's and shit. Aw, man. It's on!

Listen y'all, that tricking shit? We does it! Period. Them girls like money, we had some, and we liked fun. It works. So we know we're about to have a ball out here if they're going like this.

We pull into the parking lot in all kinds of wheels. Rental Vans, Benzes, Acura's, man we showed up. Deep! 7th Street was in that joint! They knew. I'm telling y'all, we got to the front of the hotel, and we had to look like a rap entourage!

"We need seven rooms," Mike headed the pack. Plus he had good credit.

In the end, 3 of the rooms were declined on his card, so a good amount of the young fellas ended up in 1 room together. That, was the party room. I had my own room. But, y'all knew that already, didn't y'all? Another homey had his own room too. And maybe someone else. Shit who knows. We was deep over there. It was so many of us. We didn't know who all came. Even dudes who were beefing with 1 another came. Some beef's where deaded·there. Some well you know.

We looked like stars standing in that lobby waiting for our keys to the rooms. It was at least $200,000 to $300,000 worth of watches, chains, pinky rings, bracelets, and earrings dangling from our limbs. I told y'all it was about 40 of us. So whoever didn't have diamonds on, didn't matter. People from all over stared at us, and I knew why. But 1 person in particular stared at us a little too hard. That had me staring back at him.

"Oh, that's Boo right there," It hit me. On our last run in with Boo, we we're chasing him through his projects trying to take his head off!

See, we're at war with Boo about some shit that had happened between his folks and my folks. But, most of my boy's had never seen Boo's face. And Boo, had never seen any of their faces. Only a few of us knew Boo. Like I just said; Boo had never seen us. Although he knew we're from 7th Street because of Craig Mack's loud ass.

"SEVENTH STREET in this mu'fucka! SEVENTH Street, South Philly in this mu'fucka!" he'd kept yelling, and strolling around the lobby like every step he'd took, had about $10,000 in it. Like his foot print alone was money.

"Oh word?" my young bul's piped up. Their hands automatically touching their waistline's. They were trained to go!

We'd spent the rest of that afternoon on Boo. Shit, him and his company. Lil was from 13th Street, and Mus was from 31st·Street, but had happened to be with him. Along with a female. Yall know how this goes if we get 1, we got's to get them all.

"Yo, we're going to follow them to their rooms," I'd ordered my young bul's.

"Aight Bone," they'd nodded. No words no questions. That was how we'd all moved.

We waited by the lobby until they had got their keys to the rooms they'd paid for and followed them.

***

So we're at the door to the room we'd watched them go in.

"Knock, Knock, Knock!" "Room service!" my young bul' was at the door masked up. Once they'd went into the room, we had them backed in.

I'm standing off to the side watching.

"Naa yo, that's them Seventh Street niggas yo. Do not open that door yo!" I'd heard Boo yelling from the inside.

"Call security! Them nigga's trying to kill us!" I heard. I knew that was Lil's voice right there. These boys are scared to death!

"Can you see anything in the peep whole?" I asked my young bul'.

"Na yo. They've got a finger over the hole or something," he says after checking his voice muffled through the ski mask.

"Push it open, try to go in there."

Instead of trying to push the door like I'd advised, my young bul' tried to kick it open.

"DOOM! DOOM! DOOM! It sounded.

"Yo this nigga got something against this door. A fucking… couch or something… I, I can't get it open," he says still fighting with the handle.

Boo and them were inside of the room still panicking. "I'm calling the cops yo, fuck this," I'd heard Boo's voice. He knew once 7th Street was on that ass, there was only a few ways to get them off. Calling the police was one of them. Though they weren't getting away that easily.

"Don't worry about it. Look, one of y'all stay here and wait for them to come out. If and when they do? Dump on them!" I'd left them with.

Boo, Mus, Lil, or the girl that was with them didn't come

out that room for the rest of the night!

"YOO, Boo and them just left here with the police!" One of my young bul's came to me two days later.

"What you mean?" I was lost.

"Nigga Boo and them called the police and had them escort them safely off of the property!" he said with a laugh.

"How you know that?"

"The bitch I bagged at the front desk told me! Fuck you mean!" he'd said through thick clouds of smoke. His demeanor was like I'd insulted him by asking.

"Yea. That's right. Get em the fuck up out of here! Seventh Street is down here right now. They can party some other time! Word," I smiled.

Besides that run in, we had fun! The event was good. In fact the parking lot (where we'd seen all of the action at first, the fucking, the sucking, tricking,) was so popping, we'd just started cooling out there, where all of the fun was!

"Oh shit, I ain't know Bugo was here! You see this nigga Red Bone?" somebody tapped my arm.

I'd turned to see Bugo pulling into the parking lot.

"Yea, I see him," I acknowledged. Bugo was from 7th Street too.

Bugo hopped his fat ass out of his wheels, and started talking to Puerto Rican Rick and Garsh. Bugo came in with us, but he didn't have a room. That's what I'd over heard him telling them anyway. Shit, everybody had been partying in the young bul's room. I myself even went over there a few times. It was open almost all night They had it popping!

"Look at these niggas. Uh huh. Damn she got a phat ass too," I mumbled to Craig Mack.

We can both see Jariek and Rafiq creeping into the back of a building to trick them Virginia bitches. They were pretty too.

“Yo, Bone this nigga Bugo need a room yo, look out for him,” Garsh came to me.

“Shit he can stay in the young bul’s room.” The thing about that, is Bugo better know how to joke. If not, them 7th Street young bul's are going to chew him a new ass.

Meech couldn’t take it, and he's from 7th street! Meech’s ass got the fuck up out of there quick. I'd heard he was out stealing cars now with Walt and Musty.

J Bird said he’d seen Meech driving a Honda with no keys in it. That’s how we knew he was stealing. Meech is trying to be like North Philly’s own, Maybach-O.

“Meech, if you wanna be like Maybach-O you’re going to have to do better than a Honda!”

I see J.C. pulling into the parking lot now. Lenny peeped him. Aww shit. Something might be about to happen. They haven’t seen each other yet. Lenny is mad at J.C.

Supposedly, the story is J.C. had sex with Lenny’s childhood girlfriend. I know what you’re thinking. HUH? Yea, me too. Brothers get stupid over some pussy.

At the same time Jariek is feeling some kind of way toward J.C. as well, because he doesn’t know what J.C. is going to say about him dealing with J.C.’s ex-girlfriend, Kelly. Smh!

“What’s good? How y’all?” J.C. spoke to everybody.

“What up young bul’?”

“What up?”

“What up?” Everyone spoke to J.C. except Lenny. J.C.

felt the vibe.

"Yo, Lenny, let me holla at you right quick," J.C. pulled Lenny to the side.

"Listen dawg, don't believe nothing the street's is saying. I wouldn't dare fuck ya girl."

Lenny looked at J.C., and nodded his head. "It's cool fam," they shook hands. The beef died.

Meanwhile, I'm seeing other things go on. Craig Mack was right with me.

"Bone, do you see what I see?" Mack whispered in my ear. I don't know where he'd came from, or what he'd done with his girl to get here because she was on him like white on rice. But he was here with me.

"Yea, I see them young bul."

The same females that had left with Jariek and Rafiq were now back for more. Rafiq and Jariek must've, did a good job eating their asses. That's what they do, eat ass! But, they're walking toward me, instead of them.

"Hey, Red Bone, can I speak with you?"

Now, I don't even know who this woman is. I don't even know who told her my name. She must've heard my boys call me.

"Yes sweetheart?"

"Your boy Rafiq didn't give me all of my money," she looked at me.

I'm looking at Rafiq out of the corner of my eye, and I can see him looking dead at her while she's talking to me, about him.

"Rafiq with the red belt on?"

"Yea, that's him right there," she'd pointed at him.

"How much was he supposed to give you?" I asked her, completely unsurprised.

"Two hundred and fifty dollars."

"What did he give you?"

"Sixty-five dollars, all in ones."

"Sweetheart why didn't you count the money when he'd gave it to you?"

"Cause he'd told me he was going to eat my ass and I forgot about the money," she whined.

Dumb bitch.

I looked at Rafiq. "Yo Rafiq, come here lil homey." Rafiq grinning all goofy walks over to me.

"Come on man. I know you didn't do that, did you?"

I ain't even have to ask the deed. His grin said he knew exactly what it was about.

"Bone Crusher, I ate her ass so good that bitch should be paying me!"

"Rafiq, I feel you. But it don't work like that. You can't do shit like that to these out of town bitches dawg."

"You're right Bone, I'll take care of it right now," he agreed, reaching into his pocket right then and there.

"Here you go sweetie, he got you right now," I said to her.

Rafiq then handed her the money.

Here comes Lenny trying to be nosey.

"What's your name Boo?"

"Carla," she looked at him.

"What we talking?"

"Two-fifty."

"Let's take a walk," Lenny put his arm around her shoulder as they walked off.

Lenny is a funny bul'. As soon as that girl suck his dick he's going to start flying her out to Philly and all of that. It was obvious. Hope Lenny don't marry her like he did them other girls. He gets turned out quick when it comes to them bitches.

CHAPTER 30

Lenny is a stalker!

7th St.

Speaking of Lenny's miserable ass, it's about time I shared the details of this wild ·shit Lenny pulled one day in Philly. I'll be quick.

"Yo, take this ride with me," Lenny pulled up on me. I was on the block at the time.

"Where to?"

"To one of my girl's house."

What Lenny wasn't telling me was he didn't know exactly where the girl's house was. He just knew what road her house was on. So, 25 minutes into the drive, I'm helping him look for the house!

"There it is right there!" Lenny pointed, then parked across the street in the dark! I felt like a creep!

We'd sat there for about 20 minutes, not doing anything. After a while, a car pulls up to her house. Me and Lenny are still sitting in his car, and I'm waiting for him to get out and walk over to her house. Little do I know, this bul' ain't going in her house. This creep pulled out some big ass binocular's!

Binocular's. What?

"Yo dawg, what the fuck is you doing? Fuck you get these shits from? Matter of fact, why do you even have them?"

I went in on him. Our niggas don't act like this. Not the Bone Crusher anyway. Bitch won't have me like that.

"I knew this bitch was fucking! I need to see this nigga up close," he mumbled focusing more on his target, and working the binocular's like a real pervert now.

"Then get out of the car and go up to the front door! Lenny, come on man, we don't get down like this. Let her do her! Ain't you doing you?" I tried to reason with him.

I had to hurry up. The more we sat there, the more I felt like we would get caught. And the Bone Crusher couldn't have no creep charge on his record.

Lenny is ignoring me, because he knows I'm right. I know I'm right. I know he didn't bring me all the way up here to play detective with this bitch. I know her, she's cool and all but she's not worth all of this. She must've did his ass good though. I won't ever have a bitch make me do that. I don't give a fuck how good they suck this little dick!

I had to try another approach.

"That bul' don't look like the bul' you described Lenny. That bul' is short. You said that other bul' was about six foot tall, and he walked funny!" I'm trying to get him off of this mission.

Lenny is staring hard through them binoculars. I can't believe this shit! A certified 7th Street nigga doing this shit! Smh! I guess we breed them all. It is what it is. This creep is still focused. He knows who he's looking for too. He knows this bul' from head to toe!

In my mind Lenny has been stalking both of them. He needs to stop that shit. And I can't wait until I get back down to 7th Street so I can tell the 'hood about this psycho.

"Yo, Lenny, you need some serious help."

Lenny looked at me. Pulled out his Chapstick and rubbed it on his lips real-real fast. "Bone, you're right, fuck that bitch."

I'm saying to myself, "yea aiight! Fuck outta here nigga! Tomorrow you're going to do the same shit to that bitch Linda from Delaware. Don't forget, I know you"'

Anyway, back to Virginia. Long story short we all had a real good time, and had made it back home to Philadelphia from Virginia. Safe and with good memories.

***

I have a wilder story then that about Lenny and them hoes! Peep this craziness.

One day Lenny calls me from jail. He's my nigga, I accept.

"Yo, Bone, do me a favor. Go to Linda's house for me, and check all of the cars on her block. See if any of them has a hot hood," he came over the line. No "what's up", "I need some bread", "How are you doing?" ... Nothing... Ok, cool.

"What?" This nigga wanted me to shoot to Delaware? He knew he was tripping. My expression said that to him.

"Na, because I was just on the phone with the bitch, and I heard a knock on the door. Then all of a sudden she had to hang up! I'm trying to figure out who her company is."

"Damn Lenny. Aight man, call me back in a second. I'll

get dressed."

I know. I was bugging. But, I go hard for my peoples.

So, Lenny calls me back, and my dumb ass drives to Delaware to check the hood of all of the cars on her block for him!

Awhile later.

"Hello," I answered my phone. Its Lenny.

"What happened?"

"All of the cars were cold. I don't think she had company."

"Aight, go through the back of her house and check."

"Aight." I'm here no Fuck it. My dumb ass does this too. I checked Linda's car, her neighbor's cars. I'd did the do for my man.

"Lenny, these cars are cold fam!"

"Is her lights on or off?"

"On."

"Aight, break into her house from the back and see who's in there for me?"

That was when he went overboard!

"Lenny, that's a case! I can't do that!" is this boy serious? I already went too far!

"Hello? Hello?" Lenny had hung up on me. And I'd got the fuck up out of there before someone thought I was some kind of Cat Burglar.

Anyway, back down 7th street. I couldn't break in that woman's house. That was too much. If Lenny were to ask me to pop someone, I would've done that yea. But, not break into no woman's house. Naa. You must be high nigga! I don't stalk females. Shit, females keep stalking ME! And

Porsha and Tiffany are the worst!

IT'S BONE CRUSHER, BITCH!!!

CHAPTER 31

I Boo'yowed the Love-Bug

Philadelphia 7th St.

Back on the block. 7th Street is always jumping. It's almost always something going on.

I remember one day, Herbie Luv Bug and Toby was racing to a drug sale.

Picture this:

"STOP PLAYING Toby! I seen him first! I seen him first!" Herbie's running after Toby. He has his work in his hand, and is trying to dump some of his product into his hand, so it can be ready for sale by the time he reaches the sale. Problem was, all of that was slowing Herbie down.

Toby on the other hand was faster, and he also wasn't fumbling with his pack. Herbie, see's Toby might reach the sale before he does. So do I. Right then and there I had made up mind. "If Herbie loses this sale I'ma Boo'yow that nigga!" I smirked. Mind y'all neither of them is paying any attention to me, walking up the other side of the street.

"TOBY! TOBY stop PLAYING man! I seen him first! I seen him FIRST!"

Toby wasn't hearing him. Then Herbie tried the fiend. "Ay! Come here Unc! Yo right here! I got bigger Pieces!" The fiend wasn't hearing Herbie either. "TOBY! Toby stop playing! I seen him first! Toby, you's a fucking. Aight. Aight bet! It's the fuck on! Watch!" was all Herbie could say once Toby caught the sale.

Herbie was heated. That's where I came in. I'm creeping up on Herbie. He's still arguing with Toby. Toby wasn't hearing him. He was counting the fresh money he'd just made.

Herbie's standing right next to Toby, helplessly watching him count the money. "Toby, you're really going to do me like that?"

I 1 made it up to Herbie just as he was putting his pack back in to his pocket.

"BOO'YOW BITCH! For missing that money!" I kicked Herbie right in his ass. Hard too! Good thing for him it was barely anyone around to witness it.

"Yo what the fuck!" Herbie snapped. Then turned around. "Oh naa, naa, I want a fair one Bone! Fuck that, you gotta rumble me for that Bone!" Herbie took off his jacket.

I knew he was heated, but I couldn't fight the Luv Bug. Naa. I just walked off on him. But I still had to turn around and get a look at his face. And when I did, Herbie was looking dead at me. "Bone, you best believe Ima get you back!" he promised.

"It's cool, but right now suck it up!" Herbie the Luv Bug had the Gucci look on his face. Memories.

***

I remember one time Rick was on the block. Not Puerto Rican Rick or Home Invasion Rick, (his name is self-explanatory.)

Deena was mad. "I'm tired of some damn McDonalds! You take us there every day. Rick, Damn! Your daughter is tired of that food too!" she was going off. "No, I want some Wendy's today Rick." She had her face balled up and I could tell she was settling.

Ricky Rolex was still playing like he didn't have it. And he may not have. Ricky gambled a lot. He wasn't the best at it, so he would always lose money. That still didn't stop him from doing it. In fact losing make Rick lose more money, trying to get back the money he'd lost. Just like he was about to do right now.

"Aight babe, I'ma get y'all Wendy's today. I promise. Let me hit this dice game right quick. It's sweet right now. BrandyWine is over there. He's thirsty, so he's going to bet against me. I'ma hit and pay for Wendy's today, and tomorrow! Ok? Trust me on this!" Rick gassed her head. Yall should've seen this shit!

"But you said that last time, and you still lost!" Deena wasn't going for it, at first.

"Yea, but last time I didn't have my lucky watch on!" Ricky raised his left hand and flashed his wrist watch in Deena's face. Then walked off like he had the golden ticket. And, before Deena could say another word.

I'm watching from the other side of the street! As usual, in the cut. Now, I know Ricky can't shoot. He's not better than BrandyWine and them.

I don't care how lucky he thinks that watch is Luck doesn't make shit happen around here. Will does, and Rick's will isn't strong on them dice. All of this is in my mind as I watch him diddy bop his way to the dice game.

I'd made up my mind right then and there; If this nigga loses I'ma Boo'yow his goofy ass! With that in mind, I went to watch the game and get closer to Rick just in case.

"Give me the dice! I'm shooting, who got my bet?" Ricky's rattling the dice after they handed him the dice.

"I got two hundred he crap out, first roll!"

"Me too!" dudes instantly began making bets against Rick, and they're smiling, like they've figured something out that Rick hasn't yet.

Rick paid it all no mind. "Aight. I got thirty five dollars. I can't cover all bets but I can cover some," he shook the dice harder. "I got's to crack y'all niggas today! I got's to!" he mumbled. Still shaking the dice, and staring at the spot he was going to roll them in. "Come on baby! My babies are tired of McDonald's! I'ma get them some Wendy's TODAY! WENDY'S TOD..!" he'd rolled them. Seconds later, 1 of the dice stopped spinning.

"Three! It's a three!" BrandyWine pointed at the dice. Everyone else is quiet, waiting on the other dice to fall.

"Come on baby! COME on baby!" Rick told the dice.

I'm standing behind him a few feet away. He can't see me, because he's bent over looking for the other number. I felt it was going to land on a 4. That was the number Rick needed to lose! And guess what the number was?

"FOUR! It's a FOUR! You LOST nigga!" BrandyWine was already separating Rick's money. Deena, put her head down.

Here I come. "Boo'yow Bitch! For losing Wendy's money!" I punted that nigga! Ha!

"AHHHHH!'' Khalifa fell on the ground laughing.

Crazy. That was 7th Street for you.

ITS BONE CRUSHER, BITCH!!!!

CHAPTER 32

Herbie was under pressure.

7th St.

Right after I Boo'yow Herbie Luv Bug, Him, G Hern's and a few of my other homies went downtown shopping at Doctor Denims.

I stayed on the block and caught the extra money that came through. Had enough damn clothes for the moment.

About 2 hours later, G Hern's and the fellas pull back up on the 7th Street. The 1st thing I noticed was someone missing.

***

"Oh, y'all dropped Herbie off?" I noticed Herbie Luv Bug was the missing person.

They all looked at me.

"Naa Bone, you ain't goin believe this shit !" G Hern's began.

"Believe What?" I looked from 1 face to the other.

Evidently something happened.

"Fucking Greg got pulled over by the police for running a stop sign!" Fatty shook his head.

G Hern's whipped his head at him. "Why you ain't tell me the cops was in the cut!"

"You the Driver, you supposed to see him!" Fatty sarcased.

"How? Through the back of my head?"

"Aight nigga, Damn! I ain't say you got Herbie Luv Bug locked up. I just said what happened!" Fatty defended himself.

"What? What happened to Herbie?" I cut them off.

"Yo, ya man is retarded young bul'" Far looked at me

"I'm telling you I would've never did nothing like that!" Shanky says while turning his face away.

"What the fuck happened?" I pushed.

"Na, this nigga Herbie. We gets pulled over cause I blew the fucking stop sign. But these niggas knew I was on the phone and they aint even tell me the police was watching us!" G Hern's kept defending himself.

"Why was you on the phone?" I asked now since he kept going back to it.

"Fucking Darryl called me from The Water Front County Jail in Camden! Him and Toby got locked up in Jersey, and they need bail money. So I'm trying to handle shit on the phone with them, and I blow's the fucking Stop Sign. These nigga's ain't even tell me the fucking Cop was behind me! They sitting back there in the back seat all fucking high!"

"Fuck they get locked up for?" I'm curious.

"Stealing TV's!" G Hern's told me.

“Aight, so what happened?” These 2 dizzy ass niggas. Smh!

“Na, so when we pulled over, Police pulled us all out of the car and started asking us all of them dumb ass questions.

“Where you guys headed? Do you have anything illegal on you? All that dumb shit. You know how they do. Right? So everyone else is brushing the cops off. Avoiding the bull shit. Nobody’s admitting anything.”

“Oh yea, as soon as we got out of the car, Lloyd took off! The nigga must’ve had warrants on him or something the way he was running!”

“Anyway the whole time we standing there, I can feel Herbie Luv Bug shaking next to me. This nigga was scared to death! Cop’s eventually got to questioning him.”

“Do you have anything illegal on you young man ?”

“This nigga Herbie talking about some, “HUH?”

“Yea as soon as he said that I knew he was goin do some dumb shit,” Far muttered.

“Yea, Me too!” G Hern’s looked at me. “So, police ask this nigga again.”

“Do you have anything on you young man?”

“This nigga Herbie goin say, “Yea I got something on me.” sounding all high and dumb!

“Well, where is it?” the cop tryna see through his clothes now! His eyes was moving all fast and shit. I’m just looking at this nigga Herbie Luv Bug like “What the FUCK is you doing?”

“His dingy ass goin look at the cop all sad and say, “It’s in my boot!” Bra, I wanted to suplex this nigga yo! And he’s just standing there. Looking at the cop like he was hoping to get a fucking fine or something.

"Right then and there, the cop went for his handcuffs! Herbie knew he did some dumb shit as soon as that cop reached! He knew he was going to jail! We all knew it. We knew it as soon as he said that!"

"You shoulda heard this nigga, tryna explain himself while the cop was putting the cuffs on him.

"Sir, I'm sorry Sir, I didn't think it was that big of a deal. I was just tryna to be honest with you, I…"

"But the whole time he's whining to the cop, he's moving his arms so the cop can't get the cuffs on his wrists. Now the cop gets mad and starts yelling.

"STOP RESISTING! STOP RESISTING! And all this goofy ass shit! All cause he wanted to play Honest Abe! And now he don't wanna let the cop put the cuffs on!" G Hern's looked at me wide eyed and placed a hand on his hip.

"So what happened?" I knew what happened. But I had to hear him say it.

"Fuck you think happened? They locked his ass up! He probably call me talking bout some damn bail next!" G Hern's walked off angrily.

I shook my head. Damn they done got the Luv Bug.

ITS BONE CRUSHER, BITCH!!!!

CHAPTER 33

I forgot I was Chris!

7th St.

That same night, I'm out clubbing with my boy's out at Palmer's night club in Philly. It was everything I needed it to be! Nice girls, hustlers, bad boy's, and every other type of character from my surroundings. Not long after I'd walked in, one of my old chick's noticed me.

"Chris!" I'd turned around to see who'd called me through the thick clouds of smoke, wild hairstyles, and fitted hats, my eyes landed on Shakeah. My East Oak Lane chick.

"Damn boo! How you doing?" That made me smile. I hadn't seen her in months.

I was dealing with Shakeah awhile back. Only for a few month's though. I liked Shakeah. She was brown skinned, tall, real pretty, had real nice hair, nice lips, and a phat ass! Shakeah was nice. Her problem was she was crazy! Just like most beautiful girls. Unless that's just how they get after I stick's this little dick up in them!

I was still with Jada, so I couldn't have nothing too serious with anyone else, because as I'd said before, I had 5 girlfriends. So, if Jada didn't find out and go off, 1 of them most likely would've. Even then so, a brotha could've squeezed a nice girl in his stable somewhere, if she's right.

But I won't lie as nice as Shakeah was I knew it wasn't going anywhere emotionally. I couldn't. Me knowing that, I'd told her my name was Chris, from North Philly, just in case she took me personal. And she did!

Dig how this shit went down, I'll start her story from the funny part....

"Chris! Oh Chris! I love you! I love you!" Shakeah's screaming, digging her finger nails in my back as I pound away at her pussy.

"Who the fuck is Chris?" I'm thinking to myself. Then it hit me, Chris is ME! I'm Chris! Well, to her anyway! That's who I told the bitch I was. Hah! Red Bone is too famous around Philly.

"Chris! Chris! I love you!" I let her keep screaming. Can't mess her groove up.

I'm butterball naked in this Hotel room, busting her ass! She was another 1 I fucked with just my Timberland boots on. That's my thing. I'd strap them boots on and dick a bitch down!

I stood on the floor, and had her in doggystyle, with her big ass and them wide hip's hanging off of the edge of the bed. With me standing up my Timb's could dig into the carpet, and I could throw all of my hip's into her, and wouldn't slip and inch.

"PLOP! PLOP! PLOP! PLOP! PLOP! PLOP! PLOP ! PLOP! PLOP! PLOP!" I was going on that ass.·Bul' I'm telling y'all, this bitch had some good pussy. And seeing them long legs and brown butt cheeks from the back made the Bone Crusher go harder! Now I'm holding her by her shoulder's, pulling her body back to me, as I slam my body back into hers. That bitch went crazy!

"Chris! I'm CUMMING! I'm CUMMING! Oh my GAWD!"

I kept right on pounding. "PLOP! PLOP! PLOP! PLOP! PLOP! PLOP!" Yea, I stayed in that·ass all night.

Ok, so I fucked Shakeah. Hit her with that good 7th Street dick.

Shakeah curled up and put her face in my chest. "Can you stay with me tonight Chris?"

Yea. She know. "Yea, I'm here."

Shakeah got me to stay the night with her, but it wasn't because of that 7th Street dick. This bitch had plans! Guess what she did? A Porsha and Tiffany move! This bitch done went in my pocket while I was asleep and stole $100.00 out of my shit. She got me. I Knew it was a trick to it! All of that sweet talking me her ass did. Can't believe I fell for that.

I didn't notice the money was missing until the next day, after I dropped her off down her way. And I know it was missing, because I'd counted it long before I took her to the hotel.

It's cool though. I'll get her back 1 day. She's going to suck this dick. Or something! Bitch. But for right now, she might've been hungry. I wasn't really mad though. That $100.00 wasn't nothing. And that pussy was so good, for real; she could've took a few more $100.00's!

***

"Hey," I walk's in Jada's house to play with my son.

"Hey," Jada speaks back to me.

"Hey little man!" I goes straight for my little man.

"Ahh haha bah!" he's laughing as I scoop him up. We go to the dining room.

While I'm in the dining room playing with my son, I hear Jada laughing extra hard!

"Hahah! Yea girl, you're right! That's just how they are too!"

Now, Jada is a high spirited woman. But, this time she was laughing a little too damn hard. Fuck is she on the phone with?

"Yo, who the fuck are you talking to?"

"My friend," she was vague.

"Your friend who?"

"Shakeah!" she said and then let her eyes linger on me. Like I was supposed to fold or something!

I'm MONROE'S son! Yall know the Bone Crusher played his part to the "T."

But, I didn't think it was Shakeah at first. Not the Shakeah I just met. What was the chances of that? I'd told the bitch I was Chris, from North Philly! Not the Bone Crusher, from 7th Street! How the fuck could she link that together? See, I didn't know Shakeah. I would learn about her though. And I would teach her about me.

"It's my friend. It's cool," Jada was responding to my confused look.

"Aight. I'm about to be out," I stood to leave.

"Here Bone, Shakeah wants to talk to you before you leave," Jada was handing me the phone. That's when I knew it might be her.

Jada is oblivious to this whole thing. Evidently Shakeah didn't blow the situation up yet but I didn't know what her plans were.

"Hello?" I grabbed the phone as casual as I could.

"Hey Red Bone." Yup, it was Shakeah. I knew that sexy voice.

"What?" I had to play it off. Jada was staring at me with a smirk on her face.

"You heard me. I know you're name isn't Chris. Its Red Bone."

"Aight bitch, so what? Fuck that got to do with you?" was what I wanted to say. But what came out was smarter. "I don't know what your talking about. Chris, is Farrej's real name. my name is Red Bone!"

"Huh?" Jada's face said. She's confused.

Now, I'm thinking Shakeah just might've told her that she knew me. But not that I'd sexed her. Jada would've been going the fuck off by now. So I'm figuring she didn't go that far, yet. Cool; that's room for me to wiggle.

Even if she knew I was lying. I could've been caught at the scene of a homicide, with the gun in my hand, and the barrel still smoking. I DID NOT do it! That's my story, and I'm sticking to it!

Shakeah was quiet. I took that as gold.

"Hello?"

"Yea, I'm here."

"Yea, that's Farrej's real name," I pressed.

"Oh." Yea, she wasn't 100% sure it was me. I had her ass!

"Don't let Farrej know I told you his real name," I warned

her before passing the phone back to Jada.

Jada got back on the phone with Shakeah. I got them! I know I do! Both of them bitches is dizzy. I tell them that too! They know.

"I love you little man! Daddy be back later on, kay?" I kissed my little man good bye.

"Muah!" I kissed Jada on the forehead on my way out the door.

"I'm inviting Shakeah over for dinner," Jada revealed to me, then searched my face f or an expression.

"Go head. Make sure you cook up something nice. Me and Farrej will be here," I stayed in character and kept walking to my car. The very 1st thing I did was call Farrej.

"Hello?" he picked up on the 1st ring! Yea, he seen my number on that screen. He knows.

"Yo young bul', peep this shit," I had to put him on game right quick.

Farrej knew what it was. We pulled stunts like this all of the time. Sorry Jada.

"Bul', you gotta get that Shakeah chick in order!" Farrej advised me.

"I know! I don't know how that happened! I can't wait till the next time I see her ass. I'ma put her right in her place."

"Yea, you better!" Farrej laughed.

It was crazy, because I loved fucking Shakeah's tall ass. I had to figure something out for her. In the end, she never came over for dinner. And, she'd found out who I was. Yet she didn't make another fuss of it. I guess she wanted to have access to my pockets while I slept. Yea Whatever. Work's for me.

ITS BONE CRUSHER, BITCH!!!!

CHAPTER 34

I gave her the game!

7th St.

Meanwhile I'm doing me in the hood, I heard some news which turned into a story I'ma share with y'all.

Remember Nephatia? My girl I told y'all met in the corner store back in the day? Aight, well she has a sister named Shavon I'd built a sister brother relationship with.

I got with Nephatia when Shavon was just 5 years old. It's been years since then, and Shavon has grown into a full figured woman! She was short, thick, dark brown skinned, shaped, and had a nice bubble to go with her legs.

By this time, it's been a minute since I'd seen her, but her name has been floating around the hood. A Lot!

"Yo, that lil bitch is NASTY!"

"Who, Shavon right?"

"Yea yo! Do whatever a nigga want too!" I'd over heard a few of my homey's talking.

"Word?"

"Word! And the box is good!"

"Yall talking about my folks Shavon?" I got out of the

dice game to investigate.

My boy's got quiet. They didn't know how I would take it. See, most people don't know Shavon is not my real sister, so they think I'll take it disrespectful. But, I'd already heard more than what they were saying. They had only added to it.

Later that night, I was up Shavon's way.

***

"Big brother! Hey boy! What'chu doing up this way?" Shavon was happy to see me as usual.

It's been a while since I'd seen her. And Man! She had grown up. WAY up! I see why she was a topic in the streets. It was time to big brother Shavon. FOR REAL.

"Aww ain't nothing. I came to see you! You got big girl!" I said opening my car door.

Shavon came to me, we hugged. "Yo, take a ride with me. I gotta holla at you," I gave her the eye. Meant I was serious about something.

"Alright big bro, come on," she hopped in my Acura.

It was night time, but I could still see Shavon's shape in her body dress and black stockings. Yea, she was money.

***

"Damn big bro this another one of your cars huh? You really rolling like this? Let me get some money!"

I'd turned on Mckean Street, and leaned back in my seat. I was about to give Shavon some Grade A jewels and I needed her undivided attention.

"You always need some money girl. What are you doing?"

"What'chu mean what I'm doing?"

"Here. Roll this weed up," I gave her some exotic weed. "Shavon, I'm about to give you the game sis."

Shavon looked at me, then prepared herself to listen.

"I been hearing some things about you in the streets! You fucking this dude. You fucking that dude. You do what niggas like done. You GO! Everything. All that there is to hear about a young, unmarried women, who don't really have a goal or an aim. It's ..."

"What'chu mean? I..." Shavon got defensive.

"Chill, let me finish!" I held up a hand. "I'm not hating! Like I said, shit ma about to give you some game! Niggas is talking about you!·I drove all the way up here for you! They're talking about you. Not bad, good actually. But, every time I see you, you need money. Yo need clothes. Though you still dress nice. I'm just saying, you can make some money off of the way these niggas is saying ya name. You like a sex symbol all of a sudden!

"Short hair, thick nice lips, dark ebony skin. Sis, nigga's is liking you out here. They're not supposed to be getting you for FREE! So they done had you in every way they wanted you, and after that, you back in the street's asking for help. Na! That ain't the way sis! These nigga's want to party make them pay! Real rap! These niggas spend money on a good time. And they will spend that money on you!" I stared in the eyes of the little girl I once knew.

The woman she was becoming, now stared back at me. "What'chu saying? I should be a hoe?"

“I'm saying you should make sure you’re taken care of! These niggas is having their way with you and you ain’t getting nothing out of it!”

Shavon was quiet. The realization of it all, had hit her.

“All I’m saying is, every one of them I heard say ya name would’ve paid nice money for you to party with them! It ain’t about you being a hoe. People will talk about you regardless. So, you might as well make some money off of these nigga’s.” I gave it to her, no chaser.

By that time, the weed was finished and so was the talk between us. Time was money, and I was getting back to mine. Even if Shavon wasn’t trying to get to hers.

“I hear you bro. I should’ve called you. I should’ve,” she turned to me in her seat. “I was trying to get money off of these dude’s, but they all keep acting broke!”

“Oh, ok. Yea, they will try you. Listen, come and see me when you’re ready.” I pulled up on her block. “Don’t even tell Nephatia I came through here either,” I parked up the street from her hang out.

Shavon looked at me. “I ain’t telling Nephatia shit, that bitch stole my last tampon!”

Shavon stepped out and shut the door. I backed out of her block and went my way. That, was far from the last of my seeing Shavon.

As for Nephatia, I just shook my head.

CHAPTER 35

Shavon the Hustler

7th St.

Back down 7th Street the next day. The block is crowded. Something bad happened. Through all of the commotion, I hear my name being called.

"Red Bone! Red Bone!"

"Who the fuck is that?" I'm looking around.

"It's your sister, Shavon!" O Dog, my homie, saw her before I did.

I turns around to see Shavon, walking through the crowd looking all thirsty. She knew she was on 7th Street.

"Yo sis, what's up?"

"Hey," we embraced. Shavon let me go, then looks me in the eyes, "I need some money."

"How much?" I didn't know exactly where Shavon was from our last conversation. If she still needed a few dollar's, of course I would give it to her. But, I would rather her have her own. And if she was going to be running around anyway. Hmh.

"I'm trying to get like three hundred dollars. But, I want

you to handle it for me," she looked at me.

That, told me she was with everything we'd talked about. "Oh okay, okay bet!"

Shavon came fully prepared too. This was wearing cut off sweatpants she made into shorts. They were right at the top of her thighs. You could see her camel toe! The print was bulging front the front of her shorts like it was trying to eat its way out into the air! And the top of her shorts fell right on top of her thick, smooth, chocolate, muscular thighs. Like Ebony milk. Straight on down to her strong calves, dark ankles, and pink and black Air max Nike Sneakers. Those matched her pink cutoff shorts. The belly shirt she'd worn matched both, pink and black, and showed her flat stomach. A diamond navel ring sparkled on her chocolate skin. Her whole presence exuberated sexy.

I caught myself staring. "Aight, I got you."

"Alright. Just make sure you don't call none of them stinky ass niggas. Markeem, Steph Pokey, Fat Ass Harvey, or none of them niggas. Try to get some niggas like Lil Shizz. He got deep pockets, and he likes eating my pussy," Shavon gave me her do's and don'ts.

"Aight, I got you."

"And don't call G Rap either! I don't need his creepy ass right now. Trying to role play and all that wild shit he be wanting me to do. He be wanting me to act like I'm a football player, wear helmets and shoulder pads while he acts like he's the coach, and tells me to do shit. I ain't goin through that again," she looked at me seriously. "Don't call Sha either! He creepier than G Rap! Last time I was with him, His freaky ass wanted me to tie him up and burn his nipples!

Rafiq aight though. All he wants to do is eat my ass. I can deal with that. And Puerto Rican Rick; he like them Golden showers! Him, Khalifa, Wyan, Chim-Chim, and P.G like that shit! Want me to pee on …"

"Hold on! Girl you crazy! What about J Bird?"

"J Bird is gay! Pig is too, But J Bird is something else. He be wanting me to strap up and fuck his ass with the dildo," Shavon said.

"That's crazy." I knew what she was going to say about them. I just wanted to hear her say it.

"Come on, walk with me. I turned to lead the way.

"Aight," Shavon followed me.

I took her to an empty house on Winton St. It was 1 of the low spots we'd had just for things like this.

"Aight, the first person I'm calling is my young bul' Farrej," I looked at her.

"Ok. I hope he got some money this time."

"You dealt with Farrej before?"

"One time."

"Aight, I'll make sure he has some money for you. Whoever else comes in after him, just do your thing. Everybody got thirty minutes. Tops. I don't have time to sit out here all night. I got shit to do.". I'm fronting I would sit out here all day, because I knew I was going to make money off of her.

***

Farrej fat tricking ass came to the house. "What you got here for me?" he's grinning all silly.

"You got some money on you?"

"Yea!" he pulls out like a stack. (That's a $1,000 where I'm from.)

"I got Shavon in the house with her clothes off."

"For REAL?" his face lit up. His eyes searched mines for a lie.

"A buck fifty and you got her for thirty minutes."

"Thirty minutes? How you gain charge ya man a buck fifty?"

"A Buck fifty Dawg. Thirty minutes," I stood firm.

"Yo Bone, that bitch ain't worth no buck fifty! I'll give you Fifty!"

"Na homey, This is a special day And Shavon is looking good right now."

"Maan!" Farrej began then became quiet thinking to himself. "I'll give you a hundred, and she better suck my dick too!"

"Yo, she's going to treat you right."

I turned to open the door. "You ready?" I ask Shavon.

"Yea, tell him to come in," her voice came back.

Farrej heard her, and took his dizzy ass inside of the house.

***

I spotted another trick walking past me on my block.

"Yo Rell," I called him over. I'm the Bone Crusher, he came. He knows what I'm about. "You wanna fuck Shavon?"

"Yea."

Yup. Knew I was right. I'm telling y'all, Shavon is thick boy! Even in sweatpants she would turn heads. In the hood, all a bitch needed was a phat ass. In my hood anyway. These boys are wolves. Well, most men are. But, these boys throw that bread around.

"I got you. A buck fifty," I told Rell.

Rell looked at me for a second, then realized, I was serious.

"Bet! I'll be back in two minutes." Rell ran off without another word. He knows if I said it; I mean it!

Rell was back in that 2 minutes, 3 at the most. But he was back and sweating like a Hebrew slave!

"Why you sweating like that?" I had to know.

"Cause I had to go get Andra some chicken wings from the Chinese store, then go get my kids some milk!" he forced out between breaths.

Damn, he was running for that ass. Hah! "Shavon wasn't going nowhere. She's in the house right now with somebody. In ten minutes, you can walk in and do your thing."

"Aight! Aight, bet " Rell got all excited. Rell gave me his

$150.00 with no problem.

I checked my watch. 30 minutes was up. "Doc doc!" I tapped on the door, then opened it.

Farrej was putting his shirt on. Shavon was in the bathroom.

"Farrej, walk out the back door so don't nobody see you."

"Coo1," Farrej did what I asked.

I turned back to Rell as I shut the door. In two minutes, just walk in."

Two minutes later, Rell took his tricking ass in the crib.

“Thirty minutes,” I reminded him.

“I only need ten!” Rell shot back over his shoulder.

I laughed. I'm sitting on the steps as they do them. We’ve made $250.00 so far. That's good. If this is the last person Shavon does, she’ll get $60.00 out of this $250.00. Fuck that, I'm watching this door.

“Yo Twin! Right on time.” Twin was diddy boppin past me. This fat nasty tricking ass nigga is going to pay like he weigh for Shavon. “Yo Twin, listen; I got Shavon in the crib right now,” I went at him. The tone of my voice told him what the situation was.

“Shavon? Your sister?”

“Yes, my sister.” Twin doesn't know Shavon isn't my real sister.

Just my ex-girlfriend’s sister. Me and Shavon always kept that brother and sister bond. “Twin, Shavon is in the house naked, and she’s trying to fuck!”

“How much?”

“Shavon ain't no crack head Twin. So you can kill all of those ten, twenty dollar thoughts,” I set the tone for my price. “You gotta pay like you weigh for that.”

“That's too much! I weigh four hundred pounds! Bitch pussy ain't that good!” Twin shook his head.

“That’s a metaphor Twin. You don’t have to pay that.”

“Oh! I was about to say! How much then?”

“Two fifty! And I'll make sure she sucks you off, and do what you want!”

“For Real Bone?”

“Would I lie to you?”

“You did before!”

"When?"

"That time it was a drought on coke and you said you had ounces."

"I did have ounces!"

"Yea and they were fake!"

I got quiet. "Na I don't remember that!" Had to deny that. I'm the Bone Crusher, fuck that. "I sale real drugs Twin. Now are trying to fuck Shavon, or what?" Damn everything else.

"Hell yea!" Twin dug his fluffy hand into his pocket and counted out $250.00. "Here," he outstretched his hand.

I took the money then opened the door to check on Shavon. 30 minutes was up. She was ready. "Send the next one in," was all I heard.

I looked at Twin. "Thirty minutes."

"Ok, no problem Bone." he walked in the house.

I didn't see no one walking through Winston St. So I decided to make a few calls.

I know Rafiq and Jariek is going to want her. But they're not going to want to pay me my price. So I wasn't calling them. I know I can get $300.00 for her from the right trick. If Shavon fucks a few more heads, she will have that money she wanted.

"Bone Neck! That's who I'm calling!" It hit me. He's my cousin. Bone Neck is a good dude. He's handicapped from the waist down, but he can feel orgasm's. He gets a Social Security check every month, and he should have it right about. Now. I know he needs his dick sucked.

He picked up on the 2nd ring.

"What's up cuz?"

"Yo cuz, I got this little bitch at the crib, and she said she wants to suck your dick while you sitting in your wheelchair.

"For REAL cuz?"

"Cuz, for real!"

"Who is it?"

"Shavon!" I told him.

"I always wanted to fuck Shavon too!"

Uh huh! Just the words I needed to hear. "Three fifty cuz, you can have her!"

"Word Bone? I'll give the bitch my whole check!" Bone Neck got hyped.

I started laughing. Bone Neck really will give the bitch his whole check. Bone Neck trick's every month around this time. All of the hood trick's know it too.

"Do you want me to come and get you now?"

"I'm already on my way there! I'm driving down Fourth Street!"

"Who's bringing you?"

"My wheel chair! I'm driving myself cuz!" Me and Bone Neck laughed at that.

"Aight Cuz, I'll be waiting on you."

"I'm already at the clubhouse where you was at last week, so I'll be right there in like six minutes!" Bone Neck assured me.

"Six minutes cuz?"

"Yea, six minutes. I be moving cuz!"

"Aight!" I banged on him ending the call.

***

"Time is up Twin," I opened the door.

"Bone, if I give you another hundred dollars, can I get another ten minutes?" Twin fat ass asked me.

"Yea," hell yeah! Was what I'd wanted to say.

By the time Bone Neck gets here, he should be finishing up. I looked at Shavon. "We're almost there."

"Ok," she nodded.

Back out ·side, I'm looking down Winton St, I see Bone Neck bucking traffic. Shortly after that, he was right in front of the door.

"Cuz, what's up bul'!" I reached out to hug him.

Me and Bone Neck are cool. I do wish he was walking. I know the damage me and him could've done together. Smh, life has its ways. We deal with them as they come.

"What's up cuz!" he hugged me back."

"Five more minutes," I told him.

"Cool."

While we stood there waiting for Twin to finish, I knew I would need help when it came to bone necks turn. At the same time, I seen Burn Nate, our neighborhood smoker walking past us. Perfect.

"Burn Nate, come here!" I motioned him over to us. "Help me get him into my crib," I pointed at Bone Neck.

"This your house?" he bent to help Bone Neck.

"Don't start with all the questions!" I looked at him with my crazy look.

"Aight Bone, Damn!" he joked it off as he picked up Bone Neck.

After he helped me do that, he was off. Later for him. Time is up for Twin, again. I open the door, and saw Twin pass Shavon his number. Shavon took it, and put it in her purse.

Bone Neck is in the crib now. “You cool cuz?”

“I am now,” he looked at me. Then passed me $350.00. Clean money.

“Ok Cuz, thirty minutes.” I shut the door.

As I did, I turned to see T.Y and Lil Craig smiling.

“We heard you got something for us Bone? Rell just told us.”

“Yea, I got something for y’all.”

“Yo Bone, please don’t charge us up. Look out for us!?”

“Shavon’s bills need paid. I can’t look out. But listen,” I got close to them. “I’ll tell y’all what give me a buck fifty a piece for everything.”

“Rell only paid a hundred dollars,” Lil Craig whined.

“Fuck Rell. He didn’t get everything. He only paid that to fuck. He didn’t get his dick sucked. But, if y’all only wanna fuck then give me the hundred. Come on,” I held my hand out. I was gaming them and hoping they went for it.

They went right for it.

“Na, I need the whole works!” T.Y shook his head. “I got the whole buck fifty,” he dug his hand into his pocket. I wasn’t hearing it. We need ours.

“Ok, you got next then.”

5 minutes go by, while we’re waiting on Bone Neck to finish. “Yo, pay that buck fifty. We’ll make it back,” T.Y assured Lil Craig. I guess he wanted him to enjoy himself today as well.

“Cool!” Lil Craig couldn’t wait to hear that. He’d pulled the $150.00 right out of his pocket already counted! Hah!

Niggas is wild bul'.

I took the money. Time is up... Bone-Neck should be done. I opened the door, and seen Bone-Neck kissing Shavon. I was stuck, but I didn't freeze. "Cuz, what are you doing?

"I'm trying to make love to her," Bone Neck kept his eyes on her.

Shavon was laughing. She thought it was cute Bone-Neck was trying to please her.

"Cuz, you can't make love, you're in a wheel chair," I reminded him.

"This bitch just made my legs move!" Bone Neck argued.

"Bone Neck, your legs didn't move cuz."

"Cuz, you're trippin', I know what I felt," he insisted.

"You gotta hurry up man people out here waiting."

"Can I come back?"

Since Bone-Neck is my cousin, and I charged him up I told him, "Yea cuz, you can come back tonight. It's on me."

Bone Neck looked back at Shavon, "I'll be back aight?"

Shavon giggled, and took her ass upstairs. I caught Burn Nate, the hood smoker walking past us again, and had him help me bring Bone Neck back outside.

"I need something this time Bone, I know you got me too!" Burn Nate looked at me.

"Yea I got you young bul', hold up," I promised him. I guess everybody got some love that day.

T.Y. walked in the house after we sat Bone-Neck on the curb.

"T.Y., thirty minutes young bul'."

"Aight Bone," he shot back.

"Yo, Shavon is like that!" Bone-Neck looked at Burn-Nate.

Burn-Nate started laughing. After these clowns are finished Shavon will probably have about $200.00.

My phone went off while we were standing outside. "Hello?"

"Yo Bone, where the weed at nigga?"

"I don't got no bud, but I got Shavon around here at the club house. And she working!" I told Lil' Scoop.

"I' be right there!" Scoop hung up on me.

"Oh shit here," I handed Burn-Nate something for helping me with Bone-Neck.

By now T.Y. was done. He came out, and Lil Craig went in, as Scoop was walking up.

"Right on time Scoop."

"How much?"

"A hundred, for everything." I told Scoop. Scoop gave me the money. "Cool, as soon as Craig comes out, just go right in," I directed him. Then walked over to my cousin to holla at him about them dizzy 5th Street bitches while he's down here.

***

"Yo cuz, did you see Pooh out there?"

"I saw Pooh and Ebony, and they both asked me did I see you."

"How Ebony looking?"

"She still look aight. She be with her daughter a lot."

"That's what's up. I remember me and Ebony took our

daughters to Chucky Cheese together. Ebony is good people's."

"Yea, cuz she's good people's. And she loves you too."

"What Pooh doing?"

"Nothing. In front of Monae's steps with her girlfriends. Them bitches are always there."

Craig came out, Scoop went right in.

"Shavon, Scoop is the last one." I said behind him.

"It's about fucking time," Shavon mumbled.

"Come on Shavon, are you serious?"

"Hell yea I'm serious."

"Shavon, I got ya back. Shut the fuck up and treat Scoop right."

"Fuck you Red Bone," Shavon snapped back. By then I was already on the steps closing the door behind me.

"'Yo I thought I was last?" Bone-Neck quickly reminded me.

"You're right Bone-Neck. I got you. I'll make sure she sees you."

"Aight cuz."

"Yo, do you remember when Pooh's husband Lenny came home?" I asked Bone-Neck.

"Yea I remember that."

"Yea, that was wild. I thought I was going to have to fall back and give Pooh some space. Instead she was on my heels crazy! I'm like sweetheart, chill. Go home and be with your husband." Pooh told me, "I will, but I still want to keep seeing you." Pooh was wild. But yea, she stayed letting me hit that. Pooh treated me good. I can call her right now if I wanted to. Even with her husband out of prison.

"Cuz, I remember one day I was on the phone with Pooh, and I asked her would she let me get hurt down 5th Street?"

"No! If you get hurt, they gotta hurt me too!" she answered me.

"How 'bout if Lenny tried to hurt me, would you let him?"

She said, "Lenny will get fucked up out here! We'd roll on his ass."

"You're crazy Pooh!" I told her. But I knew she had love for me though. And it was genuine. I had the same thing for her. "She's good people's," I was going on to Bone Neck.

See, Pooh can't forget a lot of things I did for her. I showed Pooh how to stay alive, and live in these mean streets of Philly. When I met Pooh, she didn't even have an I.D! I took her to Penndot to apply for that and her license. That was just a few things I did for her.

Scoop was finished, and coming out of the house now. I went in to talk to Shavon, "Hey, take care of Bone-Neck right quick. He's the last one I promise."

"For real?"

"Yea, for real. Finish Bone-Neck, and come and get your three hundred dollars."

"Bone, all of them niggas, I sucked and fucked, and that's all I made was three hundred dollars?"

"Exactly three-fifty! You know them broke ass nigga's ain't got no money."

Shavon screwed her face up at me. She knew I was lying.

"Tell Bone-Neck to bring his trickin' ass in here!" she huffed.

I go to the door to get Bone-Neck, and he's gone. I looked

around for him, and I spotted him with Pugie's smoking ass sister, Ebony!

Ebony knows Bone Neck got that check today, and she's on his head for some of it. That's cool! As long as she works for it.

"YO, BOONEE NNECCK!" I had to make sure he was good.

"I'll get at you later cuz!" I heard his voice echo back. That was all I needed to hear.

"Yo, get dressed." I turned back to Shavon.

"I told you, I need three hundred."

"I got that for you," I looked at her with sincerity.

"For real?" Shavon lit up. Then got up and started jumping up and down on the bed like a kid who had just got a scoop of ice cream.

There had to have been a few thoughts in Shavon's mind. The 1st thought, was probably the fact she got her desired amount of ·money, that told her that she was worth something. And that something was tangible. There was power there. Secondly, she could accomplish something she'd put her mind to. Shit, I was just glad to get her started there.

"You good?" I went upstairs to check on Shavon after a second.

"Yea I'm good. I like twin. He's the only one who ate my ass. I'm going to have a baby by him and lock him down," she looked at me.

"Now you're thinking." I smiled at her she was thinking long term. At least she vision it.

Twin was a good look for her. I knew he would take care

of her.

“Thank you Big brother!” Shavon put her arms around my neck.

“Ain't nothing girl. You know I got you!” I wrapped my arms around her.

See, Shavon wasn't looking at the situation like I'd pimped her. She, was looking at it the right way. Like I schooled her on how to capitalize off of what was already going on. Shavon got dressed, counted her money, and smiled at me again.

“I wanna do this more often!”

“I got you, just hit me up.”

“Alright big bro. I'll do that,” she promised me. Then went on. “Bro, I gotta go. Thanks again, and I’ll be in touch alright?”

“Aight, bet. Be cool.”

“Alright.”

Shavon was already heading for the front door.

I'm watching her leave, and thinking to myself, “this bitch didn't even wash her ass?”

“SHAVON! You ain’t goin...” she was long gone by then. The money was talking to her. She wasn't hearing anything, or anyone else.

I locked the house up a few minutes later. Now I'm walking away rewinding everything that just went down. “Damn, I can do this all day.” I pulled the money I just made out of my pocket. This was good money. It was easy. All I would have to do is find them and charge them. Shavon would do the rest.

Shavon did call me again too. A few more times. Many,

even. She also did what she'd said she would with Twin.

I saw Shavon a few months later, she was in the passenger seat of Twin's car leaning! Like Twin's shit was a Bentley or something! I couldn't hate though. Then, I would see her come through driving Twin's shit, then, eventually the baby came. To Twin.

"Damn," I said to myself. "Out of all that trickin, she got a beautiful daughter, Bless."

ITS BONE CRUSHER, BITCH!!!!

CHAPTER 36

All Star Weekend

All Star weekend, California.

It was the NBA All Star weekend at the Staples Center, In Los Angeles California. Yall already know 7th Street had to be there to see the boy Lebron James do his thing. We were deep too. About 20 of us took a flight out there!

We arrived in Los Angeles a few times by this time. But seeing the top of those huge palm trees from the high skies never got old to me. You know the Bone Crusher always got himself a window seat on the plane. My crazy look got me that. They know me. I'll back slap one of these niggas.

As soon as the plane wheels touched land, the pilot came over the intercom. "Ok ladies and gentlemen, we are now on land here at the Los Angeles Airport. Thank you, for flying with Delta Air Lines and we hope you enjoy your stay," he announces.

Shortly after that the plane stopped and me and my boys hopped out of our first class seats and into the California sun. It's rays of shining light felt good on my skin. A light breeze followed behind it. This is nice. High palm trees, beautiful weather, and exotic cars everywhere we looked. Yea, our kind of thing.

In the airport, we walked through basking in the scenery. We spotted a few celebrities in passing. But we're celebrities ourselves, so we weren't star struck. We're 7th Street. Shit, celebrities were looking at us! We mobbed through the airport like we owned it. Or like we could've!

After grabbing our luggage, we left the airport and stepped into California. The West Coast air immediately warmed us. "YOOO! YOO Right here!" I waved down the taxi I seen.

Yea, we rode in style wherever we went. 'Pull that shit over!' my attitude said like I had a $1,000 tip for him. And I just might depending on his service!

"Where to?" the driver said as the few that was with me got in the cab.

"The car rental. We need a car."

"Nah fuck that we need a Rolls Royce!" my man jumped in.

"Yea fuck that. We about to do this shit!" I nodded.

"Ok, ten minutes," the driver gassed the limo.

Sure enough, 10 minutes later we pulled to the car rental. The luxury car rental.

"Look, there go the Phantom right there!" I pointed.

The grey on grey Rolls Royce was the 1st big boy wheel I seen. Sitting on a small perch at the front of the car lot separated from all of the other cars, in all of its splendor. It was a show piece and we were seeing why right before our eyes.

"Excuse me, can we get the Rolls Royce right there?" I

went straight up to the 1st sales man I seen, after I walked inside. "And how much is the Benz right there? And the one over there?" I went off pointing at everything I knew we wanted.

"Well, okay" the man smiled, seeing that we were here to have a good time in LA.

The man noted every vehicle we wanted tallied their prices, and gave us a bulk package deal.

We paid it and 20 minutes later we were backing out in all of the fly shit we wanted to be in. Well, me and a few others anyway. Nigga's don't got money like the Bone Crusher. (Jariek, Dor, M.t, Rafiq. Yea.) I got more money than all 4 of them. We was cool though. 3 exotic wheels and a few squatters to roll around in, and we're out!

Rodeo Drive was nice. It's everything you see in the movies. Beautiful women with long legs and pretty hair, dressed like super models and carrying expensive handbags. Upper echelon cars at almost every light you could turn, and almost everyone seemed to be their own star.

"YO!" Lenny answered me on the 1st·ring.

"Yo, let's hit the Beverly Hills Mall!" I suggested.

"Aight bet!" he hung up.

"BEEP! BEEP!" we beeped to let my boy's know to follow us.

"BEEP! BEEP!" they beeped back.

From there I started asking questions. A few directions, a few highways, and some turns later, the Beverly Hills Mall came into view. It was CRAZY!

I'm seeing it all as I'm coming off of the 3 lane highway. Lamborghini's, Ferrari's, Bentley's, Range Rover's and some more shit! The mall itself was like a half of a city block long. Or more! Traffic is moving fast, and cars are whizzing past us as we're corning off of the expressway, and into the open complex for parking. There were actors, and other entertainers beside us in traffic. This wasn't 7th Street. And these weren't the neighborhood stars.

Inside of the mall, it just as big as its outside. And just as. glamorous as well. There is a certain crowd this atmosphere appeals to. The rich and the famous. From that, you can imagine the surroundings.

"Yo, check this out!" Jariek picked up a flyer off of a table we passed by. "It says," Jariek stared at it trying to formulate the words.

We all waited on him. He had our attention now.

Rafiq knew he was struggling, "Sound it out Jariek!" he encouraged.

"I'm trying to.. Pooffee i…s .. HH.. aven Ayy pottee."

"Man why you got him reading that, you know he can't read!" Indris snapped on Rafiq and walked over to Jariek. "Gimme this shit maan, damn! Told ya dumb ass to go to school." Indris snatched the flyer from him. "It says Puff Daddy is having an after party, after the All Star game! It's five hundred dollars to get in, and drinks are on the house!" Indris read it off then pocketed the flyer.

I held my laugh in. I knew that nigga went to Furness High! Ha! Dummy! "Hell yea we there." No one seen me holding my laugh.

"I'm grabbing my outfit right now!" my boys got hyped. We'd all decided right then and there we were going to the party. That gave us a reason to shop. We walked through the mall with a purpose now.

"Yo, ain't that Kyla Pratt right there?" Rafiq noticed.

"Where?" I looked around.

"In the red dress, sitting at the table right over there, he pointed subtly in her direction.

Then I'd noticed her. "Ohh. Yea, that is her."

She was wearing a 1 piece fashion dress. Might've been Channel, might've been something else. Her legs were showing, her calves were nice, and the black open toe shoes she had on accented her curves. Her hair relaxed over her shoulder's. She didn't have on any jewelry, and there was a nice little handbag on her side of the table.

And though she played a young woman on television, this was a woman sitting before me. She had a strong aura, and I could sense it from where I stood. That didn't scare me. It intrigued me.

As for me, I was in my basic 7th Street wear. Multi colored Ralph Lauren collared shirt, casual shorts and a fresh pair of 6 inch collard Timberland boot's. I had my fitted hat, but I was holding it up my hand so I could show off my shape up. And just like that, I went after her.

"Excuse me? Do I have to have on a suit to come and talk to you?" I joked lightly.

"No, you don't have to have on a suit to come and talk to me. How are you doing?" she smiled at my humor.

Her mouth. Hmh. "I'm doing good, how are you?" Yea, she was down to earth. Bet!

"I'm fine. What's your name?" she eyed me.

"Red Bone," I told her. She was getting the real me. A 7th Street nigga.

"Ok Red Bone. I'm Kyla, and it's nice to meet you," she extended her hand.

I took it. By now, I can see Rafiq and them in my peripheral vision, gawking at me like they were thirsty, and they were mad I found some water. Hating ass nigga's.

"Yes, definitely. It's nice to meet you too," I smiled.

"We're throwing an after party after the All Star game if you'd like to come?" she offered me, after we'd been conversing for a minute.

"Oh yea? I'll come through, where is it?"

"Here," her friend handed me the flyer. It was the same flyer Jariek just tried to read off of bout the after party.

"We already got this," I analyzed it to make sure. "This is the Party Puff is throwing right?"

"Yes, Puff is promoting it, but it's our afterparty. There's a few of us throwing one there. Come through you'll enjoy yourself'. And bring your friends," she extended her invitation.

She noticed my boys on the side. She knew we had money too. She could tell. The diamonds dangling from our limb's told her we could cover whatever the fee to get in the party was.

"Ok. Uhm, can I have your number so I can call you sometime?" I shot my shot. I felt comfortable enough.

"Uhm. Sweetie you're cute, but I don't know if we'll be able to work on anything serious. I'm too focused on my career," she said humbly.

I respected her grace. But as she talked, I imagined us 2 coming through the block together. I knew she was a good look. I would've stunted with this 1!

"I mean, we can work on that. I can travel."

"I hear you," she smiled. I connected her smile to my persistence. "Well, yea I can give you my number. Give me a call sometime. You're coming to my after party, right?" she was curious now.

"Yea I'll be there," I smiled back at her. I heard her career talk.

But I know she liked me. The eyes never lie.

Yall already know as soon as she passed off her number I was feeling myself. I knew she was goin give me that number. Fly ass 7th Street nigga like myself? Hell yea! Shit, I should've asked her what took her so damn long to give it to me! "Aight, bet. Ima come have a drink tonight with you. Ok?" I threw some charm at her.

"Ok," she smiled humbly.

After I got her number, me and my boy's shopped around the mall for a while longer. None of them really said anything about my meeting her. I told y'all we're stars ourselves so things like that didn't amaze us.

Eventually, we went from the Beverly hill's mall back to our hotel room. Most of us haven't slept since we arrived here. It was California, and we were enjoying every bit of it.

We stayed at the "W". It's one of the main hotels, on one of the main strip's in California. We knew it was where everyone who was anyone would be. Celebrities and stars were all over that hotel. We were in there.

The night went good. It wasn't that late when we made it back to the hotel. But as I said, we needed to get some rest. So, we tried to. I know I sure didn't get any. I was too excited about what the next day would bring.

Kyla and Puff's party wouldn't be for another day or 2. Although the All Star game was later on that next night.

***

The next day, I was up nice and early. I'd barely slept. "Yo, let's go get some breakfast?"

"Aight bet. I'm driving the Phantom!" Indris claimed. "Go head! That ain't no breakfast car anyway. Fuck I look like driving that spaceship to breakfast? Fuck you tryna prove?" I clowned Indris. He couldn't wait to be seen in that double R. "Rick, Wake up for I BOO'yow ya goofy ass! Ha! Toby, don't shit on these peoples stuff in this hotel nigga. We ain't doing that!" I went on everybody around me. Fuck that, Bone Crusher in this bitch!

"Fuck outta here Bone! Talking shit because you got an actress number yesterday!"

"You ain't get it!" I bragged.

"How you get that anyway Bone?" some dummy had the nerve.

"Fuck you mean how I get that? I'm from Seventh Street nigga!" I continued brushing my hair in the mirror. Damn, I'm a fly nigga.

"You funny as hell Bone!" Leem joked from across the room.

Leem is Meech's brother. Meech is here too. Him and Buck shot. Them dirty nigga's there normally stay on the block and try to get all of the money when we went on trips.

We convinced them to take a trip this time. Shit, Meech needed 1 after the incident with his son being threatened over his fake Rolex.

It was Markeem who'd stayed on the block to get the money this time. He said he was trying to get his money up to pay off that red Acura.

Shit I don't blame him. Him and Craig Mack. Said they were tired of being the dirty young bul's', and it was their turn to shine like us. Go for it!

I wasn't done. "Lenny, please don't stalk no bitches down here! We don't need none of these people thinking that's how Seventh street niggas get down!" I went on Lenny next.

"Oh you're really showing off now!" Lenny tried to scare me with his own crazy look.

Ha! Please! His eyes are serious, but his lips looks like he's been eating powdered doughnut's all morning. And he's staring at me, really trying to make his look work. Ha! "What nigga? It ain't my fault you're hanging in trees and spying on bitches!"

"Yea AIGHT!" was all he could say.

"Indris, get your corny ass out of that mirror! And take that nut ass shirt off! Tryna be like J.C!"

"Yooo.Yea Dreese, you do be tryna be like that nigga! Haaa! You do be tryna be like J.C though! Puerto Rican Rick was awake now.

I don't even know how all of them got in my room. Or when they came in. But, they were here now. And the jokes were on.

"Bone fuck outta here!" Toby came back. "That's why your brother Wyan running around here with Bull Dog robbing·peop1e to get high!"

"So what, that's why your dad is Cuffy!"

Toby gets mad when we say that to him. Cuffy was a crack head from 5th Street that had a limp. Toby's mother, married Cuffy. That's where the joke came from. But Toby didn't like that shit. At ALL!

"Fuck outta here! That's why your mom had that beat up ass red station wagon back in the day! I remember when y'all was driving down the street in reverse, because the shit couldn't go forward!" Toby piped up. He got me there. That station wagon was beat down! I won't lie. The whole hood knew it.

"Ay, we ain't doin that buss on our parents shit!" I checked them. "And you got me on that, but we wasn't riding backwards nigga."

"Fuck outta here! You started it. Talking about my parents!" Toby laughed.

"That was different! Anyway, let's go get some breakfast. I'm ready right now," I changed the subject.

"Where y'all wanna go?" Lenny came in.

20 minutes later, we were on the streets of California.

"Yo, I need some gas, go to a gas station." Indris came over my line after I answered his call.

"Aight bet," I hung up and lead the way. I knew all other cars would follow.

The first gas station we seen, we pulled over. I pulled into the 3rd pump. The Rolls Royce was 1st, the Bentley was 2nd, and my Sl500 convertible top 2 door Benz, was next to them. I know what you're thinking. I was thinking it too. We look like money.

As we're pulling in, I see a triple back Range Rover with black tint and black rims, parked alongside 1 of the pumps.

"Who's shit is that?" I'm thinking. And that's when I seen Nia long coming out of the store, walking gracefully toward that SUV. Fella's, when I say gracefully? I mean that! She was just as beautiful in person as she was in the movie Big Mamma's house.

She was wearing a regular. Jeans, tennis shoes, and a halter top. I'm telling y'all, God is good. I'm serious. She was gorgeous.

We parked at the pump behind her Range Rover. As I said I was 3rd, so I was at the furthest pump from her. But see, I had the·advantage·on my nigga's, because I seen her before they did. And guess what? Indris had the Phantom parked behind her at his pump!

Now, I seen Nia double take at the Phantom for only a half of a second, and that was enough for me. Indris and them are still in the car, and doing whatever it was they're doing.

Right then and there I came up with a plan, and it was time to move on it. If Nia wanted to know who owned the Rolls Royce then it was time for her to meet him.

I walked over to the Phantom like I owned it. Meanwhile, I'm watching Nia out of the corner of my eye to make sure I got her attention. "Yo, what the fuck is y'all doing? We supposed to be here on business, and y'all out here playing around in my shit! Damn I can't take y'all nigga's nowhere! Indris, get ya dirty ass out of the car and go fill the tank up. Matter of fact fill this up, fill the Benz up, and the Bentley! (I pulled out one of my toilet paper sized knots of money, and acted like I was undecided on how much to give him. Of course I was just showing off. That was the plan!) Yea, just go head and fill all of them up man cause we're going to be out here and it's going to cost me anyway. So, I might as well fill them up right now. Here just, take it all," I gave Indris the whole knot of money and waved him away with my hand. I was fronting hard. Shit, for that moment all of them vehicles were mine.

And guess what it worked! I see Nia's eyes on me out of the corner of my eye! She was looking at me !Nia long was looking at ME! The Bone Crusher! A 7th Street nigga!

I see Indris looking at me out of the left side of my perennial eye. I can almost feel the heat coming on to me off of his eyes. "Oh you got that off. Oh, you got that off!" I can hear him mumbling to me.

I ignored him, and turned to Nia like I hadn't noticed her in the least bit! "Oh, hey princess. How are you doing?" I was nonchalant. Like I didn't set this stage for this movie I was starring in.

Then I turned fully toward her, and let the diamonds in my RB piece shine in her direction. That pendant, was the initials of my name. And they were iced down! My shit was dancing when the sun hit it, and I knew it.

"Hi, how are you?" she smiled at me, Her response wasn't flirty. But hey, this was Nia talking. I'll take it.

"I'm doing all right. Ssssmm business as usual," I kept right on faking. Shaking my head as if the stress of business was just too much sometimes.

"Yea, I know exactly what you mean," she said knowingly, jiggling her pump into its place in her truck.

Behind me, I could still feel Indris staring at me! I guess because I talked all of that trash about the Phantom in the hotel. Now I was out here fronting in front of Nia. Yea damn all that.

I looked back at him with my crazy look. “Dreese didn’t I tell you to go fill the cars up with gas? I mean Now! Damnit!” I commanded him. Then looked at Rafiq and them, and folded my arms across my chest.

Indris bit his bottom lip. “You got that,” I heard him mumble before walking off.

I was on my shit, and he was going to go with it, or I was going to fuck a situation up for him the next time he had one. He knew it too. “Fuck y’all standing around for?” I looked at my other homies.

They all looked at me with a vindictive eye. “Oh yea, he really showing off now,” I can hear their whispers. But they made me look good, and walked off.

They're going kill me for that later, but back to Nia for now. I turned back to Nia, and smiled. Hopefully she didn't catch on to my game yet. She was still struggling with her pump. I guess her special edition was a bit tricky. “You okay?” she smiled at me.

“Yea, I'm cool. Business (I shook my head again.) Can I help you with that?” I nodded at her gas pump.

“Oh, no, no. That's ok, I have it.” She was sweet. That was making me want her more. I knew if I came down 7th Street with her? Bul'!

I smiled at the thought of that. But I don't feel that door open with her yet. Damn!·Don’t tell me I done fronted like this for Nothing! Shit, these nigga’s are going to grind me up for that! BAD! But, you know the Bone Crusher couldn’t let her see me sweat. I'm too far in my movie!

“Ok, well you have a nice day. Oh can you tell me where

there's a nice place to have breakfast?"

"Yea, sure. Roscoe's chicken and waffle house is good. And its close by here," she began. She then gave us directions, and bade me farewell.

Damn. I felt like I was living in the wrong part of the world. Especially if life was this glamorous on this side of the map, and the women were this humble and beautiful.

ITS BONE CRUSHER,BITCH!!!!

CHAPTER 37

Enjoying California

Roscoe's chicken and waffle house was nice. Whoever you are reading this book, you should visit there sometime. The waitresses look like super models, and the people treat you like King's! It was fun.

Puff's after party. His, Kyla's and whoever else's it was, still wasn't for another day. But there were other live events going on. Honestly, California was full of live events. Friday, there was the Rookie All Star game, Saturday was the Slam Dunk Contest, and Sunday was the actual All Star game. Between those, Shaq had his after party on a Saturday after the contest and Puff's and his host's party was on that Sunday! So, yea like I said we were partying all weekend. And every one of these events were lit! 7th Street showed up!

Kyla's event was my favorite. What can I say? I was personally invited. "When you come, ask for me at the door," Kyla told me, before we parted that day I'd met her. I just never told my boy's. So, that was exactly what I did, when we finally did show up at her party.

"Good evening guys, take any and all medals out of your pockets, and raise your hands in the air please?" security frisked us as we came up. These were top rank security men, wearing all black suits.

We did as they asked. "Okay thank you and enjoy your night," they moved out of our way and let us through after we were cleared.

Five hundred dollars to get in," the man on the door was next.

***

"Yo how the fuck did you do that?" Indris was on me when he seen me not pay the entrance fee.

"Chill. Mind ya business nigga, damn!" I smirked. "My girlfriend got me in here."

"Yea aight! Who is ya girlfriend?"

"Kyla Pratt! I told you!"

"Man that ain't ya girl nigga ! Stop frauding! I know you frauding." Indris knew I might've been joking. But he couldn't tell, because they did see me talking to her that day. "You do be fronting, but you got in here for free so I can't even hate," he gave up on finding out the truth.

The party was live! Everyone was everywhere! Celebrities hung around regular people. Danced with them, drank with them, partied with them and just had a good time. It was so blended, I could've walked over to Paris Hilton and shot my shot!·She was right there with us! And she was pretty in real life too.

“Hey Red Bone,” Kyla smiled at me when I came in. Yea Indris, take that!

“Hey sweetheart,” I walked into her open arms.

“I’m glad y’all could make it,” she smiled.

“I’m glad I could too. You know I’m trying to get close to you,” I flirted with her.

“You’re crazy boy. I like that though. You drinking?”

“Yea, I’m buying. Drinks on me.”

“Ok, uhm.” she ordered some bottles. She knew I had it. My RB piece was in her face again. And I didn’t have them little crushed up sprinkled specs of diamond’s in my shit. Those were on the insides of my piece. The outside of my joint had them stones in it!

Anyway, that whole night I danced with Kyla and her girlfriend. Bought bottles. Partied with them. They were completely down to earth. Good people. I really enjoyed myself. My boys did too. Being with NBA stars, NFL stars, and all other kinds of athletes, actors, and actresses. We had a ball.

We left the party in good spirits. When we made it back to the hotel, most of us weren’t tired, and there was a bar inside of the hotel on the main floor.

“Yo, y’all tryna hit this bar?” Lenny looked at me.

He knew I was with it. “Let’s do it,” I headed in first. Through the window of the bar, I had already seen something I liked.

The bar though it was inside of the hotel, and the hotel was lit. It was like one of the bar’s in every neighborhood. And you know what comes with those places. Neighborhood people, and neighborhood women! So technically, we were at home here too.

It's 8 of us that went in there. And y'all already know, we're tricking. Well my niggas are anyway.

"What's up boo, how you doing?" shot straight at this thick high yellow chick I'd seen from the outside. She was the reason I came in the bar. She was nice too. And she had a phat ass. I'm trying to bust that bubble!

"I'm fine, and you?" she fixed her eyes on mine.

"I'm good. Yall from around here?"

My homey's had already approached her company of girlfriend's.

"Yes. Born and raised. Where y'all from?"

"We from Philly," I spoke for us. It was obvious we weren't from around here.

"I can tell. Yall dress and talk different. It's cute though," she smiled at me. I knew I was about to bag her.

See, I don't really do the tricking thing. My homey's do. But, If I want a bitch bad enough, I know how to get past the games when I don't have time for all of the wine and dine shit.

As of right now I can tell shorty is feeling me. I can bag her off of the strength of who I am. Just as I normally does.

Rafiq and them are on their normal. I can hear them in the background. "I got three hundred right now, Right now! What's up?" All I know is the first one we find out is going, they on her.

"What y'all doing out here?"

"Tryna have some fun. Shit, we came to party!" I cut the chase.

30 minutes later, I got the light skinned chick I was

talking to on Jariek's bed, in doggy style. Yea, face down, ass up! There was only 4 of them, so we only brung 4 of us. Of course, the 1 I had was the prettiest. And she was the one who'd hollered at the rest of her girlfriends at the bar. I don't know if they'd accepted Rafiq's offer before that.

Rafiq had a slim dark skinned thing. Jariek had this tall thick thing. Sheesh! She was built too!

Ok, so if y'all know me by now; I'm swimming in this pussy. I almost drowned! Hold up bitch; Can't drown in front of the homies! Hell no! Hold on. I'm telling myself as I get in the groove. I got my Timbs on with her ass!

Rafiq is butterball naked on the other bed, piping girly down. He's slow fucking her. I guess he wanted to remember that California sex. The next thing you know, I hear, "Turn over. Get in doggystyle," Rafiq said.

Then, he starts eating the girls ass! Now, ok, the chick did look good, but she's not all of that and she's a stranger! You don't eat no strangers ass! Come on Rafiq! I know before these chick's came into this room, they'd banged about 10 dudes already! I ain't judging, but…? This is All Star weekend. They're trying to get paid, like men are trying to get laid!

"Jariek get down with the program!" Rafiq yelled.

"You know it!" Jariek yell back, and started eating his chicks ass. Did I tell y'all, the girl Jariek was hitting looked just like Oprah? It wasn't her, but she did look like her.

I was appalled! These dizzy ass niggas here! I ain't ever in life fucking women with these niggas again. I'm telling myself.

"Dock! Dock! Dock!" the door to the hotel room

sounded.

"Somebody is knocking on the door," the chick I'm fucking said. "Check the door. Somebody," she added.

Everybody ignored her, and kept right on fucking. It was a small orgy going on. But y'all know me, this little dick is done. I got mines. I'm about to leave anyway. So I answered the door.

It was Indris's sneaky ass. He knew what it was when he'd left us in the bar, so he was doubling back now. Smart move. Just like a 7th Street nigga.

"What nigga?"

"Bone, let me get parts?"

"You got some money?" I whispered to him. I'm about to make some money off of one of these bitches. And I already knew they were going to like him.

"You know it!"

"Aight, Gimme three hundred and you can fuck one of them." I promised Him.

"Here," Indris went right in his pocket and gave me the money. "Yo, don't tell nobody I was in here," he looked at me as he came in. I guess he doesn't want his wife, Joy to find out. She'll kill that nigga! Just like Kelly will kill Jariek. She probably still will when this book comes out! Ha!

I left the hotel room by this time. Saw Nate in the parking lot "T'sss, Indris trickin again," I looked at him.

"Word? Maan, Joy goin kill that nigga!" Nate's eyes grew wide.

I smiled to myself. I was telling on their asses today. They're always telling on me. Yea we're going to see how they like that!

“What room are they in?” Nate perked up. Nate thinks he’s slick he wants parts of the action.

“Eight zero three!” He wanted it, he got it. “Go head Nate, get in there and get you some! Rafiq and Jariek are up there with Indris.”

Here goes Nate again. “WHAT? Kelly goin kill Jariek! And Quilla goin kill Rafiq!” he slammed his hat down on the ground like the news hurt him!

This bul’ is fronting! Hard too! “Nate, Quilla ain’t with Rafiq no more,” I poked at his game, then watched his response.

“Yes she is. He’s still with her. They have a strong bond,” Nate reminded me. He’s still plotting though. I know his ass. He picked his hat up.

“Yea, you’re right about that.”

“That means Rafiq’s new wife is going to kill both Rafiq and Quilla!” Nate walked off, like he was going to go rescue Rafiq from the wrong he was committing. Yea aight.

“Nate, where is your sneaky ass going?”

“I got’s to tell Jariek he’s wrong! That’s wrong!” he kept walking. Determination in his strut.

I laughed. I knew I was right. “Yea, Ok Nate. Your ass is going up there to trick! I ain’t hating. Just make sure you wear a condom!”

Nate stopped mid strut to turn and look at me. “Bone, I don’t wear condoms. I goes straight in raw!”

“Oh yea! Well, you just make sure you don’t ever fuck any bitch I fuck with.” ‘Dirty dick ass nigga,’ I mumbled to myself. Rafiq and them told me what happened when Nate got up there to the room. Smh. Too funny.

***

"DOCK, DOCK, DOCK!"

"DOCK, DOCK, DOCK!" "YO!" Nate was outside of the hotel door he knew Rafiq and the fellas were in. This was after he'd just left me downstairs in the parking lot.

Upstairs, no one is answering the door for Nate, because they don't want him there. See, Nate is the type to do something with you and mention it later on. That wasn't good business.

"YO!" "DOCK, DOCK, DOCK!" Nate knocked harder. He was heated they weren't letting him in. And pretty soon he became irate!

"DOCK, DOCK, DOCK! YO! RAFIQ! INDRIS! JARIEK! Open this door!"

"DOCK! DOCK! DOCK!" he's drawing attention to the room now. Screaming like a mad man in the hallway!

***

In the room, Rafiq had got up to open the door. "Yo chill yo, don't open that door!" Jariek screamed to stop him.

"I got's to! If I don't y'all know he's going to keep banging! This nigga is crazy!" Rafiq ignored Jariek and opened the room door.

Nate walked in slowly. "Fuck is going on up in here?"

"We eating ass!" Jariek flat out told Nate!

"I'm not eating no ass!" Indris defended himself. "These two ass eating nigga's are doing that!" Indris motioned his head at Rafiq and Jariek.

“Oh, that's why this room smells like shit?” Nate was scanning the room. “You’re out of pocket!” Nate told Rafiq. Then looked at Jariek, “ You too!” He didn't say anything to Indris, because Indris would've said something bad to him.

“Man, What do you want?” Rafiq blasted Nate.

Nate spun around and eyed the high yellow chick I was fucking. Rafiq saw him and immediately put his price on her. “Three hundred!”

Still staring at his target, Nate went right into his pocket, and gave Rafiq the money. $300.00 was like the normal price of tricking for them. So Nate had already had it counted out, knowing what he was coming up to their room for! Yea, in the parking lot trying to fake it to me. Hah!

“Take her to the bathroom,” Rafiq advised him, and tried to pass Nate a condom.

Nate screwed his face up. “I don’t do that young bul! I don’t need no condom for this bitch,” he hurried toward the bathroom.

Rafiq followed him. “I might as well give you my money right now,” Rafiq says to her figuring that was his que to dump her on Nate.

The 3 of them make it to the bathroom. “Here,” Rafiq went to hand her his fee for their time and walked away real fast. He was trying to get her.

“Hold on. Yo, this is only fifty dollars,” she stopped at the door of the bathroom.

“That's all I got!” Rafiq lied.

“Make it enough,” she hands Rafiq the money back.

Rafiq went into his pocket. Nate is watching as Rafiq is

digging around the huge knot in his pocket, searching for a small bill. "Here," Rafiq hands her another bill. Nate laughs to himself.

The girl stared at the bill. "Be for real! Ten more dollars? You're crazy! The price is two hundred! Give me my money, or I'm calling my big brother!"

"Take that sixty dollars, or you don't get shit!" Rafiq snap on her.

"Yo, Dawg Just pay for it man. Damn!" Nate jump in. He knew what Rafiq intended to do the whole time. Especially when he'd found out that this girl let Rafiq have his way with her before she got her money.

"You pay for it for me!" Rafiq eyed Nate seriously.

Nate got quiet.

"I got you sis. I'll give you the rest of the money," Jariek cooled the situation down.

See, Rafiq thinks just because he's from 7th Street, that he doesn't have to pay for shit. He's funny. Jariek paid his tab, Rafiq sat there and watched him and Nate just shook his head. "That's why I don't like tricking with Rafiq!" Nate says to Jariek, with Rafiq still standing right there.

Rafiq started laughing! Nate disappeared into the bathroom with the female and didn't come back out until he was done.

That's crazy Rafiq. Think just because you eat all that ass you don't have to pay them tabs. You's a wild bul'!

ITS BONE CRUSHER, BITCH!!!!

CHAPTER 38

Lenny's always telling on us!

Virginia.

Freshly showered, I'm headed to the area of the lot we'd been hanging in. The 1st person I see is Lenny.

"Where were you?"

Something is telling me; Don't tell this clown shit! The reason is because Lenny will tell our girlfriend's everything we would do, when we would all go on trips.

"I was getting dressed nigga!"

"Did you see Rafiq and Jariek?"

Damn, he's digging. "Two hours ago." I feel childish lying to this dude, like he's somebody for me to lie to. But Lenny be on bullshit!

Lenny isn't stupid. He pulls a Chapstick out of his pocket, and rubs it around his lips quickly. His dizzy ass knows something is going on, and he wants parts. I need to get his mind off of them.

"Yo, what's up with ya daughters mother?"

"Which one?" he looked at me. I got him. "The one that changed the locks on you?"

"Yo you remember that?" his eyes grew wide.

"Are you serious? Yea I remember that! Especially after the dude she was fucking jumped through your car window trying to fight you about her! How could I forget that? I ain't goin lie dawg, she did have a phat ass. That was the best girl you've ever had."

"No she wasn't!" Lenny looks at me like I'm crazy.

I'm not about to argue with him. He knows what I'm telling him is true. He just mad because shorty changed the locks on him.

"What's up young bul'?" Jariek is coming toward us smiling.

"What'chu smiling for?" Lenny sharpened his eyes at him. He knows that smile. "I know you didn't do that to Kelly?"

"Do what? I ain't do nothing, ask Bone!" Jariek instantly pulled me in the line of fire with him. Smh!

Lenny whirled his head at me. "I knew you knew w…!" his words were lost in his anger, and he swung on me!

But, y'all know the Bone Crusher got away from his punch and laughed at his hating ass.

"I knew you knew where they was at! You play too much," Lenny's breathing all hard, forcing words out.

At the same time, I see Indris, Nate, and Rafiq are all walking out of the hotel and toward us. Lenny knew us. Like I said, we're all squad and we'd been to plenty of places. Lenny was with us on most of our trips. So he knows when we're smiling, most likely what it's about. Good memories.

"I'm telling! I'm telling!" Lenny's whining.

"Get ya snitch ass outta here!" Rafiq got mad at him.

"Did you tell Lenny what we was doing?" Jariek looked at me.

"Fuck no! You know I ain't do no dumb shit like that! If I would've told Lenny, y'all know he would've went banging on that door for y'all," I looked at Jariek.

Lenny walked off. His mind was made up. He was going to tell our girlfriend's whatever he thought went on inside that hotel.

"You're right Bone. He would've came upstairs. You think he's going to tell Kelly for real?" Jariek got serious.

"Hell yea he's going to tell Kelly! He's going to the hair salon as soon as we land! Kelly is going to fuck you up!"

"No she's not! I run that relationship!" Jariek got tuff.

"Yea aight nigga. If you tell Kelly you fucked that girl, you might get a beat down. But, If You tell her you ate that girl's ass? She's going to kill you!"

Jariek got quiet. He was thinking.

"Do whatever you want, just please don't tell her you ate that bitch ass," I warned my homey.

"You're right Bone. I'm not telling her I did nothing. It's my word against Lenny's. And she's going to believe me over him," Jariek was going over the story he was going to tell his girl.

***

I just thought of something. This isn't a part of the scene above, so bear with me. It's just another 1 of Lenny's stunts.

I remember I'd went on a prom date with another girl, while I was still dealing with Jada.

I'd never been to any kind of prom, and this little bad joint from North Philly named Lil Mia offered me to go And fellas, let me tell y'all, Lil Mia was bad. FOR REAL!

Lil Mia was short. I guess that goes without saying. Right? Well, yea. She was short. With a honey brown complexion, neck length hair that relaxed on her slender shoulders, brown eyes, a perfect nose, and perfectly even white teeth. She was petite. Ebony Magazine model type of petite. With a soft neckline and poise. And yo, I'm telling y'all, Mia turned heads. By both men and women.

I met Lil Mia at Club McDonald on Broad and Diamond street. I was on my Hyaboosa 1200. Her panties must've got soaked at the sight of me on that thing! Because that is what that was. That thing! It was a wrap after that. The woman practically threw her number at me! I'm surprised her panties didn't come with it! I was still awed because like I'd told y'all, she was bad! Once she gave me that number I was down North Philly to see her almost every free moment I had. I could've wife Mia. I swear. Because she was sure enough that material. But like I said I was still dealing with Jada, and I didn't want to hurt Mia. Although I did enjoy myself with her. In more ways than 1.

I was elated when she offered me to her room. Shit, I was too bad to make it to my own high school prom at Bok. So I was about to show off at this prom. I knew that!

My man J..C. had this ill cherry red, almost candy apple red Sl500 convertible Benz coupe. Tan interior, wooden dashboard, and chrome piping going around it, in and out. It was plush! No tints. Tinted windows night fuck up the elegance of a car like that.

Anyway, I took Lil Mia to the prom in that. Plus, I was dressed to kill. Casket Sharp, they call it. Mind y'all, we were still young. I wore a 2 piece black dress suit, with a dark red linen button down collared shirt. Diamond cufflinks, to go in the outer sleeves of my blazer. Which all fell lightly over my black wing tip shoes. Those were the most expensive thing I'd had on. My man, J.C out me on to those. J.C was 1 of the older playa's from our block, and he would show me things from time to time. Once J.C came with that piece to my puzzle, I was straight.

Lil Mia matched me. She'd worn a sheer black gown, that was damn near see through. It was an eye catcher. She'd showed up. I mean, a young man like myself couldn't ask for more.

We'd showed up, and showed off. Overall we just had a ball. Danced, talked, flirted, kissed, hugged, took photos, and did a few more things that us young adults indulged in. It was nice. Real nice.

I'd managed to make it all the way through that night, and into the next few weeks, without Jada finding out that I'd went. And I was still in good with Mia.

All of this brings me to the point I'm getting at. I'd had Lenny with me while I was going to see Jada 1 day. Now me and Jada were beefing about some dumb shit. I can't remember right now. But I do remember this.

"Hold up, lemme shoot by Jada's house right quick. Drop this money off for my child," I'd parked in front of her place. My place. Whatever. "I'll be right back." I'd left Lenny in the car.

2 minutes later, I'm walking back toward my car while Jada's yelling out of the front door, "Fuck you Red Bone!"

"Yea, whatever. Jada!" I shot back as I was opening my car door. As I'm getting in my car, Lenny is trying to get out of my car. Huh? "Lenny, where the. fuck are you going?"

"Hold on right quick," Lenny stops me from reversing. I knew something wasn't right, ·right then and there. I should've left his ass right at Jada's house. Him and his Chapstick!

This man walks up to Jada's mail slot after she slammed the door shut and puts something in the mail slot of her door "Here you go Jada."

As he's walking back to my car, I'm looking at him in complete confusion.

I'd left the photos from me and Mia's Prom night, in the glove compartment of my car. It turns out; that as soon as I'd went to see Jada, Lenny had gone through my shit and found the prom picture!

Now, here was Jada standing in the door holding the prom photo in her hand. "Oh, you went.to a prom mutha fucka? You piece of shit! Don't come home Bone! Stay your ass at that bitch's house!" Jada screams, and then power slammed her front door shut!

I just stared at Lenny for a good minute.

As I've said, that has nothing to do with California. But, I wanted to shed more light on Lenny's miserable ass. So y'all can picture his character as I give y'all our story.

***

Now, back in California, you can see why no one wanted to bring Lenny in our small orgy. Or anything that had to do with women. And look, he was heated we didn't call him! But, he was only heated because now he wouldn't be able to tell our girlfriends any details about the orgy! SMH!

By the time Lenny came back over to us, Karon and Buck Shot 2 more of us from 7th Street, are pulling in the parking lot with some girls I assume are from California.

Lenny is on his bullshit for real now.

"Karon, who's that?" Lenny jumped right on him.

"A friend," Karon mumbled.

"Does Sahida know her?"

Karon just looked at Lenny, and escorted his company into the hotel.

Buck Shot must've told the woman he was with to just stay with him in the car. That was smart. He knew Lenny was going to draw on him.

The girl Buck Shot had in the car with him looked just like Wendy Williams, but was skinny like his wifey, Soni. Buck loves them chicken heads. If Soni knew Buck was cheating she'd be out here on the next plane smoking.

Lenny walked off again. Probably looking for the other homey's to see what they're doing. What he could tell their girlfriends. When Lenny walked off Buck and his company got out of the car and went inside the hotel.

"Aww man! Look at this shit!" Nate said, looking to his right.

"Aww man! Man, come on Nate," Indris walk off and took Nate with him.

"Why did they walk off?" Rafiq looked to his right and saw exactly what they were avoiding. Craig Mack in one of Hoarse's old Coogi sweaters that we'd seen him wearing the day we left Philly to come down here!

Rafiq snapped. "Aww come on maan!" he threw his hand's in the air.

By now, I'm looking at Craig Mack shaking my head.

"Yo Mack! You can't front like that Mack! You can't fake it like that. That's too much! We on the West Side. You know better! Take Hoarse's Coogi sweater off and go put a white T shirt on!" Rafiq commanded him.

"Come out here with that hot ass sweater on. Put a T shirt on or take yo crusty ass back to Philly!" Rafiq went off.

Here goes Craig Mack. "I'm anemic!" he shouted, still strolling like he'd had the response already in his mind. He knew we were going to get his ass. "SEVENTH Street here! SEVENTH Street here!" he yelled his normal shit, holding his jeans by the waist, and stepping like every step he took had at least $15,000 in it. I told y'all how Mack is.

Rafiq was still heated.

Nate was back by now, and he'd heard Mack's excuse. "Get the fuck outta here! ANEMIC! You hear this nigga?" Nate looked at Indris. "It's like a hundred and twenty degrees out this bitch! How can you be anemic in this weather!"

"Yea Mack, you on some bullshit!"

"Yea Mack, fuck outta here with that 1."

Everyone started walking off on Craig Mack.

"Naa, chill yo. I'm for real. I am anemic. I do have thin blood!" he tried getting us to buy his story. Wasn't happening. We knew better. He was about to tarnish our image trying to keep up with the big dogs. "Yo! Where y'all going? Don't leave me. I need a ride!" Mack yelled at us. We kept right on moving.

I'll tell you what though, Craig Mack made it back to Philly. So did we all. Safe and sound.

ITS BONE CRUSHER, BITCH!!!!

CHAPTER 39

Tiffany tried to catch a baller!

7th Street.

Going out with the fellas always had its ups and downs. Although for the most part, we always had fun. Of course I didn't always just go out with the fellas. I took my ladies out too.

I remember when I took Tiffany to the BET Awards down in Los Angeles California. We weren't a couple at the time but that didn't matter. I wanted to go.

"Hello?" she picked up on the second ring.

"I'm going to the BET Awards. I'll be there in a half hour to pick you up. Be ready," I hung up the phone. I didn't ask her. I already knew she would want to come. Tiffany liked a good time too. Why wouldn't she? She knows.

***

A few hours later, I was dressed to kill. Big boy Breightlin watch on, my chipped up 'RB' pendant, some Louie loafers and a casual shirt. That was enough for·me. Showered and dressed, I headed straight for Tiffany's.

"Beep Beep!" Lenny hit the horn, letting Tiffany know we were outside of her house a short while afterward.

The door swung open, and Tiffany came out of the house, STOPPING TRAFFIC! This woman was DRESSED!

Tiffany came out of that house, wearing a dark grey body dress. The material was like spandex. And I told y'all, Tiffany is built. Natural muscles in her legs and calves. Ass phat, and her chest was plump! And Tiffany knew how to walk sexy. I mean she used to throw them hips. She used to walk like she knew she had a phat ass. Yea that's the type of shit that got my attention. That was why I brung her. 1 of the reason's anyway.

A flight fee and some Air miles later, me and Tiffany stepped off of the plane and into California. Yall already know had the window seat!

You know what I did. "TAXeeyy!" I hailed a cab straight to the car rental place again.

20 minutes later we walked in. "Hey Red Bone!" the white bul Mark even remembered me! Shit, he should've. We spent some paper with him the last time we were here.

"What's up Mark!" I remembered him too. They did us well.

"No homeboy's this time? Just you and the lady?" he smiled.

"Yea maan, I'm coolin with my baby mom this time. We need something to show up at these Award's in," I automatically scanned the cars available.

***

90 minutes later, something basic. Chrysler 300.·New series thing. We're on our way to the Kodak Theater on Hollywood Blvd where the BET were being hosted. By Will Smith, and his wife," Jada.

We got a good seat. Thanks to a few bucks and a good name. We were seated a few rows from the stage. Fat Joe was a few people to my right. The female rapper Eve sat a few people to my right. A few actors Jay Z, Free and A.J was right next to me. Pharrell and a couple of Basket Ball stars too. This shit was lit for real!

So anyway, the show starts. Will Smith is doing his thing. "I gotta use the bathroom right quick," Tiffany whispered to me and got up from her seat.

"Aight," I nodded at her. Didn't you just use the bathroom? I'm thinking to myself. Because we'd just left the hotel room. But, whatever Tiffany came back a few minutes later. Show goes on. "Guess who I just seen?" Tiffany tapped me.

"Who?" I hope it ain't no enemy. I don't feel like the drama tonight.

"Apri1 and them!"

"Oh yea? Who she here with?"

"Bill and Lil."

"Oh ok." I nodded. I couldn't hate. They were some true South Philly players. I knew them. I wouldn't go look for them though. I don't do groupie shit. They knew me. Respect shown here, Respect shown, there.

Aight, so another 15 minutes passes. Here goes Tiffany

again.

“I be back, I'm going to the bathroom,” she got up from her seat again!

“Aight.” Again? The fuck wrong with her? I’m thinking.

But, again, whatever.

10 minutes later, Tiffany is back. Mind you, I told y’all Tiffany knows how to throw them hips when she walks. I’m telling y’all she was built like a Russian race horse!

So, every time she got up to leave, the fella’s are looking at her ass bounce. And Tiffany’s throwing it side to side, on purpose! And she had on some skimpy shit! Kitty kat all bulging out the front of her outfit and all that! But I don’t care because she’s not my woman at this point.

Now, the fella’s keep looking back at me, and was exactly what Tiffany wanted!

“I'm going to the bathroom,” this chick said, again!

That’s when it hit me! “This bitch tryna catch!” I looked at her walk away this time. I mean, really studied her. This bitch was throwing that ass! Lol! No she ain’t trying this shit while she’s with me!

That was funny, I couldn’t blame her though. I got her used to fucking with winners.

This time, she was back in 5 minutes. Ha! How Ironic! I had some reality for her ass this time.

“Tiffany, Jay Z don’t want you!” I laughed.

“Shut up!” she laughed back. She knew I caught on to her game.

All that shaking her ass was doing, and Jay ain’t pay her a bit of attention. Bitches is crazy. Bitch, you’re sitting with a winner. And I’m probably the best you’re getting! I thought of saying to her. But, I didn't. I could have though. Fuck she thought she was doing? Better fall her ass back, and enjoy the show. Dizzy bitch.

$$$$$$$$$$

Aight, so the show is over. Tiffany's plan didn't work, so she's walking back to the car, with ME! Ha!

I wanted to laugh at her ass. "Bitch, fuck was you doing? You really was goin leave me for one of them niggas?" I had to ask her. "I mean damn, I got you in the building!" I joked with her. Tiff my peoples, we talk like that.

"I'm saying Red Bone, you got money. But you don't got money like they got money" she joked back. She was right though. Shit, that was entertainment money.

"I'm saying, Jay 2 though ? You kept walking past him though. Ha! That nigga wasn't paying your ass no mind!" I laughed. "You might've got that one bul'. the African dude that played in Barber shop! Or somebody like that. But not no damn Jay! Ha! On some real shit you might've blew ya own shot. And then, they seen you there with another nigga. You trippin!" I shed some light on her then laughed.

"I know right," Tiffany laughed back. "Ssss OwW! Hold on Red Bone, hold on!" Tiffany stopped walking, and held me from walking so I couldn't leave her, and so I could support her while she removed her shoe and rubbed on her toes. "My feet killing me!" she whined.

"Yea, yo ass was doing all of that super model shit. In their strutting ya stuff!" I joked.

"Shut up!" she whined.

All in all we had a good night though. We had to stop a few more times so Tiffany could rub her feet. That's what her ass gets though. Act like the Bone Crusher ain't good enough.

ITS BONE CRUSHER, BITCH!!!!

CHAPTER 40

Toby can't spell

16th and Mckean St. The bar.

It was packed. 7th Street was outside because we were throwing a get together. As usual, we were deep. And cracking jokes.

"Nigga you slow!"

"I ain't slow. I went to Bok!"

"Bone, you ain't go to no damn Bok!"

"Yes I did!" they knew I was lying. But damn them, that's my story, and I'm sticking to it.

Bok, was the vocational school around my way. Everyone knew if you went to Bok, you were smart. If you went to any of the other schools like Furness High, South Philly High, or any of these schools you were the regular simple minded young one. But as I said, Bok was a vocational school. A charter school so to speak. And even if I didn't go to Bok they couldn't prove it!

"You can ask Netta, Bobby, Manny, Martin, AND Tex! Tex was on my basketball team!" I said matter of factly.

"Man I know you Bone! Who you think you talking to?

You went to Furness!" Toby tried to blow my cover. Hating ass nigga.

"Fuck outta here Toby! You got high with Ms. Wanda!"

"Fuck outta here! I ain't know that blunt was laced! That's why you and Wyan was in disability class at the same time! Yall BOTH stupid!"

"Fuck outta here! Matter of fact since I'm so stupid spell kitchen!" I looked at Toby. This is how we kill all of the back and forth shit.

"I know how to spell it. You spell it!" Toby tried to spin it back on me.

"Fuck outta here! I asked you first!" I fired back, folded my arm's across my chest and smirked.

"Fuck outta here! It's K, I, C, H, I" he started stuttering. Yall know we went off as soon as he fucked up.

"You dumb bitch!" 1 of the 7th street girls yelled at Toby.

"You's a dumb ass Toby! Fuck you don't know how to spell kitchen! Fuck are you doing in school?" her friend joined in on Toby.

"Bitch fuck you!" Toby snapped back. "That's why your boyfriend be with Pig in the Hotel!"

Toby knows everyone knew Pig was gay.

"Yea aight nigga. I remember what you did at that pool. Don't get me started!" she glared at Toby.

"Yea aight bitch." Toby turned his head to me. "Bone, see what you started?" he pointed at the chick.

"I ain't start shit! You should know how to spell kitchen!"

"Damn Toby, how the fuck you don't know how to spell kitchen? I mean kitchen though? For real?" my homey Faizon looked at Toby.

"Fuck outta here, I do know how to spell Kit…"

And before Toby could finish his sentence, Meech came out of nowhere, crept up behind him and Boo'yowed Toby right in his ass.

"BOO'YOW BITCH! For not spelling kitchen right," Meech kicked Toby.

"Oh naa, you gotta rumble me now pussy!" Toby went at Meech.

"Oh naa, you gotta rumble me now pussy!" Toby went at Meech.

Yall should've seen this shit! 1st of all, the nigga Meech wasn't down here since Edmond pressed him for that fake Rolex he was wearing. So I don't know where he even came from. But all I seen was his short dark self creep up behind Toby and Boo'yow that nigga.

"Now you wan fight? Suck it up nigga!" Meech laughed at Toby.

Fat Cat, Steph Pokey, J Bird, and Craig Mack are all walking up toward the bar.

"Look at these dirty ass niggas here!" I hear Puerto Rican Rick mumble from the side of me.

"Man, I'm out," another voice came.

"Me too!" another followed.

"Yea, word. Ain't nobody tryna be around no rapist's," Puerto Rican Rick walked off while eyeing J bird in disgust.

That was the end of that bar escapade.

***

Down the block from the bar, I see the young bul Cheese,

lurking like he was up to something. I knew that look. I wore it myself many times.

Now, we drove past Cheese on our way home. When I eyed him, he'd turned his face. But, I knew that look in his eyes. I knew what I'd seen.

***

"Yo. Hello?" I answered my phone a few hours later.

"Yo, Cheese just robbed the Bul' Slick!" Dor came over my line. This was later on that night after we'd left the bar. I wasn't surprised. "Yea? When?"

"Like five minutes ago yo! Took all of his shit and everything! Made the young Bul take off his jacket, his shoes, and his socks! Made him walk home. Then he kicked J Brid in his ass and told him to leave them kids alone! This nigga Cheese was going crazy out there!"

"What J Bird do?"

"He ain't do shit! You know J Bird ain't doing nothing aggressive. J Bird cold bitch." Dor explained what I already knew.

"Yea I believe you though. I seen Cheese down there lurking, looking like he was waiting on a lick." Cheese knew better than to try that shit while we were still there.

"Yo, I'ma hit you later. I just wanted to give you the scoop."

"Yea, good looking." I hung up.

Damn. Shit is about to get crazy. I knew it was. And that very next day, it did.

CHAPTER 41

Porsha walked 2 miles, for $2.00

7th Street.

"Two dollars?" I screwed my face up. This bitch is always asking me for some damn two dollars. "I know you ain't walk your ass all of the way up here to ask me for no damn two dollars!" I looked at her.

Hold on visualize this. It's a beautiful day in the hood. The block is popping, the hustlers are shooting dice, the kids are jumping rope playing hopscotch, riding bikes. The normal. It's a lovely day. And here she comes with this damn $2.00!

"Yea I walked up here for that! Me and Cherika just wanna get some rice and gravy from the Chinese store," Porsha stood in front of me bargaining for her and Cherika.

Cherika went off to bother Herbie Luv bug. Seconds later, he was chasing her past me! For a second anyway.

Then all I heard was "Ahh!" I looked and saw Cherika laying in 1 of the oil spills behind a parked car.

"Ha!" the whole block went off laughing at her.

BrandyWine and Gary Akhee were running a dice game

over on the other side of the block. And of course, they were arguing.

"Who laid that ten?"

"You laid that ten!" I heard someone.

"You laid that ten dollars! You laid that! I rolled three, I brung it back, and you betted that ten dollars. I couldn't roll it again!"

"Oh. Yea, you're right! I did say that. You can roll it again. Now! What you betting nigga?" Brandywine, argued.

"Aight! Bet that beat up ass Oldsmobile you still driving around nigga!" Gary Akhee shot back

These 2 old heads stayed going at it. They were partners.

"Aight, bet it! Bet it against that old ass Bike you got? BrandyWine got in Gary Akhee's·face.

BrandyWine knew Gary Akhee's bike was his favorite possession, so he was threatening it. He's funny.

Gary Akhee got quiet. "I can't do that. I can't bet my baby," he shook his head. "Let's go bet Lil Zeke for his money?" He suggested to BrandyWine.

"Aight yea." BrandyWine looked right for Zeke. "Ay ZEKE. ZEKE come here Lil homey. You wanna go grab Saphia some clothes?" he began his hustlers pitch.

It was at that moment, the events of the day changed.

***

"Don't move PUSSY!" was all we'd heard. The sound of threat in a familiar voice was·what·grabbed our attention.

"Oh shit." came a few whispers. It was Slick. The young Bul' Cheese had just robbed the day before. He'd had

Cheese at gunpoint with his Glock Nine pointed clean at his face.

By the time we'd realized what was going on, it was too far into wherever the scene of the movie was going.

See, I knew it was going to be some shit. I know Cheese is a goon. Cheese was the type that will shoot a block up; then stand right there like he was daring someone to do something about it!

But, what Cheese didn't know was Slick was the same exact way. And he was up and coming. So yea, I knew Cheese would show his face. And I knew Slick would be right there waiting on him. Cheese was on the sidewalk negotiating a drug sale.

Slick had been in the alley way of an abandoned house, waiting for Cheese to come around 7th Street. Now Cheese had to face what he had coming.

By now, my block is so quiet you can literally hear a pin drop. All eyes are on Cheese and Slick. And Slick has his gun dead locked on his target, Cheese.

Cheese reacted fast, "Hold! Come here nigga!" he snatched the crack head he was negotiating the drug sale with as a shield. Now, it is his face staring down the barrel of Slick's finger sized gun.

Najee, immediately plead for his life. "HOLD! HOLD! HOLD on maan! I don't got nothing to do with this shit maan! All I wanna do, is ride my bike out North Philly, and get my dope! That's All I·wanna do. Please don't put me in y'all's shit!" Najee begged.

It was clear. All Najee wanted to-do was get high.

Slick wasn't hearing him. Neither was Cheese. Slick just

kept his gun aimed at Cheese and Cheese kept Najee in front of Slick's gun.

"Aww come on man!" Najee plead. "I got somebody in my chair! I got dirty ass Craig Mack in my chair!" Najee whined.

Smh! NOW he cares he got somebody in his chair. He's funny. He does that all the time leave niggas in his chair while he creeps off to go and get high. Najee will leave you in that chair with a half of a haircut while he creep's down North Philly to get some dope. I know this for a fact, because he did it to ME!

Najee had me in that chair for almost 2 hours 1 day, with half of my haircut! He's always doing that. So I know he isn't lying. But NOW he cares. Ha! Yea, If a gun was pointed at me I guess I would too!

Najee's pleas were ignored. Slick aimed at his right shoulder. Cheese moved Najee there. Slick aimed at Cheese's left shoulder. Cheese moved Najee there. Slick continued to aim for a lace to shoot Cheese. Cheese moved Najee wherever Slick aimed his barrel.

Cheese was determined to live. Slick, however was more determined for him to die. The look in his eyes says he doesn't want to shoot Najee to get to Cheese, but his patience was growing thin with aiming his gun around Najee.

"Yo Chill with that shit man! Come on man the kids are out here!" 1 of our old head's yelled.

That was Najee's signal. "Chill man! STOP! CHILL! he plead.

By now the crowd had grown, and guess who appeared out of nowhere?

Pugie, and another rat, Petey Gun! Yup! These niggas showed up to get some information. Smh! 1 of them is going to tell the cops about this.

None of that mattered to Slick. Revenge was on his face, and he was now at his boiling point. Then suddenly, he snapped.

CHAPTER 42

Life or Death for Cheese

7th St.

"Let him go" Slick stepped closer, his gun still aimed.

"Put the gun down!" Cheese demanded, holding Najee tightly.

"Let me go man!" a bead of sweat trickled down Najee's face as he plead for his life.

Slick is massaging the handle of the gun. I could almost literally see his index finger itching to squeeze the trigger. Najee was truly innocent. The bullet wasn't meant for hi. But in this case the innocent crossed paths with the guilty. A deed was done, and a choice had to be made. Slick chose.

Najee saw the decision in his eyes. "Come ON MAN! DON'T SHOOT ME, I'm on DOPE!"

'POP!' Slick squeezed the trigger over Najee's words.

***

"AHHHH!" Najee let out as a shell the size of a fingertip ripped through his shoulder, immediately opening his collar bone.

I watched the bullet go in through his collar bone and come out his back, inches away from Cheese, who was still holding him from behind. Cheese, knew, it wasn't only serious, it was dead serious. He'd held on to Najee, still.

Now it was Life or Death for Najee knowing Slick was willing to kill him to get his revenge on Cheese. Najee began squirming to free himself from Cheese's grip.

"Let me GO man!"

"MGH!" Cheese forcefully threw Najee to his left. He realized he shouldn't use his energy to hold Najee's life trying to protect his own. He had to make a run for it. Bad move. His back, becomes fully exposed to Slick.

Slick, took aim. POP! POP! POP! POP! POP! POP! POP! POP! POP! shots tore off.

Cheese made it maybe two steps away from Slick before his back was riddled with bullets. His 3rd step was a wobble, by his 4th step, he was down. Rolling over on his back, he looked his killer in his eyes. Slick stood over him, and finished taking all of his sweet revenge on Cheese.

POP! POP! POP! POP! POP! POP! POP! POP! POP!

Shell after shell sank into Cheese's chest.

'CLICKA! CLICKA! CLICKA!' the empty gun sat back.

Cheese stared off into a sky of emptiness… Slick stared back into his dead eyes… Done.

Finally satisfied, Slick tucked the gun away and ran back into the alley-way he'd emerged from.

***

"I'm HIT! I'm HIT!" I heard Najee in the background.

I turned my head to see him holding his shoulder, gasping for air like HE was the one dying! Smh.

"NAJEE, come here Najee!" I called him over to me. All he wanted was a care package. Some 'get-high'. I had him. We didn't need him complaining.

***

"Damn man, that's crazy..."

"Yea, that was crazy."

A crowd had begun to form around Cheese's dead body... Soon after, the Ambulance came to the scene with the Police.

CHAPTER 43

Slick got his revenge

7th St.

“Everyone, PLEASE, step AWAY from the SCENE, so that WE can do our job,” one policeman cleared the crowd. Other officers began to set out the yellow cones next to Slick’s gun casings.

“That’s a shame...”

“That was crazy.”

“I know right?” voices were heard as people backed away from Cheese’s corpse.

"What is HE doing over there?”

“Who?”

“HIM!” Ms. Wanda pointed. The tip of her finger was on Pugie.

Pugie, was in the middle of everything. We know what he was trying to do. Ratting ass.

“What’chu doing over there Pugie?”

Pugie ignored Ms. Wanda, and kept his thumb in his mouth, and stood right on the corner trying to gain as much information as he could. Smh.

Somewhere along the line, another argument broke out, from among us within the commotion of the crowd. Evidently a few of us held different stands on the event. This difference, would bring on another monster.

***

"He didn't have to do that young bul' like that! Over some damn money. That's the problem with the young nigga's!" Puerto Rican Rick was going off glaring at one of the young bul's standing on the block

Faizon was from 7th Street. He wasn't your typical young bul'. Faizon was a good dude. That's my man Rafiq's little brother. Faizon barely got into beef. But when he did, he handled it. Puerto Rican Rick knew this about Faizon. However, Faizon was part of the young crowd this act was attached to. And he was the one standing there right then.

"What'chu looking at ME for, I ain't do that shit!?"

"Ya BOYS did it though! Y'all ALWAYS do that shit. Come around here fucking up money. Now, we goin draw all kinds of heat through here and ain't nobody going to be able to eat!" Puerto Rican Rick snapped, logically.

"You got a point, but money ain't everything. Da fuck. Y'all act like y'all ain't have to put no work in! Y'all had to lay a man down to get some ground around here before. How da fuck else did y'all earn that respect? Fuck you talking 'bout!" Faizon snapped.

I understood him. Here, a man he knew lay dead. Killed by one of his men, for something money couldn't buy... Respect.

"You act like Slick was wrong!? Fuck outta here. THAT man was wrong! Made my boy walk home with damn near no clothes on. That man got EXACTLY what he deserved," Faizon added defensively.

"Old head get the FUCK outta here, we. Ain't tryna hear that shit!" Chris another young bul' jumped in.

Its 'HIGH Tide' all over the block now... A few people are upset Cheese lay dead. Others upset that Slick did the hit. Others are hurt by the whole fiasco. Me, stuck in the middle of the heat. Puerto Rican Rick and them are my squad. The fucked up part of it all was that I understood both arguments. In the end, I never thought this whole thing would get as heated as it was about to.

"FUCK you MEAN you ain't tryna hear that shit?!"

"YOU heard me! I ain't stutter!" Chris eyed Puerto Rican Rick. Waiting for him to move. Flinch, jump, reach. Anything.

Puerto Rican Rick wasn't a bitch... Guess what he did? Reach!

As soon as Puerto Rican Rick reached it was on... AGAIN!

'POP! POP! POP! POP! POP!'

'BOOM! BOOM! BOOM!" BOOM!'

'POOM! POOM! POOM! POOM! POOM! POOM!' all kinda shots took off at one another. From just a few feet away!

Of-course, by this time the police and paramedics had picked up the body and left the scene. Police didn't even try to ask any questions. they knew they weren't getting any answers or leads to help crack the case. Not from us anyway.

So, now, a whole OTHER war took off. The younger men·, against the few of us a bit older than them. And from this point, it was a little too late to talk this out over some weed, or night of drinks.

***

(Later that night.)

The shooting ceased, at least for the moment… Me and a few of my boys are on the block.

"Yo, I KNOW that ain't Najee's dope fiening ass?" Rafiq was looking up the other side of our block.

I turned my head in the direction Rafiq was facing… Yep, it was Najee alright… We knew him by that famous pedal bike… "Yea that's Najee crazy ass!"

"I knew that was him. That man is wild!" Rafiq laughed.

Najee was in his normal routine. On his bike ride all the way up to North Philly. He's pedaling as hard as he can, and as fast as he could. With his shoulder brace strapped around his upper body. His forearm lay diagonally across his chest, protecting the shoulder he was shot in. His speed told us he was on his way to get his dope.

I could see his wound didn't slow him down a bit. The reflectors on his bike pedals were moving too fast!

"DAMN that dope must be good!" I laughed.

"FUCK yea... Make a handicapped nigga go to the other side of TOWN to get that shit? It MUST be good! Rafiq laughed with me.

These fiends are crazy...

The shoot outs went on for a few days... People were hit, blood was shed. Revenge was sought, and finally peace was made. But not before Slick was gunned down. Slick had been gunned down in front of his mother, and his only daughter the day before we'd ended the beef. His killer still hasn't been found.

A few of the brothers and myself finally got around to the talk we all needed to have. We got the men together, and met at Lenny's hair salon 'Skies The Limit', a few days after Slick's funeral.

Keep in mind reader that I mentioned something is always going down on 7th Street. What we didn't know was ending this beef would take more effort than we knew. Mainly because the powers that be were out of our control. Police had already began to build their cases…

CHAPTER 44

Old-head's vs Young-buls.

Skies the limit-7th St.

Pugie ain't·see y'all come in here did he!?" Lenny looked at us as soon as we came through the shop's door.

"Naa man. Only nigga I seen was Toby's brother, crusty ass Doc! Smh. Out there geeking for a hit "

"Yea. Probably out there selling them dummies. One of them smoker's goin kill his ass for selling that soap one day ... I don't know what I'ma do with them two. Toby's shitting in pools, and he's selling soap! Smh!" Lenny shook his head.

"Who you telling?" I agreed with him.

Doc stayed selling bags of fake cocaine. It was his main hustle. It's how he fed his family. The rest of us older brothers filled into the salon, along with a few of the younger men. We weren't really that much older,· just older than. most of them. They were as young as 14 years old. Babies... So we had to give them the game. And it was time for them to accept if from us.·

***

"Aight fellas, we gotta end this war. It's too many bodies dropping. That's what got this war started. A body we didn't want to see drop, got dropped That boy was a kid man. And he was killed by another kid I got kids around here. A lot of us do. And I don't wanna see one of our kids get hit by one of these bullets we throwing around at each other," Puerto Rican Rick started it off.

Him, and Faizon were standing in the center of the salon. So was Chris. More of us waited outside for whatever. This could go anywhere and we knew it.

"Yea, I agree man. I understand what you were saying that day. I just wasn't trying to hear it. It was bad timing. But I feel you. Shit, I got two kids myself," Faizon spoke.

"Yea, it was just bad timing man. That's all," Chris chimed in.

Outside, a crowd was growing. News traveled the 'hood pretty fast about us meeting at Lenny's shop to cease the war that broke out among us. Soon, almost every face we knew we saw outside of Lenny's shop. The police eventually came... Not just the police, a Detective.

***

"What's going on fella's..." the detective came in wearing a smirk, four other police followed behind him into Lenny's shop.

"Fuck y'all want?" Rafiq spoke for the room. Everyone else was silent, eying the blue suits...

'Aww, shit...' The first thing I noticed was the photo in his hand... I knew exactly what that meant. They were looking for someone…

The entire shop is quiet. We don't know what these cops want. Cheese is dead, Slick is dead, a few more people got hit, and are in critical condition. And more than likely we are all in Lenny's salon right now with dirty guns on us. Or, guns period. Yea, we'd come to dead the beef, but, I knew how we got down... With these cops walking in the shop, we knew it wasn't a good thing. Especially if they wanted anything to do with the mayhem we'd unleashed on one another the past few days.

We were all still silent. The officers scanned the room, like there was a face they knew they were looking for... And, it was.

"THERE he is sir, right there!" One of them yelled pointing toward the back of the shop.

"FREEZE! DON'T MOVE! DON'T, MOVE!" the officer standing next to the Detective drew his firearm, and aimed it at the man his comrade was focused on. That, drew heat.

"HOLD UP! Fuck y'all pulling out guns for!?" someone shouted from within the shop.

"Yea! Fuck is that about!? Ain't nobody threatening y'all?!" another voice shouted.

It's a known fact that the police out here in Philadelphia will shoot, and kill civilians. We weren't having that.

"Calm down, calm down. Everyone remain calm... We have a Warrant for George, and we want to make this as smooth as we can. We don't want anyone getting hurt," the Detective tried to reassure us.

Meanwhile, his men proceeded toward the back of the

shop to arrest George... Damn, I hope it isn't about what I'm thinking. From long ago.

CHAPTER 45

I tried to blow his head off

8 months ago,
7th St.

"What!? He told y'all, y'all can't hustle out here?"

"Yea. He told me Khalifa, AND Craig-Mack that!" Markeem explained to me.

Hmh! I don't know WHO the fuck Petey Gun think's he is, but I don't like it... "Aight, y'all sit here for a second, I'll be back. Where is Petey Gun?... on the block?"

"Yea."

"Cool. I'll, be back," I walked off heated.

I don't know where the fuck Petey Gun got the nerve to tell nigga's they couldn't hustle on 7th street, but I had something for his ass.

See, Petey Gun is a gun... I can't take that from him. He was still living off of the fear he'd created in people from him shooting the bul' Kareem in his face while he was in the Chinese store playing the video game. Petey Gun walked right up behind him and almost blew his cheek out. Well, actually he did blow his cheek out.

But, fuck that. He is from 7th street, but he don't belong telling no 7th street niggas that they can't hustle out here... What?! Okay, time for us to talk...

As soon as I got on the block, I spotted Petey Gun leaning on the pay phone in front of the cleaning store I'd just bought. It was right on 7th street, and this was before I turned that old cleaning store into my joint, 'REDBONE'S Restaurant'... Yea, Philly nigga... Y'all know me.

But anyway, I'm creeping on Petey Gun while he's still on the phone… I got something nice for his ass...

A few weeks ago Petey Gun was at war with some people. He'd been shot up really bad. So bad that when the ambulance got there, they had considered him dead, and placed him in a body bag, zipped him up, and carried him on his way to the coroner!

Petey Gun fought his way out of the bag! That's how they'd discovered he was alive! And this, was AFTER he'd shot Kareem in his face. So he was playing like he was Super Man. Though I knew the sound of those shots still haunted him. And he was about to get a rude awakening as a reminder of what could happen to him again...

I slid the M-80 by his foot while he was still on the payphone. He didn't hear me creeping, and he's relaxed like he had shit in control. Wrong move. I lit the M-80

'BOOM!!!' it went off.

"WHOA!" Petey Gun immediately jumped and ducked behind the payphone. Then looked around… his eyes landed on me. I stood there eying him.

"What the fuck you do that for?"

"Fuck you ·telling nigga's they can't get money out here for?"

"I'M PETEY GUN, nigga!" he got in my face.

"And I'M BONE CRUSHER, nigga!" I got in his face.

As soon as I reached for my gun, Petey Gun reached for his....

CHAPTER 46

George went down

'POP! POP! POP! POP! POP! POP! POP! POP! POP! POP!' we heard shots. But they weren't from Petey Gun's gun or mine.

"Da fuck?" me and Petey Gun both whirled around looking behind me in the direction the shots were coming from.

We see our homey George, in the middle of 7th Street letting off every shell in his gun.

Okay, so while me and Petey Gun were arguing, I'd overheard another argument going on with George, and whoever else....

"Yea, WE the REAL Seventh street! Yea! Y'all nigga's know what it is out here..."

I caught pieces of someone saying. I remember looking around, and quickly seeing it was the Chinese bul's from down the other side of 7th St. Those boys, were into gang banging and a world of other things we didn't do down my end. But, we did do things, they weren't doing as well... Y'all already know what I'M talking about... We got that bread. Yea screw all of that other shit. They usually stayed down on their end with the bullshit. I. mean, they weren't soft, pussies, or nothing like it. I think they called themselves 'Red Dragons' or something like that…? And they were serious about it.

The thing about that, was we were 7th street. Everyone knew us. We, were serious about our thing. They knew that. I guess it came time for them to be reminded...

"Yea AIGHT! Y'all better get the FUCK from around here with that shit!" George was head first in keeping them in check.

I'm hearing the squabble take place but think nothing of it. Mind you there's always something going on down 7th street so I don't pay them any real attention. I'm busy with Petey Gun's tough ass. The next thing you know, I hear the cannon going off... And I see George in the middle of the street DUMPING rounds out of his handgun.

"AHHH!"

"Oh my God!"

"They SHOOTING!"

"GET in the house!"

People are screaming, running, ducking behind cars and trying to hide. It was crazy…

I looked back at Petey Gun... (Gotta keep your eyes on that nigga) and he's hauling ass to his car! I laughed... His ass ain't that tough! After he got in his car, he looked around and made sure he took in the scenery. I watched him look around all crazy, but I ain't think nothing of that either... I was trying to get away from that scene shit was hot.

I left within that next 10 minutes… And as I was driving

down Mckean Street away from the shooting, guess who was walking back the other way, toward the shooting… With a pencil and piece of paper, prepared to take some notes... PUGIE!

Smh! THESE niggas!

CHAPTER 47

9 months later…

9 months later...

A LOT of us got ·booked that day, but. I'll give y'all this 1st, Damn near the whole 7th Street was packed in room 108, at the Courthouse on 13th and Filbert. Police charged George· with murder after they arrested him in Lenny's shop. This was his preliminary hearing.

"I hope George beat this shit," Indris tapped me.

"Yea I hope so too. Shit he should. They don't got the main witness," I eyed him knowingly.

Everyone knew the main witness was Pugie. Well, who we thought it was anyway. And if he was the witness, he wouldn't be attending this hearing.

***

"AAGGGHHHH! Come ON man! I ain't TELL on George man! He's from Seventh Street! I'M from Seventh Street! I wouldn't do no shit like that!"

"SHUT ya bitch ass up nigga!" P.G. stood over him, adrenalin filled his veins as he thought of what he had in store for Pugie…

"Come on man, I been here for TWO day's, TIED UP, with no clothes on! Come on man. I did my dirt, but I'm a Seventh Street nigga. Don't do a Seventh street nigga like this maan, come on P.G.!!" Pugie begged.

"SHUT THE FUCK UP!" P.G. snapped... "We let ya bitch ass live long enough around here, doing ya bullshit. Now, you done fucked up... Got my man on a body... A body…?" P.G. looked at him with rage in his eyes... "A body huh...? You goin send that man away forever, huh?" he looked at him deeply. His jaw muscles clenching tighter...

"WHAT'chu doing man? What'chu DOING?" Pugie seen the look in his eyes as P.G. reached for his foot.

"Shut'cha bitch ass up!" P.G. ignored Pugie's cries, and placed the teeth of the wire cutters against his right pinky toe…

Pugie is helpless... And he had no one to call, for help. He had now, become a hostage to his own ways… That, came at a bitter price...

***

"Yea, they definitely don't have the main witness," Indris eyed me back.

George looked back at us from the defendant's seat. His dark blue prison issued clothing hung loose on his frail limbs. HE nods... His own way of thanking us for our support. I nodded back... "I got you!" I silently mouthed to him. My way of telling him that Pugie would not be joining us here in, this courtroom today, sadly... I smiled.

George relaxed... That was all he needed to hear. He crouched down into his seat and placed his leg over his lap. A smile came to his face.

"SSHhh," the courtroom hushed as the Judge walked in.

"All RISE," the man spoke the word's... Court, was now in session.

***

"AGGHHH! COME on man! That's my TOE!" Pugie stared at his pinky toe, severed from his foot, and laying in a small pool of its own growing puddle of blood... "I keep telling you man, I didn't GO to the cops for that case they got George on! Somebody ELSE did!"

P.G. snickered... "I knew you was going to mention somebody else. Ya bitch ass can't ever just wear your own weight, can you?" he chuckled again, and placed the bloody blade of the wire cutters to the next toe on Pugie's same foot.

Pugie's foot shook in agony of the pain it knew was coming. His toes wiggled... "COME on MAN! I SWEAR I ain't tell on George!" Pugie pleaded.

P.G. chuckled again. He wasn't hearing any of it. In fact, his cries were music to P.G.'s ears. P.G. had been waiting to get at Pugie. We'd kept him off of Pugie, for a few reasons. When it came to George, we unleashed him to a desire he'd long yearned for.

Pugie, watched helplessly as P.G. applied his strength to the blade of the tool. His mouth opened in horror.

CHAPTER 48

They don't have the main witness

30 minutes later.

George is slouched in his seat in good spirits. It looked promising for him. Until the D.A. pulled out their secrets.

"Your Honor, I would like to move for a dismissal on behalf of the defendant... There is no proof of the defendant being the gun man in the shooting, NONE of the shells found at the scene have his fingerprints, AND there are no witnesses!!!" George's attorney flexed.

"HELL yea!"

"It's OVER!"

"It's a WRAP!" a few of our voices went off in the courtroom.

"Ok, seeing that there is astounding evidence in your client's favor..." The Judge began pondering... "Unless the D.A. has anything else to say..." he gave them one last chance.

"I DO your Honor! The plaintiff wishes to call to the stand its eye witness," the D.A. dropped on us.

The courtroom instantly went silent, and all eyes fell on me!

"I thought you got the nigga!" George's eyes said.

"I DID! I got that nigga tied up in the fucking basement! I don't know WHO the fuck THEY talking about!??" I wanted to shout at George.

And for the moment, we all sat in shock... If it wasn't Pugie, then who was it…?

The whole courtroom was dead silent as the side door swung open, and the bailiff escorted in some goofy looking dude I didn't recognize at first. This dude was a straight meatball! A CLOWN! Rocking a red Fubu hat! Some red shades, a blue college jersey, and some yellow pants! His hat was cocked to the side, and he was diddy bopping like he was cool! Y'all shoulda seen this shit... Fuck this nigga think HE is!?

"Remove your glasses please," the Judge ordered after he was sworn in, and seated in the witness chair.

That goofy ass Fubu hat he was wearing he had already taken off. He looked familiar. But as soon as the glasses came off of his face, I recognized him instantly... So did the courtroom. They went, OFF!!!

"OHH SHIT!"

"YOU SERIOUS NIGGA?!!"

"LOOK at THIS nigga!?" everyone is pointing, yelling, screaming and some MORE shit! 7th street went CRAZY in that room.

It was COMPLETE surprise... A shock... His eyes locked

on mines and mine locked into his... I couldn't believe it. Y'ALL won't either... I was staring into the eyes, of what used to be a respected 7th street killer... PETEY -Fucking-GUN!

***

"COME on Man! I SWEAR I did not TELL on George MAN!!!" Pugie was pleading for his big toe.

It was the only toe he had left on that foot. The pool of blood beneath the foot had now become a puddle. His other toes lay in it. P.G. knelt down in Pugie's blood holding the work tool. Pugie's toe wiggled in fear of more pain....

P.G. chuckled to himself... He had Pugie ALL to himself, and he never liked him in the first place. He had been given instructions not to kill Pugie. Only to torture him. Grabbing the tool again, he focused on Pugie's last toe...

Pugie went off... "NO NO Nooo No NO! PLEASE man, come on man! Don't do it... I'll do anything... ANYTHING!!! Ask Pig!... They don't call me 'Butter Pecan' for nothing man...I'll do you right!" Pugie cried.

P.G.'s eyed turned darker... "WHAT the FUCK you just say to me?!"

"I'll do ANYTHING man, ANYTHING! Just don't cut my last toe off P.G. PLEASE!" Pugie's bitching.

His mind is made up... Pugie didn't deserve that last toe, or any of the toes on his other foot. Didn't matter how much he cried. It was vain. P.G. placed the blade of the tool against Pugie's bloody big toe... His eyes focused in, he grins.

***

“Yo, what the FUCK!” P.G. answered his phone, pissed. He'd been ignoring it for a reason. Too much fun with the task at hand. As always, somebody had to mess things up.... “WHO the fuck is this?!!” he snapped.

“It’s BONE Crusher,” I shot back from the other end of the phone. “Sorry to spoil the fun homey, but it ain’t Pugie!”

“What you MEAN it AIN’T Pugie? !It IS Pugie!”

“NO, it's not... It’s THIS. nigga, Petey, fucking, GUN! He's in there right now telling everything!”

"WHAT!!? Are you SERIOUS Bone?” P.G. was heartbroken.

“Would I call just to spoil the fun?”

“Man DAAMNN Maaan! Da FUCK! THIS nigga is ALWAY’S getting saved!” P.G looked up at Pugie.

“Come on maan, just let me go! I ain't DO that shit!” Pugie still pleaded. His body was sweating and trembling.

“I know you didn’t just shit on yourself...? I KNOW you didn’t just do some nasty, coward, cold bitch shit like that...!? I know you didn’t?” P.G. sniffed, checking his senses then turned his eyes to Pugie.

“Man let me GO mann, PLEASE!” tears fell from Pugie’s face.

“Yea P.G., let the nigga go. But, make him understand this ain't no fucking game,” I advised him, knowing P.G. was likely to kill him anyway.

“I know just the thing, listen to this...”·P.G. grinned happy to go a step further with his fun.

He placed the phone on speaker, laid it on the floor behind the wooden chair Pugie sat in, and grabbed the wire cutters by both hands... The foul stench of bodily waist and plasma filled his nose again. He ignored it and squeezed the device on Pugie's last toe with all of his might.

"NOOOOOO!!!!" Pugie screamed at the top of his voice box as he felt the dirty blade slice through his skin, veins, and bone.

On the other end of the phone, I could hear the sound of Pugie's toe being severed... So sad. A smile came across my face.

***

"ORDER in the COURT! ORDER in the COURT!"

'BANG! BANG! BANG!' the Judged tried to control the commotion 7th Street had been making since Petey Punk Ass Gun walked out in the courtroom to testify against George.

George looked back at me again, for the 5th time 'AWE' on his face. I knew what he felt... Petey Gun, could bury him. I felt his pain. I empathized with him... Too much to see. I shut my eye lids, and rubbed my brow's with my thumb and. index finger...Shit just got deep.

"State your name for the court please?"

"They call me Petey Gun in the streets," this nigga told the court like he was tough. And had the nerve to stare at me, like he still had that Gorilla in him.

"Is this nigga serious? Can't wait till I catch his bitch ass out here! I'ma push his wig smooth back!" I'm saying to myself. And Petey Gun knows it!... Don't matter though. He's a dead man walking.

Anyway, the Judge made him state his real name, and he told...Y'all should've heard this nigga 20 minutes later, telling EVERY fucking thing!

"Yea, and that's when George came out from behind Bone Crusher's Benz and started bussin' at them dudes man! He ain't have to do that to them bul's man. They was good dudes man...Good dudes. George emptied the WHOLE clip at them bul's too! Ask Bone Crusher, he was there. That was the day I told the detective about. I was in front of his store on the payphone when he tried to blow my foot off!"·Petey Gun looked at me with his 'tough guy' look.

"And was Mr. Bone Crusher the only other witness?"

"Maan the whole Seventh Street was out there! That was the same day Rafiq ate that girl ass behind that corner store... Indris was back there with him. They were tricking!"

"OBJECTION you honor, this is all semantics."

"SUSTAINED... Mr. Petey, can you please state the facts only relevant to the case in question please?" the Judge ordered.

"Yes Ma'am... And can I have some water please?"

"Stop TALKING so much you won't need none!" one of my homies yelled. Sounded like Herbie-Luv Bug. Or Buck-Shot.·

"ORDER in the COURT!" Judge snapped... "One more outburst like that and you will be held in contempt of court!" she threatened.

***

"GET ya BITCH ass out!" P.G. ordered a naked Pugie.

It was snowing, and chilling cold. P.G. drove to the Walt Whitman Bridge I-95 inter-pass and parked in the darkest part.

"Come on man you see I ain't do it. Why you goin do me

like this?" Pugie bitched.

His hands were tied together, and so were his feet... You can imagine him, trying to limp because of his fresh wounds. Hilarious! From what I heard P.G. ignored him, and got back into his truck. Angry he had been robbed of his yearning to kill Pugie. He shut the door, and pulls off.

"HOW I'MA GET HOME!!!?" Pugie yelled at the screeching vehicle.

***

Back in the court house, Petey Gun had given well enough evidence for the judge to bound the case over for trial. There was nothing we would be able to do.

In the weeks to come, Petey Gun hid out somewhere. Very well, I say with much knowledge... (We couldn't find that nigga NO WHERE!) He appeared back in America in time for George's trial… Smh!

I'll tell y'all about that outcome, in part two of this Memoire... I had to make a Part two... Too much to tell.

ITS BONE CRUSHER, BITCH!!!!

CHAPTER 49

George got a thong on…? Naa…

7th St.

Fast forward. 8 months later, we're in Lenny's hair salon trying to dead the beef we had going on before another body was dropped, and that's when the cops strolled in.

"Fuck yall want?" Rafiq addressed them.

I saw the piece of paper the detective was holding and automatically knew they were looking for someone. Poop, came to the head of my exit. I squirmed in my seat fighting to hold it in me. I cannot shit on myself in front of these niggas, Noooo, NO!

You're probably laughing. It's cool. It might be funny right now. But at that time, I was involved in enough shit to get LIFE if that piece of paper the detective was holding had my name on it. I'm telling yall now; I was SHOOK! I sat myself in that chair with my butt muscles clenched as tight as I could hold them.

Keep in mind, cops don't come to your neck of the woods looking for someone who has a gun charge. Some fines, or court cost. Maybe some child support issues. Dumb shit.

When they come with a WARRANT! It's serious! Me knowing the shit I was involved in, what?

I remember a bead of sweat trickling down my face. There were people outside everywhere. The hair salon is packed, I got my gun on me. It was just wild. I just knew they were coming for me.

"There he is Sir!" 1 of the detective men yelled.

As soon as the rookie cop pointed in my direction, I turned my head and acted like I was looking out of the window. 'Don't look back. Don't look back.' I kept saying to myself. That wasn't realistic I had to! So I did and saw the cop walking toward me. Damn! It's over. Na, it can't be over. It can't be. 'Oh Allah! If you let me out of this, I swear, I will go to Jumu'ah every Friday from now on. I'll stop treating Porsha and Tiffany the way I do, and I PROMISE to…" I began to pray.

Meanwhile, the cops are still focused on their target. "FREEZE! DON'T MOVE! DON'T MOVE!" the officer next to the detective drew his service weapon, and aimed it in my direction. That, almost made the poop I'd been holding in come out!

"HOLD up! Da FUCK yall pulling out guns for?" someone shouted.

The cops drawing guns brung more tension in the room . Of course..

By now, the police were doing my man George dirty! See, George was wearing some Spider Man drawls beneath his clothes. None of us knew. We'd only found out because the cop that arrested George was holding him by his waistline so tight he gave him a wedgie.

"Ooohhhh!" the people sounded. That's how I knew they'd seen it too. Damn George. Sorry it was you, but glad it wasn't me!

That was fucked up though. Had my boy handcuffed like that. Dragging him by his draws. Looked like my, boy had a thong on. Smh.

Alright, It is almost a Riot going on on 7th Street. Everyone was outside. At 1st they all came outside to make sure the beef between us was being settled. Mother's came to watch over their youth, and father's had come to do the same. Uncle's, aunt's, everyone. And before we knew it, we were everywhere.

Coming out of the salon it was mayhem. People are everywhere supporting our people. Smoker's, jogger's, worker's, the mail man, bum's, grandmother's, grandfather's, pedestrian's AND Civilian's. And we all knew 1 another. Or were at least familiar with each other. Even though our hood wasn't always in agreement, seeing the police harass George put us on the same page. So, basically, it was everyone against the police.

"GET the FUCK off of me! LOOSEN these fucking cuffs! They too fucking TIGHT! And let go of my fucking drawls! WHY the FUCK are you holding my drawls? Da FUCK are you gay?" George snapped, yanking himself away from the cop, who'd yanked right back at his arm's, harder.

"STOP RESISTING! That is your LAST warning!" the cop pulled his huge black flashlight from his leather belt, and prepared it as if were going to swing it across George's face. Na, not down 7th Street!

"THAT is POLICE BRUTALITY if you hit that man with that light!" 1 of our grandfather's yelled at the cop.

"Yea And we're ALL watching!" the elder woman next to him added. Must've been his wife.

Then, I see Ms. Wanda out of the corner of my eye, creeping out of an alley, and coming across the street toward the cop! "That boy ain't do nothing. Yall don't have to do him like that!" she went straight at the cop.

Now, I don't know what Ms. Wanda was doing inside that alley, but she looks spaced out. And she has her left hand balled up in a fist.

The cop took that as a threat. "Ma'am, get BACK! Get BACK!" he warns her all the while keeping his eye on that hand.

The funny thing was Ms. Wanda kept that hand balled into a fist. "NO! Yall are harassing a good young man!" Ms. Wanda waved that fist in the cops face as she got up close to him.

The cop took that as a threat. "What is that in your fist Ma'am?"

"NOTHING! Don't worry about what's in my fist! Worry about the way you treating this young man! You can't treat him…!" she quickly put that hand behind her back, and continue going at the cop.

She was almost in the cop's face now.

He's still holding George, and watching her hand. "Ma'am, I told you to get BA..!" he let go of George, grabbed Ms. Wanda, and went for the fist behind her back.

It's so much other commotion going on with the other officer's trying to keep control of the masses, everyone was occupied with their own fight, no one is paying attention to Ms. Wanda and the cop. Well, 1 of the other cop's took after George as the officer that cuffed him went after Ms. Wanda.

The cop had hold of her hand, but evidently Ms. Wanda had the death grip on her clenched fist. Whatever she was holding, she was not about to let go.

"What's in here! WHAT'S IN HERE?" the cop was yelling at her fist. He has her fist and both of his hands trying to pry the fingers on it open! Yall should seen this shit! Him and her, wrestling over her fist!

"Oowww!" Ms. Wanda screamed. Her ass ain't open that fist though!

Now I'M wondering what the hell is she protecting so hard? Whatever I'm on her side. "Let the lady go! Let the lady go!" I warned the cop.

He ignored me!

"Oh you ignoring me?" I looked at ·the cop with my crazy look. He doesn't know what it means. I could tell because he ignored my look too! OK. Yall know I had something for his ass. One Bone Crusher coming right up!

"Let my mom go!" Ms. Wanda's daughter Sai screamed at the cop. "You're hurting my mother! Let go of my mom!" her other daughter, Sai's sister Ranieasha jumped in.

I don't know where the hell they came from.

Out of the corner of my eye, while all of this was going on·,·I see my uncle Apple Cider, my cousin Marlow's father? Peek both way's, andd come out of the same alley I seen Ms. Wanda come out of. Aww! They're creeping! AWWW! Wait till I tell the hood THIS shit!

I'M still looking at the cop, trying to figure out exactly

how, or what I wanted to do to the man, and I hear G Rap behind me!

"I'm with you Bone! I'm with you cuz!" he came up behind me, shadow boxing like he was in the ring!

"ONE TWO G Rap! ONE TWO!" G Rap's brother my other cousin Sha hyped G Rap up.

"I got it! I KNOW what the fuck I'm doing!"

"You DON'T know what you doing! Matter of fact Watch out I got em! I got em!" Sha came in front of G Rap and me to face the cop.

The cop had to let Ms. Wanda go to deal with Sha.

Ms. Wanda only cared about whatever she was holding. So when the cop let her go, she pulled her fist close to her chest and hurried off. "HEY you! FREEZE!" I seen the next cop go right after her.

The cop in front of me squared off with Sha. White boy stance.

Shit it looked like Sha was going to give us a show, so we sat on the curb to watch it.

"Yea, this that Seventh Street shit right here boy," Sha started dancing in front of the cop. Shuffling his feet, and throwing his hands like he was "Apollo Creed' in the movie "Rocky."

After dancing around like some corner boxer, Sha finally swung. I can't front the cop looked scared to death!

Sha swung some ole wild Hay Maker shit. The cop ducked it, and came back with a power punch that landed right on Sha's eye. My mouth dropped! And guess what Sha did? Went straight to sleep. In midair, while he was still standing! Then, Sha went crashing over face 1st to the cement.

"OWW! Damn Sha!" the smoker bul' Burn Nate touched his own eye. "I KNOW that shit hurt! That shit LOOKED like it hurt!" Burn Nate joked. "All that time Sha was faking like he could fight I knew he couldn't fight. Out here tryna be like his dad." Burn Nate looked at me and G Rap, then turned to Sha. "YOU ain't CHEW nigga! WAKE yo ass up and go home!" he yelled at Sha, who by now lay between 2 parked cars snoring.

G Rap seen his brother Sha laying there between the car's, and went WILD! For REAL! The man damn near lost his fucking mind!

This man literally leapt from a standing position onto the cop! I'm talking BOTH feet off of the ground, knee's in the air, finger's open like claw's, arm's spread, and face full of COMPLETE RAGE! I mean, his TEETH was even showing!

Yo, the way he landed on that cop's back and started going crazy, was like he was trying to tear his head off of his neck. No, CLAW it off of his neck!

"YEA get em G Rap! GET EM! TAKE his head off!" our crack head uncle Cider came out yelling.

I'ma hollar at him later. I don't know what the heck him and Ms. Wanda were doing in that damn alley?

"Watch OUT Cider!" I warned my unc. I was about to Boo'yow this cop. Yall know me. Fuck it!

I back up a few feet, got a running start and was about to kick this pussy as hard as I could. I took 1 step, another, another. A few more. Got my momentum up, cocked my boot back. And, "Pfff!"

I was tackled! By a DIFFERENT fucking cop! "You are UNDER arrest! For the attempted assault on a fellow police officer! You have the right to remain silent! Anything you say, CAN and WIIL be used against you in a court of law!" he had me on the ground.

The punk got me from my blind side.

In the end, 3 cops had G Rap on the ground, folded up like a pretzel.

Ms. Wanda, and a few other people were arrested as well. Although they'd gotten us out of there before, I really had the chance to see who the other's actually were. I'm almost sure they're from 7th Street though.

But, I did see Lenny and Rafiq, looking out of Lenny's salon window as we got booked shaking their heads side to side. Aww, wait til I catch the both of them.

Sha finally woke up, and was sitting between the same 2 parked car's holding his right eye, and shaking his head side to side.

Burn Nate stood in front of him, demonstrating with his own hands as he explained to Sha what he should've done. "You was supposed to DUCK, Throw the HOOK, and SLIDE out on him with the JAB! That's what you were SUPPOSED to do! THAT'S how you fight! I don't know WHAT the fuck YOU were doing!" Burn Nate put his hands up in frustration.

Sha, just kept right on shaking his head.

"If I would've knew you couldn't fight I would've BEEN took ya work! Fuck you doing out here on these corner's if you can't protect ya shit?"

Burn Nate went on. "Then goin have the NERVE to jump

in that man's face! Like you LIVE like that! YOU something else! You deserve that right hook."

Sha, just kept right on shaking his head.

The cop who'd arrested me, finally jumped in the driver's seat after more police arrived to clear the rest of the crowd out.

I still didn't see who else was booked with the rest of us I did see get booked. I did see more people though. Fuck it, we went with a fight. They know us.

ITS BONE CRUSHER, BITCH!!!!

CHAPTER 50

Everyone was sentenced

7th St.

6 months later.

It was time for the rest of us to go back to court. It had been decided by everyone that we would all take the case to trial.

We all had the same Judge, went in the same Courtroom, at the same exact time.

In the end, everyone lost trial! Now, we all stood in front of the Judge waiting to be sentenced.

The judge had the paper work in her hands. I can't say their real names, so I'll say their nick names. But, everyone knows who they are. Here were the dispositions.

"Fat Cat, J Bird, Wyan, and Puerto Rican Rick, You four are being charged with Sexual activity with a minor. You guys are old enough to date women in your own bracket. I hereby sentence you three to 3 years in an up state correctional facility, to be served in its entirety! Bailiff, please escort them out of my Courtroom!" the Judge ordered.

"Meech, you are being charged with Child Abandonment.

For leaving your son in the presence of an armed felon, for a fake Rolex watch. This was uncalled for, un explainable, and extremely selfish. You will be sentenced to five years, and loss of visitation rights for one year!"

"Craig Mack, my officers informed me of your repeated Coogi sweater offences, and also the stench of your feet at the time of your arrest. Uncalled for! I now order you to see a Physiatrist, and serve one thousand hours of community service to be served immediately!" she then pointed her finger in Craig Mack's direction, "You know you don't wanna see Boo again!"

I didn't even see Craig Mack at the scene with us! Crazy.

"Markeem! You mister, are a bad image to these children! You're stealing food from the neighborhood charity, you're drinking all of the fruit juices, AND you go to the school yards to pick on the grade school children! This behavior is Pathetic! I'm sentencing you to two thousand hours of community service, sixty days jail time, no work release, and you will ever serve the free lunches again! We'll see how tough you are after the men in C.F.C.F.·have a turn with you!" the Judge wrinkled her nose at Markeem. I laughed. I been told his ass about that creep shit.

"Doc! You're fortunate. You're one of the only one who's walking free this day. And that's only because my officers chose not to charge you with the dummy bags of cocaine you were in possession of that day. I gotta tell ya, I'm sick of you and this dummy bag thing! This is the fifth time you came in front of me with this! First it was your Father, Cuffy. Now, It's YOU! What is it with you guys!" she looked at Doc.

Doc's sitting there looking all scattered the fuck out like, he needed a hit. He just shook his head. "It's hard out there your Honor!" he tried to reason.

"That's no excuse, get a Job!"

"A JOB?" Doc fixed his scattered look on her. "Bitch, are YOU high!" his expression said. "Your Honor, THAT'S how I SURVIVE out here! I can't get no job. How I'ma get high?" Doc shrugged his shoulders and looked at her. It didn't cross his mind how damn dumb he sounded. Smh.

"You'd better figure it out young man. Otherwise I'll help you figure it out!" she threatened him with her stare.

Judge Mary then slang the folder in her hand across her desk, put a hand on her fore head, and fixed her eyes on G Rap. "How many times have I told you about those ears of yours?"

"A lot, but your Honor, that's how I was born!"

"Don't matter, six months!" 'BANG!' the Judge banged the gavel. She was tripping today! Guess she had enough of seeing us in here.

"Mister Earl! Aka, Bone Crusher, Aka Red Bone! You again.

I can tell this won't be good. Oh well, fuck it.

"Traffic Courts looking for you. Child Support's looking for you, AND you have an open gun case! What do you have to say for yourself? Cause I can tell you right now, you aren't leaving here a free man today," this woman got on ME now.

I KNEW I wasn't going home. These people always want me for something. "Your Honor. Naa Nothing. Never mind." I was about to tell her to suck this little dick. Changed my mind.

"Yea, never mind. It didn't matter what you were about to say. Your money can't get your ass out of this two years I'm sentencing you to!" she screwed her f ace at me and then banged the gavel 'BANG!'

Yea fuck you too. Dizzy bitch!

"Ms. Wanda! I am shocked to see you here honey, What happened?" she went to Ms. Wanda. "I thought you were cleaning yourself up?"

"I am," Ms. Wanda plead.

"Well, what is the excuse for your behavior that day?"

See, what we didn't know was Ms. Wanda was hiding in that alley with my smoking ass uncle Cider, and she had just took a mean blast before she came across the street to get in that cop's face that day we were arrested. She was acting like that, because she was high! And the reason she'd had her hand in a fist, was because she had just filled, the pipe with another hit, and she was hiding it from the cop!

I'm just listening as it all comes out while the Judge talks to Ms. Wanda. I had an idea, but I didn't know all of this.

"And your also charged with assault on an officer? Why did you swing on the officer Wanda?" the Judge looked at her.

Ms. Wanda turned her face away from her.

"Answer me, I'm asking you a question?" she persisted.

"He broke my pipe!" Ms. Wanda mumbled toward her, then turned her face away again.

"Well what were you doing with a pipe?"

"Nothing. I…"

"Why was there drug paraphernalia in it?"

"Huh?"

"HUH?" the Judge mimicked her. "I see you're not serious about your recovery. I'm going to help you I'm giving you TWO YEAR'S jail time for the crack pipe and drug paraphernalia police found in your possession. This is time for you to get yourself together, and…"

The judge didn't even finish her sentence before the uproar came.

"THAT'S CRAZY! Two years for a damn crack pipe?" Ms. Wanda's daughter Sai looked at her other daughter Raniesha, then Keena her other sister.

"Naaa. That ain't cool. That, ain't cool at all!" she shook her head. "How is two years in jail supposed to help her?"

"I guess she won't be making no platters tonight!" O Dog, 1 of my homies, had to be the 1 to make a joke.

THAT's 7TH Street for you.

ITS BONE CRUSHER, BITCH!!!!

Last words and Shout Outs!

This book, was a 7th Street book. Most of the event's in it are true, but as you can tell I added some entertainment for the reader. But don't get it twisted though, I'm still that nigga. Smack a mu'fucka around! Yea, ask about me! Smallest nigga in the jail, Biggest heart! Big Knife Big heart! Shot out's to all my folks on 7th St. Starting with Marlow, Mike, Tammy, Tina, Kia, Rocky, Shock Q, Tisha, Aisha, Renae, Tamika, Baleen, Rasul, T.J, Kenny, Tree, Brittany. Shizz, D, Mark Madness, Craig Mack, O Dog, Mark Dat, Chris, Faizon, Rollin, Karon, Buck Shot, Lavon, Zeke, Quan, Pokey, T J, Grim Pokey, Dor, Mecca, Tiffany, Hanifa, Martina, Lil Martina, Zeen Peen, Tanya, Kia, Vita, Wydia, the OTHER Wydia, Ms. Brenda, Honey, Sharon (Rest In Peace homegir1,) Tie, Quindeis, Rodneika, Aunt Carmella, Aunt Rachel, Aunt Vicky, Erica (Shock Q baby mom), The RIGG's family. Heavy and Tike. Ebony, (Lenny's girl.) Malcolm, J lip, Kiesha, D.J Earl, Dirty O Mar, Rahmi, Ike, Moo Moo, Troy, Rest in peace to my Ant Mutter, my snake ass brother Wyan, (who don't be sending that bread up here!) My cousin Sha, who ain't get at me yet! (Whas'sup bul'? Get at me cuz. You know how we rock nigga! Major love for you bul!) Nikki, Tameka (Titan·St.) heat, Jeva,·Greg, Marquan (Pizza Pretzel! Send that bread up here for I beat you up nigga!) Lil Wyan stop playing before I slap you young bul'! Toby, I hope you got them bowel's tight now nigga! Doc, stop selling them dummies! Meech! You be with Meek

Mills! I know you got a real Rolex by NOW!

Craig Mack, you better not still be the dirty young bul'! You better be buying ya own sweaters now nigga! Big Lip Nate, You ain't no 7th Street nigga. Give that mink back Lenny stop stalking them bitches! Hanging in trees with ya wild ass. Smh! Markeem, you ain't getting that Block Captain job again, so don't even apply! J Bird, leave them kid's alone. You Creep! Gerald AKA Banks what up!

Next, shout out's to my other folks, Uncle Leonard! Aunt Shirly, Uncle Edward (Rest In Peace) Uncle Jessie, Aunt Mutter, Aunt Tracy 20 St Uncle Cyder, Uncle David, Uncle Chew, cousin Dollar, Rest In Peace to Day Day.

Key Key and Mone what up? Rest in Peace to Uncle George! Aunt Rosa Lee, Ms. Marleen, Rest In Peace Grand mom Gene! I Love you more than LIFE its SELF!

My Grandpop Willie Mixson! Rest In Peace Old head! See yo u in the hereafter, Inshallah! And Rest In Peace to My Grand mom too! I don't Know her name because she died when I was young. But I love you!!!

Real quick, R.I.P to Ms. Jerry, and Ms. Vowel.

Oh let me get these other names from 7th Street before I forget, and they ask me some dumb shit like WHY did I forget them? Then I got to lay hands on people! lol. Shot out to Geno, Old head Ramon, Wayne Jones (Rest in Peace homey!) Heem, (Rest in Peace to Jersey too!) Lodge, Nut, Fat Bul, the Twins, and Rest in Peace to Donny too! D Giger, Nate, Jay Ralph what's up! Kenny, Rome, Chris Mack, Poop Man, Faith, Cory, Ms. Wanda you know I love you! Ms. Linda!

If I didn't mention·ya name yall know what it is, 7th

Street for LIFE! Its Red Bone bitch!

Shout out to my 13 St. people! Shaneen, Naja, Tasha, Sharon and Shatema!

My Up Town sweet heart Shakeah, Carla from Brick Yard.

My North Philly sweetheart Erica! Running Hand's ON Hand's Off hair salon, doing the illest hair styles. Lil Mia from Diamond St, shout out to you!

My other friends Big Butt Renea, and Sexy Vita, GET AT ME!

Back down south Philly. Shout out to 5th Street! Bone Neck what's up cuz? Saddiq keep ya head up, they can't keep a good nigga down! Raheem, Rest In Peace Lloyd, I love you Aunt Robin! Jassmin, Tifa, Presious, Ebony, Pooh what's up homey! Midget, Dawud, My Dad Hard Rock, Monae, Baby Doll, Ivan, Bun, Stormy, Rest IN Peace to Joe Black, Andre, Montrell, Saleema, Soni, Eidi, T 90, Tiffany, Ulonda, Kiesha and Kim, Iyana, Houston, Robert L, Kareem, Carlos, Darell, Don B, Yusuf.

To the ones I ain't mention yall know I still got love for yall. I just can't remember everybody right now. Tanya you know I got love for you! Tell ya husband Lenny I ain't mad at him for talking that fly shit. Don't hate the player hate the game. It's a cold thing!

Shout out to my PEOPLE's Muff! I LOVE you homegirl! for real! I respect EVERYTHING you did for a man since I been down. You the woman a man can really get ahead with! You been here with me since the beginning, and I recognize you as a true friend, and I appreciate that!

Shout out to ya folks April, Bia, Teniesha, Ebony,

Brenda, Jeff, Rae, and Nicole. Much respect to all yall!

Shout out to Porsha and her squad, Andrea, Cherieka, Taria, Mi Mi, Fat Channell, Erica, Jaimie, It's a lot of yall chicken head's to mention. I can't remember all of yall, but yall know its love.

Porsha, we had a lot of up's and down's and all that, but one thing I will say about you is no matter what we went through you never took it out on your child. You took good care of our daughter I love you for that. You a strong woman, and I tip my hat to you for it. But bitch don't get it twisted, you cross that line you going feel these palm's! Better raise my daughter the right way!

Now. Time for the REAL nigga part of the talk.

For all you niggas out there, partying all night, popping bottles, popping tags and all that fly shit, and yall got down from Day 1 niggas, that got some time, kept their mouth shut, and took that shit on the chin like a real nigga was supposed to, and yall ain't send him a DIME to make sure he had a bar of soap to wash up with some fresh socks to wear, some clean under clothes, and some cosmetic's to keep himself fresh with? You ain't right my nigga.

You in the club with a $5,000 watch on and ya man is in jail starving. Yall done left that man for dead. Just like them hoes did. And yall know jail is like modern day slavery! So a man will forget who HE is fucking with that place! Nigga's don't bother to send a nigga no flicks of his loved ones, no letter's to let him feel that love, and will BARELY answer his call when he's trying to reach out to you! Yall niggas is foul! And yall hiding it behind that shine.

Yall supposed to make this shit easy for a nigga to do. Sometimes yall all we got! Yall all a man might have. And yall shitted on him! Its men that turn into women in here, nigga's eating out of other nigga's food trays and all kinds of shit going on! Aight, given that's what they get. But what does a real man get? The nigga that ain't tell on yall, that ain't turn gay, that ain't go crazy YET! And just kept it real. WHAT does HE get?

From one real man to another. Look out for yall peoples!

And all of yall that's booked, be patient with yall folks. It ain't always as easy as it may look for people. Remember they have bills and kids out there too.

Lenny, I appreciate everything you doing for my daughter out there bro. That's real nigga shit.

7th St for life! The movie·will·be coming soon!

Shout out to my Easton PA peoples! Lucy S, Fountain, Cory, Scott, Rest In Peace to Mr. And Mrs. Ransom, Fat Cenica, Tina, Jennifer, Chuck, and you know I can't forget about the Robinson family. Kim I got major love for you! For all of yall! Yall showed me love when I was out there. Love yall for them good times, real rap!

To my Passyunk sweet heart from Passyunk Projects, GET AT ME! You know who you are! LOVE!

George, Rest In Peace to you and your Wife's newborn. May Allah make it easy for you, Ameen.

Anybody else who's tryna get at me, my ADDRESS is

EARL MOORE 63586-066

Federal Correctional Institution Hazelton

PO BOX 5000

Bruceton Mills

Wv, 26525

Also, Shout out to the illest editor, SHEED WHITE! You took my pen game to another level·akh! When his novel drop's a few months from now, yall gotta support him!

Shout out to Joy and Kelly. This is just a book. Don't kill my boys.

I'm out!!!
Its Bone Crusher, Bitch!!!

R.I.P. Hoarse 7st

R.I.P. J.C 7st

R.I.P. W-Daddy 7st

R.I.P. Malo…

R.I.P. Danny

R.I.P. Tiffany

R.I.P. Earn…

R.I.P. Lisa
I love you Lisa… You know what it is.

R.I.P. Rob

R.I.P. Cuz

#tbt RIP ERN aka Stunna u will never b
forgotten homie See More

Earn… R.I.P….

R.I.P. Far…

R.I.P. Rob…

R.I.P. Cheese

R.I.P. Herbi Luv Bug

7st…

Meech (with the shades on) hiding that fake Rolex! Jariek… T-Murder… 7st.

Tyshon

Leem and Meech

Aunt Jackie…

Red-Bone

Duweit!

Bub, Mal, Meech, and Leem…

7st goons…

I see you Heem… 7st.

I see you Uki!

7st.

7st

I see you O-Dogg, 7st

Ralphy 7st

Fat-Bul, Darryl, Shanky, Bugo, T-Murder…

7st!!!

7st

7st…

Ebony, Brenda, Big April, and beautiful Tiffany!

5st… I see you Midget and Montrell.
Rest in Peace to the twins and Rick…

Nadia

Pooh… 5st

CONGRATULATION'S TO:
PEYTON

My #1…!!!

Peyton

Park-Way Prom… Another one I snuck off too… BOSS!
RedBone and Aisha…

Faizon… 7th.

steph7pokie 1w

53 likes

Steph pokey…

71 likes

Gerald 7st…

7st…

Tasha

Chris and Fiz…

Shatema

5st Ivan and Shaleen

7st…

Kia, G-Rap, Tanya, and Toby

Nice-Town and 7st.

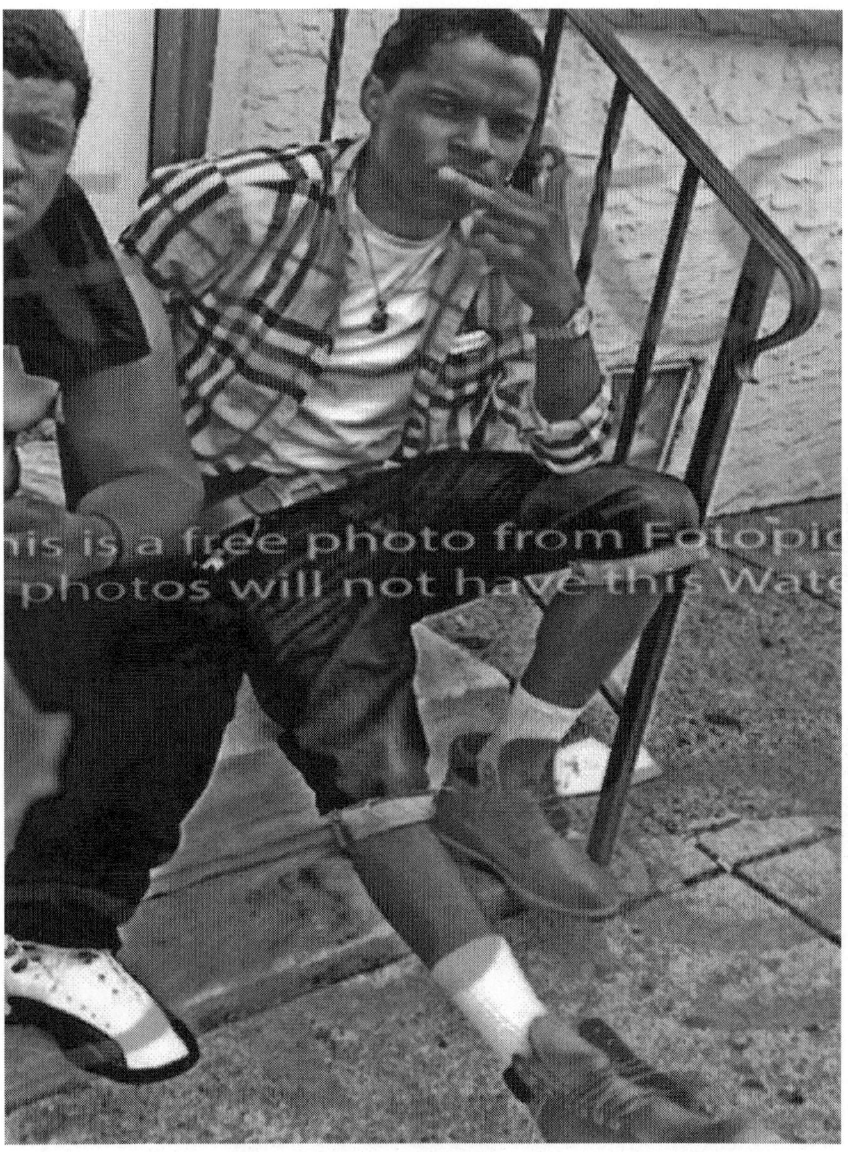

Lil-Zeka and Pizza-Pretzel

Zai and Quana… I love yall!!!

Porsha…

G-Dub and 7st…

Wyan-Wyan Wiggles… Aka SNAKE Aka Wyan-Wyan-Knot…
(my nigga always's got a knot full of 1's tryna make it look big!)

Old-Head J.C!! Rest in Peace!
Mark and Gary-Ahkee

Fitz and Daddy D-Wop…

Ontavious, Rell, Cuz, and some 7st young goons…

7st…

Diquanna Aka Boog and her sister…

T.Y and Dae'ru… 7st.

Mark and Rolland… 7st.

I see you Black-Jesus!

7st…

E-Boogie…

7st

Tiffany A.K.A. Muff… Little Chain Chain LOL

Shakeah…

My nigga, Dirty ass Spud.

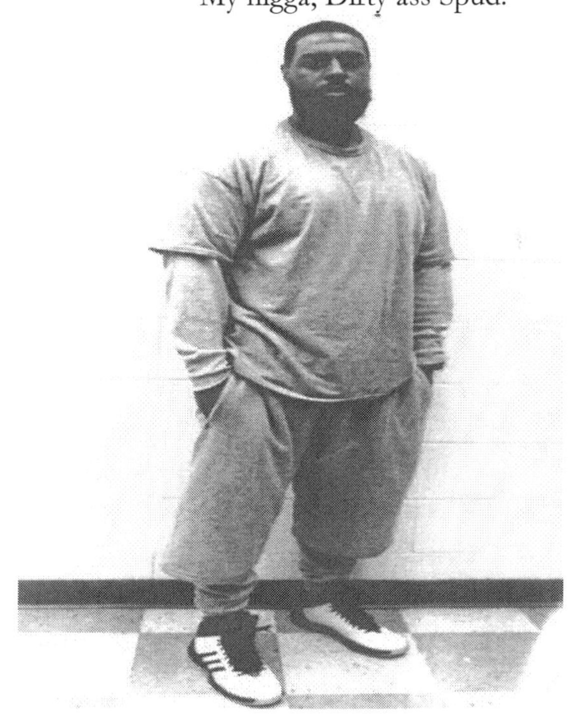

Sidiq, what's up cuz!!?

Sexy ladies Nadia and Janae…

7st… Doc what's up young-bul'!
You still my man, I just had to get you!

Black-Nate and beautiful Sai

18 likes

boawbias_7 Power circle. $$$

chinky_eyes23 My brothers

7st Power-Circle

I see you Mark-Dat… 7st!

Aisha

Lil-Rick, Raniesha, and Puerto-Rican Rick…

Lenny and Hoarse…

I see you Tisa!

7st…

7st...

7st…

7st…

7st…

I see you Karon, Melvin, and Tree. 7st

7st doing us…

Fat-Cat, Zai, Raniesha, and Sha

RedBone… 7st.

Levon Lodge, Fitz, 7st

Ricky Rolex, what's up Boy! Tameeka, Aisha and 7st!!

Quan and Monae, 7st.

Jada.

7st… Jada

7st, Leem… See you young bul.

Sexy Shakeah

F-Dog and Toby

April and Brenda

ABOUT THE AUTHOR

Bone Crusher hails from the South side of Philadelphia. 7th Street. Incarcerated on KING PEN trafficking charges, a 30 year sentence holds him from his freedom. His sentence is the outcome of the stories presented in this memoire. His message; Know the result of the choices you make...